Published by Liot Literary June 2016

© Fran Connor

The right of Fran Connor to be identified as the Author of this work is asserted in accordance with the Copyright, Design and Patents Act, 1988.

www.connorscripts.com

ISBN – 13: 978-1533678744
ISBN – 10: 153367874X

Other novels by Fran Connor

The Devil's Bridge
Sophia and the Fisherman
Someone to Watch Over Me
Elbourne House
Her Man In Havana

This novel is entirely a work of fiction.
The names, characters and incidents portrayed in it are the work of the author's imagination. Any resemblance to actual persons, living or dead is entirely coincidental.

Acknowledgements

My thanks to my wonderful partner Vivienne for her valuable advice and support in creating this novel.

© Cover by Aidana WillowRaven

WillowRaven Illustration & Design Plus

http://WillowRaven.weebly.com

Editor

Philip Newey

Chapter One

A little Saxon church, built by Earl Godwine in the eleventh century, huddled in a fold in the rolling Hampshire Downs. Driving rain from a sky as dark as a dungeon swept across wheat fields and meadows while damp sheep sought refuge under sturdy English oaks. It lashed against the ancient, leaded windows as if it were a bo'sun with a cat o' nine tails, and howled like a tormented soul through the bell tower. For over eight hundred years this building had serviced the spiritual needs of the community of Eagledown and withstood tempest, war and pestilence. It would survive this storm.

Richard de Mornay stood on the cold flagstones, grateful for the thickness of his knee-length boots as he faced a simple altar that bore a white cloth and a brass cross. The weight of responsibility hung heavily on his broad shoulders. He felt the grey, stone walls were contracting to imprison him, but he would do what was right today for his friend Algernon, and not least for Peggy. Brushing invisible specks from his coal-black jacket, he stretched up to his full six-feet height and cast his green eyes around the congregation. His face, uncluttered by facial hair apart from the dark sideburns that came down to his earlobes, was both handsome and kind. The sides of his mouth bore permanent wrinkles from his ever-present smile, even on this momentous day. This twenty-one-year-old was the prime catch in the quiet corner of rural Hampshire over which he would be lord and master in four years if he survived Africa.

The busy tongues of ambitious mothers in the area had not ceased their malicious attacks since news of the wedding escaped.

Richard smiled at his mother seated in the front pew on his side of the flower-bedecked aisle, Lady Adele de Mornay. She wore an elegant blue-and-white dress that did not hide her good figure. She smiled back, fingering a lock of her prematurely grey hair. Her smile did not fool Richard. He could sense her unhappiness. As her hand held the order of service, it trembled. He knew why. The reason sat next to her in the form of his father, Lord de Mornay, with his belly straining the buttons on his black frock coat; his cheeks not ruddy from the weather but from the silver flask he kept inside his jacket.

An ivory Chinaman's head hung from his gold watch chain. His silver-topped ebony cane lay propped against the corner of the pew. Richard remembered well the beatings he had taken from that cane in his younger years and suspected his mother still suffered blows from it, though she always denied that her husband mistreated her. Now Richard was a grown man he knew his father would not dare lift it to him.

Next to his mother sat Penelope, his seventeen-year-old sister, wearing a fashionable pink dress. Her jet-black hair hung down in ringlets tied with pink silk ribbons. There was just a hint of water in her green eyes. He knew why. It rankled with Richard that his sister should suffer because of the dire consequences that had brought him to the church on this English summer's day. He kept his smile though his heart was breaking for what Penelope had lost.

Lady Luisa Bonchurch, Richard's aunt and Adele's sister, slipped in next to Penelope.

'Problems?' asked Richard, pacing along the front of the family's pew.

'No, just some last minute adjustments to the wedding breakfast.' She adjusted her stylish maroon dress with white lace edging, covered partly by a crimson-lined black cape. The cape had saved her perfectly coiffed, long, chestnut-coloured hair from damage by the rain.

'Why is it called a wedding breakfast when it will be eaten in the late afternoon?' asked Penelope.

Richard shrugged.

'I have no idea!' Lady Luisa smiled her gentle smile that radiated from deep within as she fidgeted with her wedding ring: a symbol of what she had lost to the pitiless sea.

'I'm going to miss you, Aunt Luisa when we go to Africa,' said Penelope.

'Me too,' said Richard.

'I'll miss you all too,' said Lady Luisa.

'Except for father,' Penelope whispered.

Lady Adele sniffed.

Lady Luisa gave a non-committal smile, showing perfect teeth in her fair complexion that belied her forty-three years. She picked up an order of service from the shelf in front of her pew.

Church of St Thomas, Eagledown, Hampshire
Tuesday 24th June 1862
The Marriage of:
Margaret Mary Crabtree
to
Richard George de Mornay

'I like Peggy. I've never thought of Peggy's real name being Margaret. It sounds so strange when I think that I've known her all my life as Peggy.'

'Me neither,' said Richard.

'She will always be Peggy to us. It is just convention in these circumstances to use the full name,' said Lady Luisa.

'Why must convention always take precedence, Aunt Luisa?'

'That is how society works, Penelope. Convention. Without it where would we be?'

Penelope shrugged. 'Convention often stops us from achieving what we want.'

Richard nodded agreement.

'We have the privileges of position and wealth. It comes at a price. That price is living according to social convention.' Lady Luisa clasped her silk-gloved hands in her lap.

'Well, when I am of age I shall jolly well do as I please, within the limits of propriety, of course.'

'Of course, Penelope.' Lady Luisa squeezed her niece's arm.

Richard looked to the far side of the aisle. Algernon, with his muscular frame contained by his grey jacket and his blond hair tied back in a ponytail, glared back at him from the front pew. Richard winced at the memory of the names his erstwhile friend, and soon to be brother-in-law had called him after he and Peggy told Algernon and her father about her condition. The words 'betrayal', 'dishonour' and 'rake' still rang in his ears.

Richard saw the Eagledown servants at the back of the church on his side of the aisle under the watchful eye of Humphreys, the butler. The ex soldier's eyes met Richard's. As the two men looked at each other for a moment, Richard wondered what Humphreys was thinking. Richard remembered how this unusual butler had taught him to ride, swim, fight in unarmed combat, and shoot. All he got from his father when he was a boy were beatings.

His thoughts were drawn back to the present when he heard the organ strike up its wheezy tune and saw Peggy coming down the aisle on the arm of her father, following the robust Reverend Smythe.

Richard marvelled at how lovely she looked in the blue silk dress that his mother had given her. Though only five feet tall and slim—except for a slight bulge in her tummy—she radiated something special as she proceeded along the aisle carrying a posy of meadow flowers picked that morning on the estate.

Her father did not look well. His daughter was helping to hold him up. His grey frock coat hung on his stick-thin frame and his pallor was evidence of his consumption. Richard knew the man had not much longer to dwell on this earth and that he had forced himself from his bed to give his daughter away. He wondered if he should have told him the truth, and had nearly done so, but the knowledge of the terrible consequences that could ensue had persuaded him to keep quiet.

Peggy arrived at his side. The tomboy he had chased across the Downs had grown into a young woman with a sparkle in her blue eyes. Her indomitable spirit would not be fazed by the events that led to them standing before the altar. No, not Peggy. She would pull through, Richard hoped.

His mind wandered with little comprehension of the progress of the service, but he managed to say the right words at the right times. He was thinking about Africa.

Before long, the ceremony was over and Richard led his bride from the church. Outside the rain still drove down onto the church and its graveyard. Richard and Peggy stopped in the narthex to shelter while the small congregation gathered around. That is, all except Algernon. He stayed inside the church.

Richard offered his hand to Mr Crabtree. 'I appreciate your coming today, Sir. I know how difficult it must be for you.'

Mr Crabtree took Richard's hand in his bony fingers. 'I only wish my dear wife was here to see our daughter married. I shall see her soon in Heaven and tell her about today. I ask only that you treat my daughter well, Sir.'

'I shall, Sir. You may count on me.'

'I believe I can, Sir.'

The wind and rain eased and then stopped.

Richard took Peggy across the churchyard towards the lane outside where a carriage and two white horses waited, courtesy of Mr Belchamber of the Winchester livery stables. As they passed the grave of his grandfather and grandmother, Richard glanced at the inscription.

General Sir Richard Edward Philip Elphinstone KCB
1776–1851
And his beloved wife:
Lady Caterina Isabella Elphinstone
1783–1854

'I must live up to his expectation of me,' said Richard.

'Thank the Lord he bequeathed Eagledown to you, or your father would have got his hands on it.'

'Well, as it is, Aunt Luisa has control until I am twenty-five. He trusted her and I trust her. It is good for her to run the estate. Being a widow must be a lonely existence.'

'And when you're twenty-five you will be Sir Richard!'

'And you will be Lady Margaret Mary de Mornay!'

'May I not be Lady Peggy? Or just plain Peggy? I ain't . . . I'm not really cut out for high tea with society ladies.'

'You may be Lady whatever you wish and the ladies will love you. My mother and aunt love you.'

'They're special. Not all the ladies are like them. I'm just a tenant farmer's daughter. I won't fit in with high society.'

'Peggy, we will work it out. Remember that I shall never let you down. I not only owe you that, but it is also what I want to do.'

***

The ride through the Hampshire countryside in the damp summer evening was a sombre affair for Richard but he didn't let it show. Peggy sat beside him. The wedding breakfast had been subdued and they were both relieved to be on their way to the hotel in Winchester.

Mr Belchamber pulled the horses up outside the Georgian façade of the Downs Hotel, overlooking the River Itchen. He helped them with their luggage and bid them good evening.

Richard found a man sitting behind a polished wooden counter writing in a ledger with a quill and ink.

'Good evening. Mr and Mrs de Mornay. We have a reservation,' said Richard.

The man looked with rheumy eyes over his half-moon spectacles. Richard thought he must be at least seventy years old.

'Ah, yes. The newlyweds.' He pinged a silver bell on the counter.

A boy in a blue uniform with brass buttons and red piping appeared.

'Take these guests to the blue room,' said the man, handing the boy a key.

The boy slipped the key into his pocket, looked at the two suitcases and blinked. Then he bent down and picked one up in each hand.

Richard took the heavier one from him.

The boy smiled a 'thank you' and led them along a corridor, up a flight of stairs and along another corridor with yellow walls and a red carpet. He stopped outside a brown, varnished door, turned the key, and stepped inside.

A four-poster bed stood with the head against a wall. The aspect from a mullioned window was of the River Itchen meandering through the countryside. A sofa with a flower-pattern cover sat next to the opposite wall. The boy opened a door revealing a bathroom with brass taps and a big white bath. There was also a lavatory. The bathroom floor was tiled in black and white while the walls were blue.

Richard handed the boy a shilling. 'Thank you, Sir.' He closed the door behind him.

Richard turned to Peggy. 'Are you hungry?'

'Not really. You?'

'No. Not after what we ate at the wedding breakfast.'

'I'll unpack. I expect you're used to servants doing that for you,' said Peggy.

'No, Mama always made Penelope and I do our own packing and unpacking.'

'You're lucky to have had such a good mother to bring you up. It stopped you from being one of those horrible boys we used to fight from the village.'

'She made up for my father.' He laughed, making Peggy grin too. 'You, me, Algernon and Penelope against the world!'

'Not forgetting Napoleon,' said Peggy.

'Yes, I will miss rabbiting with that hound.'

'Richard! You think you hid your gentle ways from us. We all knew you hated to kill anything. That's why, in all the times we hunted with Napoleon, we caught bugger all. Oops! Sorry! I'll have to watch out when I'm dining with the gentry.'

'Don't go changing anything about yourself, Peggy. As for the rabbiting, I didn't know I was so obvious.'

'That's why we all love you, Richard. Because you care. It's fortunate that your kindness didn't extend to the horrible boys. You've always stood up for people being bullied or downtrodden. I shall always be grateful for what you did today.'

Richard felt his face colour and his skin temperature rise. All he could manage in reply was, 'Harumph.'

Peggy laughed and turned her attention first to her suitcase and then to Richard's, emptying the contents into a solid oak wardrobe.

'Shall we go downstairs anyway and have something?' said Richard.

They settled for two glasses of champagne in the guests' lounge served by the old man. It appeared to Richard that they were the only guests. He had a good view through the French doors to the terrace, river, and a pleasantly laid out formal garden, giving way to the rolling fields and hills in the distance.

The rain of the day had turned into a sunset that seemed to have the heavens on fire.

As he sat watching a magpie on a wall in the evening glow, he wondered about the wildlife in Africa. He had heard much about the animals and hoped to see elephants and lions. If the camera he had ordered was waiting at the harbour, he would be a happy man. He cringed when he thought of how his father would decimate the wildlife on safari.

The summer evening's light faded to black. 'I suppose it's time to retire,' said Peggy. 'Is that what you say, "retire"?'

Richard nodded.

She slipped her arm through his as they climbed the stairs.

In the bedroom, they looked nervously at each other.

'I'll take the sofa,' said Richard.

'Richard, in the eyes of God and the law we are man and wife. There's no need for you to take the sofa. I'll get ready first.'

Richard watched her gather her nightclothes and go into the bathroom. While she was in there, he changed into his nightshirt and climbed into the bed.

Penelope came out of the bathroom dressed in a long, white, linen nightdress and a shawl around her shoulders. He could see her embarrassment.

She slipped into the bed next to him.

They both sat propped up on pillows.

'Richard.'

'Yes.'

'I know it would have been more convenient for everyone if I'd done something about it.'

'Peggy, it is your decision and I respect it.'

'I did go to a woman in Winchester who I'd heard would help girls in my condition. But I couldn't go through with it. I couldn't kill even in these circumstances. I'm sorry, Richard.'

'There is nothing, absolutely nothing, to be sorry about, Peggy. I understand. I would not have wanted you to kill him or her.'

'You're such a good man, Richard. I don't deserve you.'

'Peggy, you deserve far better than me.'

'I do thank you for asking me to come to Africa with you and your family, but you know I couldn't possibly bear to be near your father. And I just know I'm not cut out to live in society. I'm a country girl, Richard.'

'There is nobody in society who is better than you, Peggy. Never forget that. I have to go. Mother has to go with him because she is his wife and would be arrested for desertion if she left him without being able to prove just cause.'

'I would have thought the beatings were just cause.'

'Not in the eyes of the law, even if she could prove it. And he would marry Penelope off to the man who paid the most. I can't let that happen, Peggy.'

'I know, Richard. You have the weight of so many people's troubles on your young shoulders. I'll be all right. Algernon and I have been running the farm since father was taken ill, and when he passes, we will continue to work it if that's acceptable in the tenancy.'

'It is. I saw to that and Aunt Luisa agrees.'

'I told my father the truth.'

'But, Peggy . . .'

'I had to tell him, Richard. He will not tell Algernon.'

'Your father spoke some kind words to me after the wedding.'

'He holds you in great esteem, Richard.'

'You will make a good mother to the child, Peggy. Of that, I am sure. I wish I could be with you to help bring him or her up.'

'You've done so much for me.' Her hand trembled.

'What's wrong, Peggy?'

'I'm embarrassed, but I have to say this because I know what a gentleman you are. If you want to claim your—conjugal rights I think they call it—it would be wrong of me to deny you. You're entitled after all you've done.'

'Peggy, dear Peggy, I love you so much, but as a friend and perhaps as if you were my sister . . .'

'And I think of you as more of a brother than a husband.'

Richard smiled. 'That is indeed a compliment, Peggy. We have been friends since our mothers let us play together when we were babies. And then as Algernon and Penelope came along we were a great team. The fearless four. What times we had, Peggy. What friends we were. And what friends we will continue to be.'

'Richard, I thank you. Shall we go to sleep?'

Richard nodded and patted her hand. 'And someday, perhaps, Algernon and I will be friends again.'

They lay down side by side. She kissed him on the cheek.

Chapter Two

Victoria gazed around the vast, white-walled refectory of the place that had served as her home for the past sixteen years. She looked at the date board on the far wall that for the last two years had been her responsibility to chalk up daily.

Tuesday 24th June 1862

The date filled her with hope. Tomorrow she would be sixteen years of age and free of this orphanage. Free to make her way in the world. Free from the grip of Tweedale and his harridans. She would not miss this dark house. Deep in her heart, though, she felt a pang of sadness that she would be leaving many of her friends to the mercy of the regime. Not that any mercy was found within these walls. There was nothing she could do for the inmates now.

She thought about the wide world out there. A world where people lived happily. Nothing bad would happen out there. It would not have the horrors that the walls of the orphanage contained. But her knowledge of the outside world consisted only of visits every Sunday to the church under the watchful eyes of the harridans.

Her fingers traced her initials, carved on the scrubbed pine table five years ago, next to those of her twin, Edward. When she recalled the beating she had taken for the carving she still felt sick.

She still missed him. The horror of his death kept her awake at night in her twenty-bed dormitory as she listened to the whimpers from the other girls. No tears fell from her eyes. There were no tears left.

The rain swished against a row of arched windows. Victoria sat with the other children. As usual, they waited for the excuse that passed for dinner.

A sea of green, with the girls in gingham and the boys in green, checked shirts, all spotlessly clean, hardly moved an inch. One candle lit each table. Each table held ten occupants. At the top end of the room, a staff dining table stood on a raised dais. Had it not been for the rain, staff would have a view out of the windows across the gardens and lawns of Gravestoke House: tended by the toil of generations of orphans. Life here was better than the workhouse.

Well, that was the opinion of the trustees who founded the orphanage. Many would disagree not least the residents.

They sat on their benches with their arms folded and their sad eyes raised to Mr Tweedale, Master of the House, on the dais.

He squirmed his skeletal frame out of his oak chair with its high back and armrests. His bony hands clasped in front of him, he wheezed, 'For what we are about to receive may the Lord make us truly thankful. Amen.' Spittle formed at the sides of his mouth as he spoke through thin lips on a face that looked as if it had not seen the sun in years.

In a quiet drone, the children chanted, 'Amen.'

Victoria stared at the man. She could not hide her extreme disgust of him and the cruel way he kept order, with a stick and solitary confinement for alleged miscreants. Her pale face gave away her feelings. The beatings he had given her she could not count on all her fingers and toes. She did not know when or how, but some day, she determined, she would return his cruelty with interest. This she would do for the sake of all who had suffered at his hands: even if she hanged for it.

'You're sixteen tomorrow. You can leave this hell hole,' whispered a girl, another inmate of this awful establishment, sitting beside Victoria.

'At last,' said Victoria, her mouth moving like that of a not-so-good ventriloquist.

'Will they replace Katy?'

'Don't know.'

Victoria caught sight of one of the two harridans who kept strict order at mealtimes coming her way. The woman wore a long, grey skirt and matching top that bulged under her fat belly and thick arms. Had she seen an infringement of the refectory rule of silence? Victoria steeled herself for the blow. It did not come. The leather strap the woman carried whacked a boy across his shoulders on the next table.

Victoria stopped whispering. She felt guilty at the relief that she was not the target.

Outside the rain turned to hail. It drubbed on the windows as the fingers on the washboards did in that Stygian place of toil.

The kitchen staff dolloped a greasy stew into the children's little wooden bowls. They did not take much. Even Oliver Twist would not have asked for more. That was not because of the 'no speaking' rule.

To fill the space in her belly that the stew had not, Victoria lifted a wormy apple from a pile in the centre of the table. With eyes darting around for the harridans, her hand slipped down to her black ankle boot. Gently she curled her fingers around a small knife with a deer's foot handle. Victoria knew the punishment would be far more severe than a strap across the shoulders if she were caught with a knife. Slowly, she raised the knife and put the apple in her lap. With both eyes checking for the harridans, she dug out the living creatures from her fruit. Her imagination replaced the apple with Tweedale's throat. Her knife safely back in its place, she ate the rest of the apple as she glared up at the staff table.

Tweedale and his guest, whom Victoria knew was Captain Rodney Woodward, tucked into sausages and mash, washed down with local cider. Victoria saw Woodward look around the room at the orphans. His thick lips dripped with saliva. It made her feel sick.

She could see a tattoo on the back of his right hand showing the feet of a woman. She guessed his jacket's sleeve covered the rest of a naked figure.

The hailstones built up on the sills and scratched at the glass as if they were souls escaping from Hell.

Victoria could not lip read so she was unaware of what the two were discussing, though she had no doubt it was about her because they were looking in her direction.

***

An image of Jesus with his arms outstretched hung above a leather armchair in the master's room. Under the picture were the words: *Suffer the little children to come unto me.*

Tweedale's interpretation of the word 'suffer' differed considerably from that meant by Jesus.

Woodward sat in the leather armchair. Tweedale sat behind a polished mahogany desk, fingering a large, leather-bound Bible.

The hailstones still rattled the windows. It would be a wild night out on the Downs.

The two harridans from the refectory stood motionless like gargoyles against the wall.

Light from an oil lamp on the desk and another on a bookcase cast a glow. The burning wicks gave off an acrid smell to go with the musty odour of books and damp carpet. The wind blew through the guttering, making an unearthly wail as if someone had fallen into the terrifying darkness of a Downland bog. It drowned out the steady tick-tock of a grandfather clock against the wall behind Tweedale. The atmosphere hung like a blanket as if the room held a dreadful secret.

'Cash in advance,' said Tweedale.

'Don't trust me?' said Woodward.

'I trust nobody but Our Lord.'

'Hypocritical bastard!'

'Pay up.'

Woodward climbed to his feet and made his way over to the desk. His rough hand went into a deep pocket in his black coat that still had salt stains from his last voyage. He lifted out a small pouch that he dropped on the Bible.

Tweedale snatched it from the book, pulled the leather retaining strap, and looked inside. He drew out a bundle of notes and counted them.

'All here.'

'Of course, it's all there. Now let's get on with it. It's a dreadful night out, and it's a long way to Southampton.'

A knock silenced the room.

Tweedale pocketed the pouch.

The taller harridan stepped towards the door and pulled it open.

***

'The master sent for me.'

'Come in!'

Victoria stepped into the master's room. The harridan shut the door.

'You know Katy had the opportunity to go to Australia to train as a governess?' said Tweedale.

'Yes, Master.'

'Well, with her death, this kind man is still willing to take an orphan and have her trained as a governess over there. How would you like to replace Katy?'

Victoria's tummy turned to mush. Her legs buckled but she managed to stay upright. She looked at the window. The shortest harridan stood next to it: no way out through there. The other harridan stood by the door: no escape that way.

Victoria took a deep breath. 'Really? That's marvellous, Master. Are you sure you want me? There are so many other girls more suitable than I.' She managed to smile at Woodward.

Woodward returned it with a sly grin. 'Do not be modest, Victoria. You would be perfect.' His voice struck fear into her more than his appearance. A gruff voice as if he had glass stuck in his throat. An unmistakable voice that she would never forget.

'When am I to go, Master?'

'Tonight. Sorry for the short notice, but Cap'n Woodward sails on the tide tomorrow.'

'That's wonderful, Master. I do not know how to thank you.'

'Just work hard and make something of yourself and that's all the reward I need for the years I've spent making you into a finished and educated young woman.'

'I'm so excited, Master. May I go and pack?'

'Of course.'

Victoria dragged up a smile from somewhere and headed for the door.

'Please go with Victoria and help her prepare for her journey,' Tweedale instructed the harridan standing guard at the doorway.

***

Once Victoria had left, Woodward said, 'She seems as though she's going to be easy to handle. I didn't expect her to be so willing.'

Tweedale's hand felt the money pouch in his pocket. 'She's your responsibility now.' He looked over at the other harridan. 'You'd better go too and make sure she doesn't do anything foolish.'

'Yes, Master,' said the harridan, slapping her calf with her leather strap while she gave a wicked grin.

'I'll wait for her in the carriage,' said Woodward, standing up and striding towards the door.

Tweedale opened the great Bible. A ream of white pages lay at the back. On the pages were lists of orphans, their birth dates, their arrival dates if different, the dates they left or if they died while at the orphanage. His finger ran down the list to 1846.

Edward Sillitoe: born 25.6.1846 (died from drowning 16.5.1855)
Victoria Sillitoe: born 25.6.1846
Mary Sillitoe: died 27.8.1846 aged 16 years

He wrote next to Victoria's name: *'Left to make her way in the world: 24.6.1862*

***

Victoria marched down the long corridor with its grey flagstones that many hundreds of little feet had trodden over the years. The other harridan caught up with her colleague and together they escorted Victoria to her dormitory at the far end of the ground floor.

A huge window dominated the room. The hail lashed against it, echoing across the Spartan accommodation. The poorly fitted frame let in a rivulet of water that ran down the sill and whitewashed wall to puddle on the cold stone floor.

A single candle on a pine table in the centre cast an eerie light that flickered shadows on the walls. The pervading smell of carbolic no longer irritated Victoria's nostrils. It was yet another smell she had become used to over the years.

She didn't show her disappointment at finding the dormitory empty. Victoria would have to do this alone. The other children would be working in the basement or washing up in the kitchen. She opened a wooden locker beside her bed and stuffed the only other dress she owned into a threadbare blanket from her five-feet-by-two iron bed.

'Well, that's me packed and ready,' she said with a smile on her face and terror in her heart.

'Hurry along then. Cap'n Woodward is waiting,' said the tall harridan.

Victoria put her bundle under her arm and with one harridan in front and one behind set off back along the corridor. As she passed what served as the girls' ablutions, she said, 'I'm so excited I need to go to the lavatory. Is that all right?'

'I suppose so, but hurry up yer skinny little cow,' said the shorter escort.

As best she could, Victoria concealed the shake in her hand as she thumbed the ablutions door handle down and pushed it open. Inside this vast, cold washroom, the one cubicle that served as a lavatory had two sides, no door and backed up against the wall. Privacy was not on the agenda at the orphanage. As usual, the window above the privy lay open to let out the smell. Water from the driving rain and hail came through the window, soaking the sill and floor. Victoria stepped carefully through it towards the hole that served as the privy.

'May I close the window while I go, or I'll get wet through?'

The harridans nodded.

Victoria reached up to the window and in one mighty effort dragged herself up onto the sill, threw her bundle out of the window and jumped out after it.

She landed on a patch of wet undergrowth that broke her fall. Sharp branches scratched at her skin. With her heart pumping so hard the palpitations filled her ears, she ran as if the Devil was after her towards the only place that offered a way over the eight-foot-high brick wall surrounding Gravestoke House. Her legs felt weightless. Fear gave her wings as she bounded the wall, using an old oak's gnarled trunk as a launching pad. She heard the harridans' shouts as she hit the ground on the other side, but she soon disappeared into the blackness. The hail stung her face, but her terror drove her on.

With no sense of time, she hurried on until she found herself in a narrow country lane. A pungent smell of wild garlic filled the damp air. An occasional scurry came from the high banks as mice and shrews ran for cover at the sound of her iron-tipped boots crunching along. Victoria felt safer knowing her knife was in one of those boots. She decided that if Woodward, Tweedale, or the harridans found her, she would kill them if she could.

The hail turned to rain and then stopped. A break in the clouds let a faint moonlight through. Victoria kept walking, her pace determined, her ears tuned to any sound that someone may come after her. Her eyes searched ahead. Inside she felt sick.

A little way on, she saw the spire of St Agnes's church rising out of the dark surroundings. She knew the church well. All the orphans had to go there every Sunday morning to listen to the long, boring sermons and sing mournful hymns. Tweedale always read the lesson from a Bible that lay on the back of a brass eagle.

She drew nearer the church. Her ears detected nobody following. *I'll say goodbye to Edward.*

Noiselessly, she slipped the catch on a five-barred gate that led into the graveyard. The moon slid behind a cloud, leaving Victoria in darkness. Her trembling hands felt their way through the gravestones until she reached the back of the church. There were no gravestones here. This was where the orphans found their final resting place: in paupers' graves with no markings other than a small stone bearing a number. The graveyard did not scare her. She had seen death often enough at the orphanage. Victoria knew the dead could not hurt her: only the living could do that.

Victoria saw the freshly dug earth that would cover Katy. There were no funerals for the orphans. They were just carried away on a cart and buried. Somewhere, now overgrown with grass and weeds, would lie Edward. She knelt down and put her hands together. 'I'm going away, Edward. I have no choice. I'll be sold into something awful if I stay or I'm captured. Someday I'll come back and buy you a headstone. I don't know where you are down there, but I shall find you.'

The moon escaped from the cloud. Victoria looked at the weeds and grass that stretched as far as a perimeter brick-and-flint wall. 'You're down there too, Mother. You died when you were the same age as I am now. I'll find you if I can and give you a headstone. I don't know how I'll get the money, but I promise it will be honest. I shall not be a thief.'

With her only other dress wrapped in the blanket under her arm, she slipped out of the graveyard and strode out to face whatever the future had in store.

Chapter Three

After an hour trudging through the night, and soaked to the skin, she found a fisherman's hut by the River Test. She would not have chosen this spot if there had been an alternative, but the fear and walk had worn her out. Curled up in a ball on the floor of the hut she quickly fell asleep.

The next morning she woke to feel the chill of wet clothes clinging to her. She peered out. No other person could be seen along the pleasant riverbank, and now the sun shone instead of rain. *Perhaps this is a good omen.* Victoria peeled off her wet clothes and hooked them on the low-hanging branch of an oak tree. Her grey woollen dress had kept relatively dry in her bundle, so she slipped it on. While she waited for her other clothes to dry, she found a shallow part of the river and plucked up enough courage to use the clear, Chalk Down water to drink and wash her face and hands. Water scared her. It had since Edward drowned, and she had nearly suffered the same fate.

She sat down to wait for the sun to do its job. She watched two swans gracefully sail up and down the river. Victoria imagined life would be better if you were a swan instead of an orphan.

While she sat waiting, she checked her purse. She always carried it with her. Things went missing at the orphanage if you left them lying around. Seven pence. However many times she counted it, she could never make it more. *Not much to show after all the years spent in the orphanage. Swans don't need money.*

Her gingham dress soon dried in the heat of the morning. She swapped it for the woollen dress. As she walked away from the river, along a path lined both sides with brambles, Victoria picked the berries and ate them to fill the void in her tummy. The happy hum of bees filled the still air. A wood pigeon cooed its gentle lament. In a sycamore tree, a blackbird called for his mate. This idyllic summer's day epitomised all that was good about the English countryside. *I'm so glad to be alive and free.*

In the distance to the east she could see Gallows Hill. *I will not go that way.* Gallows Hill chilled her blood. *Perhaps that's my fate.*

As she tramped along, she wondered what she would do to earn a living. She certainly could not go back to the orphanage. She could not accuse Tweedale or Woodward of anything because she had no proof, though she knew she would not have been heading for Australia to train as a governess. A much less respectable career was earmarked for her: of that, she was sure. Some girls mysteriously left the orphanage without notice and were never heard of again. Her thoughts flitted through her troubled mind. *Perhaps the ones in the paupers' graves are the lucky ones. No, don't say that. Life is precious. You must live it honestly, and as best you can.*

Her discussion with herself came to an abrupt halt. She heard a sound. A breaking twig. Victoria spun round. Too late. Someone grabbed her. Strong arms forced her face down into the wet ground. Rough hands roamed over her dress, reached into her pocket and lifted out her purse. Her small bundle they rifled but found nothing of value. From the breathing, she reckoned there must be two of them: one holding her down and the other searching. *What else will they do?* She struggled and kicked, but the strong hands were too much for her. She tried to reach for her knife but her arms were pinioned by her captor.

'Let me go, yer cretins.' Her fear soon calmed as she looked up to see two men in ragged clothes running away. Now she had no money at all, but at least they had not hurt her. *They're not working for Tweedale or Woodward, or they would have taken me prisoner.* She climbed to her feet, dusted herself down, and shed no tears of self-pity.

Way off in the distance she could see the spire of a church. She could reach it without crossing Gallows Hill. With her eyes fixed on the landmark she set off at a stride, her senses tuned in case of another attack.

By one o'clock, she found herself in a small market town, Motsford. That was the time on the clock tower she limped past on blistered feet. The cobbled main street led to a green surrounded on four sides by white-walled houses with black beams and thatched roofs.

On one side of the green stood The Jolly Farmer. Its painted sign portrayed a fat, bearded gentleman smoking a clay pipe as he sat in a leather armchair.

Calling up her courage, she stepped inside. She had never been in a public house before. The smell of sawdust, sweat, tobacco, and ale made her feel queasy. A few farmhands stood around the bar with clay pipes and pewter mugs in their grubby hands. She felt their eyes undress her. In one corner, four men in corduroy trousers played dominoes. They looked up at her as she passed by. A cocker spaniel sat at the feet of a man in a tweed jacket reading a newspaper. The dog glanced up at Victoria and then laid his head down on his forelegs. His master did not stir from his paper. Behind the bar, a man with a beard and an enormous belly wiped a pewter mug and hung it on a hook over the counter. He was not the same man as the one on the sign outside, but there was a likeness. She made her way towards the bar.

'Excuse me, Sir. I'm looking for honest work. I can cook, clean, read, and write. And I'm good with children.'

The man just stared at her for a moment and then let out a huge guffaw. 'Go see Madam Clara down at the crossroads. She's a few young ladies work for her. She'll find you something to do.'

The farmhands joined in the laughter. The domino men clapped. The man with the newspaper raised his eyebrows, and then went back to reading. Victoria straightened up, fixed her eyes directly ahead, and marched towards the door. Her tummy held a whole flight of butterflies, but she was not going to let these people know that. She had her pride.

'Come back to my place, dearie, and I'll find you something to do,' said a balding, fat man among the farmhands to more jeers and laughter.

She did not look at him. As she passed, he pinched her bottom. The insult flattened the butterflies. Anger built in their place. It rose to her throat and then came out on her tongue. 'How dare you!' The ridicule changed to a round of applause as the man reeled from a slap across his fat jowl.

'Wait a minute, Miss,' called the bar owner. 'No offence, Miss. Just a bit o' fun. Go and see Mr Jolyon down at the big house, last on the left going out of town. He's looking for a governess or childminder.'

'Thank you kindly, Sir.'

***

The house looked enormous to Victoria. It was not as big as the orphanage, but forty children lived in the orphanage and probably only one family in this big house. It was not like the thatch-roofed cottages around the Green. This one was of red brick, three storeys high, with a black slate roof.

She lifted the latch on a wooden gate that led to a neat garden bordered by red, white, and yellow roses with perfect lawns on either side of the path to the front door. Her work in the orphanage was enough for her to know that whoever tended this garden knew their business well.

Victoria was unsure whether she should find the tradesman's entrance or pull the bell chain at the front door. She plumped for the front door after slipping her bundle under a privet hedge.

A woman she took to be Mrs Jolyon opened the door. Victoria was not in the habit of criticising people, but she thought the woman a little 'blowsy'. Too much make-up covered her slightly chubby face. Her long, well-cut blue dress and matching top, with a set of pearls at her neck, were evidence enough that she was not the maid.

'Yes?' said Mrs Jolyon shaking her head.

'I understand there is a position as governess or child-minder available and if so I would like to apply,' said Victoria in her best posh voice.

'You a governess? You must be mad. Clear off.'

'Please, Ma'am, do not be put off by my appearance. I'm a respectable young lady, but I've had some misfortune lately.'

Mrs Jolyon sniffed. 'Hm-mm. We do need someone quickly. Well, my husband will have to decide. You had better come in. Make sure you wipe your feet.' Mrs Jolyon held the door open for Victoria.

The first thing that struck Victoria about the interior of the house was the perfect tidiness. Nothing was out of place and there was no hint of dust.

'Stand there. I'll find my husband,' said Mrs Jolyon, ushering Victoria into the parlour.

Left alone Victoria looked around the room. A row of books lined a bookshelf. She read the titles. All were religious tomes and three were Bibles. She shuddered at the thought of the evil, Bible-reading Tweedale.

Through the window, Victoria could see into the back garden. It too was perfect. Even the beans at the far end paraded in lines as straight as the Queen's guards. Sitting on a swing at the side of the garden was a girl of about fourteen in a white dress, swinging back and forth. There was something sad about the girl. No signs of laughter or excitement. She just sat there gently rocking forward and back, while looking far off into the distance. Victoria had seen that look on children at the orphanage after they had been to the basement.

'Who sent you?' said a man's voice from behind.

Victoria turned to see Mr Jolyon. She presumed it was Mr Jolyon standing in the doorway. He stood about five feet three inches, just an inch taller than Victoria. His black jacket and pinstriped trousers, with a cravat at his skinny neck under a beaked nose and ruddy complexion, suggested to Victoria that Mr Jolyon was a banker or some other important business person. It was not a wild guess. Men dressed like Mr Jolyon visited the orphanage. He had a kinder face than the visitors to that sad place.

'I heard from someone in the village, Sir,' said Victoria, as politely as she could muster.

'References?'

'I'm afraid not, Sir. This would be my first post, but I can assure you I am accomplished. I have looked after children, Sir.'

'Let me have a look at you.'

Victoria blushed at his scrutiny.

'Twelve times six?' said Mr Jolyon.

'Seventy-two, Sir.'

'Capital of France?'

'Paris, Sir.'

'Who is the British Prime Minister?'

'Don't know, Sir.'

He laughed. Victoria suddenly felt more at ease.

'The first four books of the New Testament?'

'Mathew, Mark, Luke and John, Sir.'

'You may do. We'll give you a trial. Where is your luggage? You'll have to live in.'

'Please, Sir, I will fetch it.' Victoria eased past Mr Jolyon, who still stood in the doorway. She felt his body next to hers. She opened the front door and recovered her bundle from under the privet hedge.

'Hmm, luggage?' said Mr Jolyon now watching her from the front door. 'My wife will see to it that you are appropriately attired.'

Mrs Jolyon showed Victoria her room in the attic. An iron bedstead with a clean mattress, a wardrobe and a washbasin and jug on a washstand were the only items of furniture. That did not worry Victoria. For the first time in her life she had her own room.

Five minutes later Mrs Jolyon returned with three dresses, two skirts, and two blouses. 'Dinner at eight in the dining room. Mr Jolyon has asked that you join us. He insists on being prompt.'

Victoria examined the clothes carefully after her employer left. They seemed in good condition: no fleas or lice and no fraying.

Victoria selected a blue dress. She did her best to make herself look as respectable as possible because she was to dine with the family that night. She could not believe her luck. Mrs Jolyon did not seem overly friendly, but Mr Jolyon had a pleasant laugh and he had smiled at her. *I hope the little girl will be nice.*

At eight precisely, Victoria descended the stairs and walked as elegantly as she could into the dining room. A large mahogany table with eight seats stood in the centre on a Persian carpet. A mahogany sideboard held plates and glasses on display. What took Victoria's eye immediately was a collection of ten different pistols on the wall. She did not know much about guns, but they looked real.

The girl she had seen on the swing was not there. *I would have liked to get to know her. Mrs Jolyon must be in the kitchen.*

Mr Jolyon strode into the room and offered Victoria a glass of red wine.

'I'm not used to drinking wine, Sir.'

'Good,' said Mr Jolyon taking a gulp of his own. 'Mrs Jolyon and our daughter have had to go over to see Mrs Jolyon's mother.

She is not well.' He seemed a little offhand. Not as friendly as he had been that afternoon.

'Oh! In that case, would you like me to prepare the supper, Sir?' said Victoria, alarm bells ringing in her head.

'That will not be necessary. She's left a cold collation. I keep telling her that we should employ a cook, but apart from having help from a daily cleaning woman, she prefers to do everything herself. More wine?'

'I have not finished this one yet, Sir.'

'Well, put it down and fetch the supper from the kitchen.' He seemed preoccupied about something.

Victoria headed for the kitchen and found an enormous room with a cooking range and a scrubbed pine table. On the table, under a cloth, were a plate of cold meat and a basket of bread. She carried them back to the dining room and placed them on the dining table.

'Sit and eat.'

His manner seemed abrupt. Victoria began to think that this was not such a good job after all.

She sat with one eye on Mr Jolyon. Her mind drifted into thoughts about escape routes as Mr Jolyon droned out a prayer for the food.

Then he heaped his plate, poured more wine, and guzzled his supper.

Victoria picked at the cold meat. She had never had the opportunity to eat meat like this before. In fact, she had seldom eaten any meat before that was not rotten. A creeping fear ruined her appetite.

'Come on, girl, eat something.'

Victoria took a deep gulp of her wine. It made her cough. 'Would you excuse me, Sir, I do not feel very well.' She jumped to her feet, ran upstairs to her room, and slammed the door. There was no lock. She wondered if she could put the wardrobe in front of the door, but she could not budge it. Then she heard footsteps on the wooden stairs.

Victoria sat on her bed, trembling. She was alone and at the mercy of Mr Jolyon. He was not very big, but he had all those guns and that frightened her. She touched the handle of her knife in her boot for reassurance. *It will be no match for a gun.*

The sound of a knock on her door made her jump. 'What do you want?'

'Open the door, please.'

'Why?'

'I said open the door, girl.'

The air of authority in Mr Jolyon's voice told Victoria she had better open the door and do her best to keep the unfolding nightmare under control.

Gingerly she opened the door. There stood Mr Jolyon with a plate of cold meat and a glass of wine. He pushed past her, placed the food and wine on her washstand, and walked back to the door.

'I suggest you eat the meat. You look like you need a good meal. Mrs Jolyon will be back in the morning and then you can start work with our daughter.' And with that, Mr Jolyon walked out of the room and closed the door behind him.

Victoria sat frozen in fear on the bed for an hour listening for his return. He did not come. She ate the meat and left the wine.

The night ticked away slowly. Victoria saw the sun come up.

***

With a beating heart, Victoria came down the stairs at seven thirty. In the kitchen, she saw Mrs Jolyon and the girl sitting at the pine table. Both seemed happy and content. No sign of the worries they showed yesterday.

'Excuse me,' said Victoria.

'Ah, there you are, Victoria. We are so sorry to have left you last evening. My mother has a fever. Her maid came over to tell us that she had woken up. We just had to dash off to see her. I thought you would be resting and did not want to disturb you.'

The girl looked up. 'We thought Grandma was going to die, but she's not going to die.'

Victoria could see the happiness on her face. What she had taken yesterday for something far more sinister was simply worry about her grandma. She would have to rein in her silly fantasies.

'I hope my husband was not too much of a bore. He can be at times.'

Mr Jolyon came out of the pantry carrying a jug of milk. 'Who are you calling boring?' He laughed his nice laugh, as he put his hand around his wife's waist and kissed her on the cheek. 'I may have sounded rather bad tempered last night. It was the worry about my mother-in-law but that is no excuse. Please accept my apologies,' he said to Victoria.

Victoria thought she had much to learn before she judged people.

Mrs Jolyon introduced her daughter. 'This is Elizabeth. Elizabeth, this is Victoria. She will be looking after you. Say hello!'

'Hello,' said Elizabeth, climbing to her feet and offering her hand to Victoria.

Victoria shook it, charmed by her good manners. All looked promising for the future. Victoria's smile went deep inside.

'The reason we need a governess or someone to look after Elizabeth is because I have to go away for a few weeks. Up north to run one of our banks there as the manager has been taken gravely ill. It is only temporary until they find a full-time replacement, but my wife has a lot to do and it would help us if you looked after Elizabeth.'

'Oh,' said Victoria.

'What's wrong?' said Mr Jolyon.

'I was hoping it would be a permanent post, Sir.'

'It will be if you do your job well.' He said it with a smile and Victoria could tell he meant it. The way he treated his daughter and wife showed her what a kind man he was and she looked forward to impressing him.

Later that morning, Victoria wrote out a test for Elizabeth to see how much she knew. The results were encouraging. She was good at arithmetic and reading, and her writing skills were excellent. The age difference between Victoria and Elizabeth was only two years, but one had been brought up in a safe environment and the other had to fend for herself to survive the rigours of the orphanage. The disparity showed. Elizabeth was intelligent and eager to learn. Just like Victoria. While the other children at the orphanage had shirked their lessons and avoided as much reading and writing as possible, Victoria had soaked up everything from the visiting teachers.

'How did you learn all this?' asked Victoria.

'I had a nice teacher. Miss Grant. One day she was teaching me and the next she was gone. Mother said she had stolen something and had been dismissed. Since then Papa has given me lessons. He knows so much!'

A family dinner that evening went well. Mr Jolyon included Victoria in the conversation. Even Mrs Jolyon seemed to warm a little to Victoria's presence. Elizabeth contributed well to the talk and impressed Victoria with her maturity.

Victoria settled in. Mr Jolyon proudly showed her his garden and the silver cups he had won for his vegetables at the annual town fair. She grew fond of Mr Jolyon with his kind manner and happy smile. Mrs Jolyon was always just a little standoffish. She treated Victoria well, but there was always an invisible barrier between them.

One morning Victoria plucked up enough courage to ask Mr Jolyon why he had so many guns on the wall.

'Oh, they're nothing to do with me. They belonged to Mrs Jolyon's late father. Her mother won't have them in the house.'

When Victoria had been at the house for two weeks, the time came for Mr Jolyon to set off up north. Taking leave of his wife with a big kiss and a hug to his daughter, he gave Victoria a friendly smile. She could not help thinking of her first night at the house and the terror she had endured without cause.

***

A few days later Mrs Jolyon arranged a horse and trap to take Elizabeth and Victoria for a picnic in the woods. Mr James would be there at eleven thirty to take them and keep them safe. Nobody messed with Mr James. His wife had made them a lovely home in a village house, but everyone knew he still had the strength and temper of a gypsy as, indeed, he was.

Victoria, Elizabeth, and Mrs Jolyon busied themselves in the kitchen. Ham sandwiches, a pork pie, jelly and lemonade were all packed into a hamper and they were ready. They had even packed extra for Mr James.

'I wish I could come with you,' said Mrs Jolyon.

'Why don't you?' said Victoria. 'Perhaps the man can come back tomorrow to fix the boiler.'

'I do not think so,' said Mrs Jolyon.

A knock at the back door sent Elizabeth off to open it. A look of disappointment crossed her face when she saw it was not Mr James.

'Morning, Miss. I've come to fix the boiler.'

With his smart jacket and trousers and his polished shoes, Victoria did not think he looked much like a boiler man.

'I'll make you a cup of tea before you start,' Mrs Jolyon offered.

A knock on the front door sent Elizabeth in that direction. This time, it was Mr James. He hoisted her into the trap. Victoria carried the hamper.

'Have a lovely time,' called Mrs Jolyon from the front doorstep. She waved them off and closed the door.

The leather seat in the trap smelled of, well, leather. The horse smelled of sweat. Mr James smelled of something odd, akin to carbolic and roses. Victoria reckoned his wife had made him clean himself up before he escorted two young ladies to a picnic.

Mr James pulled the rig to a halt outside the village shop and climbed down. He came out a few minutes later carrying a brown paper bag. He climbed back up into the driver's seat and handed the bag to Victoria. Inside were sweets.

'Oh thank you, Mr James.' She offered him one and then gave the bag to Elizabeth.

Mr James called out to the horse. 'Walk on.'

'Where were you before you came here?' asked Elizabeth.

'In an orphanage.'

'You seem to have an excellent education.'

'The trustees ensured we had visiting teachers. If an orphan was interested, they did try to help as much as possible.'

'Was it a nice orphanage?'

'No.'

'Oh.'

'It was very strict and the man in charge was cruel.'

'That should not be allowed. If I were in charge of such a place, I would make sure it was a safe place for the orphans.'

'I think you would, Elizabeth. Tell me, why do you not go to a school where you could meet other girls your age?'

'Because there isn't one near here and Papa won't allow mother to send me to boarding school. She wanted to, but he forbade it.'

'Would you like to go?'

'Not when Papa is here. He looks after me and we have a lot of fun.'

'And your mother?'

'Well, I'd better not say anything.'

'Why not?'

'Look, Victoria, I don't want to sound spiteful or make accusations, but I am sure that the governess before you did not steal anything. I don't know what happened but she left suddenly.'

'It does sound strange, but I'm sure there's a reasonable explanation.'

'I'm not.'

'What are you going to do when you're older, Elizabeth?'

'I don't know. Get married I suppose. How about you?'

'I'd like to meet a rich man who would look after me.'

'What about love?'

'What about it?'

'Wouldn't you want to marry a man that you loved, Victoria?'

'When you're poor it puts a different slant on things.'

'I shall marry for love.'

'I hope you do, Elizabeth.'

People waved to them as they passed. As they trundled through the streets under a blue sky with little puffs of white cloud Victoria felt that at last she had found safety and happiness in the Jolyons' home. She cast the doubts about Mrs Jolyon from her mind.

They passed a pond where two swans glided as serenely as galleons across the still water. They reminded her of her first morning away from the orphanage when she slept by the River Test. She had watched a swan glide along the river and thought the swans had a better life than her. Now she was not so sure. She had found sanctuary in a nice house and a good job. The fright of the robbers on the footpath came back and she shuddered at the memory. Now she was safe.

In a side street, Victoria saw a small boy rolling a hoop using a stick to keep it going. Another memory trickled into her mind. The children were not allowed to play that game or any others in the orphanage.

'Well now, my young misses, I knows a lovely spot down by the river where you can have your picnic,' said Mr James in his deep voice with a trace of gravel, or so it seemed to Victoria.

'That would be splendid, Mr James,' said Victoria.

'Yes!' said Elizabeth.

Crack!

Victoria felt a sharp jolt and found herself flying through the air. She hit the ground with a bump that knocked the wind out of her. With a shake of her head she looked around and saw Elizabeth lying beside her, still and silent, face down.

'Oh no! Dear God, no.'

First Victoria moved her own legs and arms. Relief flowed when she realised she was uninjured. On her knees, she crawled over to Elizabeth and saw that she was breathing. She rolled her onto her side and she opened her eyes.

'What happened?' asked Elizabeth.

'I don't know. Can you move?'

Elizabeth pushed herself up onto her knees. 'Yes, I think so.'

Victoria saw Mr James in the road, climbing to his feet and rubbing his elbow. He grabbed the reins of the horse.

'Jesus! Sorry, Miss. Is you both all right?'

'I think so. What happened?'

'A wheel fell off. Thank the Lord you lassies ain't hurt.' Letting go of the reins, he strode over to the two girls and lifted Elizabeth to her feet. Then he helped Victoria up. 'I'm so sorry. You sure now, you ain't broken anything?'

Victoria checked herself and Elizabeth. Though their dresses were smeared green, she and her charge were not physically injured.

'It'll take me a couple of hours to fix this. You'd best be getting off home if you're sure you're both all right,' said Mr James.

'That's fine, Mr James. We'll have the picnic another day,' said Elizabeth.

Elizabeth and Victoria walked home carrying the picnic hamper between them.

Nobody locked their door in this quiet town except at night, so Victoria and Elizabeth let themselves in through the front. Victoria put down the hamper. She was glad to get rid of it.

'I'll go up and change out of these clothes,' said Elizabeth, climbing the stairs.

Victoria strode off to find Mrs Jolyon, whom she thought would probably be in the kitchen with the boiler man. Indeed, she was. Victoria opened the kitchen door to find Mrs Jolyon on her back across the pine table, her drawers on the floor and her skirts up around her chest. The boiler man's trousers were round his ankles and he was pumping hard.

Victoria looked in horror at the sight. She knew some boys and girls at the orphanage did it though she had not. She was shocked to see her employer in this position and thought about kind Mr Jolyon so far away. She did not know what to do. Had Mrs Jolyon seen her? If not, she could pretend that she never saw anything. Then her eyes met those of Mrs Jolyon.

'Oh my God, not again!' screamed Mrs Jolyon.

Victoria slammed the door and stood in the hallway, wondering what on earth she was going to do.

Flustered, Mrs Jolyon burst out of the kitchen, now fully clothed. 'Come with me, Victoria, I need to talk to you.'

Victoria followed her into the kitchen. The boiler man now wore his clothes and a sheepish look.

'You did not see anything,' said Mrs Jolyon.

'I did not see anything,' said Victoria.

'You can't trust her,' said the boiler man.

'You're probably right,' said Mrs Jolyon.

'I won't say a word, honest,' said Victoria.

'Too risky,' said the boiler man.

'Yes,' said Mrs Jolyon.

'Please, Ma'am, I won't say anything.'

'Go and get your things. I'm afraid you will have to leave,' said Mrs Jolyon.

'But . . .'

'And do not think you can blackmail us, young lady. We'll say you were dismissed for stealing, like the other one,' said the boiler man.

Victoria knew she would have to go. 'May I have a reference, Ma'am?'

'No, that could complicate matters if you were dismissed for stealing,' said the boiler man.

'Get out now,' said Mrs Jolyon. 'And leave the clothes I lent you behind. Do not speak to Elizabeth on the way out.'

Chapter Four

Three days later, with nothing to eat since leaving the Jolyons' home, Victoria found herself in Southampton. Never before had she seen so many people. She marvelled at how the horse-drawn carriages managed to avoid each other in the busy streets. Fancy ladies with well-dressed men strolled the pavements among rougher locals. An odour drifted on the breeze. It wasn't pleasant. As it seeped into her nostrils and caught in her throat, her empty belly retched. She had nothing to bring up. The smell bore a resemblance to the privy back at the orphanage though this was many times worse. It grew stronger as she wandered down a street and through an arch that bore heraldic shields. They were just like the shields she had seen in the books she had read about knights in shining armour rescuing damsels from evil men. *I wish someone would rescue me.*

Beyond the arch she recognised, again from books, rows of ships' masts on the other side of a long wall. The smell must be the mud flats. A feeling of dread overtook her. *Ships. Woodward. I must be careful.*

A blond woman leant against a wall by a gate. Her face was painted, and her clothes gaudy and few. Victoria knew exactly what she was. She did not look down on anyone unless they meant her harm. For a few moments, she pondered if it was safe to approach her. A quick look up and down the street did not give her cause for alarm and the ache in her tummy spurred her on. She stepped across to speak to the woman.

'Excuse me, but could you tell me where I can get honest work?'

'No honest work around here, dearie.'

A man in a top hat and a well-tailored morning suit came out of a building opposite. He carried a black cane with a silver head. Everything about him exuded wealth, including his bulging belly and coiffed, mutton-chops whiskers. His arrogant manner, as he strolled along the pavement, suggested authority.

'See that gen'lman over there, dearie? Ask him for a shillin' an' he'll give you one.'

'Why would he do that?'

'He's one of them philanthro . . . pillanthr . . . Oh, a bloody do-gooder.'

'A philanthropist?'

'Aye, one 'o them.'

Victoria crossed the street and ran after the man. She caught up with him and tugged his sleeve. 'Excuse me, Sir. Would you please give me a shilling? I have not eaten for three days.'

'Clear off!' said the gentleman.

'Please, Sir. I understand that you are a philanthropist.'

The gentleman turned. 'Perhaps. You're young. That could be worth a shilling. Come down here,' he said, walking into an alley.

'Where are we going, Sir,' she said, following him.

'I think you need some help, young lady. I'm going to take you to someone who will give you something.'

'Thank you kindly, Sir.'

'My pleasure. Always happy to help the less fortunate.'

Things are getting better. This is lucky, meeting him. He'll help me.

He continued down the alley with her still following. A bin held stinking vegetable waste that a rat was enjoying. Water dripped from a pipe in the grey wall, making a puddle across the rough passageway. A cat sat on a high windowsill with its eyes on the rat. Victoria could see no doors at ground level. An uneasy feeling came upon her.

They came to the end of the alley where it was blocked off by a brick wall. *Oh, no!* Shock and fear shot through her body like a cold knife. *How could I be so stupid?*

She turned to run. The gentleman grabbed her by the hand and tripped her with his cane. She rolled over and jumped to her feet. As hard as she could, she kicked him in the leg. 'Take that yer bleedin' cretin.'

He let go of her and dropped his cane. 'Ouch! You little vixen! I'll teach you!' He slapped her across the face, making her lip bleed and her cheek sting. He raised his hand to strike her again.

She lashed out and caught the side of his face with her fingernails, drawing blood that flowed freely from three deep claw marks in his cheek. Then she kicked him hard in the shin, following that up by stamping down with the heel of her boot on his toes. Quick as lightning she kicked him again just behind his knee. Her hand went down to her boot for her knife.

'Come here, you guttersnipe.' He managed to grab her hand before she had a chance to draw her knife. He threw her against the wall. She banged her head, making her woozy. The impact shot pains down her shoulder.

Again she kicked out at his leg, but this time without the same ferocity, feeling sick and disoriented. The impact with the wall had taken its toll.

Still her mind raced to find a way of escape. He stood between her and the open end of the alley. He had her by the throat with one hand.

'Now, young lady. As I said, I'll introduce you to someone.'

She watched in horror, gasping for breath, as he undid the buttons on his trousers with his free hand.

'Leave me alone. I'll scream,' she managed to plead.

He slapped her face again and followed it up with a knee in her stomach. 'If you scream, young lady, I will cut out your tongue.'

She squirmed and writhed but he was too strong for her. With all her might she brought the heel of her boot down again on his toes. Though she tried to scream it came out as a feeble croak due to the pressure on her neck.

He let go for an instant and hopped on one foot. Then he punched her in the face.

White dots appeared before her eyes and she swayed. *He's too strong for me. Please, God help me.*

He went to grab her by the throat again. She pushed him backwards but she could not get around him to escape. Again he grabbed at her. This time he caught her dress at the neck and gripped tightly. With a jerk, he threw her to the ground. She fell on her back. Looking up she saw an ivory Chinaman's head on his watch chain as he finished unfastening his trousers, keeping a knee on her chest to stop her getting up. His hands went up her dress.

She kicked and struggled but he was too strong for her. With all her strength, she pushed upwards but still she could not shake him off.

'Now just lie still. This won't hurt. Well, maybe it will, but just lie still if you want to live,' he said. Victoria could smell alcohol on his breath and some sort of perfume or scent from his greasy hair.

'Don't, please.'

'Shut up.' He slapped her across the face again.

The blow stung. Everything seemed to drift in a haze. For a moment she lay still, unable to fight anymore. She waited for the dreadful experience that would surely befall her at the hands of this brute. Then a little voice inside her head pulled her back from the brink of unconsciousness. Her anger exploded. A tingle went down her arms and legs.

'No, you bastard. No!' Victoria reached down to her boot and curled her fingers around the deer's-foot handle of her knife. Fear clawed at her chest as she gulped a deep breath. Her whole being seemed to gain strength. *I won't let him!* As quick as a mosquito she stabbed him in the thigh of the leg that held her down. She pulled out the knife and stabbed him again so quickly he had no time to react to the first incision. With a mighty push, she threw him off her and onto his back.

Now she was on top of him with her knife at his throat. The red mist of anger and fear clouded her vision. 'You fuckin' pig. I'll make sure you never harm another girl.' She gripped the handle of her knife, ready to slit his throat.

'No, don't, please. I'm sorry. I'm sorry.'

'I'm gonna slit yer gizzard, you bastard.' Then she heard a voice inside her head. *Don't do it. It's wrong. It's murder. Don't.*

'I have money, take it,' he said, shaking all over.

'You think yer bloody money can get you out of the shit? Yer miserable life ain't worth nothin' after what you tried to do.' She pressed the blade hard against his Adam's apple.

'Don't kill me. Please don't kill me,' pleaded the gentleman. He was now the one with terror on his face. 'Please, don't kill me,' he begged. 'In my pocket. May I put my hand in my pocket.'

'Don't do anything stupid or you'll have another mouth,' she said, easing the pressure on his throat to allow him to reach into his pocket.

He reached into his jacket and pulled out four crowns, two half-crowns, a shilling, and two sixpences. He dropped them on the ground. 'Look, it's all yours. Take it. Spare me.'

'I'm not a thief,' said Victoria. 'I'm taking the shilling because you had a feel.'

She picked up the shiny coin, jumped to her feet and ran out of the alley. At the end, she turned and looked at the gentleman.

He was on his feet, brandishing his cane in one hand and trying to stem the blood flow in his leg with the other. 'I shall have my revenge on you someday, you guttersnipe.'

Victoria ran as fast as her legs and lack of food would allow until she had put a good half-mile between her and the alley.

***

Tuppence from her shilling bought some bread and cheese that she ate as she walked north out of Southampton. As it slid down into her belly, her hopes lifted. With it came confidence. She had escaped from Woodward and Tweedale. She had overpowered a big man who wanted to defile her. Starvation was still a possibility, but for now she had enough money to eat for a week. *Unless I get robbed again. This time, they'll not succeed. I shall kill them even if it means the gibbet for me.* Realising the police may be after her for stabbing the man, she left the road and made her way along a path through the woods. The trees gave her shelter from the warm sunshine.

She almost died of fright when a doe shot out from behind a bush across her path, but otherwise she saw no living creature. She could hear many birds in the trees and named each one as she heard its song.

***

Victoria found herself walking alongside a railway track. There were two sets of lines. It was easier than going through the woods. She stopped to rest for a while as the sun made her tired and the adrenaline from her close encounter in the alley subsided. Sitting on a fungi-encrusted, fallen tree trunk surrounded by bushes, she heard men's voices. Her priorities were to avoid being a victim again or being caught by the police for stabbing the gentleman. She ducked down behind the tree trunk.

Two men shuffled along the track. Each carried a barrel. She could not understand what they were saying as they spoke in a foreign language. As her ear tuned in, she decided it must be French. Victoria could not speak French. She could only speak English, but she had once read some of a French Grammar book one of the teachers left at the orphanage. She watched the men bury the barrels under one of the tracks and then run a length of wire off into the woods opposite her.

Are they going to blow up a train and kill people? What can I do? I can't stop them. Or can I? Which way should I go? Which way will the train come from? I can't get past them without being seen so I shall have to go that way. She looked up the track and then, keeping to the undergrowth, she scrambled in that direction, away from the men.

In the distance, she heard a train whistle. As fast as she could she ran through the brambles and bushes towards the sound. Her foot caught in a rabbit hole. She tumbled over and over through the undergrowth. Her precious pennies fell out of her pocket and scattered. Unhurt, she climbed quickly to her feet. Her hand went to her empty pocket. She hesitated. *Without my money, I may starve.* The whistle sounded again. *No time to find my money.* She took a deep breath and carried on running towards the train whistle.

Out of sight of the men, around a bend, she broke cover and ran on to the track. A train headed her way on the line where the men had buried the barrels. She heard the chug-chug of a mighty engine and felt the ground vibrate. Running as fast as she could she waved her hands in the air frantically. The train kept coming, belching out black smoke from its stack and steam from the side. She ran down the same track, waving and shouting. Still the train came on. Two flags billowed in the wind on the front of the train.

Now the train was about two hundred yards away. A great, black, noisy beast, and it was coming straight for her. Victoria stopped running. She stayed on the track, waving her arms and shouting so loud a fishwife would have been jealous.

Then a terrible screech and sparks filled the air. She turned to jump out of the way but her foot caught under the rail, causing her to fall sideways onto the track, the track that carried the mighty engine.

There was no time to roll out of the way. It was almost on her, skidding along the tracks in a shower of sparks. Victoria closed her eyes and waited for the massive iron beast to take her to the Afterlife. *Please, God, I'm a good girl. Let me come into Heaven.*

When the train did not crush her she opened her eyes. There, only two feet away, stood the buffers of the great iron monster.

The driver, a man in a blue overall with a black peaked cap, leapt from the engine and came running at her. 'You stupid girl. Trying to get yourself killed?'

Then she saw policemen, some carrying rifles, jump from a carriage and run towards her. *They're going to shoot me. No, they're going to arrest me for stabbing the gentleman.*

A man in a suit called to the policemen. They stopped. He approached Victoria alone. 'What's going on?' he said.

'Please, Sir, there are men back there, and I think they're going to blow up the train. They've put barrels under the track. You must believe me, please.'

'Thank you. Do you know who they are?'

'No, but they're foreign. They may be French,' said Victoria, looking up at the man.

She struggled to release her foot. The man bent down and helped her. Now free, she stood up. Her foot hurt. Her shoulder and face hurt from the alley incident. The fear of being mangled by a train was the last straw and she collapsed, but managed to look up.

The man signalled to the policemen. They came running. He sent them down the line. Then the man picked her up and carried her to the side of the track where he sat her on the embankment

'Just rest here for a moment and then we will have a talk,' he said. Victoria liked his voice. It had a gentle and kind burr that she recognised as a local Hampshire accent.

A few minutes later, she heard shots and a massive explosion. Above the trees a huge pall of smoke rose.

Then the policemen came back carrying two bodies. She looked away as they reached the train.

One of the policemen said. 'Frog anarchists I think.'

'You've done very well,' said the man in the suit to Victoria. 'I'm Inspector Forbes from Winchester, and I think our important passenger would like to meet you.'

The inspector, holding her under her arm, led her along the track by the side of the train. It had three carriages: all were immaculate and painted green. He stopped at the steps to the central carriage. 'Wait here,' he said and climbed aboard.

Victoria tried not to watch the bodies being loaded into the first carriage, but her eyes were drawn to the scene. *They would have blown up the train and killed lots of people on board, including the important person, whoever he is. I had to do it.*

Inspector Forbes stepped off the train. 'You're going to meet someone very important. Mind your Ps and Qs and everything will be fine.'

The inspector handed Victoria up the step to a butler in a tail coat standing at the door. He pulled her into the carriage.

Victoria's mouth fell open when she looked inside. Never had she seen anything like it, with its heavy, red-upholstered furniture and tapestries. Sitting in an armchair was the important person after whom she was named.

Victoria bobbed a curtsey.

'I understand that I have you to thank for saving my life, young lady,' said Queen Victoria, dressed in black and looking sad.

Inspector Forbes came in. 'Yes, Ma'am. It would have blown this train clean off the tracks and everyone with it.'

'Please sit down,' said the Queen.

Victoria looked at the inspector. He had been asked to sit down, she thought. He shook his head and pointed to a dining chair opposite Her Majesty and nodded to her to be seated. *Oh my goodness. I'm being told to sit in the presence of the Queen.*

'Now, tell me all about yourself,' said the Queen. 'But first we must get you some tea and biscuits. That's all we have, I'm sorry to say.'

Victoria sipped her tea and munched her biscuits as she told of her life, leaving out the bits that she thought would get her arrested. The Queen tut-tutted about the thieves who stole Victoria's life savings.

When Victoria finished her short life history, the Queen said nothing for several minutes. Victoria wondered what the great woman was thinking.

An elegant lady sat in a corner throughout, watching but saying nothing. The Queen beckoned her over and whispered something that Victoria could not hear.

The lady disappeared into the rear carriage. She came back a few minutes later with an envelope, writing paper, pen and an address book.

Her Majesty leafed through the book until she found what she was looking for, wrote something on the paper, sealed it in the envelope and handed it to Inspector Forbes.

'Please deliver this letter with Victoria,' said the Queen. 'It's so difficult these days keeping up with who's who, but the person to whom this letter is addressed I do know well and she is very reliable.'

'Yes, Ma'am,' said the inspector with a smile.

'I'm very grateful to you, Victoria, for saving my life. You have had an unfortunate time in your short life and I have, I hope, done something in gratitude that will make things better for you in the future.' She waved her hand.

The inspector took Victoria's elbow and led her to the rear carriage. She looked back over her shoulder at the Queen. Her Majesty looked sad. Victoria knew why. Everyone in the country knew why. The death of Prince Albert, only a few months earlier, had broken her heart.

The Queen called, 'Good luck, and thank you again.'

The train chugged backwards into a station ten minutes down the line and made an unscheduled stop, throwing the stationmaster and his staff into a panic.

Inspector Forbes and Victoria alighted.

The train chugged away, back in the direction of Salisbury from where it had come. Victoria looked at the centre carriage. The Queen sat by the window and waved to her. Victoria waved back.

***

The inspector found a pony and trap with its owner, a jolly little man with a big beard, outside the station. A flash of the inspector's warrant card and half a crown soon had them on their way.

'Where are we going?' asked Victoria as they trotted sedately along a Hampshire country lane.

'To a new life for you, young lady.'

In the distance, on the side of a gently sloping hill, Victoria saw a grand house. It looked to her like the Greek and Roman temples she had seen pictures of in the teacher's encyclopaedia. Beyond the house, far away to the west, she recognised the outline of Gallows Hill. Her active brain worked out that she had travelled half a circle to end up on the opposite side of Gallows Hill from the orphanage.

Cows munched in green meadows, birds sang in the trees and the gentle sun shone down on Victoria. She did not know where she was going. *If it is to that magnificent house to be a maid, I would be so happy. Perhaps the Queen has found me a job as a governess at that house or some other. It would not be for the owner's children. Such a job as governess to the aristocracy would go to someone far more qualified than I. But it could be for their staff, perhaps, I hope. That really would be marvellous but a little too much to hope for, so I'll settle for being a maid.*

Wobbling around a bend came a fat constable, all eighteen stone of him. He jumped to the side to avoid the pony and trap and fell into a ditch on the side of the road.

'Blasted fool,' said the constable checking his limbs. He picked grass and twigs from his uniform and climbed out of the ditch.

'You all right, Constable Hemingway?' said the driver, desperately trying not to laugh and then giving in.

'Damned fool, what do you think you're doing riding at that breakneck speed? Sorry, Miss. Oh, sorry, Inspector.'

They left the constable brushing off his uniform.

The pony and trap pulled up at the open gates of the house she had first seen from a distance. This grand building stood at the end of a long white drive. Victoria read the name on the gate pillar: Eagledown House.

As the pony and trap halted at the bottom of steps leading up to a massive oak door, Victoria looked all around. The gardens had perfect symmetry. A fountain with a nude woman's statue filled an enormous, shell-like bowl from an amphora the figure held under its arm.

The oak door opened. A strong-looking man, probably in his late forties, strode down the steps to the pony and trap. His hands looked large and his shoulders well muscled. He seemed a little out of place in the tailed coat, striped trousers, white shirt and white tie. He had sparkling green eyes.

The inspector climbed down from the pony and trap and handed down Victoria.

She looked at the big man and curtsied. *Today I spoke to the Queen and now I'm in the presence of a man who must at least be a lord to have such a great estate. Tweedale and Woodward will not get me here.*

The big man grinned at Victoria. 'I'm Humphreys, the butler. And what may I do for you, Sir?' He turned his attention to the inspector.

'I have a letter for Lady Luisa from Her Majesty. May we see her?'

'I do believe a letter from Her Majesty would allow you to see the mistress, Sir.' Again a huge grin creased his tanned face. Victoria liked him. She hoped she would be working for him as a maid. He looked kind and would not beat her or make her work more than twelve hours a day. He did not appear bothered by her unkempt appearance. He left them standing in the entrance hall and came back a few moments later.

Humphreys ushered Victoria and Inspector Forbes into a drawing room. Victoria took in the surroundings immediately. Portraits of people on the walls, tapestries, carpets, a huge marble fireplace and a black, lacquered sideboard exuded the wealth of the owner. *All this will keep me busy if I'm to be a maid here.* But she did not mind hard work and the lady, sitting on a wing-back chair near the fireplace cross stitching a rural scene, looked lovely in a long, white dress fringed with lace.

'Ma'am, Inspector Forbes and Miss Victoria,' said Humphreys. Then he stepped out of the drawing room, closing the double doors behind him.

'I believe you have correspondence for me from Her Majesty,' said the lady, holding out a delicate hand.

Inspector Forbes slipped the envelope from his inside pocket and handed it to her.

She used the blade of a pair of scissors to slit the envelope open. 'How is Her Majesty, Inspector?' she said, glancing at the letter.

'Fair to middling I'd say, Ma'am. I do not think I'm talking out of turn if I say she's still suffering her loss terribly.'

'Poor woman. I know how she feels.' The lady read the letter.

> Dear Luisa,
>
> I remember how kind you have been to me. I do not think anyone else understood what I was and what I am still going through. Enough of my problems: I believe I have the opportunity to repay your kindness now that you are the Chatelaine of Eagledown until your nephew is of age to inherit.
>
> I am sure the estate under your direction will continue to hold one of the finest herds of cattle in Europe.
>
> I have sent a young lady to you, Victoria. She saved my life from assassins. Due to the current political climate, I am afraid that cannot be acknowledged.
>
> She has had a troubled short life and it would please me if you could take her on as your companion and bring her up into society.
>
> I know only too well how lonely you are since your dear Robert was lost at sea and you find yourself alone in that huge house, now that your family have gone to Africa. Yes, I do keep informed as to what is happening!
>
> I am sure that she would repay your kindness by bringing a little light back into your life.
>
> Victoria R.

Lady Luisa Bonchurch looked up and smiled. 'Thank you, Inspector. I think that will be all. If you are hungry, please go along to the kitchen and Cook will make you a bacon sandwich or anything else you wish.'

'Thank you, Ma'am,' said the inspector. He turned to leave the room and smiled at Victoria.

She smiled back.

Victoria felt her tummy rumble. *Dare I say something? She looks kind. If I do not, I will stay hungry.* 'Please, Ma'am, may I go with the inspector for a bacon sandwich? I've only eaten some bread and cheese in the last few days. Her Majesty gave me a cup of tea and biscuits, but I've not eaten a meal for days. I would be very grateful if I could go with the inspector to have a bacon sandwich, Ma'am.' She bobbed a curtsy.

'Certainly not,' said Lady Luisa. She pulled a bell cord by the fireplace.

Not so good here after all.

Humphreys appeared in the doorway.

'Please bring the young lady a bacon sandwich,' said Lady Luisa.

Victoria looked around to see who the young lady was and wondered, *Why can't I have a bacon sandwich if she's getting one?* She surprised even herself with such selfish thoughts. But she found she was alone with Lady Luisa.

Humphreys made his exit. Lady Luisa gestured to Victoria to sit down.

'Now tell me all about yourself,' said Lady Luisa.

Victoria launched into her story, still with a little resentment at not getting a bacon sandwich, until her eyes lit up when Humphreys returned with one on a silver tray and placed it on her knee.

And Victoria did—almost—tell all between mouthfuls of sandwich. She left out the name of the Jolyons in case she was wanted by the police for stealing, and the incident with the 'gentleman' in case she was wanted for stabbing him.

'You poor girl,' said Lady Luisa after Victoria had finished her story. 'Now, what to do with you?'

'I can cook and clean, Ma'am. I could help the governess if there are any children. I'll do any honest work, Ma'am, if you'll let me stay here.'

'Victoria, I do not think you realise why you are here.'

'Her Majesty, I believe, wanted me to have honest employment so she sent me here.'

'No,' said Lady Luisa.

Victoria's spirits sagged. *Just when things seem to be going so well, like at the Jolyons' home, it goes wrong.* Though not given to self-pity she felt more than a little of it as she sat in that warm, dry drawing room, thinking that soon she would be out on the street again. *Why did the Queen go to all that trouble just to get me a bacon sandwich?*

Victoria watched as Lady Luisa pulled the bell cord again. *This is it. I'm going to be thrown out now. Is it worth pleading? No. I'll keep my dignity. How unfair life is!*

A maid appeared in the doorway dressed in a long black dress, white apron and white hat.

'Jane, please take Miss Victoria to the green room. It will be her bedroom.'

'Yes, Ma'am.' Jane bobbed a curtsey.

'Oh thank you, Ma'am. I'll be a good worker. I'll work as many hours as you need.' Victoria curtsied with an enormous grin of relief on her face. She would not be thrown out on the street. *I'm going to be a maid in a posh house!*

'I think you misunderstand, Victoria. You are not here to work. You are here to learn how to be a lady and take your place in society. And I have a feeling it will be fun teaching you,' said Lady Luisa.

Victoria's eyes widened and her mouth fell open. 'Me? A lady? Oh my goodness!'

Jane led the lady in training up an ornate wooden staircase to the first floor and along a corridor with paintings of birds and animals on the walls. The carpet, a deep red, felt soft under Victoria's feet. Jane opened a door and guided Victoria inside. The room was half the size of the dormitory at the orphanage. The dormitory held twenty beds. This room only one. *A big bed with four posts and a roof!*

'This will be your room, Miss,' said Jane. She opened another door and Victoria peered in. An enormous white bath took up the centre. Black and white tiles covered the floor and a toilet stood in the far corner. Not a hole in the floor like the orphanage. She had seen an inside toilet before—the Jolyons had one—but not as fancy as this one, with blue-patterned country scenes.

Victoria's face filled with concern. The smile that had lit her face when she realised the huge bedroom was hers disappeared.

'What's wrong, Miss?'

'A house this size must have a lot of people wanting to use the privy. They will be in and out all night.'

Jane laughed. 'No, silly! I'm sorry, no, Miss. The bathroom is for you only, as is the bedroom.'

Victoria's mouth fell wide open again.

Jane opened a wardrobe. Empty. 'If I know Lady Luisa this will be full of the finest clothes for you very soon.'

Victoria could not believe her luck.

Jane turned the brass taps to fill the bath. Victoria backed up against the wall.

'Whatever is the matter?'

'Please don't make me get in there. I don't like water.'

'But you have to bathe, Miss.'

'Can you make it so there's only about that much in then?' said Victoria, holding her forefinger and thumb three inches apart.

'I suppose so,' said Jane with a puzzled look.

When the bath had the right depth, Victoria gingerly slipped off her clothes and climbed in. She screamed when Jane poured water over her hair.

'It's all right, Miss. I understand. Put your head back and the water will run down your back and not your face.'

Jane eventually managed to get Victoria bathed and her hair washed. She gave her a clean dress. 'This used to belong to Penelope,' said Jane.

'Who is Penelope?'

'Lady Luisa's niece.'

'Does she live here?'

'She did until very recently. She's off to Africa with her family.'

Clean, dressed and ready, Victoria made her way back to the drawing room. As she came down the stairs, she met Humphreys going in the opposite direction.

'My word you do look lovely, Miss.'

Victoria blushed and smiled.

In the drawing room, she found Lady Luisa still working on her cross stitch.

Lady Luisa smiled at her new protégé as Victoria bobbed a curtsey. 'You do not have to do that for me, Victoria. I will teach you to whom you curtsey and to whom you should offer your hand. First of all, we need a name for you to call me. Lady Luisa is too formal for everyday use. Aunt makes me sound like an old fuddy-duddy.

'Jane told me your name is Lady Luisa Bonchurch. You're a pretty lady. May I call you Bonnie?'

'Splendid! Yes, that would be wonderful when we are alone or with friends. But on formal occasions, or when we have stuffy visitors, I think we will have to be a little more formal. So at those times perhaps you had better call me Aunt, much as I dislike that epithet, even though my nephew and niece use it and I love them both dearly.'

'Yes, Bonnie!' Victoria had not been in the presence of a real lady before and expected that they would be frighteningly posh and stern. Bonnie was neither. She seemed a gentle and kind person. Victoria could not wait to start learning how to be a lady.

Chapter Five

On Victoria's first full day as a 'young lady' she came down for breakfast at eight, roused from a deep sleep in her feather bed by Jane. She had bathed in three inches of water, cleaned her teeth and dressed in the dress that Jane had given her the previous day.

Bonnie, dressed in blue, sat at the far end of the breakfast table in the dining room. Victoria took in her surroundings. More paintings of people hung on the yellow walls. Three sets of windows looked out across a terrace to landscaped gardens full of roses and other bushes. She smelt the unmistakable odour of fresh bread baking and a slight whiff of beeswax from the heavy table and a huge sideboard laden with plates and dishes. Humphreys smiled at Victoria as he held an upholstered chair for her so she knew where to sit.

'Good morning, Victoria. I hope you slept well,' said Bonnie.

'Good morning Lady Luisa, er, Aunt, er, Bonnie, er, is this a formal occasion?'

Bonnie smiled. 'No.'

'Good morning, Bonnie,' said Victoria with a grin. 'I slept very well, thank you.'

'And what would Miss Victoria like for breakfast?' said Humphreys.

'I don't know Mr Humphreys. What can I . . . may I have?'

'Well, there's scrambled egg with smoked salmon, devilled kidneys, sausages, bacon and eggs and I do believe we have some smoked haddock that would go nicely with a poached egg,' said Humphreys.

'I would like bacon and eggs please, Mr Humphreys.'

Humphreys smiled and left to fetch her breakfast.

Bonnie looked over at Victoria. 'Well done. Now, about Humphreys . . . He's the butler. We call him Humphreys, not Mr Humphreys. It's just the conventional way things are done.'

Victoria thought for a moment and then looked up at Bonnie. 'I understand. But I am sixteen years old and he's, well I don't know, a lot older. It seems disrespectful for me to call him Humphreys. If you don't mind, I would like to continue to call him Mr Humphreys.'

'Victoria, if you wish to call the butler "Mr Humphreys" then please do. I think that is quite charming.'

They smiled at each other. Humphreys arrived with Victoria's bacon and eggs.

***

Victoria's first day of 'lady training' involved a tour of the estate, starting with the house. After breakfast, Bonnie took her along the main corridor that led from the drawing room, past the dining room and two other reception rooms. Many of the paintings on the green walls were of heroic battle scenes. Victoria did not know much about battles. She knew about Waterloo, but that was the only one.

Bonnie opened a door and led Victoria inside. The walls were dark wood-panelling with brackets to hold candles and shelves of books. A large desk with a green leather top overlooked the gardens at the side of the house, and a captain's chair, also in green leather, sat by the desk.

Victoria gazed out of the window. Most of the plants in this area of the garden were rhododendrons. In the corner of the room stood two cane fishing rods and a landing net, together with a pair of waders. The room was obviously a man's, thought Victoria. A stuffed bird sat in an enormous glass case on a table by a marble fireplace.

'That's a funny looking bird, Bonnie. I haven't seen one like that before. What is it?'

'It is a Dodo.'

'Do they live around here?'

Bonnie laughed. 'No. They lived on a tropical island somewhere. It is believed they are extinct now. One of my ancestors brought this one back from his travels around the world.'

'I'd like to travel around the world.' *But not as the guest of Woodward or Tweedale.*

'Perhaps someday you will.'

'Whose room is this?'

'It was my father's but Richard has some of his things in here. That oar for instance,' said Bonnie, pointing to an oar on the wall above the door.

'Richard? Who is he?'

'My nephew. He is, or will be, the owner of Eagledown. My father left it to him.'

'Where is he?'

'He's in Africa.'

'Oh, is his sister Penelope?'

'Yes.'

'Jane said the family were all in Africa. When are they coming back?'

'When Richard is twenty-five.'

'And when is that?'

'In four years. My goodness, such a lot of questions.'

'I'm sorry. Should I not ask questions?'

'Please carry on asking them. You need to know all about Eagledown.'

'This Richard, is he rich?'

'Yes. He will own Eagledown and all the tenant farms when he is twenty-five. And he will be Sir Richard then.'

'Oh, that is interesting.'

'He is married.'

'Oh!'

'His wife, Peggy, lives at Abbeyhill Farm.'

'When she's not in Africa?'

'She isn't in Africa.'

'So Richard is in Africa but his wife is in England?'

'Yes. It is complicated and I don't understand it myself.'

'Oh, I see. Well, actually I don't see.'

'Let's move on.'

Among the paintings on the wall, directly over the fireplace hung a huge painting of a soldier on a horse with another soldier standing alongside, holding the reins. The light from the window gave the colours more lustre.

'That's my father,' said Bonnie.

Victoria heard footsteps in the corridor outside.

She looked closely at the soldier holding the reins. 'That looks like . . .'

'It is,' said Bonnie. 'He was my father's batman. When they were in India, they were cut off after an attack, without horses. Papa had been speared in the leg. Humphreys stood over him and fought off the enemy, with his bare hands when he ran out of ammunition, and then carried him for three days to safety.'

Humphreys passed the door with a tray.

Victoria called after him. 'Mr Humphreys.'

He stopped, turned and, with a smile, entered the room.

'You are a very brave man, Mr Humphreys,' said Victoria. 'Doing what you did and then carrying a man all that way.'

'No, Miss. I had to carry the guv'nor. He knew the way back and I didn't.'

Victoria was sure she saw a twinkle in his green eyes. 'I think you're teasing me.'

Humphreys bowed, smiled and continued on his way.

'Does anyone use this room now, Bonnie?'

'I occasionally do for the accounts. But it is a little drab for my liking.'

At the end of the corridor a door led out into the rear yard. Bonnie and Victoria crossed the gravel to stables at the far side. Victoria counted ten boxes.

'That's a lot of horses, Bonnie.'

'Not all are occupied.'

Bonnie lifted the latch on the wooden door at the near end of the stable block. Inside Victoria smelt the fresh hay and not so fresh horse droppings.

Victoria jumped backwards when the black head of a horse poked out nosily from the first box to examine the visitors. Bonnie had come armed with sugar lumps. The horse nibbled them from her hand.

'What's her name?'

'Solomon!' said Bonnie.

'Solomon?' Victoria looked underneath the horse. 'Oh! Bugger! Er . . . sorry.'

'You try it.' Bonnie handed Victoria two sugar lumps.

Victoria was unsure. She had not handled horses before and this was a big one with huge teeth. She closed her eyes and held out her hand. It tickled as the horse helped itself to the treat. Opening her eyes, she said, 'This is a beautiful horse. Do you ride him?'

'No. He belongs to Richard.'

'What happens when Richard and his family come back? Will we have to leave?'

'I do not know.'

'Well, he's not due back for four years. That gives us plenty of time to find somewhere else. Perhaps I'll marry a rich man and then I'll be able to take care of you.'

'I think we are getting a little ahead of ourselves. Anyway, do not think of marrying for money. Marry only for love.'

'You can't eat love and it won't put clothes on your back or a roof over your head.'

'Are you sure you're only sixteen?'

They both laughed and then stopped when a rustle in an empty box startled them.

A gangly lad a couple of years older than Victoria stuck his head above the lower half door. Another head popped up beside him. Her blond hair full of straw and her blouse open, she ducked down again.

'Er, this is Jake the stable boy,' said Bonnie with embarrassment. 'And that's Abigail, one of the maids.' She took Victoria by the hand and led her out of the stable into the yard.

'It's all right, Bonnie. I know what it's all about!'

Bonnie recovered her composure. 'Do you ride?'

'I've never tried.'

'Then you shall have your first lesson this afternoon. I'll have Tess saddled up for you.'

They spent the rest of the morning in and around the house. Victoria marvelled at the orangery with its pond in the centre, home to a myriad of brightly coloured fish.

Humphreys brought them lemonade as they sat in the garden watching the birds. Victoria impressed Bonnie by knowing most of the birds' names, from a sparrow to a heron that flew overhead.

'Where did you learn all that?'

'We had to tend the garden at the orphanage. I watched the birds and the teacher lent me a book so I could see what they were.'

'What is your favourite bird?'

'The swan. We didn't have any swans at the orphanage. But I've seen pictures of them in my book. And I did see two on the river. They're so beautiful and elegant.'

'Swans partner for life. Did you know that?'

'No. They stay together always?'

'Until one dies.'

The thought seemed to sadden Bonnie.

'Are they allowed to find a new partner when one dies?'

'Yes, I think so. Perhaps some find another and some do not.'

Victoria wanted to give Bonnie a hug. She was not sure if it was the right thing to do, but it felt right. So she did, much to Bonnie's surprise, and the elegant Bonnie hugged her back.

That afternoon Victoria and Tess were introduced to each other. After two hours, Victoria had mastered how to get the horse to go in the direction required without her falling off. It seemed so unnatural to ride side-saddle but Bonnie insisted. Together with Bonnie—Jake following up just in case—Victoria rode out across the estate.

A herd of Herefords grazed on the lush pasture.

'This is a very special herd, Victoria. The estate makes a lot of its income from breeding and selling them on,' said Bonnie.

'What makes them so special?'

'It's their history, their bloodline. It goes back a long way. We've won many prizes with them.'

'They're a sort of cow aristocracy then?'

Bonnie laughed. 'I had not thought of it that way but, yes, perhaps they are.'

'We'd best take good care of them.'

***

Bonnie did as the Queen had requested. It did indeed bring her happiness as she involved herself in the training of Victoria. The young woman's accent already had the hallmarks of the upper crust ... When she was not excited. A Tartar of an elocution teacher ironed out the few tell-tale expressions. Every time he left, Victoria and Bonnie convulsed with giggles at the man's complete lack of humour.

Jake taught her how to ride side-saddle and astride, though the latter was frowned on by Bonnie so they did it away from the house.

Not on Solomon. The horse was far too temperamental for a novice to handle. She rode Tess, a gentle grey mare. It did not take long for her to master the rudiments of riding. The horse seemed to take an instant liking to her. Soon, not content with a quiet trot through the Hampshire countryside, she had Tess galloping up and down the miles of bridleways, across open fields and over fences, and she did not do this side-saddle.

Hours spent in the library brought Victoria a wealth of knowledge. Bonnie used the same room for deportment lessons. Not only did Victoria get to read the books, she had to walk up and down with one on her head.

A kind old lady who always smelled of lavender came twice a week to give Victoria piano and singing lessons.

Humphreys taught her all about which knife and fork to use, which glass to drink from, how an estate ran 'below stairs' and how to address all the different social ranks that she would meet. Victoria enjoyed her time with him. He was almost the father figure she never knew.

***

One year after Victoria's arrival at Eagledown, Bonnie decided the time had come for her first foray into upper-class society.

Not a cloud appeared in the sky as the multi-talented Jake tapped two horses pulling the carriage along a winding lane. Ahead, nestling on the side of a hill, Victoria saw an imposing Georgian mansion.

Jake manoeuvred the horses through tall, wrought-iron gates and along a gravel driveway to the front of the house, where he brought them to a skilful stop, jumped down and opened the carriage door.

First he helped Bonnie down and then Victoria. A few butterflies flitted around Victoria's tummy as she looked at her surroundings. A parasol kept the warm sun from her discreetly made up face under her perfectly coiffed hair. She looked down at her white shoes and just the slightest exposure of her ankles under white silk stockings. Her pastel blue dress, cut in the latest fashion, helped her confidence. This encounter could set the tone for her future. If she failed then all the hard work of so many people would be for nothing.

Jake gave her a smile and then jumped back on the carriage and drove away.

Victoria could hear the garden party at the rear of the house. She smiled to see the familiar face of Lord Peter Abbott, a regular visitor to Eagledown House, as he strode down the steps from the house. Victoria placed him in his early fifties. The mutton-chop whiskers on his ruddy face always made him look cheerful, though she knew that inside he carried a great sadness. Bonnie had told her that he had been a widower for ten years since his wife and children died of cholera in Shanghai. The dashing lord had been a soldier and diplomat, and now he was Bonnie's good-natured rival in the cattle business. Hopefully, in Victoria's opinion, he was also her benefactor's suitor; though Bonnie would never admit to such an idea. Currently, he held the first prize for his Hereford bull, but Bonnie would take it from him eventually, with a lot of luck.

Lord Peter kissed Bonnie's hand. Victoria offered her hand. He took it gently and gave a slight squeeze and a smile. Then he led them both around the house to the gardens. A white marquee stood in the middle of perfect lawns bordered with box hedges and, on the far side, with a rose garden. People stood about, the ladies in fashionable dresses and hats, the men a field of grey in morning suits. All seemed to be drinking champagne.

A butler offered a tray of champagne to Bonnie and Victoria. 'May I have something else, please, perhaps a glass of lemonade?' said Victoria.

The butler nodded acquiescence and disappeared into the marquee.

A knot of well-heeled guests stood by a magnolia tree, champagne glasses firmly held in one hand and little biscuits with caviar in the other. They were all busy talking, but none of them appeared to be listening.

Lord Peter interrupted their interlocution. 'You all know Lady Luisa; I would like to introduce her niece, Miss Victoria Sillitoe.'

'Oh darling,' said a fat woman in a big hat. 'I thought Adele only had Penelope and Richard. Of course, Sillitoe, you could not possibly be Adele's.'

'You must be Robert's sister's child,' said a tall, thin woman dressed in pink, looking down her nose at Victoria. 'Though I did not think he had any siblings.' She laughed like a crow.

'I do not believe I know the Sillitoes,' said a man with grey hair and a long beard.

Victoria felt the anger swell up inside her as they discussed her in her presence.

The knot of people looked at Victoria, and not with kindness. An atmosphere hung over the gathering as though they were vultures waiting to tear their victim to shreds, albeit metaphorically. This was her first trial. She must not let her anger show.

'Is it not so frightfully difficult to keep up these days with who's who? Even Her Majesty remarked to me on that fact when I travelled with her last year,' said Victoria, turning to take her lemonade from the tray with which the butler had returned.

Lord Peter and Bonnie stifled a chuckle and the three of them moved on, leaving the vultures to ponder if they would suffer social repercussions after being rude to someone so well connected.

The rest of the garden party greeted Victoria kindly. Soon she felt completely at ease in this company. She did not put a foot wrong. Staying well clear of politics and religion, she captivated all who spoke to her. Even the vultures mellowed. Perhaps not because of her undeniable charm; more likely out of the desire to be in the presence of someone who moved in royal circles.

***

Another year slipped by with Victoria watching the changing seasons as they brought the bright, fresh colours of spring, the deep shades of summer and the reds and browns of autumn. The winter brought snow and ice, but Victoria enjoyed the evenings sitting by a roaring log fire in intellectual discussion with Bonnie on subjects ranging from politics to geography and ancient Greece, with its myths and legends.

Sometimes she would play the piano for Bonnie and sing. The staff would find some excuse to be near to hear her, particularly Humphreys.

By the time the next spring filled the meadows with wildflowers, Victoria had blossomed into a beautiful young lady who could ride, hold an intelligent conversation, play the piano and sing as sweet as a nightingale. She had become a sought-after guest at soirees and a delight to accompany to Ascot, Henley and Cheltenham.

But High Society was not enough for Victoria. Her farming enterprise started one morning over breakfast.

'Bonnie, I need to earn some money.'

'Whatever for? Do you not have all you need here?'

'Yes, but I want to buy a headstone for my brother's grave and my mother's, if I can find them.'

'An admirable idea, but you do not need to work. I will give you the money to buy the headstones.'

'Thank you, Bonnie, but that is not what I want to do. I want to earn the money to pay for them myself. Please do not be offended. I am grateful for the offer, but you do understand?'

'I do indeed. What work did you have in mind?'

'If I may have a patch of ground I shall grow vegetables that I will send to the market. When I have raised enough money from that, I will buy sheep. I will breed the sheep, and when I have enough of them, I shall sell them and buy the headstones.'

Bonnie clasped her hands in front of her and laughed. 'Victoria, you never cease to amaze me!'

With the help of old Jonah, Eagledown's retired chief gardener, and Jake, Victoria soon had a thirty-by-fifteen-yard vegetable plot ready for planting.

Jonah contributed some plants and seeds from his own smallholding and showed Victoria how to plant them and make sure they had plenty of water.

Every morning, after breakfast, Victoria would dash off to her plot to see how much her crops had grown. There were carrots, cabbages and potatoes to start her foray into market gardening.

***

Victoria wandered into the stables looking for Jake. She found him brushing down Solomon.

'Jake, when you're in town could you please pick up these things for me? I need them for the vegetables.' She handed him a note.

He stared at it and shook his head.

'What is the matter?'

'Can't read, Miss.'

'Why?' Victoria wondered why she did not know this already, but she had had no cause to ask him to read anything before. She felt a pang of guilt. Not knowing seemed a failure on her part to fully understand what happens on an estate such as Eagledown.

'Never learned, Miss. Too busy to go to school.'

'But it's so important to be able to read and write.'

'I get by, Miss.'

But getting by was not something Victoria would tolerate. She felt a responsibility. 'Would you be willing to learn if I taught you?'

'I would, Miss, and so would some of the others. There're lots of people can't read and write.'

How could I not know this? I've been too selfish looking after my own interests. Well, from now on I shall jolly well make sure I think of others.

Victoria turned on her heels and marched back to the house. A quick search found Bonnie in the drawing room with Reverend Smythe, the local vicar.

'Excuse me interrupting, Aunt Luisa, but I've just been talking to Jake. Did you know that he and many others on the estate cannot read or write?'

'Yes.'

'I did not, and I think they ought to learn!'

'There is talk of making schooling compulsory, but I'll believe it when I see it,' said Reverend Smythe, wiping tea from his walrus moustache.

'With your permission, Aunt Luisa, I would like to teach them.'

'In addition to your new farming enterprise?'

'Indeed so. I have plenty of time. I just need a suitable building.

'Victoria, I have absolutely no objection to your taking on this task if you feel you are up to it. I'll see what I can do to find a suitable building on the estate. But please remember, this is a working estate and the staff will have to do their school work in their own time.'

'Oh yes, of course, Bonnie . . . I mean, Aunt Luisa. Thank you. I'll leave you in peace now.'

The vicar smiled.

***

Victoria found an old barn down the slope from an irrigation dam by a stream in a fold in the landscape. Bonnie gave her permission to convert it into a schoolhouse. With Jake and other men from the estate, she set about her mission. Soon she had a classroom. The whitewashed walls reflected plenty of light from the windows that Jake had skilfully installed. Oak beams held the pitched ceiling under a slate roof. Jake even made a blackboard. Trestle tables made do as desks. An odd assortment of chairs, rescued from various parts of the estate, provided the seating.

She sat on the irrigation dam, looking down on the schoolhouse. Her school would start the next morning. She felt pleased and proud that she would contribute something useful. Bonnie hadn't really the heart to make the workers learn in their own time and allowed three hours, two mornings a week, for school lessons.

***

Bonnie had already eaten most of her breakfast by the time Victoria arrived in the dining room on the first school day. Though she had hardly slept all night, Victoria had drifted off to sleep just before the time to get up and had been roused by Jane.

'I'll have the smoked haddock please, Mr Humphreys, with a poached egg.'

'Yes, Miss.'

'All set for your students?' said Bonnie.

'I hope so.'

Victoria tried not to bolt her breakfast and then made her way over to the stables to ride Tess to the schoolhouse. Jake had saddled her already.

A gentle rain fell as she passed her vegetable plot and then the irrigation dam. Her ride was slow as she pondered the coming day. She tied Tess to a rail outside the schoolhouse and went in.

Jake had beaten her to the school. Abigail and several other men and women, ranging from their early twenties to their fifties, sat at desks. They stood as Victoria came in.

'Please sit down.' Victoria handed out slates and chalk. 'Anyone know what the date today is?'

'Saturday, Miss,' said Jake.

Victoria smiled and chalked on the blackboard.

'Saturday, 25th June 1864.'

She did not tell them it was her birthday.

Then a memory shot through her. *Two years exactly since I escaped from Tweedale and Woodward. Someday I will have my revenge. No, don't say that. If you hate, you are the loser. I must not let hate rule my life. Look how well it has turned out for me.*

***

The school prospered, and within a month Victoria had fifteen students. They had no money. Victoria made it plain that she did not want payment of any sort, but these were proud people, if poor, and insisted. Each student gave one hour per week of their own time to work on Victoria's vegetable plot, and soon the plot trebled and then quadrupled.

Then Victoria had another bright idea. She read in a magazine about the 'Rochdale Pioneers' and how they had set up a cooperative movement in that town. She decided to make her vegetable project a cooperative. The result was a little money for the workers and a little for Victoria. Not enough yet to buy the headstones, but she was going in the right direction and would get there soon. She felt her brother and mother would not mind waiting a little longer for their headstones if it meant that some of the living poor could improve their lot.

***

Bonnie and Victoria were to be guests at a dinner given by the Middletons who lived a few miles away from Eagledown in a lovely Elizabethan house with views for miles. Lord Peter escorted them while Jake drove their carriage. Victoria liked Mr and Mrs Middleton. Whenever she met them at social functions, they always made a point of talking to her. Mr Middleton was particularly interesting and knowledgeable about birds. He had travelled in China and Africa. His study held a broad range of paintings of birds that he had done himself and a collection of eggs that fascinated Victoria.

The late July evening felt warm and the sun still had a couple of hours before it disappeared over the horizon. They stopped at massive, wrought-iron gates. A long white drive led to the house. The garden looked lovely. It had always looked good on her previous visits, but she had not been here for several months and now it looked very different: more beautiful and more colourful.

Victoria found herself noticing gardens more and more as she expanded her vegetable enterprise.

Mr Middleton, tall, with the bearing of a military man, strolled down the steps at the front of the house to greet them. His wife, in a fashionable pastel-blue dress that failed to disguise her wide hips, followed.

Hands were shaken, bows and curtsies exchanged before the party went inside, through the house and onto a large terrace overlooking the gardens. On the terrace, they were met by the other fifteen guests.

A butler served champagne. A maid dispensed mouth-watering hors d'oeuvres.

At the far side of the lawns stood a walled garden that Victoria knew would contain the vegetable plot. Taking Mr Middleton aside, she said, 'Would you mind terribly if I took a look at your vegetable plot. I am really interested.'

'So I hear,' said Mr Middleton with a chuckle. 'Go ahead.'

Discreetly she placed her champagne glass on a stone table and made her way across the lawn to the walled garden. A wrought-iron gate lay open. Through the doorway, Victoria could see the tidy rows of lettuce, onions and runner beans. She stepped into the garden.

Over by the far side a gardener weeded a row of tomatoes. He was so preoccupied with his task that he had not noticed her come in. A gravel path led through the garden to where the gardener worked and she strolled over to chat with him about herbs. She wanted to improve her herb garden.

'Excuse me,' said Victoria.

The gardener looked up, taken by surprise. He doffed his flat cap. 'Sorry, Miss, I didn't see you come in.' Then their eyes met. He blinked.

'Mr Jolyon?' said an astonished Victoria.

'Victoria?'

Victoria could feel his embarrassment. 'What are you doing here?'

'It's a long story, Victoria. I'm sorry, Miss, I should say, looking at you. You've done well. I'm so pleased for you.' His manner showed he meant it.

'It is still Victoria. I have a long story too. Can we swap them?'

And so Mr Jolyon explained how his wife had paid a woman to say he had an affair with her. She divorced him for adultery, compounded with cruelty. With her lover, his boss who had been the 'boiler man', they managed to take his house, his savings and accuse him of embezzlement. She shot him in the leg with one of the guns from the display in the dining room and claimed self-defence because he had attacked her, which, he assured Victoria, was a lie. He went to court for the alleged embezzlement and the alleged attack on his wife. Fortunately, the jury found him 'Not Guilty' on both counts. It still ruined his chances of ever working in the banking business again. She had not wanted Elizabeth so they had both been thrown out on the street. He had managed to get this job while Elizabeth worked for the Middletons as a kitchen maid. They lived in a two-room apartment over the stables.

Victoria listened intently. When he had finished his sad story, she patted his arm. 'I'm so sorry for you.'

'I'm sorry for what happened to you. I tried to find you when I came back from the job up north. I just knew you would not have stolen anything. I was beginning to suspect my wife. You were the second governess she sacked for stealing. It just did not seem possible. And then it all fell apart.'

Victoria cut her story short, just to say that she had been lucky and taken in and educated by Lady Luisa Bonchurch. The assassination attempt on the Queen she was ordered never to divulge.

Victoria curtsied to Mr Jolyon. He bowed to her. Then she leant forward and kissed him on the cheek. 'I shall think of something, Mr Jolyon. You deserve more than being a gardener.'

'It's honest work being a gardener, Miss . . . Sorry, Victoria. Though it is hard and Elizabeth finds being a maid is very hard too. She never complains.'

That night, in the carriage on the way home, Victoria resolved she would help Mr Jolyon and his daughter if she could. For now they were safe with the Middletons, though not in circumstances that suited.

Chapter Six

'Easy now, Nkosi, easy,' said Sipho, Richard's Zulu guide, slipping a cartridge into the large-bore rifle's breech with fingers as black as a moonless night.

Richard looked at a bull elephant standing high on the red earth track. Its trunk swayed like a pendulum in a grandfather clock as the giant head and tusks moved from side to side. Three female elephants and two babies followed the big male, perhaps confident of its protection.

'I should have brought the camera,' said Richard.

'Nkosi, we are hunters. And that thing you had us carry, it is very heavy. I'm glad it is back at the camp, safe.'

Last night's storm had laid the dust. The damp still hung in the air although the sun had blazed all day. It was late afternoon, and the lazy buzz of insects awakened from their slumbers filled the air. Richard swatted a mosquito on his neck.

'Shsh, Nkosi. You will scare him.'

The tusks would bring Richard a good sum back in Cape Town, though he would rather shoot the animal with a camera than a gun.

Sipho handed the rifle to him.

Richard felt its weight. It had the capacity to kill the great beast if he hit him in the right place.

'Remember, Nkosi, shoot him in the ear hole or you will wound him and make him very angry.'

Richard turned to see Penelope only ten yards behind him. They were all in danger, Penelope, Sipho, Mthungi and himself, if he could not gauge where the hole was under the giant, flapping ears.

Richard controlled his breathing as Sipho had told him. He knew the elephant could not see him or the rest of the party. The long grass hid them. He would have to step out onto the track to get a clear shot. Then the beast would see him and perhaps charge.

He made the final step out to the track with the rifle levelled. Richard brought the sight up to the point where the bullet would impact. The bull elephant had still not seen nor sensed his presence.

Richard's finger closed on the trigger. He took another breath. The animal still swayed its head and tusks, apparently oblivious of the danger. Then Richard stopped. He lifted his eyes from the sights and looked at the family of elephants.

'What's wrong, Nkosi?' said Sipho, coming to the edge of the long grass and whispering.

'I do not want to kill him.'

'But why, Nkosi? He's worth much money and you will have a trophy. It is the biggest elephant in these parts.'

'But why kill him?'

'That is what we are here for, Nkosi. We've tracked him for three days.'

The elephant now sensed the presence of the hunters. He trumpeted so loudly that Richard felt the ground vibrate beneath him. For a moment he thought the beast would charge. He raised his rifle ready to shoot and then realised it would come head on at him. His chance of shooting it in the ear was lost. But then it turned and shepherded its family away from him, down the track and out into the veldt.

'I am glad you did not shoot him, Richard. I'm glad you have not changed,' said Penelope, stepping on to the track in her safari coat, long dress and knee high boots.

'Nkosi! What kind of a hunter are you?' said Sipho.

'A wise one,' said Mthungi, a bearer with a broad grin on his black face.

Sipho shrugged. 'So far we have killed nothing. You have used that thing on legs to capture what you say will be pictures but we have no game. You have paid me to find you game, Nkosi. I have found you the biggest elephant in these parts and you did not shoot it. Will I still be paid, Nkosi?'

'You will, Sipho, I shall see to that.'

'Then I do not care if you take pictures or shoot as long as I do not have to carry that thing. I am a warrior. It is woman's work to carry such things. But if you will shoot something, we could get an antelope unless you are now against eating meat?'

The hunting party made its way along the red dirt track. Sipho stopped and signalled them to get down.

Off in the distance, Richard could see the peculiarly shaped horns of an impala above the long grass.

'If you shoot this one, Nkosi, we can eat it tonight,' said Sipho.

Richard waited for the animal to come out of the long grass into the shorter grass at the side of the track. His breath went shallow again just as Sipho had told him. A hundred yards away the reddish-brown male impala was now clear of the long grass and continued its skittish walk, all the while looking around for predators.

With his finger on the trigger, Richard squeezed slowly.

Bang!

The shot hit the unsuspecting animal just below the ear. For a moment it didn't move, and then slowly tumbled over onto its side.

'Good shot, Nkosi,' said Sipho with a big grin.

'Good shot, Nkosi,' said Mthungi.

'Please take it back to camp and have it prepared for dinner tonight,' said Richard. Now he had shot the animal he intended to make use of it or the kill would have been pointless.

'But are you not coming back to camp with us, Nkosi?' said Sipho.

'No. I think I will stay out here.' He turned to his sister sitting on a rock. 'You go back with them. Keep mother company.'

'No, I'll stay out here with you if you don't mind. Mama is fine. She will be reading a book and enjoying the absence of father.'

Richard and Penelope watched as Sipho and his companion tied the beast's legs and then put a pole between them to carry it back to camp, just over the low hill about a mile to the south. Richard reckoned it must weigh in the region of a hundred pounds. There would be enough for all to eat and still have some left over.

'Nkosi, be careful. There are lions out here. Keep your gun close,' said Sipho. 'And don't forget to shoot if one comes near or you will be its meat tonight.'

'I will, Sipho. Don't worry.'

The two guides hoisted the animal up on the pole and, with one end each on their shoulders, headed back to camp.

Penelope smiled. 'It is beautiful out here, don't you think? But terrible too. Death stalks the veldt in the guise of man, but also the beasts kill.'

'That's profound, little sister!'

'It makes you like that, out here.'

The rolling land spread out before them as far as the eye could see. Only a few acacia trees rose above the swaying grassland.

'It is not as beautiful as Eagledown.'

'We'll be going home in a year.'

'Yes. You will be twenty-one and I will be twenty-five and old enough to inherit the estate at last. If grandfather had stipulated I could inherit at twenty-one, we would have been saved this isolation.'

'You, maybe, but father would still have made mother and I come here. I am so glad you came with us. You still haven't told me how you scared off that Boer to whom father was trying to marry me.'

'I told him you had three children by different men.'

'What? Richard!'

'Well, would you have rather married him?'

'No, but couldn't you have come up with something more—I don't know—less horrible. What will people think of me?'

'It worked. Last time I saw the burgher he was getting on his waggon and heading back to his laager.'

'Does Father know what you said?'

'Yes.'

'How did he take it?'

'Not well, but he wouldn't dare try anything with me now.'

'He will be back in town when we get home. Pity he doesn't stay in Durban.'

'And he will be coming back to England with us, I'm afraid.'

'Why?'

'He wants to get his hands on Eagledown.'

'He must know he cannot do that.'

'I think he is desperate. We both know he has made some bad investments over here.'

'Just as he did with the estate he inherited. He is bad, Richard. Bad! It should have been kept to pass down to you. But instead he squandered it all and tricked Mama into marrying him with the hope of getting his hands on Eagledown. Well, thank goodness Grandpapa saw through him, that's my view.'

'I don't need his inheritance. I have Eagledown.'

'And you will make sure Mama is cared for too. I know that, Richard, and she knows it too.'

'This conversation is becoming too deep, little sister.'

'That's the effect he has on me. On you too, and Mama.'

'I cannot stop him coming back. If I could it would mean leaving Mama with him. We cannot do that.'

'No, we can't.'

'You know I will look after you.'

'I know, Richard. It has been a long time. I miss Algernon.'

'Penelope, when we get home you will be free to marry him if you both still want to. Father cannot stop you when you are of age.'

'With the bad blood between Algernon and you I doubt he will want to marry me.'

'I am so sorry, Penelope.'

'I must say it did come as a shock to me too, you and Peggy. I didn't think you were, you know.'

'Penelope . . . No, it doesn't matter.'

'What?'

'It doesn't matter.'

'I hate that. When someone is going to say something and then doesn't and says it doesn't matter. What doesn't matter?'

'It doesn't matter.'

'Richard! Never mind. Let's change the subject. You are right. We are getting too profound. What did Peggy have to say in her last letter? I know you got one just before we left and you didn't mention it. Did she say anything about Algernon?'

'She said he is working hard on the farm.'

'Is that all?'

'She said he was missing you.'

'Really?'

'Yes, really.'

'I wonder if he does still want to marry me. I was only seventeen when he proposed last time and father refused.'

'You were rather young.'

'Perhaps he has found someone else.'

'Perhaps.'

'Thank you, Richard. That is a great help!'

'Don't mention it!'

'What else did she say? How is your daughter?'

'Alice is coming up for three. She is doing very well, Peggy says.'

'It must be hard to have a daughter of three and never to have seen her.'

'Penelope . . .'

'Yes?'

'No, it doesn't matter.'

'Richard! I know you want to tell me something. You have wanted to tell me something ever since we left England. Something about you and Peggy. What is it?'

'No, Penelope, I cannot tell you.'

'You are so irritating! It's just as it was when we were children. You and Algernon with your secret den, and you wouldn't tell Peggy and me where it was. But what you are not telling me now is far more important than that, isn't it?'

'It will all come out in time.'

'I hate brothers!'

'Why? How many do you have?'

'Only one, thank goodness.' She gave him a playful punch on the arm.

He put his free arm around her while the other held the rifle. 'Do not worry, little sister. It will work out for all of us.'

'When we get back I expect Peggy will be coming to live at Eagledown. If Algernon and I marry I can live at Abbeyhill Farm and we can be your tenants.'

'I do not think she will be coming to live at Eagledown. She will be staying at Abbeyhill.'

'Why?'

'Because.'

'What does that mean?'

'It doesn't matter.'

'Richard!'

'If you and Algernon do decide to marry, I shall make sure you have somewhere to live.'

'He hates you so much because of what you did to Peggy. I doubt he would accept anything from you.'

'Penelope, we will have to wait and see what happens.'

Their conversation came to an abrupt end when both heard a scream.

'What was that, Richard?'

'I don't know. It came from over there.' He pointed at an acacia tree some two hundred yards away.

'I think there is someone there. I can just see the top of a head,' said Penelope.

'I think you are right. Stay here.'

'Not likely. I am coming with you.'

They made their way through the long grass, Richard out in front, taking great strides, and Penelope half running behind to keep up, with her skirt and boots slowing down her slight frame.

As they neared the acacia tree, the grass stood shorter and they could see an African boy of about twelve holding on to the trunk and moving slowly around as if keeping the tree between himself and something in the grass. The boy was black but his face was painted white.

Then Richard saw what the boy was trying to keep away from. A lioness was working its way round in a circle, keeping up with the boy's turns.

'Oh my God!' said Penelope.

Richard could see the lion was so intent on its prey that it had not noticed the newcomers.

'Shoot it, Richard. Quickly. Before it gets the boy.'

'I don't want to shoot it.'

'You can't let it take the boy, Richard.'

'I know, but I don't want to shoot it.'

'What are you going to do then? Let it take the boy?'

The lioness heard the talking and turned its head towards Richard and Penelope.

Then Richard's heart missed a beat. Not one lion, two, the second having been hidden by the grass.

The first lion gave a low growl as it looked at Richard and Penelope. Then it turned to look at the boy, as if deciding which would make the best meal. Its companion moved closer to the boy.

Richard had one shot in the breach of his rifle and four more bullets in his pocket. Would he have time to reload if he shot one of the lions? Did he need to kill either lion? He glanced over at the boy. He seemed to be pleading with his eyes for Richard to shoot the predators.

Richard made a decision that he knew may be wrong, but he had to try. He pointed the gun in the air and pulled the trigger.

Bang!

The sound echoed across the veldt. Both lions roared and turned their full attention to Richard.

He remembered the cats at Eagledown. They ran away from danger if they could, but when cornered they would hiss and stand their ground. He wondered if it was the same for lions. They had plenty of opportunity to run away, but would they? Were he and his sister a danger or supper to them?

With fumbling hands he decided to find out. Richard reloaded and fired into the air again.

The lions turned and ran into the grass, out of sight.

Richard reloaded just in case.

The boy dashed over to Richard and threw his arms around him. Richard could not understand what the boy was saying, but he gathered he was mighty grateful.

There was no point asking the boy what on earth he was doing out there alone on the veldt. With sign language, he conveyed to the boy that he would take him back to camp.

***

Richard and Penelope came into the camp with the boy walking between them. In the gathering dusk, a collection of insects had taken to orbiting a hurricane lamp.

A fire of embers under a triangular frame roasted two haunches of meat.

He checked his step when he saw the fear in the faces of Sipho, Mthungi and the porters. There was no mistake in Richard's mind. They were scared. Why?

'What is wrong?' asked Richard.

'The boy,' said Sipho.

'What's wrong with the boy?'

'He's Xhosa.'

'So?'

'That paint on his face. He's on an initiation test. You've interfered. They will not be happy.'

'Who?'

'The warriors who would be accompanying him.'

'I didn't see any warriors.'

'Why did you bring him here?' said Sipho.

'Because the lions were going to get him.'

'It is part of his test. You shouldn't have. There will be trouble.'

'They would have killed him.'

'Better they killed him than the Xhosa kill us,' said Sipho.

'Do not be ridiculous. Ask him where the warriors are?'

Sipho said something to the boy in a tongue unknown to Richard. The boy replied.

'What did he say?'

'He got separated from them and lost in the long grass during the storm.'

'Then they won't be mad at us for saving him, will they?'

'I don't know, Nkosi. I don't know.'

'Ask him where he lives and tell him we will take him there.'

'I can't go there. They're Xhosa. I'm Zulu,' said Sipho.

'Well, find out where he is from and I will take him there,' said Richard.

Lady Adele came out of one of the three tents erected in a line. 'What is going on Richard?'

'We have another mouth to feed. This boy was out on the veldt and we had to bring him here or he would have been taken by the lions.'

'Oh, the poor mite.' Lady Adele strode over to the boy. 'Why is his face painted white?'

'Apparently it is an initiation test,' said Richard.

'What? Leaving him to be eaten by the lions?' she said.

'No. He became separated from the escorting warriors during the storm.'

'Then you had better take him home,' she said.

'Yes, that's what I was explaining to Sipho but he said he couldn't go there because they are Xhosa and he is Zulu.'

'Ridiculous! We will take him to his home,' she said.

Richard smiled. It was not often he saw his mother so forthright and playing the memsahib, because she was usually in the shadow of his father.

***

Richard lay in his tent with his rifle loaded by his side. The boy slept on the floor at the bottom of Richard's camp bed. Outside he could hear the last spits from the dying embers of the fire as the remains of the impala burned. Somewhere in the distance a creature howled. A cacophony of insects ebbed and flowed.

Richard's original plan was to set off with the boy in the morning to the village alone, while Sipho and the other porters led Penelope and his mother back to the town twenty-five miles to the south. That was his plan. The women were having none of it. They were coming too. So Richard's plan was now for them all to head back to the town, taking the boy with them, and to make arrangements for his return when they got there. He was unwilling to risk the safety of his sister and mother out on the veldt or in a native village where a friendly reception could not be assured. He knew that the British under Sir Harry Smith had almost destroyed the Xhosa civilisation.

***

Richard woke with the sunrise. A damp, cool air filled the tent. He looked for the boy but he had gone. He dressed and stepped outside.

The boy was kindling some dying embers into a fire. He looked up at Richard and said something.

Richard had no idea what he was saying so he just nodded his head.

Sipho and Mthungi came out of their tent, and soon after Penelope appeared from her quarters.

'We had better make an early start, Nkosi. The boy's escort may be looking for him and if they find him here, we will have difficulty fighting them with so much cover around. We need to get out onto the veldt,' said Sipho.

'Sipho, I have no intention of fighting anyone. We have saved the boy from certain death and I do not believe his people will have anything other than the deepest gratitude for that,' said Richard.

'Nkosi, you are Englishman. I am African man. Do not tell me what the Xhosa will do.'

Sipho had a point, but Richard could not bring himself to believe that the boy's people would cause them harm in the circumstances. But he also had the safety of his mother and sister to consider. 'All right. Let's pack up quickly and be on our way. Sipho and Mthungi, make sure the rifles are loaded and the ammunition to hand.'

'Do you think we are in danger, Richard?' said Penelope.

'I do not know.'

His mother appeared at the entrance to her tent. 'What is going on? All this noise has woken me.'

'We are moving on, back to town. Now,' said Richard.

'We haven't had breakfast yet, Richard!'

'Mother . . .'

Richard saw two figures coming out of the undergrowth behind his mother's tent. The men wore loin cloths of animal skin and carried spears and shields.

A quick glance over at Sipho told Richard that the guide did not have a loaded weapon: just the rifle and a cartridge in his hand.

Mthungi likewise was in the process of loading.

Richard had left his loaded rifle in the tent.

Two more warriors appeared from the undergrowth and then two more. All were armed with spears.

They must be Xhosa. It was him, Sipho and Mthungi against the six. If the other four porters joined in to help the odds were better, but he could not see them. Perhaps they had melted away at the sight of the warriors.

A warrior, six feet tall with bulging muscles in his arms and legs, stepped towards the boy who looked up and ran towards the man, flinging his arms around his legs, shouting something that Richard could not understand. This warrior then barked out something to his companions.

The other five warriors let out a cry—something like 'Ugh!'—and advanced towards Richard with spears pointed. They jabbed the weapons forwards and backwards as if making stabbing motions.

'Ugh!' again and they came on.

Penelope screamed. Lady Adele put her arms around her daughter.

Richard threw a look towards Sipho to see if he had loaded the rifle. If he could get one shot off it may slow down the others enough for him to dash into his tent and grab his weapon. The odds would be better, though still against them. It was a slim chance, but he didn't have much choice. He took a deep breath. With blood surging around his body to prepare him to fight, Richard kept his eyes fixed on the warrior. He cleared his mind of any reluctance to kill in the full knowledge that it was kill or be killed.

To Richard's surprise, Sipho wore a grin. Had he turned against him to save his own life?

The warriors moved closer, still jabbing the air with their spears and chanting, 'Ugh, ugh.'

One of the warriors was now near enough to stab Richard. If he was to die, it would not be without a fight. Richard fixed the warrior with his eyes and moved first to his left and then to his right. The warrior followed him with his spear.

'Do not do anything, Nkosi,' shouted the grinning Sipho.

But Richard continued to move to the left and then to the right. A second warrior had now come within stabbing distance.

Richard looked over at his mother and sister, helpless in front of their tent. He did not want to imagine their fate.

Suddenly the warriors stepped back and raised their spears in the air. The one to whom the boy had run moved forward.

He said something to Richard but it was beyond his comprehension, partly because it was in a language he did not understand, and partly because the blood pumped around his body with such force he could hardly reason.

'They are honouring you, Nkosi,' said Sipho.

It took seconds to sink in but it did. Richard looked at the warriors. They were smiling and waving their spears in the air.

'That one is the boy's father and he is thanking you for saving his son,' said Sipho. 'They are not going to kill us!'

The boy's father stepped forward and said something.

'He says that you are a brave man. The boy says you scared the lions away. You are a mighty warrior if you can chase away lions and he salutes you.'

Richard did not know what to say. He looked at his mother and sister, who still appeared terrified.

'What is the correct response for me to give, Sipho?' said Richard.

'Don't worry, I'll say something good.' Sipho gave a long speech to the warriors.

The warrior father reached into a pouch that hung from his leather belt. Richard hoped he was not going to offer something unpleasant.

In the man's big hand, Richard saw some rocks. One was an opaque, greyish white, the size of a pea, and the others—seven he counted, each about the size of a thumbnail. Richard could see the gold in them.

The warrior told him through Sipho that the rocks meant nothing to the Xhosa but he knew that the white men killed each other for them, so he could have them without killing anyone. He put the rocks in Richard's hand.

The boy said something to Richard and then the warriors disappeared back into the undergrowth, taking the boy with them.

Richard strode over to his sister and mother. They hugged each other in relief.

Chapter Seven

On Victoria's twentieth birthday, Bonnie came to sit with her at breakfast. 'I have a surprise birthday present for you, Victoria,' was all she would say.

Jake pulled the pony and trap up at the front of the grand house and helped Victoria and Bonnie in. Off they went along the narrow country lanes for nearly two hours until Victoria started to recognise the scenery. Goosebumps on her arms and a sickly feeling in her tummy grew and grew as they continued the journey. They came round a bend and there it was: the forbidding edifice of the orphanage.

'Why?' said Victoria.

'Do not worry. You will soon see.'

Jake pulled up outside the main door. Victoria looked at the bleak house and the perfectly tended gardens. A small bunch of curious but solemn children looked out from behind a hedge.

Victoria did not want to go in. It held too many unpleasant memories. Bonnie took her by the arm and led her up the steps to a black door with Jake beside them. Jake rattled a brass knocker. Footsteps echoed on flagstones in the hallway. Victoria took a deep breath.

The door opened. A boy aged about ten greeted them. 'The master is expecting you.' He stood aside for them to enter.

He led them to the master's room. Tweedale sat behind the same desk in the same clothes and with the same spittle around his mouth that Victoria remembered so well.

The boy did not enter the room. He waited in the doorway. Victoria sensed the fear on the boy's sullen face, confirmed by his shuffling feet.

'Good morning, Lady Luisa, Miss,' said Tweedale with a slight bow of the head as he rose to his feet.

Victoria watched his narrow eyes run over Bonnie's face and body. He then turned his penetrating stare on her. He did not seem to recognise her, or least gave no indication that he did.

'I understand from the trustees that you are now in charge of this establishment, Ma'am. I'm sure you will find it an extremely well-run orphanage with happy and contented children.' Tweedale rubbed his bony hands together with an insincere deference to the visitors.

The boy at the door coughed.

'I think we will be the judge of that,' said Bonnie. 'We will have a look around.'

'Of course, Ma'am,' said Tweedale as oily as ever. 'I'll show you what we do here.'

'I think not. This young man will show us,' said Bonnie, pointing at the boy in the doorway.

'Well, I'm afraid that would not be proper, Ma'am. You see, we are so very careful to ensure our charges come to no harm, so no visitors are allowed unless escorted by staff on the premises,' he said.

'Mr Tweedale, I am now the benefactor of this orphanage and I am authorised by the trustees to take whatever measures I see fit. I believe you will find that puts me in the "staff" category. Please carry on with whatever you are doing and we will not bother you any further until we have finished our tour.'

Tweedale's spittle ran from the corner of his mouth and onto his chin.

Bonnie took Victoria by the arm and led her towards the door.

'I must insist . . .' said Tweedale, striding over to the door and putting himself between it and the two women.

'Please get out of my way, Mr Tweedale,' said Bonnie.

'I cannot allow you to wander around the orphanage unaccompanied.' He stood in the door and spread his arms, crucifix-like.

'Jake!' said Bonnie.

Jake grabbed Tweedale by the scruff of the neck and threw him into the room.

'Please show us around the orphanage, young man,' said Bonnie to the boy, who now had a grin on his face.

The master sat down on his chair and put his hands over his face.

First the boy took them to the laundry. Victoria watched the anger on Bonnie's face at what she saw. Children as young as five bundled dirty washing into enormous boilers. Others pulled out washed clothes from boiling water with their bare hands. And the clothes were not those of children. Clearly there was a laundry business in progress with the children as unpaid workers.

In a long, stifling-hot room, they found four girls aged about ten sewing clothes. A pile lay in a corner with price tags on them.

In the spotlessly clean kitchen, she discovered rotten meat with maggots being put into a huge pan to be boiled up for lunch. The cook was a fat woman in a crisp white apron who must have joined after Victoria left because Victoria did not recognise her.

Victoria's memories of the orphanage had played a trick on her. She thought she remembered how bad it had been for the orphans, but it was worse.

In a locked room in the basement, they found a girl of six. She had obviously been there for some days and there were no toilet facilities. A piece of mouldy bread and a mug of water sat on a filthy bunk. It was a sharp contrast to the spotlessly clean orphanage upstairs.

'Why are you in here?' said Bonnie.

'I broke a plate, Ma'am,' sobbed the little girl. 'So I'm in silly tree confinesment.'

Bonnie looked at Victoria and mouthed, 'Solitary confinement?'

Victoria nodded.

Jake clenched his fist.

Bonnie held out her hand and led the little girl from the cell.

The two harridans that Victoria had escaped from came along the corridor. They both carried leather straps.

Victoria could not stop a streak of fear shooting through her body.

'How dare you lock a child up like this?' said Bonnie.

'You'd better ask the master that,' said the taller harridan.

'And why are you carrying those awful weapons?' said Bonnie.

'Protection from the little bast— Self-defence,' said the shorter harridan.

'Take us back to Mr Tweedale, please,' said Bonnie to the boy.

With the little girl still holding Bonnie's hand, they made their way back to the master's office.

Tweedale sat behind his desk. He glared at the wall and floor, everywhere but into the eyes of the three visitors.

'I found this child locked up in filthy surroundings with only bread and water. What do you have to say to that?'

'It's a regulation punishment that's carried out in all orphanages,' said Tweedale, mopping his forehead with a linen handkerchief and glaring at the little girl.

'I'm a very busy woman, Mr Tweedale. It appears that the trustees must also be very busy, for they have not done much to help the orphans here. I do not have time to keep a check on you.'

'I understand, Ma'am. I'll make any changes you recommend immediately.'

'Because I am so busy I am delegating the supervision to this young lady,' she said, pointing to Victoria. 'She will ensure that everything is run for the welfare of the children as a priority.'

'Of course, Ma'am,' said Tweedale.

He clearly had not recognised her.

'I believe you know Miss Victoria Sillitoe?' said Bonnie.

If it was possible, Tweedale went paler. 'You!' I thought . . .'

'You probably did, and you thought wrong because I am here now.'

'You are in charge now, Victoria. Are there any changes you would like to see?' said Bonnie.

Victoria said, 'Mr Tweedale, you have one hour to pack your belongings and get out of your very comfortable cottage here. If you need longer, I will ask the orphans to assist you.'

'You'll regret this. You'll regret this very much.' Tweedale pointed a bony finger at Victoria.

'And those two wicked women you use to instil fear in the children are going too,' said Victoria, folding her arms across her chest and staring at Tweedale.

'I'll get my revenge on you, Victoria Sillitoe.'

Smack! Tweedale shot backwards from a hefty blow delivered by Jake.

Tweedale rubbed his jaw. 'No need for that. I can cause you a lot of trouble, young lady, and you too, Ma'am.' He held out his hand in defence to keep Jake away from him.

Jake stepped forward.

'No,' said Bonnie. 'Mr Tweedale, if you would rather not end up in a shallow grave out on the Downs or crab food off the Isle of Wight then I suggest you retire from this establishment forthwith and never bother Miss Victoria again.'

Victoria looked in amazement at her benefactor. She had just threatened to murder Tweedale! And she looked as if she would do it.

***

The countryside had begun to ripen for the harvest. Golden fields and fruit-filled orchards under a blue sky as far as her young eyes could see made her glad to be alive. And Victoria's mission made her even happier. The shadow of Tweedale had not gone, but it had faded.

She found Mr Jolyon in the walled garden after first calling at the house on the pretext of seeing Mrs Middleton. The butler had, of course, told her they were not at home, as she already knew. That was why she had chosen this day and time.

She asked if she could have a look at the vegetable plot as she was thinking of making alterations at Eagledown.

Victoria guided Tess along a gravel path to the walled vegetable garden, making sure the mare did not step on the immaculate lawn. As she tethered her to a rail jutting out of the garden wall, she caught the sweet scent of the jasmine that crept up the red brick.

Mr Jolyon raised his cap to Victoria when he saw her glide through the rose-arch entrance, her face lit by a huge smile. His smile in return was genuine. His downfall had not flattened him. He still had his pride, his faith and his sense of humour.

'Good to see you, Miss Victoria. What brings you to these parts?'

'Please, I'm still Victoria! You bring me to these parts, Mr Jolyon.'

'Sorry, you are such a young lady that I forget. You have come to see me? Why ever would you want to see me?'

'I need a favour. I need someone who can run a forty-bed orphanage, manage the accounts and deal with people at every level of society. And most important of all, I need someone who is kind.'

'And you thought of me? That was very kind of you.'

'I also need a young lady with a good education who can teach the orphans.'

'I know just such a young lady.'

'I know you do, Mr Jolyon. The job comes with a three-bedroom cottage, a garden and a reasonable salary. Do you think you would be interested?'

'When would you like us to start?'

Victoria had to hold back a tear of happiness at the sight of Mr Jolyon's face. This surprised her. She did not shed tears when things went wrong, but she was about to shed them out of joy.

She arranged to meet Mr Jolyon and Elizabeth at the orphanage in three days to settle them in. Meanwhile, she scribbled out a note for Mrs Middleton and told her the truth about poaching her staff. She hoped Mrs Middleton would eventually forgive her.

***

Now that she had satisfied herself that the Jolyons and the orphanage were happy she decided to accept Bonnie's offer to arrange a prospective suitor to call upon her.

The colours of the rainbow emitted by a glass bauble bounced around the stuffy, mausoleum-like room, adding a welcome ambience. In a corner by a portrait of some distant ancestor on a white horse, ticked a grandfather clock. Victoria looked up at Bonnie's relatives gazing inquisitively down from their paintings. She thought they were looking at her, ready to pass judgement on the suitor about to call. She fidgeted.

Bonnie took her hand and shook it gently. 'Do not worry!'

'I cannot help it.' Victoria wriggled in her seat like a ten-year-old waiting for a magic lantern show to begin.

A young man followed Humphreys into the drawing room. His black hair shone with pomade and a well-trimmed moustache in a tanned, handsome face gave him a dashing appearance that was unfortunately betrayed by his almost feminine gait.

'Mr Charles Hamilton of the Edinburgh Hamiltons, Ma'am,' said Humphreys. He backed out of the drawing room, closing the double doors behind him, but not before managing to give Victoria a little smile, unseen by Bonnie and Charles Hamilton.

'Good day, Lady Luisa, Miss Victoria. So good of you to see me.' His voice came as soft as silk on bare skin. It had a slight Scottish lilt.

Bonnie ushered Charles to sit in a Louis XIV chair opposite their settee. 'The Edinburgh Hamiltons? I have not seen them for ages.'

'Yes, M'lady. I mean . . . er, you have not?' He crossed one pinstriped leg over the other and adjusted his white cravat.

Victoria could see a tremble in his hands as he put them on his lap.

'Your mother and I were at school together.'

'Yes, M'lady. Indeed, she remarked upon that fact when I told her I would be calling upon you and Miss Victoria.'

A bead of sweat escape from his hair and trickled down his sideburns to his cheek, to plop on his black frock coat.

'Your mother was jolly good at sports from what I recall,' said Bonnie.

'Yes, M'lady. Er . . . She remarked on that fact when I told her of my visit to see you. I . . . er . . . understand you were also rather good at sport.'

Bonnie smiled. 'Only croquet I'm afraid. And do you play any sports, Mr Hamilton?'

'Hmmm . . . er . . . had some rowing success at Oxford.'

'Splendid. Have you travelled at all?'

Victoria watched as another bead of sweat dripped through the pomade.

'Er . . . Europe, India; and I spent a couple of years in Texas, M'lady.'

'As a cowboy?' said Bonnie.

'I did try my hand at that. Jolly good company the chaps on the ranch. Had to leave in rather a hurry though when their war broke out.'

'Yes, a dreadful business. Thank goodness it is over.'

'Indeed, M'Lady.'

'And now you are in the banking business, is that correct?'

Victoria shuffled in her chair. *I should help the poor man. He's terrified.*

'I'm a director at Empire Bank,' said Charles, putting his forefinger in his collar to loosen it. His face had gone from tanned to red.

'Have you been to Paris, Mr Hamilton?' said Victoria with a smile, in the hope that it would ease his discomfort.

'Paris! Ah! Yes, I have. I spent two months there painting in Montmartre,' said Charles.

'You are a painter?' said Victoria.

'Not a very good one, I'm afraid,' said Charles with a smile.

'Do you ride to hounds?' said Bonnie.

'Not if I can avoid doing so,' said Charles, at last settling down a little.

'Glad to hear it. Frightful way of treating animals in my opinion,' said Victoria.

Bonnie took a deep breath.

Humphreys brought high tea. Bonnie poured.

Charles' hand still trembled slightly as he held the saucer.

'Do you shoot, Mr Hamilton?' asked Bonnie.

'Not really.'

'Are you a good dancer?' said Victoria. As she said it, Bonnie gave a slight cough as a warning.

'I do dance, but not very well.'

Victoria thought that if he was trying to sell himself, he was not doing an especially good job. It made her like him, a little.

Charles took his leave.

After he had left, Bonnie looked at Victoria and raised her eyebrows. 'Well? You seem to have made an impression on him. The poor man almost lost his tongue!'

'He is nice but . . .'

'He is presentable and very eligible,' said Bonnie.

'I am not sure about . . . Well, I do not know how to say this . . . Do you think . . .?'

'Victoria, Charles Hamilton has a gentle way with him but that is not an indication of what you are thinking. I can assure you that any young man I allow to call upon you here will have been vetted by my contacts. Charles Hamilton would make any woman proud to be his wife.'

'He is certainly rich.'

'Perhaps you will warm to him.'

'Perhaps! I like him, but I doubt that I could love him.'

'Sometimes love comes like a hurricane and sometimes it glides into your life as a balmy breeze.'

'At the moment, it is dead calm on the love stakes.'

'I am sure you will find your rich man and you will love him!'

'Well, we have the other problem. Richard and his family will be here any day now. What are we going to do?'

Chapter Eight

Richard leant on the rail of the ship as it steamed along the coast of Spain. He thought about the four years he had been away from Eagledown. What would he find on his return? He ran his hand over his clean-shaven face, tanned from the African sun. His strong hands held the ship's rail.

'Good morning, Sir Richard,' said Penelope, coming to lean on the rail next to him.

He laughed. 'It sounds so strange.'

'It is your entitlement now that you are twenty-five.'

'I do not know if I will ever get used to it.'

'I'm sure you will! Are you nervous?'

'About what?'

'About being the master of Eagledown and all that comes with it.'

'A little. How about you?'

'I am nervous about seeing Algernon again. I do not know how he feels about me now after so many years.'

'If there is anything I can do to help?'

'You could tell me the secret you keep from me. What is it, Richard?'

'No, I am sorry, Penelope. I can't tell you.'

'You are irritating!'

'I know.'

'Well, whatever it is, it must be very important. I expect I shall find out some day.'

'Dear little sister, I would be surprised if you did not. But for now, may we change the subject?'

'How long before we get to Southampton?'

'The day after tomorrow.'

'I am looking forward to seeing Aunt Luisa. I wonder what her companion, Victoria, is like?'

'Probably nosey like you!' said Richard.

Penelope gave him a playful punch on his muscular arm.

'What are you going to do with that diamond and the gold rocks the warrior gave you?'

'I don't know.'

'You could have it made into a ring for Peggy.'

'Probably not.'

'Why not?'

'Stop fishing!'

'What are we going to do about Mama and Father?'

'I'm not sure we can do anything. If we can get him to leave her at Eagledown and move far away, it would be one solution.'

'Do you think she would leave him?' said Penelope.

'Ask her.'

Lady Adele de Mornay strolled along the deck, her face still marked by sadness and a lack of laughter.

'Where is he, Mama?' asked Richard.

'Playing cards.'

'I don't know why he did not stay in Cape Town,' said Penelope.

'Too many debts and people after him. But I think we all know the real reason he's come. He wants to try to take control of Eagledown. That will be over my dead body,' said Richard.

'You really should not say that, Richard,' said Lady Adele.

'Mama, I cannot understand why you put up with him,' said Penelope.

'I have no choice.' She smiled sadly.

'You could stay at Eagledown and he could live somewhere else,' said Richard.

'I do not think so. He has no money of his own. He has squandered all of it and mine too. He will want to live at Eagledown.'

'Is that what you want, Mama?' asked Penelope.

'What I want is unattainable, so I must make the best of what I have.' She strolled on along the deck.

Richard looked at Penelope. 'When we get to Eagledown I will do what I can to get rid of him.'

'Be careful, Richard, you know what he is capable of.'

***

Bonnie and Victoria sat in wicker chairs on the lawn near the terrace of Eagledown, with a view across the estate bathed in late-summer sunshine. Way off in the distance Victoria could see her sheep. She had nearly a hundred now, all of the Hampshire Downs breed which provided good wool and meat. Victoria had become something of a celebrity in the sheep business though her flock was small. Few, if any, ladies were involved in sheep rearing.

An oak tree provided shade so their parasols lay unemployed on the grass. Humphreys brought them lemonade and placed the glasses and jug on a wicker table.

'Thank you, Mr Humphreys,' said Victoria.

He nodded, almost absent-mindedly, and returned to the house.

Victoria could not fathom what it was, but she felt that something troubled Humphreys. Since learning that the de Mornays were on their way back to Eagledown, he seemed a little nervous. Or was it something else? She did not know.

'Bonnie, I hope I'm not being silly, but is something worrying Mr Humphreys?'

'What makes you think that?'

'I don't know, really. I just get a feeling that all is not well.'

'I haven't noticed anything. Shall I ask him? Do you want to ask him?'

'Probably best not to, Bonnie. I am sure he will tell us if we need to know.'

'So, how is your farm enterprise going?'

'Very well. The vegetables are bringing in enough to pay our overheads and leave us with a tidy profit. The sheep are doing marvellously. I was going to speak to you about that. I have enough money to buy my brother's headstone and I was thinking of going over to the orphanage to see if Mr Jolyon can help me.'

'Splendid.'

'Do we know when the de Mornays arrive?'

'No. Soon, perhaps tomorrow. Certainly within a week.'

'So we will be moving into Marlsham House?'

'Probably. I need to live close to make my contribution to running the estate, and I do have a half share in most of the enterprises here. Except, of course, yours! You need to stay close too.'

'Do you think they will want the land back that I have taken?'

'I doubt it. We will just have to wait and see.'

'Why do you not marry Lord Peter? He wants to marry you. Then you would not have to worry about where to live.'

'Thank you, Victoria, but that is my business if you do not mind.' Bonnie took a sip of her lemonade.

Victoria knew Bonnie well enough to leave the subject there. 'It will feel strange not living here. I have come to like it very much.'

'Yes, I grew up here. It is my home. But we have to move with the times. The estate belongs to Richard and he is free to do with it whatever he wants.'

'I don't like the sound of his father.'

'I do not think he will be living here. Much as that pleases me, I am sorry that means my sister will have to go with him wherever he decides to settle.'

'Even if she does not want to?'

'I am afraid so. That is life as far as we women are concerned.'

'Well, it just is not fair. I shall never be subservient to a man.'

Bonnie laughed. 'I do believe you could be right.'

In the still morning, the sound of horses' hooves and wheels on the gravel drive at the front of the house travelled to where they sat.

'I wonder who that is,' said Bonnie.

Jane dashed out of the house through the kitchen door and across the lawn to where the two women sat with their lemonade.

'Whatever is the matter?' asked Bonnie.

'They're here, Ma'am.'

'Who is here?'

'Mr Richard, Ma'am.'

'Damn! Oh, I do beg your pardon, Bonnie,' said Victoria.

Bonnie gracefully climbed to her feet. 'Hmm mm. Go about your business, Jane, and leave this to me.'

Bonnie walked serenely through the house with Victoria alongside. Victoria wondered if all she had heard about Lord de Mornay was true, and if Richard was as handsome as Bonnie said he was.

Humphreys stood at the main door on the top step. A carriage pulled by two horses halted on the drive.

Bonnie slipped by Humphreys and made her way to the bottom step. The carriage door opened and Victoria saw a tall young man with a shock of unruly black hair climb out and embrace Bonnie. He was indeed as handsome, perhaps more so than advertised.

The young man reached into the carriage and helped a young lady down the step. *Penelope,* said Victoria to herself. Next came an older woman. This must be Lady de Mornay. Richard held her hand as she descended from the carriage.

Bonnie hugged Penelope and Lady de Mornay. Richard and the three women climbed the steps.

A black riding boot with a brown top stepped down, followed by the rest of the man. Victoria gasped. She recognised him at once. She could see the ivory Chinaman's head hanging from his watch chain. He stood on the gravel and then came up the steps behind his family.

He walked with a limp. *A limp from when I stabbed him. Will he recognise me?* She turned towards the house.

'Do come in,' said Bonnie, with her arms around the shoulders of Richard and Penelope.

'And you can get out of the habit of inviting us into our own house,' said Lord de Mornay.

Richard shot around, his face flushed and angry. 'My house, not yours.'

Lord de Mornay huffed and puffed. Richard turned back to walk in with the two ladies.

Victoria looked at Humphreys. He seemed to be smiling as his eyes met those of Lady de Mornay, who quickly averted her gaze.

'Please bring tea, Humphreys,' said Bonnie as the party sat down in the drawing room.

'I'll leave you to talk family business,' said Victoria, still with her face turned away from Lord de Mornay.

'No, please join us,' said Richard. 'And Aunt Luisa, would you please introduce us properly to this young lady.'

'This is Victoria of whom I wrote in my letters. She is my companion. Victoria, I would like you to meet Lord de Mornay and his family, Lady Adele, Richard and Penelope.'

Victoria knew she would have to offer her hand. She offered it first to Lady de Mornay, then Penelope, Richard and finally Lord de Mornay.

Lord de Mornay looked at her carefully. Victoria's tummy turned over in fear, mixed with disgust. Then she realised his look was not one of recognition. No, it was something else. She felt her flesh crawl.

The party all sat down again.

'Now, Aunt Luisa, I received the updates on the estate. I have to say, you have done an excellent job,' said Richard.

'Thank you, Richard.'

'I do think the idea of a school is excellent,' said Lady Adele, speaking for the first time.

'Victoria already has most of the estate workers reading and writing. Jake is doing particularly well,' said Bonnie.

'No good will come of teaching the lower orders to read and write. Next they'll be getting ideas above their station,' asserted Lord de Mornay.

'Why should they not be allowed to learn if they wish?' asked Bonnie.

'I hope they're doing it in their own time then,' said Lord de Mornay.

'I do not know what your plans are, Aunt Luisa, now that we are home. I would be very pleased if you would stay on here at the house to help me with the estate,' said Richard.

Lord de Mornay interrupted. 'That will not be necessary. I will make sure everything runs correctly.'

'As I said, Aunt Luisa, I would like you stay on here at the house. Penelope will also be staying. I hope Mama will too. Unfortunately, my father is looking for alternative accommodation.'

'Now just a minute . . .'

'I was going to ask if we may stay at Marlsham House,' said Bonnie, 'but I would like to accept your kind offer.'

'That would be ideal,' said Richard.

'Where am I and your mother going to stay then?' said Lord de Mornay, his face red and his temple throbbing visibly.

'I hoped Mama would stay here with us,' said Richard as Humphreys brought in tea on a silver tray.

'She's coming with me,' insisted Lord de Mornay.

Lady Adele put her hand up as if to calm Richard. 'I'll go with him. It is for the best.'

'Then as Aunt Luisa will not be using Marlsham House would you like to use it, Mama? It will mean you are close.' Richard put the emphasis on *you* both times.

His father grew even redder. 'It'll do for now until my assets are transferred back here.'

'What assets?' said Richard.

'This is no way to treat me, your father. I've offered to run the estate for you and you have refused. You do not think you have the experience to run it, do you? And as for Luisa . . . Why on earth are you allowing a woman to be involved? Really, it is all too much!'

'Under her tutelage, the estate has blossomed. I need it to continue like that. Humphreys, please arrange for my mother and father to be taken to Marlsham House along with their luggage.'

Humphreys bowed and exited. Lord de Mornay's throbbing temple looked fit to burst; he jumped to his feet and stormed out.

***

After lunch, with only Lord de Mornay absent, Richard took his leave of the ladies and headed over to the stables. He smiled to himself when he remembered how much he had missed the distinctive smell. African stables had a different ambience. Solomon seemed to recognise him immediately, though he had been away four years. Richard saddled his horse and led him into the yard.

Victoria wandered out of the house. 'Where are you going?'

'To see my wife,' said Richard, jumping on Solomon and trotting off.

Richard guided Solomon gently into a farmyard. Ducks and chickens scattered out of their path. He stopped by a rail outside a row of stables and slipped the reins around a post. A brown-and-white mongrel dog loped out of the stables, spotted Richard and bared its teeth.

'Don't be stupid, Napoleon,' said Richard.

The dog came over, gave Richard a good smelling and then licked his hand. The dog had aged well since he, Peggy, Algernon and Penelope used to run with him over the Downs.

A maid answered Richard's knock on the farmhouse door. 'Oh, it's you, Sir. Madam has been expecting you. Please come in.'

Richard stepped inside. He liked the feel of the house. It did not have the grandeur of Eagledown but it had a calm ambience. The maid showed him into the parlour. A bookcase stood at one end and a sewing machine on a table at the other. A scatter of rush mats covered the stone-flagged floor.

Peggy sat in front of an unlit log fire, knitting. She had put on some weight. At her feet sat a little girl, playing with a tabby kitten. A big man leaned on the fireplace. His shovel-like hand held a clay pipe.

'Good day, Mr de Mornay, or should it now be Sir Richard,' said the man, offering his huge hand.

He took it with a smile.

'This is Luke,' said Peggy.

The little girl looked at Richard. 'Are you my daddy?'

Peggy blushed.

'Alice . . . Come on, Alice, let's feed the ducks,' said Luke. He hoisted Alice onto his shoulders, kissed Peggy on the lips and carried Alice out of the room.

'Poor little girl,' said Richard. 'How much does she know?'

'Only what we agreed.' Peggy stood and kissed Richard on the cheek. 'I heard you had arrived.'

'News travels fast around here!'

'Indeed it does. Come, tell me all about Africa.'

The maid brought tea and biscuits while Richard regaled Peggy with his adventures in the Dark Continent.

When he had finished, Peggy said, 'Luke has asked me to marry him. We've been living together now for two years. Could we divorce? Is it possible?'

'It is possible, but we need grounds. It would make me so happy if you were happy.'

'Could you divorce me for adultery?'

'Probably, but I will not hear of it. I am not going to give the old crows any ammunition to denigrate you. I will make suitable arrangements for you to divorce me. I will find someone to be the co-respondent.'

'You're such a good man, Richard, but I don't want another woman's reputation ruined for my sake. And remember, a man may divorce his wife for her adultery alone, but a wife may not divorce her husband for adultery only. There has to be more to it, such as cruelty or desertion.'

'Well, I went off to Africa and left you for four years, so that could be described as desertion. If I am caught in adulterous circumstances, that should be enough.'

'I expect so but, Richard, I really don't want a woman's reputation ruined.'

'Do not worry. Leave it to me.'

'How is Penelope?'

'She missed Algernon and I think she would like to see him soon.'

'It's such a shame. She was young, though.'

'Well, she's old enough now to do as she pleases, and if Algernon wishes to call on her, he is most welcome.'

'He's too headstrong, too fiery. I'm not sure he could bring himself to go to Eagledown now you're the master there.'

'Well, we both know what he is like. If he ever found out the truth . . .'

'He won't from me.'

The door opened. In stepped Algernon. 'You! Get out of my house.' He pointed a riding crop at Richard.

'I was just leaving.'

The two men eyeballed each other as Richard passed Algernon.

'Algernon, Penelope is back, and if you wish to call on her you are most welcome,' said Richard.

'Get out!' said Algernon.

'Please, Algernon, I invited him in,' said Peggy.

Richard walked out of the house and climbed on Solomon. He rode hard all the way home, going over in his mind what the future may hold for him now that Peggy had settled on her way forward.

***

Dinner that night at Eagledown was informal. Bonnie dined at Lord Peter Abbott's with other local cattle breeders. Richard had been invited to discuss arrangements for the forthcoming county agricultural show with them, but he decided to leave it to Bonnie. Lady de Mornay dined with her husband at Marlsham House. Only Richard, Penelope and Victoria sat down in the huge dining room.

Victoria had not had the opportunity to speak to Richard since he returned from visiting Peggy. She hardly knew him, but the struggle to keep her jealousy in check showed on her face.

'Are you going to introduce me to your wife?' said Victoria over the French onion soup.

'Perhaps,' said Richard.

Humphreys filled her glass with a light white wine from their own vineyard.

Suddenly the door burst open and in dashed Lady Adele. Blood poured from her mouth and a swelling closed her right eye.

'Dear God!' Richard jumped to his feet.

Panting after her came Lord de Mornay, brandishing his silver-topped cane and his face red with rage. 'Get back home at once, woman.' He lifted his cane to hit Lady Adele over her head.

Richard sprinted through the dining room, knocking over a table and an expensive vase. He tripped on the edge of a Persian rug and fell heavily against the wall.

Humphreys stepped between Lord de Mornay and his wife.

'Out of my way!' Lord de Mornay raised his cane at Humphreys.

Humphreys punched Lord De Mornay full in the face with a tremendous right and followed it up with a powerful left, and then another right before Lord de Mornay buckled to the ground, his face a bleeding mess.

Penelope put her arms around her mother and pulled her to the far side of the room, away from Lord de Mornay. Victoria bent down to Richard.

Lord de Mornay spat out a tooth, raised himself to his knees and made to stand up.

'Stay down or I'll knock you down again,' said Humphreys.

Victoria looked at the butler. He was no longer the quiet and kind man she had come to know and like so much. He stood over Lord de Mornay with murder in his green eyes.

Richard recovered and stood up. 'Let him get up, Humphreys. And then show him out, please.'

Humphreys grabbed Lord de Mornay by the scruff of the neck, hoisted him to his feet and dragged him out of the dining room. Lord de Mornay whimpered but made no attempt to resist.

'What on earth happened?' said Richard to his mother as her injuries were tended to by Penelope.

'Another argument. Just because I said I was going to the agricultural show with you.'

Humphreys came back into the dining room, closely followed by Jane carrying a bowl of water and pieces of linen. With Penelope, Jane cleaned and dressed Lady Adele's wounds. Humphreys watched—worry all over his face.

'He's got to go tomorrow. Mama, you will stay here at the house,' said Richard. He had recovered from his fall with nothing hurt but his pride, after his mother had been saved by the butler and not him. 'Thank you, Humphreys. I do hope this does not cause a problem for you.'

Lady Adele looked up and tried to smile. 'Thank you,' she said to Humphreys.

To lighten the tone of the evening, Penelope brought her violin into the drawing room to accompany Victoria on the piano. Bonnie arrived home and joined them. The mood called for Mozart. Victoria played the Andante from his piano concerto No 21. All Bonnie's hard work in making a young lady out of Victoria could be summed up in that beautiful tune.

***

The next morning, Victoria walked Tess around the yard. The horse had new shoes, fitted the previous week, but one of them seemed to be causing problems and she thought it may be necessary to bring back the farrier.

She looked up as a pony and trap trotted into the yard. Constable Hemingway held the reins. She liked him. He was not the dolt he sometimes pretended to be, but it always made her smile when she thought of that first day on her way to Eagledown when he had fallen in the ditch. A man in a suit, coat and hat sat alongside the constable.

Four years had passed, but Victoria had not forgotten the kind face that had brought her to Eagledown. That kind face now sent a signal that she was not to identify him. She knew not why, but she obeyed. Sitting in the back of the trap, Lord de Mornay sported a black eye, what looked like a broken nose and a fat lip.

'Good morning, Miss Victoria,' said the constable. This is Inspector Forbes from Winchester. Lord de Mornay here alleges . . .'

'There's no "alleges" about it, man. He assaulted me.'

'As I was saying, Miss, Lord de Mornay alleges he was assaulted here last night and suffered GBH, er . . . that's grievous bodily harm.'

'You had better wait here,' said Victoria. 'I will go and find Sir Richard and Bon . . . Lady Luisa.'

Victoria strode with purpose to the back door of the house, making sure not to run or show any sign of panic. She found Richard in the gunroom cleaning his Purdey twelve bore with which he only shot clay pigeons.

'The police are here, Richard, about last night. It looks as though your father has made a complaint.'

'Mama is still in bed. Please get Jane to help her dress and bring her down to the drawing room.'

Victoria found Jane in the kitchen and gave her instructions. Then she found Humphreys in the boot room.

'The police are here about last night, Mr Humphreys. I think Lord de Mornay has made a complaint against you. You had better hide.'

'No, Miss. If they want to arrest me then so be it. I'll not run. I know I did nothing wrong.'

Victoria went back out into the yard and showed the policemen and Lord de Mornay into the drawing room. Richard joined them. She still did not know why she could not acknowledge Inspector Forbes.

'Can I help you?' asked Richard.

'Lord de Mornay alleges—' began Constable Hemingway.

'Stop saying "alleges", man. I have been assaulted by the damned butler!'

'Lord de Mornay alleges that Mr Humphreys assaulted him here last night,' said the constable.

Humphreys stepped into the room. Lord de Mornay slunk behind Constable Hemingway.

'Well go on, man, arrest him.'

Inspector Forbes spoke for the first time. 'Lord de Mornay, we have to ask some questions first. Please sit down and keep quiet for a moment.'

'Do not dare speak to me like that. I'll have you know I am a very good friend of the chief constable,' said Lord de Mornay.

'Well, maybe you are, Sir, but we still have to investigate this matter properly, so sit down and shut up!'

Constable Hemingway scratched his nose to cover a smile.

'Mr Humphreys, did you assault Lord de Mornay yesterday evening in the dining room here?' inquired the inspector.

'Yes, Sir.'

'He was defending me.'

All eyes turned towards the door. Lady de Mornay, supported by Jane, stepped into the room, her bruised face set hard in a glare at her husband.

'I'm entitled to chastise my wife and servants. You heard what he said. He admits assaulting me. I demand you arrest him at once.'

'Lady de Mornay, I'm afraid I have to ask you a few questions. First of all, did Lord de Mornay inflict those injuries on your face?'

'Yes, he did.'

The inspector pointed at Humphreys. 'And you say this gentleman protected you. How?'

'My husband tried to hit me with his cane. Humphreys hit him to stop it.'

'Had Mr Humphreys not intervened, what would have happened?'

'Lord de Mornay may well have been looking at a murder charge. Had he succeeded in hitting me on the head with that vicious cane I would surely have died.'

'Rubbish. I merely waved the cane to make a point. I would not dream of hitting her with it,' said Lord de Mornay, safely behind Constable Hemingway.

'Lady de Mornay, do you wish to make a complaint of assault against your husband?'

'I'm not sure if that would be allowed in law,' she said.

'Neither am I, Ma'am, but if you wish to make a complaint, I will see what we can do about it.'

'I do not think so, Inspector, but thank you. I would just like Lord de Mornay out of my life.'

'Now you just wait a minute, Inspector. I made the complaint first. I have been assaulted by a servant. I demand something be done.' Lord de Mornay, his face red with bluster, stepped out from behind the constable. Humphreys took a step forward. De Mornay retreated to his previous sanctuary.

'Clearly Lord de Mornay was assaulted by Mr Humphreys. Looking at the injuries to Lady de Mornay, and having heard what has been said, I am of the opinion that no further action should be taken. Lady de Mornay has no wish to pursue a complaint against her husband and Mr Humphreys prevented a serious assault taking place. I bid you all good day,' said the inspector.

'Come back. I demand you arrest Humphreys,' weaselled Lord de Mornay.

'We're leaving, M'lord. Should you wish to come with us you are welcome, but if you wish to stay and accept the hospitality of these good people, then please do so,' said Constable Hemingway.

Humphreys stepped to one side to allow de Mornay free passage to the door. As the two policemen passed through the door into the outer hall, Lord de Mornay turned and said in a low voice to the others, 'You'll regret this. Believe me, you'll rue the day you interfered, Richard, and you too, Humphreys. I never forgive.' He strode quickly through the door after the policemen.

'You'll move in here immediately, Mama,' said Richard. 'Humphreys and Jake will collect your belongings.'

'Thank you, Richard. I suddenly feel as if a great weight has been lifted from my shoulders.'

Victoria slipped out of the house and found Inspector Forbes looking at the view while Constable Hemingway helped Lord de Mornay into the pony and trap. Victoria stood alongside the inspector out of earshot of the transport. 'Good to see you, Sir. I'm not sure why you did not want me to acknowledge you.'

'I'm very pleased everything has worked out well for you. The constable briefed me on the way here about how you've made a real contribution to the local community. I did not want de Mornay thinking I had any prejudice, so I thought it better we did not let on. But, on second thoughts . . . who cares!'

She held out her hand and he took it in both of his. They smiled at each other.

'What the devil . . .?' De Mornay stood in the trap, hopping from one foot to the other.

'An old friend!' The inspector released Victoria's hand. 'If ever you have any difficulties do not hesitate to contact me in Winchester.'

He climbed aboard the pony trap. The constable cracked a whip and off they went.

De Mornay, from the back of the trap, said, 'I'm going to make trouble for you, Inspector. You're in on it with those criminals at Eagledown. By the time I'm finished with you, you'll be pounding the beat instead of being a high and mighty inspector.'

Inspector Forbes turned to Lord de Mornay. 'Your Lordship, would you like us to drop you at your house to collect your belongings, as I understand you are moving? If you would like that, then would you kindly shut up or you will be dropped somewhere else—like off a bloody cliff—now shut up!'

Chapter Nine

A buzz of excitement filled Eagledown as Richard and Bonnie gave instructions and advice to the workers for the agricultural show. Gilbert, their Hereford bull, would be up against Lord Peter Abbott's Oliver. First prize would boost the value of the winner and the ego of its owner or, in the case of Gilbert, owners.

Jake spent the whole of Thursday brushing down Gilbert and polishing his horns and hooves. Victoria could not help laughing at the gentle way Jake dealt with the massive beast.

Friday came. In front of the barn on a cobbled square, Richard lined up all the farm workers, with Jake in the centre holding a rope through a ring in the nose of Gilbert. It looked so funny to Victoria. Some of the men had string tied around their trousers just below the knees. The women wore bonnets and were all of a fuss as they straightened their dresses and jockeyed for position in the front line.

A wooden box held a camera with a length of black cloth on the back. The contraption stood on a tripod. The line faced south and caught the glow of the morning sun. Victoria knew the smell of the dung heap beside the barn would not find its way into the final photograph.

She stood next to the camera, watching with fascination.

Richard put his head under the black cloth and shouted, 'Stand still and do not move.' His right hand came round to the front of the camera and lifted off the lens cap.

The line-up stood still. Even Gilbert seemed to sense the importance of not moving.

'Right, finished.' Richard replaced the lens cap and came out from under the black cloth.

'When can we see it?' asked Victoria.

'Just as soon as I have it developed. Probably tomorrow as we have so much to do today.

Jake and Richard loaded Gilbert into a cattle truck pulled by four horses. Lady Adele, her face nearly back to normal and the blemishes covered with subtle make-up by Jane, climbed into the trap next to Bonnie, Penelope and Victoria to wait for Richard.

With the bull safely aboard the truck and Jake in charge of three farmworkers to help him with the animal, Richard climbed into the trap and off went the party to the agricultural show.

The warm August sun danced patterns from the cotton-wool-like clouds on to the Downs. The ladies sported their parasols and waved at the locals as the trap made its way along the narrow country lanes with the cattle truck close behind.

Victoria marvelled at the sight that came into view. Marquees stood in lines with military precision with just about every country craft on display. Pens at the far side held cattle, horses, pigs and sheep.

Richard parked the trap and left one of the workers to look after the horse. The four ladies and Richard made their way through the throng of visitors to the judges' tent. There Richard handed over his paperwork and the entry fee to Squire Galbraith, a large, jolly man with a handlebar moustache.

Some rough-looking boys hung around the beer tent. They sniggered at Victoria as she glided by. She could not hear what they said, but she could imagine. It did not worry her. Today was far too beautiful a day to be bothered with immature boys.

'Adele, look over there. They have a cross-stitch tent. Shall we have a look?' said Bonnie.

Lady Adele nodded and smiled. Victoria had not seen her smile much since she had arrived back from Africa.

'If you do not mind I think I'll look somewhere else. Cross stitch is not exactly high on my "must see" agenda,' said Richard.

The ladies laughed.

'Nor mine actually,' said Victoria.

'Nor mine,' said Penelope. 'There is a musical instrument exhibition on in one of the marquees. I would like to see it.'

'We'll come with you,' said Victoria.

'No, really. I shall be fine on my own. I would not wish to bore you and I do want to spend some time looking at the exhibits.'

'Well if you are sure you are all right on your own,' said Richard.

'There are many people here, Richard. I shall come to no harm.'

'We are booked into the restaurant tent for twelve thirty. Let's see, it is ten thirty now. Meet there at twelve fifteen?' said Bonnie. The older ladies headed off to the look at the cross-stitch display.

Penelope smiled and walked away towards a marquee with a huge replica of a violin at the entrance.

Victoria saw a young man with blond hair enter the musical instrument venue ahead of Penelope.

'What would you like to see, Victoria?' asked Richard.

'Perhaps we could have a cup of tea over there by the refreshment tent and think about it.' She had longed to question him about Peggy but held back for fear of being thought too nosey. Perhaps now, here, she could lightly broach the subject.

As they strolled over to the tea tent, they met Mr Belchamber, a stocky man of about fifty years with whiskery mutton chops who had taken Richard and Peggy to their honeymoon hotel four years ago. 'Good day, Mr de Mornay, er, Sir Richard, Miss Sillitoe. Enjoying the show?'

'Indeed, Mr Belchamber. Are your horses in the show today?' asked Victoria.

'They are, but that scoundrel Phipps took off this morning, leaving me in the lurch. He's stolen some of my best harnesses too. Dreadful shame. Never liked the lad but he knew how to handle horses. And now I don't have anyone to help me get them ready for the show so I expect I'll have to pull out. And how am I going to manage back at the stables?'

'There are plenty of boys running around this place. Could you not hire one of them?' said Victoria.

'No. They're all layabouts and wouldn't know a day's work if it bit them on the . . . if it bit them.'

'Good luck, Mr Belchamber,' said Richard and led Victoria towards the tea tent.

Sitting on a hay bale with mugs of tea, Richard and Victoria watched the world go by.

'Tell me to mind my own business if you like but I do not understand why Peggy is not living at Eagledown. She is, after all, your wife.'

'Indeed she is. I am very fond of Peggy.' He sighed and looked at Victoria with sad green eyes. 'We are going to be divorced.'

'Divorced? If you are very fond of her, why are you getting divorced? Is she not fond of you? Does she not love you?'

'You said for me to tell you to mind your own business if I like. I would not put it so rudely but shall we just say it is a subject I do not wish to discuss.'

Far from feeling put down by his refusal to talk, Victoria felt a ray of hope. She had liked Richard from the moment she met him. He was everything that she wanted. Could she dream that at some time in the future he and she could make a life together? Perhaps!

Victoria saw a young lad, about fourteen, sitting on a hay bale. He wore a mournful expression. As she would not be getting any more information from Richard, she decided that the young man needed help, her help. 'Excuse me, Richard. I would like to see what is troubling that young man.'

'Never happier than when you are helping someone, I hear,' said Richard with a smile.

She walked over to the youth and sat on the bale next to him. 'Hello, what's the problem?'

'I'm down from North Wales lookin' to find work. I don't like it up there in the mines. The way they treat the workers and the pit ponies ain't nothin' less than criminal. So I thought I could get a job but nobody is takin' on.'

'Do you know anything about horses?'

'Not really. I worked with the pit ponies. I know about them.'

'I should think that pit ponies and horses are more or less the same.'

'Nah, Miss.'

'Wait here.'

Victoria jumped to her feet and called Richard over. 'Did you see where Mr Belchamber went?'

'Yes. Into the beer tent to drown his sorrows I expect.'

'Please fetch him here.'

'What are you up to, Victoria?'

'Please.'

Richard strode off and came back a couple of minutes later with Mr Belchamber in tow.

'Hello again, Mr Belchamber. You said you had lost your stable boy. This young man knows about horses and is looking for work.'

'Thank you, Miss, but I don't know about horses. I know about pit ponies.'

'What's your name?' said Mr Belchamber.

'Jamie Hardcastle, Sir.'

'What do you know about pit ponies?' said Mr Belchamber.

'I used to look after them in the mines. But the bast . . . the owner mistreated them. I caught him floggin' poor old Deidre, my favourite pony. So I kicked the bug . . . I kicked him in the shin. He gave me a bloody—sorry, Miss—a good hiding and sacked me.'

'You kicked your employer for mistreating a pit pony?' said Mr Belchamber.

'Yes, Sir. It's wrong to flog ponies.'

'You'll do for me, lad. How do you fancy working with horses and me?'

'Thank you, Sir, but I don't know about horses, only pit ponies.'

'You'll learn and you can start right now. How about it?' Mr Belchamber stuck out his hand.

Jamie Hardcastle's grin spread across his face. He shook his new employer's hand and wiped back a tear.

A tour of the site took Victoria and Richard to the sheep pens to watch a race between two sheep shearers. A shady man in a peaked cap collected bets from the gathered farmers. Victoria looked at their speed. *Not much faster than me.* She had sheared some of her own sheep, having been taught by a visiting shepherd and Jake.

'Would it be too unladylike if I had a go?' said Victoria.

'What? You must be joking. You're hardly dressed for it,' said Richard.

That was enough for Victoria. She marched over to the judge, reached into her small handbag and took out a shilling: the entry fee for the competition.

The judge, a jolly man with a big belly, gave her an incredulous look. 'Are you joking, Miss? I know who you are, but . . .'

'Indeed I am not joking, Sir. My money is as good as anyone's. I demand the right to compete.'

The judge beckoned over a tall, skinny man dressed in a long, brown, linen coat. 'Lend this young lady your coat. She's on next.'

The man frowned but divested himself of his coat and handed it to Victoria. She slipped it on. The hem touched the ground.

Then the judge looked at her pretty footwear. 'Slip these over your shoes,' he said, handing her a pair of galoshes that were several sizes too big. Victoria pulled them on.

'The squire has put up some prize money and the entrance fee will be added to that. The fastest three share the money equally,' said the judge.

'Splendid.'

The shearers in the ring finished to applause from the watching crowd. The judge looked at his timepiece and smiled. 'That puts you in the lead,' he said to the taller of the two contestants leaving the arena.

Victoria found herself in the ring pitted against a wiry young man with two fingers missing on his right hand.

Her coat donor opened the gate and brought in two sheep. Victoria had not expected this. She thought the sheep would have been restrained for her but no, she would have to catch one before she could shear it.

Her opponent chased a sheep down and turned it. Victoria had trouble running in her long dress and even longer coat. She cornered her sheep and managed to turn it to the cheers of the audience which had now swelled as the word had got out that a 'lady' would be shearing.

With both sheep now restrained the judge blew his whistle and pressed the button on his timepiece.

The two missing fingers did not seem to hamper Victoria's adversary. But Victoria clipped away just as she had been taught with considerable dexterity with her small hands. A quick glance upwards at the crowd froze her blood. There, among the watching farmers and workers, were two faces from her past and one from the present. Tweedale, Woodward and Lord de Mornay were in conversation. The sight made her fingers fly through their task.

Halfway through shearing she lagged behind by a few inches as the crowd roared encouragement. Three quarters of the way through she had caught up. And with a final flurry she had the fleece off seconds before her opponent. The crowd went wild. The judge pressed his timepiece and smiled.

Victoria walked out of the ring to tumultuous applause to be met by Richard. She looked all around, but the three men were gone. An ominous feeling came over her. She decided not to say anything to Richard at this stage. He had enough worries with his impending divorce.

'Well, I must say, Victoria, you are full of surprises,' said Richard as she took off the brown coat and galoshes.

'Well done, Miss,' said the judge.

Remarkably, Victoria's dress and shoes were untarnished. With Richard, she wandered off to see what else the show offered with a niggling feeling that she could not disperse.

They came across a coconut shy. A man in a straw boater and striped blazer beckoned them to have a go. 'Penny for three throws. You get to keep the coconut if you knock it off its stand.'

Richard bought three wooden balls. His first missed by inches. His second missed by a foot and the third clipped the top of the coconut but failed to dislodge it. He shrugged.

Victoria decided to have a go. Handing over her penny, she received her three balls. She imagined the first coconut was Tweedale's head. Her first shot knocked it off its stand. The second target she identified as Woodward but missed it by a whisker. The third was Lord de Mornay. She hit it, but it failed to fall down.

In the marquee hosting the vegetable competition, she found Mr Jolyon and his daughter. They were with two orphans, a boy of about thirteen with two front teeth that a rabbit would have been proud of and a girl of twelve who had evidently not been living on a meagre diet. They had just finished laying out their entries. Victoria kissed Mr Jolyon and Elizabeth on the cheek. 'Are these the orphanage entries?' she said, looking in amazement at the biggest pumpkin she had ever seen.

'Yes, grown by these two little terrors,' said Mr Jolyon, patting the two orphans on the head and receiving beaming smiles in return.

Three fans of carrots, a cucumber and three huge tomatoes made up the rest of the display. Victoria could see the happiness the new management at the orphanage had brought to the previously awful place. She wondered what Tweedale would be doing and quickly shoved him out of her thoughts. She did not want to think of that dreadful man.

The morning flew by and soon it was time for lunch. Victoria and Richard met Penelope, Bonnie and Adele for a cold lunch of smoked salmon, with a salad that had been grown at the orphanage. The proceeds of the sale bought extra treats for the orphans; Mr Jolyon indeed had made his mark. Rumour had it that the salmon had been supplied under the table from a shifty character who frequented the River Itchen, but nobody seemed too concerned.

'What time will the cattle results be posted?' asked Bonnie.

'Not sure. Perhaps after the meal tonight,' said Richard.

'Do we stand a good chance?'

'I should say so.'

Lord Peter Abbott sat at the adjacent table with his entourage. He overheard the discussion. 'Your bull, Gilbert, a fine specimen. I'm sure you will pick up second prize.' He laughed.

Victoria thought it a pleasant laugh. It was not mocking. He was just having a joke. She noticed Bonnie's face. Though Victoria had little experience of love, indeed none at all, she recognised the signs. It filled her heart with gladness to think that kind Bonnie had a suitor. *Just what on earth is keeping them from actually getting on with it?*

'I am looking forward to the ball tonight,' said Lord Peter.

Richard said, 'Yes, we will collect our first prize!'

After lunch, Victoria and Richard wandered through the exhibitions. Penelope had gone off on her own again. Victoria saw her talking to a young man with blond hair. She had seen the man go into the music exhibition earlier.

'Who is Penelope talking to?'

'Algernon, Peggy's brother,' said Richard, taking a deep breath.

'Oh! Is that a problem? I do not wish to pry but I have heard talk about him.'

'No, Victoria. It is not a problem for me. I do wish they would come out in the open though.'

The sheep shearing had finished and they watched the judge nail up the results on a post.

'Well done, Miss,' said the judge with a big smile.

Eagerly Victoria slipped her finger down the list to find there were twenty-four entrants. She had come third.

Handing her a brown envelope, the judge said, 'Your winnings, Miss. Don't spend it all at once!'

She smiled back at him and then noticed a man standing by the sheep pen. He stared at her. It was not an aggressive stare. She did not feel threatened. No, it was a strange, sad look. Dressed in a heavy black suit with a collarless shirt and flat cap he did not look well. *Half starved.*

Richard noticed too. 'What's your problem?' said Richard to the man. There was a hard edge to his question, almost aggression.

The man shook his head.

The judge said, 'He came fourth.'

A thin woman dragging two children appeared from behind the stock shed. 'You got third place, Miss. We was 'oping Arthur 'ere would get a place. We could do with the money. 'E's been out of work for quite a while. 'E don't mean you no 'arm, Miss. 'E can't speak, Miss, on account of he ain't got no tongue.'

'Oh! Look, I'm so sorry. I joined in the shearing just for a bit of fun. I didn't expect to win a prize. Please take the money.' Victoria proffered the envelope to the woman.

The man shook his head.

'That's very kind of you, Miss,' said the woman. 'But Arthur 'ere won't take charity. Thanks all the same.' She took the man by the arm and with her two children looking back at Victoria, wide-eyed, set off towards the exit.

'Stop!'

The woman turned to Victoria. 'We ain't done nuthin', Miss. We don't mean no 'arm.'

'I'm sure you do not. I need a shepherd.'

Richard said, 'Victoria, you cannot go around hiring people you don't know. We have no idea who these people are or where they are from. By the sound of her she isn't from around these parts.'

'Where are you from?' asked Victoria.

'Lancashire, Miss. He was workin' on the moors with sheep for an estate, but the owner sold up and the new ones didn't want 'im around 'cos of 'is problem, like with speakin' an' all. There's nowt in cotton mills neither due to that war in America. No cotton, even though it's over.'

'Please wait there for a moment.' Victoria took Richard by the arm and led him a few feet away, out of earshot of the family. 'I would like to help them. They seem desperate, but they are proud. You have empty farm cottages. I will pay him for shepherding if you give him a cottage, and she can work in the big house. How about it, Richard? Will you help these people?'

The sparkle in her eyes destroyed any chance he had of refusing. 'You win.'

Victoria's face broke out into a huge smile as she stepped over to the family and spoke to the man. 'I would like to offer you a job as a shepherd. I have a large flock and I need someone who knows what he is doing. We can provide you with a farm cottage and a reasonable wage.'

What happened next cut deep into Victoria's heart and took her completely by surprise. The man fell to his knees and burst into tears.

His wife crouched down beside him. 'God bless you, Miss.'

After introducing the family to Jake and arranging for them to go back to Eagledown with him, Victoria and Richard continued their perambulation around the show. They stopped to watch children enjoying a Punch and Judy fight.

She caught Richard looking at her. *What is it? Disapproval at entering such a labourers' competition? Annoyed because I hired that poor man? No. There's something else in his green eyes. I hope it is attraction because I can feel attraction to him creeping up inside me. But he is married. But they are going to divorce.*

By four o'clock Richard had rounded up his mother, aunt and Penelope, and together with Victoria herded them back to the pony and trap. They had to get all the way home, change and come back for the ball. Jake and the workers would stay behind to load up the bull and other equipment and the new family for the Eagledown estate.

***

Victoria stepped into the vast white marquee. She marvelled at the transformation. Where it had held country crafts, it now held a sea of round tables, each set with white linen and places for ten people. Most of the tables were already full. A quartet played on a raised stage with a garland of flowers along the front.

Richard held Victoria's chair as she seated herself. Penelope, Lady Adele, Bonnie and Richard took their seats. Soon they were joined by Lord Peter and four of his guests to make up their complement of ten.

Lord Peter lifted his glass of local champagne. 'May the best bull win!'

'Indeed!' said Richard.

'What do you think of the wine?' said Lord Peter.

'Almost as good as the one we make,' said Richard in full knowledge that Lord Peter's estate had supplied it.

Lord Peter laughed. He had a wonderful laugh in Victoria's opinion. His ruddy cheeks plumped up and the laughter came from deep within. It was infectious. Everyone around the table laughed. Victoria felt she was in for an enjoyable evening with this jolly company.

The evening seemed to fly by. Soon they were finishing their coffee and port. For a change, the men and women stayed together, unlike the society dinners where the ladies were shepherded into the drawing room while the men had their port and cigars.

Squire Galbraith rose to his feet, and a low murmur of anticipation crept through the assembled crowd. Even the kitchen staff came out of their field kitchen to hear the results.

The squire started to read. 'First prize for the vegetable produce goes to . . .' A pause. He milked the tension. 'Gravestoke House Orphanage!'

Victoria had not seen Mr Jolyon at the dinner. Now she saw him make his way from a table on the far side, holding the hands of the two orphans she had met that afternoon. On the table he had just left, Elizabeth clapped her father.

The squire handed a scroll and a rosette to Mr Jolyon, but he did not take it. He pulled the hand of the boy to receive the scroll and the hand of the girl to collect the rosette. That little gesture confirmed—not that it needed confirming—she had made the right choice in giving Mr Jolyon the master's job at the orphanage.

As she looked around the rest of the room, she spotted Charles Hamilton with his parents and some other well-heeled guests. He had not pursued Victoria as it was clear to both of them that they were not suited, though they liked each other.

Then her attention was drawn to another table where Lord de Mornay sat with several fat, middle-aged men who were obviously well off by the look of their clothes. At the same table were three women to whom Victoria was not being uncharitable in her assessment that they were of easy virtue.

A long list of prizes was dispensed to a variety of recipients. Some were grandly dressed and some in workmen's clothes. They had congregated by the entrance, unable to afford the cost of the dinner.

The last prize on the list was the highlight of the show. The prize bull. The squire tucked in his belly and tried to make his chest stand proud of it but failed. He looked around the room and rested his gaze on Victoria's table. Surely the prize would go to Lord Peter. He had won every year since he had first entered, ten years ago. Richard and Bonnie would be disappointed. So would she. But if they were to be beaten by anyone it could not be by anyone nicer than Lord Peter.

'And the prize bull is . . .' That pause again. Richard took a deep breath. Bonnie sat serenely, but Victoria knew she was doing her 'swan' act underneath. Lord Peter put his hand on the table to stand up and collect his prize. 'Gilbert from the Eagledown estate.'

Lord Peter sat down with a bump and shock on his face. Richard looked amazed. Victoria felt the excitement. Though she had not been involved in anything related to the bull, she felt such pride at their success.

Richard went to climb to his feet and collect his prize. Then he stopped. 'You collect it, Aunt Luisa. It is thanks to you that the herd prospered and produced Gilbert. You collect it, please.'

'That is very kind of you, Richard, but no. You must collect it. You are the master of Eagledown and it is you who must receive the prize.'

Richard smiled. Victoria sensed that he had done the decent thing and offered the opportunity to Bonnie, but deep down she knew how much it meant to him to go up to the stage and collect the prize. She watched him walk between the tables and climb the stage steps. The squire handed a scroll and a rosette to him. Richard shook his hand and returned to his table.

Lord Peter had not said anything. Victoria could see the disappointment on his face. Bonnie patted the back of his hand.

As Richard returned to the table, Lord Peter stood up. 'Congratulations, Richard.' He shook Richard's hand and then sat down.

The quartet struck up a waltz. Richard passed the rosette and scroll over to Bonnie. She took it for a few moments and then passed it back.

'May I have the pleasure of this dance?' said Lord Peter, rising to his feet and holding the back of Bonnie's chair. He offered his arm and together they made their way to what passed as a dance floor: a raised platform of planks that, to be fair to the men that put it there, was adequate.

Victoria watched Lord Peter whisk Bonnie around the dance floor. They made a lovely couple, and she hoped that his being beaten in the prize-bull competition would not ruin it for them.

Victoria wondered if Richard would ask her to dance. She hoped so. 'May I have the pleasure of this dance?' Victoria did not recognise the voice. She turned to see a young man standing behind her chair. His blond hair and wispy moustache, together with his elegant militia officer's scarlet uniform, suggested he was indeed a young gentleman.

'Hmmm . . .' said Richard, clearing his throat. 'May I introduce Harry Ratcliffe, Victoria?'

Harry Ratcliffe held the back of Victoria's chair. She did not want to dance with him. She wanted to dance with Richard. But Bonnie had taught her the etiquette of such occasions well, and she could not refuse. 'Thank you.' She rose to her feet and was led to the dance floor.

He took her around the dance floor like a professional. He certainly impressed her with his expertise. 'I've heard a lot about you, Miss Victoria.'

'Oh!'

'I mean . . . you've been teaching farm workers to read and write. That's an awfully dangerous thing to do, is it not?'

'No.'

'And I understand you are involved in the running of Gravestoke Orphanage?'

'Yes.'

'Do you ride with the hounds?'

'No.' Then she remembered her training. She was being rude. He was only trying to be nice. 'No, I do not ride with the hounds. I do not really like to see the foxes killed in that way. I understand they must be kept down, but there is no need for me to be involved.'

'Of course. It is perfectly acceptable for a young lady to be squeamish about such matters.'

'Mr Ratcliffe, not wishing to see an animal torn to shreds is not an indication of squeamishness. It is something else completely. Oh, I say, the music has stopped. Thank you very much for the dance.'

She stepped away, forcing Ratcliffe to follow and offer his arm to escort her back to her table.

As she sat, he clicked his heels together. 'Thank you, Miss Victoria.' Then he strode away.

Victoria waited for Richard to ask her to dance. 'May I have the pleasure of this dance?' She recognised the voice and turned to see Charles Hamilton.

She smiled and climbed to her feet. She saw what she thought, hoped, was a tinge of jealousy on Richard's face. Charles led her to the dance floor. Another waltz. He was not as good as Harry Ratcliffe, but she did not mind.

'Is there a young lady in your life yet, Charles?'

'I'm afraid not. That is where I would like your help, if I may be so bold as to confide in you.'

'Of course.' *Confide. How interesting!* She did not know why people trusted her with their innermost secrets, but she had a reputation for keeping them.

'As you have some involvement with Gravestoke House Orphanage I believe you may be able to help me.'

Startled, Victoria's feet went out of step, nearly causing them both to fall. 'I am afraid the girls at the orphanage are much too young for you, Charles.' She felt a deep disappointment. Though she did not think of Charles as someone she could find happiness with, she thought he was a decent and upright young man. Now he seemed to be interested in young girls. Perhaps deep down he was another of those high-born perverts.

Charles was not blessed with lightning intellect, but the look on Victoria's face was enough for him to work out he had bungled what he had tried to tell her. 'Oh dear! No, I did not mean any of the orphans. No, no, no. It's Miss Elizabeth. I have only seen her from afar and we have not been introduced, but I caught her eye earlier and my heart missed a beat. I think I am in love and I do not even know her.'

Victoria scolded herself for making such a hasty assumption. 'You would like me to introduce you?'

'Would you? Oh, would you Victoria?'

The music stopped. With Charles in the lead, Victoria gently guided him over to the table where Mr Jolyon sat with his daughter.

'Congratulations, Mr Jolyon, on your prize. Well deserved,' said Victoria.

Mr Jolyon beamed. 'Thank you, Victoria. It's these two little terrors who won it really.' He smiled at the two orphans.

'It would not have happened under the previous management. Of that I'm absolutely sure,' said Victoria.

'When are you coming to the orphanage again? There is something I found that I need to show you. I was a little flummoxed this afternoon and forgot to mention it.'

'Tuesday, if it can wait?'

'I think so.'

'May I introduce my friend Charles Hamilton? Charles, this is Elizabeth and her father, Mr Jolyon.'

Mr Jolyon stood and shook hands with Charles. Elizabeth stood and offered her hand. Charles took it gently and bowed. She smiled.

'Mr Jolyon, may I ask your daughter for the pleasure of the next dance?'

Mr Jolyon smiled. 'Of course.'

'Miss Elizabeth, may I have the pleasure of this dance?'

The quartet had begun yet another waltz. Elizabeth and Charles made their way to the dance floor, leaving Victoria stranded without an escort back to her table. Suddenly Charles stopped and turned, having realised his faux pas. Victoria laughed and waved him on.

'Allow me,' said Mr Jolyon as he escorted her back to her seat.

Victoria had not drunk much champagne. She had taken several glasses of water. The tight corset and water eventually made it necessary for her to seek out the powder room. As was customary, all the ladies suddenly decided they needed to go too.

Though a great deal of effort had been put into making the marquee a grand venue for the ball, the powder-room facilities were, to say the least, basic and a good hundred yards' walk. Victoria's case was the most pressing so she waited afterwards outside for the others. The atmosphere inside offended her nostrils. She had come a long way since her days of using the privy at the orphanage.

The facilities for the gentlemen were no better, and separated from the ladies' by a box hedge. At first, the voices on the far side of the divide were of no interest to Victoria but then she recognised one. Lord de Mornay; and then the person he was talking to, Harry Ratcliffe.

'So, Harry, you've given up on Victoria then?'

'She's obviously not interested in me.'

'Call yourself an officer, a beau, a man of means, a rake? Have some backbone! Ask her for a dance again. Woo her. I've heard she's a lively little filly between the sheets.'

'Really? I thought she was a proper young lady.'

'Listen, I know what I'm talking about. She's just playing a game with you to make you think she's hard to get. She ain't. She's been through most of the farmhands in her schoolroom, over the desk I understand. Ask her to dance and by the end of the evening, you'll have her drawers down. I guarantee it!'

'This is hardly the place. I mean, where?'

'The barn over there. Tell her you'd like to show her a sheep or a lamb from a rare breed and she'll be with you. One more thing, she likes it rough. She pretends not to want it, but she expects the man to be forceful and take her while she puts up a token resistance.'

'Well in that case. Yes. She does have something about her that suggests locked up passion. I'll give her a good tupping over in the hay bales. What ho!'

'That's right, my boy. Get in there. Fill your boots!'

Victoria contained her anger. Instead of going off like a rocket, she just stood in quiet fury. The other ladies made their way out of the powder room and together they strolled back to their table. Victoria's demeanour, quiet as a mouse, went unnoticed by her companions.

Victoria sipped a glass of champagne and watched as Harry Ratcliffe walked between the tables towards her. Her fury she still kept contained, but her knuckles turned white as she gripped the champagne flute.

'Miss Victoria, may I have the pleasure of this dance.' Harry Ratcliffe offered his hand.

Victoria stood up. Suddenly her pent up fury exploded. It shot down her right arm into her fist. She smashed Ratcliffe on the nose with a blow that would have felled a heavyweight champion; well, at least, a bantamweight like Ratcliffe.

He fell backwards, clutching his face to stop the blood pouring, without success. Jumping to his feet, he raised his fist. 'You bitch!'

Smack! He went down again with a blow, this time from Richard.

'I do not know what the hell is going on but do not dare raise a fist at a woman in my company,' said Richard, standing over the prone Ratcliffe.

'You'll regret this de Mornay,' whimpered Ratcliffe. 'My father will see to it. You won't get away with this. You're welcome to your trollop!'

He grabbed Ratcliffe by the front of his scarlet tunic and propelled him out of the marquee, where he threw him to the ground again. Ratcliffe did not make to retaliate.

The rest of the company at the table sat dumbfounded. Richard strode back to his table. Everyone at the other tables watched his progress. The squire signalled to the quartet to play something, quickly.

Richard sat down, took a deep breath and raised an eyebrow at Victoria.

'I overheard him discussing me with your father. Apparently I am of easy virtue and Ratcliffe was advised to ... Well, you can imagine.'

'Dear God! What are the young people coming to these days?' said Lady Adele.

'That's a hell of a punch you pack, young lady,' said Lord Peter.

'I'm not sure that was part of your training, Victoria,' said Bonnie with a frown.

'Well I think he jolly well deserved it,' said Penelope.

The rest of the guests in the marquee returned to their own conversations now the excitement was over.

Victoria wondered if she had ruined her standing. All her training and she had behaved like a guttersnipe. There was no way that Richard would want anything to do with her now, she thought. Her mind drifted off. She was far away when suddenly she heard, 'May I have the pleasure of this dance?' *Richard's voice. Oh my!*

Victoria's heart skipped a beat. She looked up at Richard. He held Penelope's chair and helped her to her feet. Her hopes crashed, but then she saw him hand Penelope to a young man of whom she had not been aware while her mind contemplated her social gaffe.

Richard then took hold of the back of Victoria's chair, raised one eyebrow at her and smiled.

He held her tightly as they moved gracefully around the dance floor. Each time he moved his hand on her back it sent a tingle down her spine and legs. His lips were so close. She longed to kiss them.

Victoria looked into his eyes and he looked back at her. There was no mistaking the signals they were sending. She could hardly believe it. He wanted her.

Chapter Ten

Victoria arrived at Gravestoke Orphanage on Tuesday as agreed with Mr Jolyon at the agricultural show. Jake drove the carriage and acted as her escort. She felt safe with him.

Her mind was still full of the evening at the show when Richard had danced with her and, in an unspoken exchange, they had communicated their mutual attraction. Eagledown was a busy place and events had conspired to keep them from being alone. She did not dwell on the incident with Ratcliffe.

As the outline of the imposing building came into sight, she gave a little shudder. She knew it was now a place of refuge for children and not a nightmare, but the memory of her years spent under the old regime crept back into her mind.

Jake halted the carriage at the main door which immediately opened, and two happy children dashed down the steps. Victoria recognised them as those who were with Mr Jolyon at the agricultural show.

'Mr Jolyon is waiting for you, Miss,' said the girl.

Victoria followed the children into the orphanage. Jake stayed with the carriage.

The room that Tweedale had once used was now transformed. Paintings by children hung on the walls. Cricket bats stood in a wire basket in the corner. The huge, leather-bound Bible had been consigned to a shelf.

Mr Jolyon stood up and smiled. He bowed to Victoria and she smiled back.

'Thank you for coming. You asked me to see if I could track down which pauper's grave held your brother. I have found it.'

Victoria could hardly contain her happiness and it broke out all over her face. 'That's wonderful news, Mr Jolyon. Now I can erect a headstone.'

'There's a problem with the grave of your mother.'

'I understand. It was quite some time ago. It must be difficult to identify the plot in question, but thank you for trying.'

'No, Victoria. That's not the problem. I have the record in the Bible that gives the date of your mother's death, as in all the cases of children who died in the orphanage. I have even found the record of the payment to the undertaker to bury the body in the churchyard in a pauper's grave. But when I checked the undertaker's records and the church register to identify the plot, I found no record of her.'

'What does that mean?'

'Please don't get your hopes up, Victoria. I think perhaps I have stumbled upon something. It may be that your mother was not buried in the churchyard.'

'Oh my goodness. Do you mean she was sold to the men who buy dead bodies for scientific experiments?'

'The Resurrection Men? Possibly.'

'Oh, no!'

'That is one possibility. Another is . . . Please remember that this is just guesswork at this stage.'

'Please, Mr Jolyon.'

'The other possibility is that she did not die.'

Victoria's hand went to her mouth in surprise. 'What do you mean?'

'We know that Tweedale sold girls and boys to be indentured workers or worse to Woodward. He was going to do that to you. I am just examining the possibilities, but so far it is not unlikely that your mother was sold to Woodward or someone before him.'

'Oh my God! Can the undertaker help?' Victoria could not decide if this was good news or bad.

'No, the one who had the business when your mother is alleged to have died is dead and his son took over. He was willing to let me look at all the records and I cannot find anything that relates to your mother. So I did some more checking, and there are several anomalies regarding girls aged around sixteen who seemed to have died but have no graves. They do not appear in the parish register of deaths.'

'My mother could be alive?' Victoria sat down and took a deep breath. 'After all these years, my mother could be alive?'

'It's possible but please do not get your hopes up, Victoria. We have no way of knowing what actually happened.'

'But it is possible.'

'It is.'

'We need to report this to the police,' said Victoria.

'Not yet. I need to make more inquiries. We do not have enough evidence for the police.'

Mr Jolyon passed Victoria a piece of paper bearing the number '78'. 'This is where your brother is buried.'

Victoria stood and kissed Mr Jolyon on the cheek. 'I cannot thank you enough, Mr Jolyon. You must know how much this means to me. Please keep me informed regarding your inquiries into the missing girls.'

'Of course.'

'And I really would appreciate it if you could carry out more inquiries regarding my mother. If there are any expenses incurred, please do not hesitate to tell me so I may reimburse you. And I know how busy you are, but if you could help me . . .'

'Victoria, whatever I do could never repay the kindness you have shown to my daughter and to me.'

'Is there any chance of ascertaining who my father is or was?'

'No. I'm afraid there is no birth certificate. There should have been. I cannot find one, and there is no reference to anyone being your father anywhere in the orphanage.

'I suppose that I should register myself.'

'I believe that would be necessary. If the registrar needs anything from me, such as the Bible records, then please do not hesitate to ask.'

'Thank you. Is Elizabeth here? I'd like to say hello.'

'No, she's out with that charming young man Charles Hamilton to whom you introduced us at the show. They've taken some of the children on a picnic.'

Victoria raised an eyebrow and smiled.

'I do hope so,' said Mr Jolyon.

***

Victoria sat deep in thought as Jake brought the carriage to a stop outside the church of St Agnes. She had been here many times and looked at the paupers' numbered stones; that is, the ones visible among the overgrown ravages of nature. Never knowing under which her brother lay upset her every time. Now she had the number.

With the help of Jake, she pulled aside brambles and weeds. There was no elegant way to do it. Sweat congregated under her arms and on her upper lip. Some ran down the back of her neck. Her hands suffered pricks from thorns and stings from nettles. After hours of labour, she found the one bearing the number seventy-eight.

Jake stepped away and went back to the carriage, leaving Victoria to her thoughts.

'I have found you, Edward. I have earned the money to buy you a headstone and I did it honestly. I am going to have it made and put in place as soon as I can.'

She put her hand on the stone.

Then she raised her eyes to look around the churchyard. It looked so different in the sunshine, compared to that terrible night she had fled the orphanage. So much had happened since then. She was a lady and not without her own income. She felt a pang of guilt that her brother could not share her happiness.

***

Jake had a stonemason friend and arranged for the headstone to be made quickly.

Three days after finding his grave, Victoria stood at Edward's last resting place as Jake and his friend erected the stone.

This part of the graveyard, so long neglected, had been transformed. Victoria had paid local workmen to clear the rest of the brambles, cut the grass and plant flowers and trees. The paupers' section now looked grander than the area where the more affluent lay. And she had achieved it with her own money, by growing vegetables and raising sheep.

Richard stood by her side with Bonnie, Penelope and Adele behind. Mr Jolyon, Elizabeth and Charles Hamilton stood on the other side of the grave. Humphreys stood unobtrusively in the background.

When the stone was in place, they all quietly left Victoria with her thoughts.

'I kept my promise, Edward. Now I have to find mother's grave. I shall do it, if there is one. Mr Jolyon is making inquiries. It may be that our mother is still alive. I do not know how to find her if she is. If she is alive, I hope she is in good health and good circumstances. And I will try to discover who our father is. Perhaps I shall have to loosen Tweedale's tongue to learn the truth if I find him.'

She touched the stone and the writing:

Edward Sillitoe
born 24.6.1846
died 16.5.1855
Beloved brother of Victoria and son of Mary

Victoria placed a posy on the grave. 'I kept my promise, Edward. I shall find out what happened to our mother too. I am so sorry you cannot share my good fortune.'

Chapter Eleven

Victoria sat in the school room at her desk watching her students copy Shakespeare's Henry V speech before the Battle of Agincourt. She smoothed down her simple but heavy grey dress, having worn this particular one as it seemed in keeping with her role today as a school mistress. It felt damp from the rain, even though she had worn an oilskin on the ride over.

Her thoughts kept drifting back to Richard. She knew he would not make any advance towards her while he was married to Peggy. And she knew it would be against convention for her to say anything to him about how she felt. But she longed to do so. For now she would have to get by with daydreaming about his taking her in his arms.

Jake sat at the front alongside Bathsheba, the milkmaid. She wore a red neckerchief. On his other side, sixty-year-old Margery, a cleaner, sat with her eyes fixed in concentration. Behind were three farmhands and behind them were two drovers and the pig man. Abigail had a fever so she had stayed at home.

Victoria loved being a schoolmistress. At last she was doing something useful to repay the kindness that had been shown to her.

Richard had paid for paper and pencils, rather than having to use the old slate and chalk. It had not been difficult to persuade him. Though he had not said it, she felt in her heart that he would give her the moon if he could. *If only we could be together for a short time. I do so want him to hold me in his arms and kiss me. I know that is wicked because he's married, but he doesn't love Peggy and she doesn't love him. He married her because he got her into trouble. He's such an honourable man. Why, oh why, is life so complicated?*

Heavy rain pounded the window frames and rattled on the slate roof, as if it were trying to force its way inside. The sound brought her thoughts back to the school room. Though eleven o'clock in the morning, it appeared more like night with the sun blotted out by dark clouds.

Victoria went to the window and looked out. 'Dreadful weather,' she said to no one in particular.

'Indeed it is, Miss,' said Jake. 'If it carries on like this, we'll have to make sure all the sluices are open or the dam could burst. Should be all right for a while, though.'

'Are you sure we are safe here? I mean, if the dam is weak we are downstream.'

'It's fine, Miss, for now. I checked it on the way over. It's got another three feet to rise before there's a problem. It shouldn't get to that height until later today or tomorrow if it keeps raining. But I'll just go up and see that it's all right, Miss, if you wish.'

'Thank you, Jake.'

Jake climbed into his oilskin coat and put on his hat.

Victoria's thoughts drifted away from the weather to the threat that Harry Ratcliffe had made after Richard punched him. Could he actually make things difficult for Richard? His father was very high up in the banking business. Her knowledge of banks was limited, but what had happened to Mr Jolyon at the hands of his nasty wife and her banker lover told enough of their power.

The students scribbled away.

Jake opened the door and stepped out into the rain.

Boom! The windows rattled. Dust fell from the ceiling. The ground shook. Everyone ducked.

'What the . . .' said Jake, jumping back into the school room. 'Look out,' was all he managed to say as a deluge hit the school building with such force the back wall collapsed inwards onto the drovers and pig man.

In seconds, the schoolhouse was full of rising water. Victoria jumped onto her desk, but the strength of the water knocked her off into the swirling vortex.

Round and round the room she was pushed and pulled by the raging current. She felt herself being sucked down. The force was too strong for her. It caught her dress. She felt as if she were attached to a heavy weight. As she went underwater, she knew she could not get back up. Terror filled her heart and brought back the terrible memory of her brother drowning. She kicked and kicked and scrabbled with her hands, but it was to no avail. The current had sucked her under and she could not get out of its grip. Her lungs felt fit to burst.

Her head hit something hard underwater. Her leg scraped against something sharp. Still she fought but she could not reach the surface. She felt herself being held against a wall by the force. Which wall? She did not know, but perhaps she could use it to pull herself upwards. *No. I am going to die.*

Suddenly, the wall collapsed outwards, spilling the contents of the school, including Victoria, out into a raging torrent. Like a cork she found herself shooting to the surface, just long enough to gasp a breath of precious air before being dragged under again. The weight of her dress pulled her down and down as she tumbled along under water. Sheer terror gripped her. She would die: drowned as her brother had drowned. Then something within took over. She would survive. Life had so much to offer. She would not depart from it yet. Kicking and flailing she ripped off her dress, all the while turning and twisting in the maelstrom. Free of the encumbrance at last, she fought her way back to the surface in the whirling current.

A fallen oak lay across the path of the surging water. Its massive branches and weight held firm, with the current swirling around it but unable to shift it. She could see the tree ahead. *If only I could . . .* Victoria grabbed at a branch with both hands and clung to it with all her might. The force of the flow pulled it from her grasp and dragged her under again. She caught the stub of a branch under water and hung on to it, but she could not keep hold against the superior force. Branches ripped at her skin as the current forced her through. Then she received a blow in the stomach. She had been thrown against a thick branch. With tiring hands and bursting lungs, she managed to hold on and somehow get to the surface on the far side of the trunk. The tree trunk provided some lee. Gripping for dear life she pulled herself up onto the trunk that was only half submerged. A body rushed by. She could not see who it was or do anything. It was too far from her reach. Then another body came past, then another, which this time she recognised as Bathsheba from her red neckerchief.

She could see deep cuts on her arms as she held on to the tree trunk, but she felt no pain, only the panic and the urge to survive.

Victoria tried to edge along the tree trunk to dry land, but at the base of the trunk, near the exposed root ball, the water flowed fast and over the trunk, making an escape that way impossible.

Clinging to the trunk with her rapidly depleting strength, she saw Jake swimming for all his worth to keep afloat and heading straight towards her. As the water sucked him under the trunk, she just managed to grab his collar with one hand and keep his head above water. The pull of the current on Jake's heavy frame threatened to topple her in after him.

Jake managed to shout, 'Save yourself. Let go.'

But Victoria would not let go. She hung on with all her might and prayed for divine help. She managed to pull Jake up far enough so he could grab the tree trunk and pull himself out.

They sat on the trunk, wet, cold and terrified, unable to save anyone else. Soon the water subsided and the dam emptied.

Victoria looked up the hill to see Richard on horseback with other farmworkers by his side, dashing down to them.

He jumped from Solomon and dived into the slowing flow, powering through until he grabbed the trunk and pulled himself up. He threw his arms around her.

'My God, are you all right, Victoria?'

'I am, but I'm afraid the others may not be.' She clung onto him tightly. Shivers ran through her body.

He took off his coat and wrapped it around her.

'She saved my life, Sir,' said Jake.

***

Back at the house, in the drawing room, Jane brought a bowl of hot soup and bread to Victoria, now wrapped in a thick dressing gown. Her teeth still chattered, partly from cold and partly from fear.

Richard strode into the drawing room. He had not changed and stood in his wet clothes. He wore a worried expression. 'It looks like the dam has been blown.'

'What do you mean, blown?' asked Victoria, putting down the now empty bowl of soup, unable to comprehend.

'Blown up by someone deliberately.'

'What? Oh my God. Why?'

'I have many enemies.'

'What about the others? Did any of the others manage to get out?' Victoria was still in a state of shock.

'Only you and Jake so far. We've found three bodies and the men are searching for the others.'

'Who on earth would blow up the dam? That's murder!' Victoria's mind raced with the horror at the knowledge that someone meant to kill her.

'There's one obvious suspect, but I'm afraid there are others too.'

'Who?'

'My father, he's the most likely. Then there's Harry Ratcliffe or his family. There's Lord Peter and there's Algernon.'

'I can understand the first two but not Lord Peter or Algernon.' She couldn't think why either would want to kill her.

'Lord Peter lost to us at the show. It has cost him a lot of money because our bull will be more in demand than his.'

'That is ridiculous, Richard. He would never do such a thing.'

'Then there is Algernon. The bad blood between us has festered over these past years.'

'I do not know him well, but I do not think he would do that.'

'Well, I'm not accusing anyone at this stage. I've sent for the police. They will have to find the culprit. Anyway, more importantly, are you all right?'

'Thank you, yes. I think I am. I do not know how I managed to survive. Someone must be watching over me.'

'Jake says you saved his life.'

'To be honest, I cannot remember much about it, other than one minute gasping for air and then finding myself on the tree trunk.' Victoria's hands shook uncontrollably.

Richard sat beside her and put his arm around her shoulders.

Victoria's mind went back to the awful time when Edward fell in the mill pool and disappeared in the drag from the sluice. She had dived in after him and searched underwater to no avail, before being caught in the drag herself and pulled down. She had managed to pull herself up the bars, but she could never forgive herself for not saving Edward.

***

The man stepped into the Bear and Ragged Staff out of the driving rain and shook his wet coat and hat. He made his way through the drinkers around the beer-sodden bar. Their merry chatter stopped as soon as he came in. Nobody looked at the newcomer. In this place, you minded your own business or you may not live to regret it.

'Whisky,' said the man to the barman. He took his drink through to a back room and sat down on a wooden chair at a table sticky with stale beer. Another man sat in the half-light given off by an oil lamp. He sipped at a pewter mug of porter. Spittle formed at the edges of his mouth.

'Nice job at the dam,' said the visitor.

'You didn't tell me there would be people there. I didn't mean to kill anyone.'

'You've been well paid for it. Since when did you care about anyone?'

'Yes, well, it's my neck.'

'I've got another job if you're interested.'

'What?'

The two men sat up close and whispered for several minutes.

'You know someone who will do it? Has to be someone not traceable back to me if they are caught,' said the newcomer.

'Yes.'

'Here. More when the job's done.'

The man put his hands under the table to take a bundle of bank notes from the whisky drinker.

***

Victoria sat at her dressing table in her night attire while Bonnie combed her long hair. Circumstances still conspired to prevent Richard and Victoria being alone together though they had managed to exchange looks. She could not stop daydreaming about him. But she always came back to the obstacle that he was married, and whatever she felt for him she knew she must not let things go any further until he and Peggy divorced. And she knew that could take two years.

'So how are you now, Victoria?' said Bonnie.

'So so. I cannot help shaking when I think how close I came to drowning. And I cannot help feeling so sorry for those who drowned. Is it my fault? They would not have drowned if I had not started the school.'

'Do not ever think that, Victoria. It was not your fault. Whoever blew the dam, it was their fault and I hope they hang for it.'

'Who could it be? Obviously Richard's father is the prime suspect but the police say he has a cast-iron alibi. It could be the Ratcliffes. Or Algernon. He hates Richard. Or it could be Lord Peter. He lost out when you won first prize with Gilbert.'

'It could not have been Lord Peter. And I do not think Algernon would do such a thing. I have known him for years. He is a hot head at times. I remember from when he used to come over and play with Richard and Penelope, but I can't imagine he did it. No, I think Lord de Mornay must be involved in it somehow.'

'I never mentioned it at the time, but at the agricultural show I saw Tweedale talking to Lord de Mornay.'

'Now Tweedale is someone I would suspect. But why would he do it?'

'To get back at me?'

'Possibly.'

A knock at the door and Jane stepped in. 'Sir Richard's compliments, M'lady, but he would like to see you in the farmyard if possible.'

'Good grief! At this time? What is the problem?'

'Don't know, M'lady. Mr Humphreys just told me to fetch . . . er . . . ask you to join Sir Richard in the farmyard.

Bonnie put down the hairbrush. 'I have to go.'

Victoria slipped her long overcoat over her night clothes and followed. Bonnie stopped at her bedroom door, went in and came out again in a warm coat.

Out in the farmyard, by the stables, Miller, the gamekeeper, stood with his shotgun levelled at two men. Richard stood by the stable door examining something that Victoria could not see well in the faint light of the moon.

'What's the problem, Richard?' said Bonnie.

'Miller caught these two out in the Herefords' field. They're not poachers. They had this with them.' He showed Bonnie two dirty rags. 'What do you think we should do with them?'

'Shoot the beggars,' said Miller in his broad, Hampshire burr.

'That may be a little extreme,' said Bonnie. 'I know these two scoundrels; Edwin and his boy Billy. What are you up to?'

'Please, M'lady, we meant no harm. Just out after rabbits,' said Edwin.

Victoria looked at Edwin. She did not like what she saw. His eyes seemed too close together, with his eyebrows meeting over a hooked nose. Even though she stood six feet away from him, she could smell his bad breath. She felt happier knowing Miller had his shotgun trained on him. Billy looked frightened. About sixteen, she estimated, with sunken cheeks and staring eyes.

'They didn't have no snares, nets or ferrets, M'lady. Don't reckon they is after rabbits no how. I caught 'em sneakin' up on the cows with them there rags in their hands,' said Miller.

'Why the rags, Edwin?' said Bonnie.

'Dunno, M'lady.'

'If I may say somethin' about that, M'lady, I reckon these rags have somethin' on 'em. Disease. Probably foot and mouth. They were definitely after doin' somethin' with them rags,' said Miller.

'You had better start telling us the truth or we'll call the police, if Miller here doesn't shoot you,' said Richard.

'You'll not shoot us,' said Edwin. 'I ain't afraid of Miller.'

Whack!

Miller smashed Edwin in the face with the butt of his shotgun. 'Well, you fu . . . Well you should be,' said Miller.

Edwin fell backwards against the stable wall, blood gushing from his nose. Billy wet himself.

'No need for that yet,' said Richard. He took Bonnie by the elbow and led her out of earshot of the two prisoners. Victoria came with them. 'What do you suggest we do, Aunt Luisa? I thought you would know how best to deal with this.'

'They are just a couple of small time crooks. If they were looking to infect the herd they would not be doing it for themselves. We need to know who put them up to it.'

Richard stepped back to the captives. 'Who put you up to this?'

'Ain't tellin' ya,' said Edwin, mopping the blood from his nose with his sleeve.

'We will send Jake for the constable,' said Richard.

'Tell 'im, Dad. We're going to end up in prison again if you don't. Tell 'im.'

Edwin darted his shifty eyes from Bonnie to Richard and back to Bonnie. 'We don't know 'is name. All I know is that we was paid to rub them there rags on as many cows as we could.'

'Not good enough,' said Richard. 'You'll be going to prison unless you tell me the name of the person who hired you.'

'God's 'onest truth. On my mother's life. We do not know 'is name,' said Edwin.

'Is that right Billy?' said Bonnie.

Billy shifted uncomfortably on his feet. Victoria thought he was weighing up whether he was more scared of Lady Luisa, his dad or the person who hired him. 'That's right, M'lady. We don't know 'is name.'

Richard took Bonnie to one side again. 'If we have them locked up we will never know who hired them,' she said.

'So what are we going to do?'

Victoria had listened quietly to the proceedings and now decided to have her say. 'Why not threaten them and reward them at the same time. They're a couple of ne'er do wells. Money will loosen their tongues.'

'What do you mean?' said Richard.

'Let me explain things to them.'

'All right,' said Bonnie. 'This should be interesting.'

'Now listen to me, you two. We want to know who hired you. You say you do not know his name, so what did he look like?'

'Can't tell, Miss. It were dark,' said Edwin, his shifty eyes showing an interest in Victoria.

'We have a proposition for you. You say you do not know who hired you. I do not believe you. However, we are prepared to give you the benefit of the doubt. You have five days to return here with the name of the person who hired you, and when you do that you will be given five pounds. If you do not come back and give us his name you will be reported to the police.'

'Five pounds you say?' said Edwin.

'Yes, and if you have his name now you can leave with the money,' said Victoria.

'Don't know 'is name, 'onest,' said Edwin. 'We'll find out and come back.'

'I'd rather shoot 'em,' grumbled Miller.

***

Bonnie and Victoria pruned the trees in the orangery. Victoria breathed in the pleasant scent that the plants exuded. In the centre, a fish pond held tench and goldfish.

'So much for giving those two villains a chance,' said Victoria.

'It's only been one day, Victoria. We gave them five.'

'I think I may have been mistaken in giving them five days. They will probably make a run for it. They seemed more scared of who put them up to it than of us.'

'There is not much we can do about that now.'

'Perhaps we can.'

'What do you mean Victoria?'

'Oh, nothing really. Just thinking out loud.'

'Well, don't you go getting yourself involved.'

***

In a lane near the Bear and Ragged Staff, a cloaked figure waited in a dark recess of a long brick wall around the cemetery. A hand fingered the blade of a knife with a deer's-foot handle.

Edwin and Billy sauntered along the lane with small packs on their backs, both unsteady from drink. As they passed the recess, a hand shot out, grabbed Edwin by the neck and put the knife to his throat.

'What the . . .' said Edwin, just about managing to speak as his assailant tightened the grip around his neck and punctured the skin by his Adam's apple with the knife.

Billy stood frozen to the spot.

'Listen to me, cretins,' said a woman's rough voice. 'I reckon you is making a run for it. Well, I'm on to you.'

'What's it to you?' said Edwin, keeping very still so the knife did not penetrate any further.

'I want to know who put you up to trying to infect the 'erd at Eagledown.'

'What's it to you?' said Edwin again.

The knife sawed at his throat, drawing blood from the superficial wound.

'Wait, wait,' said Edwin.

'Tell 'er for God's sake, Dad. She's a crazy woman.'

'Aye, that I am,' said the cloaked figure.

'Straight up, don't know 'is name,' said Edwin.

The knife cut deeper.

'Tell 'er, Dad. Tell 'er.'

'Tweedale,' said Edwin. 'Used to be some sort of master at an orphanage.'

Victoria's blood ran cold. She loosened her grip on Edwin, poked the knife in his back and said. 'Clear off and do not come back or you'll be worm food.'

Edwin backed away. The moon came out from behind a cloud. He could see her face in the dim light.

'Thought it were you. We'll meet again and next time . . .' said Edwin, just before he ran off, closely followed by his son.

Chapter Twelve

Richard and Victoria raced their mounts through a newly cut field, heading for an old oak tree standing alone on the far side. The thrill of the ride excited her in a way she had not expected. Ahead by half a length, she reached the finish line.

'Well done, Victoria. You certainly know how to ride.'

'Are you sure you didn't let me win?'

He smiled. She looked into his green eyes and her whole body reacted. The effect of the hard ride had made her warm, but now she could feel her nipples against her chemise. Down below she could feel something too. Not all of this was from the thrill of the chase. His eyes held hers. *Take me in your arms. Kiss me. Make love to me. I want you*, she said it to herself, though she was sorely tempted to say it aloud.

They dismounted and Victoria bent to pick a meadow flower.

If he could sense what she was thinking, she did not care. There was nothing she wanted more at that moment than to let him lower her to the ground, remove her undergarments and take her virginity. She had held on to it throughout her time at the orphanage—only just on some occasions. Now she wanted to lose it to him. That he was already married had completely gone from her mind as her lust and love took over.

A hazel hedge separated the field they were in from the next. As they looked at each other, their intense, silent communication was interrupted. ''Scuse us, Guv'nor.'

Richard looked over at a gap in the hazel hedge. He saw an elderly woman with a younger one by her side.

'Is you the master of this estate, Guv'nor?' said the old woman, slipping a scarlet scarf from her grey hair and fastening it around her neck.

Her companion—about the same age as Victoria—had black hair down to her shoulders. Her eyes were almost the same colour.

This young woman scared Victoria. She was beautiful, but she was more than that. There was a magnetism about her. Richard's eyes were drawn to her bare shoulders and cleavage. Victoria felt the deep pangs of jealousy tear at her.

'We'd like to stay a few days, Guv'nor, if that's all right with you,' said the old woman.

The young woman smiled to reveal perfect teeth.

'How many are you?' asked Richard.

'Four caravans—ten people, give or take,' said the old woman.

'Where are you camped?'

'Follow us,' said the young woman, turning and walking away, closely followed by her elderly companion.

Richard and Victoria followed on foot, leading their horses by the reins.

In a little fold surrounded by trees, they came across a gypsy camp. A fire burned in a pit, but nobody else was around.

Victoria counted four brightly painted caravans.

Richard whispered to Victoria, 'They are real gypsies, not tinkers. What do you think?'

'You are the master, Richard. If you want these people on your land, it is your decision.' She could not hide the jealousy in her voice or the anger that her first real sexual experience had been thwarted.

'My name is Rawnie,' said the young woman. 'I'll make sure there ain't no trouble from the men. We'll respect your land.'

'All right. You can stay, but if there is any thieving I'll bring the constable.'

'We are honest folk—we're not thieves—we work,' said Rawnie with her hands on her shapely hips.

'Glad to hear it,' said Richard.

'I'll tell you your fortune if you wish, Guv'nor,' said Rawnie. 'Or is there anything else you'd fancy?' She laughed as she bent over to stir something in an iron pot on the fire.

She wore nothing under her chemise, exposing her large but firm breasts. A sickly feeling built up in Victoria's tummy as she saw Richard take in the view.

They mounted their horses and trotted away from the gypsy camp. Whatever may have happened had they not been interrupted by the gypsies would not happen now. The mood was gone.

'I had better tell the workers that I have given the gypsies permission to stay or they will be harassing them. Let's race back home.'

'No, you go, Richard. I would like to ride a little more.'

They parted without another word.

***

Victoria rode Tess through a wheat field as yellow as egg yolk. A skylark hovered high above, but she hardly noticed its song, so dark and troubled were her thoughts. With the passion of the moment gone she felt guilty that she would have been an adulteress but for the interruption of the gypsies. What really tugged at her conscience was the knowledge that she had wanted him so much. And the way he had looked at the gypsy woman, Rawnie, still rankled.

Then her thoughts went back to her encounter with Edwin and Billy and what she had told Inspector Forbes and Constable Hemingway about Edwin naming Tweedale. The father and son criminals had vanished and there was no trace of Tweedale. She omitted her use of the knife to elicit the information, leaving the police officers wondering why Edwin had been so helpful.

As she came to a five-barred gate, she leant over to release a big iron catch to let Tess through. The next field held Gilbert, the prize bull, in a meadow rich in wild flowers and busy bees. Gilbert had the field to himself today. His harem Victoria had seen several fields back. She had heard Richard talking about giving him a rest now his value had risen considerably.

Off to her right, an oak wood sloped upwards. A movement up there caught her eye. She dismissed it as probably a deer. She had no interest in it anyway, so dark and bleak were her thoughts.

Oblivious to any danger, Victoria coaxed Tess forward. Gilbert looked up at the visitors to his field and then continued to eat the grass.

Victoria saw the great animal suddenly convulse, fractions of a second before she heard a bang. Gilbert collapsed to the ground. It seemed like slow motion to her. She could see a hole just below his right ear; blood poured from the wound. The bull twitched, his breathing heavy, and then gradually lighter until seconds later it ceased. Gilbert lay still.

Victoria looked up the hill to where a puff of smoke hung in the air like a will-o'-the-wisp. The bull was between her and the shooter. *Was I the target or Gilbert?*

With her eyes fixed on the smoke, she kicked Tess and off they went in a charge towards the hill. She had no idea what she would do when she got there. Get there she would, and confront the killer of Gilbert or her would-be assassin. Tess raced up the hill as if she were a Grand National champion, with her rider gripping her sides by her knees so tightly to keep from falling, grateful she wasn't riding side-saddle. Victoria saw a figure jump to its feet and turn to run. It stopped. It was still too far away for her to recognise who it was. Her blood ran cold as she saw it bend down on one knee and level a rifle. Victoria saw a puff of smoke and then felt Tess stumble and crumple to the ground, throwing her off.

She picked herself up just in time to see the figure dash off into the woods. She tried to stand to give chase but fell down with pain in her left ankle. Tess lay whimpering with an enormous gash in her shoulder. Victoria ripped off her riding jacket and shirt. Limping over to the horse she stuffed the shirt into the gaping wound to stem the flow of blood.

Kneeling in her camisole, next to her horse, Victoria spotted a rider coming at a gallop. There was no mistaking the horse. Solomon was at full throttle with Richard urging him on.

He leapt from his horse. 'I heard a shot and saw the bull go down. Then Tess. Are you hurt?'

'Someone up there in the wood . . . He shot Gilbert and Tess.'

Richard looked at Victoria crouched by her horse, desperately trying to stop the blood flow. Even though preoccupied with the horse she saw his gaze on her underwear. She could not help a frisson of excitement shooting through her body before she grabbed her discarded riding jacket and pulled it on. Their last near encounter still lingered in her mind.

'Stay here. Which way did the shooter go?' said Richard.

'Do not be bloody stupid, Richard. He shot my horse. He will shoot you. We need to do something for Tess.'

A man rode towards them. There was a deer slung over the back of his horse. As he came nearer, she recognised Algernon. In a holder on the side of his saddle, he carried a rifle. The two men stared at each other.

'Stop it and do something useful, you two,' she said.

'What happened?' asked Algernon, climbing off his horse.

'Someone shot our bull and then poor Tess here,' said Richard.

'Did you see who did it?'

Victoria looked at him. He was about the right height. The shooter seemed to be heavier, though. But it could have been Algernon. She did not get a good look at the culprit.

'Yes,' she said, wanting to see his reaction.

'Good. Shooting a horse; that's wicked,' said Algernon.

'Not to mention my bull,' said Richard.

Algernon bent down to Tess and looked at the wound. 'I'm afraid it is serious. I don't think she will make it.'

'What are we going to do?' said Victoria to both men.

'Only one thing we can do,' said Richard.

'I hate to agree with anything you say, de Mornay, but you're right,' said Algernon.

'You're not going to shoot her, are you?' asked Victoria. Her brave charge at the shooter was now replaced with fear for her horse.

'I'm afraid so,' said Richard.

'Do you want me to do it, de Mornay, if you're still squeamish about killing animals?'

'No. If I may borrow your gun . . .'

Algernon slipped his rifle from the holder. Richard held out his hand. Victoria stepped forward and took it from Algernon. Her fingers closed on the manufacturer's name, 'Snider-Enfield'. It meant nothing to her.

'She is my horse and she is injured because of my stupidity. I will do it.'

'One of us can,' said Richard.

'Is it loaded?'

'Yes,' said Algernon.

With determination written all over her face, she limped towards Tess, carrying the rifle behind her back. 'I am so sorry, Tess.'

The horse's big, brown eyes rolled to expose the whites. Gently Victoria put the rifle barrel just below its right ear, pulled back the hammer and squeezed the trigger. The horse's head jumped with the impact of the bullet. Its whole body shook, quivered and then lay still. Richard lifted the gun from Victoria's hands and passed it to Algernon. Victoria fell to her knees, but no tears would come.

Algernon climbed back on his horse. 'I'm sorry. She looked an excellent horse.'

Richard helped Victoria to her feet and then on to Solomon. The horse did not buck or bolt. Perhaps it sensed her grief. With Richard walking ahead holding the reins, they headed back to the house.

***

Victoria and Richard busied themselves in the stables, packing away the tack belonging to Tess. Constable Hemingway waddled in.

"'Scuse me, Miss, Sir, I've finished checking over where the shooter was up on the hill. I found one cartridge that had been fired recently in the exact spot from which you said he had fired the second shot at you, Miss.'

'How does that help?' said Richard.

'Well, Sir, I'm not sure it does. It belongs to a Snider-Enfield rifle, but there are a lot of them about. They're ex-military. It's definitely an army-issue cartridge.'

'So we are looking for an ex-soldier?' asked Victoria.

'Not necessarily, Miss, but possibly.'

Victoria remembered the name on Algernon's rifle that she used to shoot Tess. *Yes: 'Snider-Enfield'.*

She decided not to say anything at this stage, but alarm bells were ringing in her head. Algernon came upon the scene very soon after the shots were fired and he had the same make of gun that was used.

'I suppose my father had an alibi?' said Richard.

'He did, Sir. Playing cards with three other peers of the realm no less.'

'The ones that he owes money, I expect,' said Richard.

'I don't know, Sir. I'm not allowed to look into private finances.'

'That is a shame. I doubt his creditors would want him locked up before he pays off his debts.'

'I will mention it to Inspector Forbes, though I doubt he'll be able to do anything.'

'Is there anything else that helps?' asked Richard.

'No, Sir. Except perhaps: the shot at the bull was a difficult one, but the shot at the charging horse of Miss Victoria, well, that must have been some marksman. The man we are looking for is probably an ex-soldier, though not necessarily. He is an excellent shot. I know your father has an alibi, but is he a good shot?'

'It may sound strange, but I do not know. He went big-game hunting in Africa. I never went with him. When we lived in England he shot deer, but I was never with him.'

'Did he serve in the army?'

'No.'

'Well, that doesn't rule him out entirely,' said the constable.

'Thank you for your help. Please let us know if you come up with anything else.'

'Yes, thank you,' said Victoria.

The constable bid them 'Good day' and climbed aboard his pony and trap. The animal seemed to be complaining about the weight it had to pull as they trundled up the drive.

'So, Richard, we have our suspects. There is the obvious one, your father, but he seems to have an alibi. Then there is Algernon, who lives nearby and was in the area when the shots were fired. I did not say anything to the constable, but the rifle that Algernon lent me was a Snider-Enfield. Then there's Lord Peter. He lost out at the show when your bull got first prize. Though the prize money on its own isn't much, the value is enormous as it attracts breeders to the estate.'

'You seem to know a lot about the economics of farming.'

'Bonnie is an excellent teacher.'

'I don't think Lord Peter would do such a thing, but I suppose we cannot discount him. Algernon, well he's a bit of a hothead at times, but I don't think he would do it either. No, I think it must either be my father who pulled the trigger or he hired someone to do it for him.'

'I agree with you, Richard, up to a point, but I do not think we should discount the others.'

***

Abigail handed Jake his tin of sandwiches and a bottle of porter. She could not hide the worry on her face. One hand went to her pregnant belly and with the other she stroked his face. 'Why do you have to go?'

'They've been so good to us. I have to do my bit. We can't afford to lose any more bulls. It's all right. Don't worry. I'll be home at sunrise.'

'It's dangerous.'

'You go off to bed now and look after the little one.' He patted her bump.

'Please be careful, Jake. I don't know what I . . . we . . . would do without you.'

'Nothing's going to happen. We've got Ben in the next valley and Miller in the woods. Nobody can get through. Now off you go to bed and I'll see you in the morning.'

'Where will you be tonight?'

'Why?'

'I'd just feel happier knowing where on the estate you'll be.'

'On the hill overlooking the farm buildings. Now please, go to bed.'

Abigail kissed him on the cheek and then on the lips. She turned and went to go indoors as he set off along the lane. Then she stopped and watched him disappear into the darkness. A dark foreboding filled her senses. Only when she could see him no more did she go back inside.

Abigail climbed the rickety wooden staircase to the bedroom. She lay in the bed but could not settle. She got out and knelt by the bed with its patchwork quilt she had spent many hours making to keep Jake warm. *Please, God, keep him safe.*

Her fear would not go away. She did not know why God had given her this foresight. Was it a curse or a boon? Her mother and her grandmother had the premonitions and some of them had come true. Some people dismissed such things as foolish at best and fraud at worst, but Abigail felt there was something in this gift or curse. Her mind went back to the deluge at the schoolhouse. That morning she had gone down with a fever and that had saved her life. Had the fever come to save her? She did not know, but from what her mother had told her, the gift sometimes acted in mysterious ways. She thought of her great-great-grandmother, burnt at the stake for being a witch. That was the curse part of the gift. She must not ignore the feeling that had crept into her mind. *If I don't do something, Jake will die. But what can I do?*

Abigail lifted her long coat from a hook on the bedroom door and pulled it on. As she made her way along a dark path lit only by the half-moon and stars, she wondered how she would get anyone to believe her. *I've had a premonition that Jake will die. That would sound crazy. But I must try. Miss Victoria may believe me. I'll see Miss Victoria.*

Eagledown House stood in darkness except for an oil lamp that she could see through a basement window, standing on the kitchen table. Abigail knew the house well from her time working there as a maid. Now, she sometimes helped Cook when Lady Luisa held large dinner parties. With a silent prayer, she tried the outside door of the corridor that ran the full length of the basement. It fell open to her touch. She stepped in. A quick search of the kitchen found a candle. She lit it from the oil lamp.

Her fear gave wings to her legs and soon she found herself in the corridor outside Victoria's room. *If I knock, I'll wake everyone up. They'll think I'm mad.* She turned the porcelain door handle of the room and went in. The draught from the door blew out her candle.

In the dark room Abigail's eyes strained. A gentle sound of breathing led her to the bedside. She sat on the bed.

Victoria woke with a start. 'What the . . .'

'It's all right, Miss Victoria, it's me, Abigail.'

'What on earth are you up to?'

'Please, Miss, I know it sounds stupid, but I have this terrible feeling that something's going to happen to Jake. I can't say how I know. I don't know how I know. I just know I know.'

'Just a minute, Abigail . . . What are you talking about? What's going to happen to Jake?'

'I don't know, Miss. I just know.'

'What are you talking about, Abigail? Where is he?'

'He's out on guard duty tonight.'

'So are many other men from the estate. He will be fine. Don't worry about him.'

'But I can't help it, Miss. I have this feeling. I know it sounds daft, but I'm scared. Something's going to happen to Jake.'

'No, it isn't. Go back home. It is the middle of the night. You should not be out in your condition.'

'I can't, Miss. I hoped you would help me. I'll go on my own. I have to do something.'

'Abigail! This is nonsense. Go home.'

'No, Miss. I'm going to find Jake on my own if you won't help me.'

'Do you know where he is?'

'Yes. On the hill overlooking the farm buildings.'

'You are in no condition to be traipsing around the estate at this time of the night. Go back home. I will see what I can do.'

'But Miss . . .'

'Abigail, please. Go home. Leave it to me.'

'What are you going to do, Miss?'

'I'm going to wake Sir Richard and the two of us will find Jake and make sure he is all right. Really, Abigail, this is ridiculous.'

'I know, Miss, but I'm scared.'

'Now go home.'

'Are you going to wake Sir Richard and go to Jake?'

'That is what I said, Abigail.'

'You promise?'

'Abigail!'

'Sorry, Miss, but I'm not going home until you promise to wake Sir Richard and go to Jake.'

'For the last time, Abigail, go home. I promise. All right?'

'Thank you, Miss.'

'You can thank me by going home and looking after yourself and your baby.'

Victoria slipped her legs out of the bed, reached into a drawer and pulled out a lucifer. She lit Abigail's candle and then one on her bedside. She threw off her nightgown, pulled on a pair of silk bloomers and quickly dressed in her riding skirt and jacket.

***

Outside in the corridor she ushered Abigail away home. Then she tiptoed down to Richard's room as quietly as possible. There were guests in the house that she did not want to wake. Dr O'Reilly and his wife had stayed after dinner that night, as had the squire and his wife.

A gentle tap and then she entered. She felt butterflies in her tummy at the sight of him fast asleep like a little boy. Putting the candle on his bedside table, she shook him by the shoulder. He moaned but did not wake. She shook him again. Slowly he opened his eyes. He sat up with a jump when he saw Victoria in the candlelight.

'Er . . .'

'Do not get excited, Richard. I am here for your help. We need to go and check on Jake out on the hill.'

'Why?'

'Because we do. Trust me.'

'What is this all about?'

'Abigail thinks Jake is in danger.'

'How?'

'It is complicated. Just get up and come with me.'

'Why does she think he is in danger?'

'Will you get up and do as I say or do I have to stand here all night arguing with you?'

'It's the middle of the night. Since you are here . . .'

'Richard! Get up and come with me. Now!'

'If you say so. Would you like to turn around while I get out of bed? I am naked.'

Victoria blushed and turned. She heard him climb out of bed. Though the candle gave off a weak light, she could plainly see Richard in a full-length mirror on the far wall. She moved her gaze away but then felt drawn back to the image. His muscled torso and strong arms made her feel weak at the knees. First he pulled on a pair of breeches and then a white shirt.

'You can turn around now.'

On the way out of the house, Richard led Victoria by the gunroom where he picked up a heavy revolver.

'Is that wise?'

'I have no idea what this is all about, but if we are going around the estate in the middle of the night and there is a problem, then we may need it.'

Picking their way carefully in the moonlight they made their way towards the hill overlooking the farm buildings.

***

Jake found his vantage point where he could look down on the outlying farm buildings. He could make out the silhouette of the huge barn that held the new bull and hay bales for the winter. He wanted to help Richard. Jake's job depended on the estate continuing to make money. Whoever the lunatic was who had targeted Sir Richard he could not be allowed to succeed and throw so many people out of work. So he sat on the hillside to watch with his home-made club of oak.

A rustle behind made him reach for the club. A rabbit sat terrified in the moonlight, looking at him. Jake opened his sandwich box and wolfed down a Cheddar and pickle doorstopper.

Though a countryman and often out when dark, he had not sat so quietly before. The fauna surprised even him. Scurrying mice, an owl on the prowl for the mice; two deer and a badger came close to him in the first few minutes of his vigil.

Jake opened his porter and took a sip. Suddenly he heard a twig break behind him. He twisted his head round. He grabbed his club and just managed to say, 'You!' before he took a blow to the head. As he lay looking up at his assailant, he felt dizzy. He tried to get up, but his arms and legs did not seem to work. 'I knew it would be you. Why? Why cause all this trouble and the deaths of those innocent people?'

'And that's not all. I'm going to burn the barn.'

Two more blows crashed down on Jake's head. Jake saw bright lights before his eyes. All went dark and then white as he stepped onto the path to the Afterlife.

***

Victoria and Richard found Jake. His still body lay on its back with eyes that did not see the millions of stars above.

'We are too late. Dear God, we are too late,' said Victoria, bending down to feel for a pulse at his neck. She felt a faint one; so faint as to be hardly there. 'He is still alive but only just and for how long?' She looked at her hand—warm and sticky. Jake's blood was seeping into the earth and taking his life with it.

Richard pulled the revolver from his belt and fired four shots into the air. Miller came running within minutes, closely followed by farmhand Ben and Victoria's shepherd, Arthur.

'Ben, you run back to the house. Doctor O'Reilly is staying there. Bring him here at once.'

Victoria noticed how calm and commanding Richard had become in the face of this tragedy. She looked down the valley at the barn. Flames shot out of the roof. 'Oh no.'

'Victoria, you stay here with Jake and Arthur. Miller, you come with me.'

Richard and Miller raced down the hill towards the barn. Victoria bent down to Jake and held his hand as she watched the fire spread along the roof of the barn. 'Arthur, you wait here for the doctor with Jake. I cannot do anything for him. Maybe I can help down at the barn.'

Arthur nodded.

She picked up her skirt and ran down the slope.

Richard and Miller were nowhere to be seen. The barn doors stood wide open. Inside, flames licked at the hay bales and rafters. At the far end, her eyes picked out movement but could not make out who it was.

'Who's in there?' said a voice behind her.

Victoria turned to see Humphreys. 'Richard and Miller.'

Humphreys dashed into the barn. Victoria ran in behind him. At the far end they found Miller, dead as mutton, with a massive beam across his back. Then she saw Richard. He lay on his side with a rafter across his legs. For one terrible moment she thought he was dead and all her aspirations with him. Her heart almost burst with joy when he moved.

Gordon, a young bull raised to replace Gilbert, stood with his back to the end wall, his nostrils flared and head down. There was terror in his eyes.

'Get out. Get out. Save yourself,' said Richard.

'Get the bull out, Mr Humphreys,' she shouted back over the thunder of fire and falling debris.

The way they had come in no longer offered an escape route. Flames crept towards them.

She grabbed the beam on Richard's legs and with a strength that she did not know she had, hauled it from him. He tried to stand but could not. She threw him over her shoulder. Victoria looked over to her left and saw a door. 'That way,' she called. 'Get the bull out.'

Humphreys took hold of a ring in the bull's nose and coaxed the terrified animal towards the door.

They reached the door as the flames shot higher and higher. Victoria felt the heat on her face. Her riding skirt caught on a timber as she struggled with Richard over her shoulder. She let it rip off.

At the door, Humphreys gave it a kick. It did not budge. Jammed. They stood there, trapped. Flames all around with no escape. Then Victoria had an idea. She lowered Richard to his feet and propped him against a support.

The bull pawed at the earth floor in a panic, terrified.

Victoria picked up a burning spar and rammed it hard into the rump of the bull. The bull roared and charged straight at the door. It went through the wood like one of Nelson's broadsides. Victoria and Humphreys between them dragged Richard away from the burning barn.

Outside in the farmyard they gasped for breath as they laid Richard down. He tried to stand but fell down. Victoria leant over him in her silk bloomers. The flames from the barn shone on her. He smiled.

Very soon the yard filled with farmhands, scurrying back and forth with buckets of water, but the barn could not be saved.

***

In the drawing room of Eagledown House, Victoria sat with a blanket around her waist, sipping a cup of Cook's chicken soup. Bonnie and Adele fussed around her.

Doctor O'Reilly came in. 'Richard will be all right. No permanent damage. I am afraid Jake is . . . I do not think he will live through the night. His wife is with him. She needs looking after too.'

'Thank you, Doctor. So fortunate that you were here tonight,' said Bonnie.

'What can we do?' asked Adele. 'The loss of lives is more important than the loss of property. It may be that we have to take the law into our own hands. It is plain who is doing all this.'

'We cannot prove anything, Adele. We must leave it to the police to do their job,' said Bonnie.

'I know the police are doing their best, but they are restricted in what they may do. It is my fault. Perhaps he is doing this to get at me,' said Adele.

'It is not your fault, Lady Adele. Most definitely not your fault. If it is him, and I firmly believe that he is behind it, your husband is getting at Richard, not you,' said Victoria.

'We must make sure we do all we can for Jake and Abigail. That is our priority for now and whoever is behind all this will be caught in the end, I am sure,' said Bonnie.

'How many more people will be hurt until then?' said Adele.

'Tweedale is probably involved in this. If anyone deserves to die, then he does,' said Victoria.

'Nobody deserves to die,' said Doctor O'Reilly.

'If I had a gun I would shoot him dead,' said Victoria.

'Victoria!' said Bonnie.

'All right. But something needs to be done. For now, I agree, we must look after Jake and Abigail,' said Victoria.

Chapter Thirteen

Early the next morning Victoria knocked on the door of Arthur's cottage.

Bridget opened the door. 'I'm sorry, Miss, Arthur ain't in. He's gone over to the far field to check on the sheep in case them buggers who fired the barn have done something over there.'

'Actually, it is you I have come to see, Bridget.'

'Me, Miss? Whatever can I do for you?'

'Have you heard about poor Jake?'

'Yeah, Miss. Bastards. Such a nice lad. Passed away yet? No chance. Poor bugger . . . sorry, Miss.'

'By some miracle, he is still alive. Can you do anything for him? You have a way with potions, I have heard.'

'Well, Miss, I don't think so. You see, what I do is bring down fevers and the like. They said poor Jake's skull is bashed in. I ain't got no potions for that, I'm sorry, Miss.'

'Could you try, Bridget. Please?'

'Course I will, Miss. I would've offered but with the doctor and that being there I didn't think my services would be needed or welcome. And probably not useful either. But, Miss, if I can do owt, I will.'

The two women hurried over to Eagledown House and the red guest bedroom where Jake lay in a huge four-poster with Abigail by his side holding his hand. His breathing was shallow.

Abigail stood as Victoria entered. She waved to her to remain seated.

'Doctor says he's unconscious, Miss,' said Abigail, wiping a tear from her eye.

'Do you mind if Bridget has a look at him,' said Victoria.

'I don't care who has a look at him if they can help, Miss.'

Bridget stepped forward.

'Can you do anything for my Jake?'

'I don't know, Abigail. I'll try.'

Bridget bent over Jake and felt his bandaged head. She put the two fingers of her right hand against his neck. Then she put her ear to his lips and listened.

Meanwhile, Abigail climbed to her feet and walked around the room, holding her pregnant belly.

'Not long now, Abigail,' said Victoria.

'What, Miss?'

'Not long now . . . the baby.'

'Oh yes, Miss. Don't know what I'll do without Jake. We'll be for the workhouse me and the baby.'

'You know Sir Richard and I would not let that happen.'

'You're both so kind,' said Abigail. 'But I can't work and look after the baby.'

The door opened and in walked the doctor. 'What are you doing?'

''Scuse me, Sir, but I'm just seeing if I can 'elp poor Jake here.'

'I wish you could. I know what you are. I am afraid there is no hope,' said the doctor, not unkindly.

'His skull ain't broke,' said Bridget. 'His brain is probably swelled. That's what's keeping him unconscious. We need to bring down the swelling.'

'So you are a surgeon now?' said the doctor, this time with an edge in his voice.

'She is trying to help,' said Victoria.

'I know. But Jake's injuries cannot be cured by mumbo jumbo and potions.'

'Can you cure 'im?' said Bridget.

The doctor shook his head. 'Don't be impertinent. I've bled him, but it has not helped.'

'I'll be back,' said Bridget, marching towards the door.

'Do not come back. There is nothing you can do,' said the doctor. 'This is all superstitious nonsense.'

''Scuse me, Sir,' said Abigail, 'it ain't nonsense. I knew something was going to happen to Jake. I had a premonition and that's why I went to Miss Victoria. If I hadn't then Jake would have died up there on the hill. So it ain't nonsense, Sir, if you'll beg my pardon. Things is not always as clear as we may think.'

The doctor said nothing. He took Jake's pulse, shook his head and left.

Abigail sat down on the side of the bed and took hold of Jake's hand.

Victoria sat in an armchair to wait for Bridget.

Bridget came back with a muslin bag in one hand and a bucket of water in the other as she pushed the door open with her foot. 'Now, Miss, Abigail, I'll need both of you to help with this.'

'What are you going to do?' said Abigail.

'First off we have to bring down the swelling. That will need you, Abigail, to apply this 'ere bag to his forehead and crown. You, Miss, I need to massage his feet.'

'Massage his feet? It is his head that is hurt,' said Victoria.

'I know, Miss, but please trust me.'

'I do,' said Victoria.

'Got to admit though, Miss, I don't know if what I'm doing will work.'

'Will it do any harm?' said Abigail.

'No, it won't do no 'arm, love.

Bridget dipped the muslin bag in the bucket. A strong smell of herbs filled the room from the bag. She handed it to Abigail.

Gently and with all her love, Abigail dabbed the muslin bag on Jake's forehead and crown.

Victoria rolled up the sheet, blanket and quilt at Jake's feet. Bridget showed her how to massage them, turning them carefully round in circles while pressing her fingers into his soles.

Victoria took over.

Bridget took a phial from her skirt pocket, pulled out the cork and held it to Jake's lips. She managed to get a small amount into his mouth.

The doctor walked in. 'What on earth . . .? I forbid you to use your potions on this poor man.'

'Please, Doctor, let Bridget try. There's nothing else anyone can do for him,' said Victoria.

'Certainly not. I will not have my patient treated by some . . . some . . .'

'Witch?' said Bridget.

'Quack. Charlatan,' said the doctor. 'Leave him be at once.'

Victoria stopped massaging Jake's feet. She pulled herself up to her full height and looked the doctor straight in the eyes. Just as she was about to order him from the room, Jake coughed. And then he coughed again. All eyes looked at him.

Slowly Jake's eyes opened. All he could mumble was, 'What happened?'

Abigail sobbed tears of joy. The doctor wore an expression of amazement. Bridget smiled. Victoria, for once, stood speechless.

***

Victoria decided she must turn detective and find the evidence to stop the person targeting the estate from ruining it. Miller had been murdered, Jake severely injured and the estate was headed towards bankruptcy. She wanted Richard so much with or without his wealth, but in her heart she knew that he would never be happy if he lost Eagledown. *No*, she said to herself, *I must find out who is responsible and I will start with Lord de Mornay.*

Jake's mind was blank for the period between leaving home and waking up after the attack. Victoria questioned the doctor at length to find out if his memory would return, but the prognosis was that it would not come back. She would have to find out who was behind the attack by some other means.

As Victoria came along the corridor outside Richard's office, she heard Bonnie and Richard talking inside.

'How long can we keep going?' asked Bonnie.

Victoria stopped walking and listened, quietly so they wouldn't know she was there.

'I doubt more than three months if we can't get a loan to tide us over.'

'Have all the banks refused to lend to the estate?'

'Yes, all of them.'

'Why? We are a sound investment. If we can catch the lunatic who is trying to destroy Eagledown, we will be back in profit soon.'

'I am afraid it is all down to Harry Ratcliffe and his father. After that altercation at the show, they have conspired with their cronies and we are blackballed everywhere.'

Victoria felt the shock of realisation that her lack of control by hitting Harry Ratcliffe had such severe repercussions. Lord de Mornay would have to wait. First she needed to undo what she had caused.

***

Charles Hamilton was not difficult to track down. She found him paying court to Elizabeth at the orphanage.

Together with Mr Jolyon and several orphans, they were picking vegetables in the garden.

Mr Jolyon looked up as she approached. 'Hello, Victoria. So nice to see you here.'

The men both bowed to her. Elizabeth smiled.

Victoria said, 'I have come to see Charles about a delicate matter. May I take him from your company for a few minutes to discuss something regarding business?'

She could see a trace of apprehension on Elizabeth's face. 'I can assure you it is strictly business regarding Eagledown estate,' said Victoria.

Victoria led him over to a bench on the side of a well-kept lawn under the old oak tree that she had used all those years ago to scale the perimeter wall and escape the clutches of Woodward. It all looked so peaceful and pleasant now.

'Charles, I have a favour to ask.'

'Anything for you, Victoria. I'm so grateful to you for introducing me to Elizabeth. I am going to ask her to marry me but please do not say anything to anyone yet because I have not yet summoned up the courage to propose.'

'Charles! Ask the girl right away after our discussion or you could lose her to some other man. She is a very attractive and intelligent young woman.'

'Indeed. Well, I'm glad that's off my chest. Now, what can I do for you?'

'Eagledown is in dire trouble. They need a loan. Harry Ratcliffe's father has ensured that no banks will offer the facility. It appears that your bank, Empire Bank, has refused too. It is not because the estate is a risk. It is because I punched Harry at the agriculture show and Richard punched him again when he raised his fist to me.'

'I have not been paying much attention to the bank recently with other things on my mind. And I doubt if something like a banking loan would be brought to my attention. I am a director, not a manager. What do you wish me to do about it?'

'I wish that you arrange the loan needed.'

'The banking system is run by people who all know and trust each other. Though we are in competition, we also make sure we work together. It does not surprise me that Ratcliffe Senior managed to get everyone to refuse Eagledown, including my own bank.'

'So you cannot do anything about it?'

'I did not say that. I will look into it. In fact, no. When I have finished here later today, I shall come over to Eagledown and talk with Richard and arrange the loan myself.'

Victoria leant over and kissed him on the cheek. 'One more request. Please do not tell Richard I had anything to do with getting you to arrange the loan. I do not want him to feel embarrassed or indebted to me.'

'I'll think of something to keep you out of it.'

Together they walked back to Mr Jolyon and Elizabeth.

'Mr Jolyon, Sir, may I speak with you alone?' said Charles.

'I suppose so,' said a puzzled Mr Jolyon.

Victoria stood with Elizabeth and watched the two men go to the bench where Victoria and Charles had discussed the loan. They saw Mr Jolyon nod his head and hold out his hand. The two men shook and then walked back.

Victoria smiled.

'What's going on?' said Elizabeth before they arrived.

'I don't know,' said Victoria.

Charles bowed to Elizabeth. 'May I talk with you alone?'

Elizabeth was trembling.

Charles and Elizabeth walked over to the old oak tree. Charles went down on one knee and then Elizabeth threw her arms around him.

'Thank you, Victoria,' said Mr Jolyon.

'He just needed a little push.'

***

Victoria managed to get Richard to stay in the drawing room that afternoon by playing the piano for him and singing. She even roped in Penelope to help her.

Humphreys came in. 'Sir Richard, Mr Charles Hamilton wishes to call upon you. Are you at home?'

'Hamilton? What does he want?' said Richard.

'He didn't say, Sir.'

'I will see him in my study.'

'Yes, Sir.'

Richard marched off.

'What is going on?' said Penelope.

'Probably some boring business matter.'

Through the open door a few minutes later they saw Bonnie coming downstairs and heading for the study.

'I wonder what Charles Hamilton wants with them? I do hope he is not going to make the estate bankrupt,' said Penelope.

Victoria could see the alarm on her face. 'I doubt it will come to that.'

Victoria carried on playing the piano while Penelope accompanied her on the violin.

After about an hour, Victoria caught a glimpse of Charles leaving by the main door. A few minutes later Richard came in, followed by Bonnie and Humphreys.

'We have had an extraordinary stroke of luck. Charles Hamilton of Empire Bank is in dispute with the Ratcliffes and to show his displeasure with them wants to break an embargo on loans to the estate that they contrived to ruin us.'

'That is marvellous news, Richard,' said Penelope.

Victoria smiled.

Bonnie raised an eyebrow.

'Come on, Aunt Luisa, we have a lot to do now that we have the backing of Empire Bank,' said Richard.

Victoria gave a little shrug. 'I would appreciate some fresh air. Would you care to join me, Penelope, while Bonnie and Richard continue with their business plans?

'Yes, I would enjoy that. Shall we take the pony and trap or ride?'

'I think we should ride.'

'We will see you at dinner then,' said Bonnie with a smile before following Richard to sort out the finances of Eagledown.

***

They saddled their horses and off they went, with Victoria riding astride and Penelope riding side-saddle.'

'You are amazing, Victoria,' said Penelope as she trotted her horse alongside Victoria on a sunken lane with the scent of wild garlic in the hedgerows.

'I do not know what you mean.'

'You know perfectly well. You arranged for Charles Hamilton to help out Eagledown.'

'What makes you think that?'

'Victoria! I am not a stupid girl. It is obvious you persuaded Charles Hamilton. I am sure Aunt Luisa knows it too. Probably Richard has guessed too. Perhaps he will not say anything for fear of embarrassing you but I know he would be extremely grateful.'

Victoria began to feel warm and blushed at the thought of Richard knowing she had helped him. Then she saw a rider in the distance, skirting a field and coming in their direction. As he came closer, she saw it was Algernon.

'Good day, ladies,' he said, doffing his flat cap.

'Good day, Algernon,' said Victoria.

'Hello,' said Penelope.

Victoria could sense there was some kind of non-verbal communication going on between Penelope and Algernon. It was only a feeling but a very strong one. 'Oh, I say! Look at the lovely meadow flowers. I shall pick some for the table tonight if you would excuse me for a moment.' Victoria dismounted and trod over the field to a display of flowers on a bank near the surrounding hedge.

As she picked the flowers, she stole a glance back at Penelope and Algernon. They were in deep conversation and laughing, though Victoria could not hear what was said. After a few minutes, the bunch of meadow flowers was as much as she could carry. Victoria made her way back to her horse.

'Well, it was nice to see you today,' said Algernon, doffing his cap and bowing to both ladies. He trotted his horse away.

Victoria looked at Penelope.

'What?' said Penelope.

'Nothing.'

'What?'

'None of my business.'

'All right, but do not tell anyone. Promise!'

'I don't know what I am promising.'

'Victoria! Promise that if I tell you a secret you will not tell anyone.'

'Should you tell me if it is that secret?'

'I just have to tell someone, Victoria, or I shall burst.'

'All right. I promise. What do you want to tell me?'

'It is about Algernon and I.'

'Now there is a surprise.'

'Please, Victoria.'

'Sorry. Go on.'

'Algernon and I. We have been meeting secretly. He still loves me and I love him. He has asked me to elope with him but I said I would only get married in our church. He does not legally have to ask for my hand in marriage as I am of an age where I may do as I please, but convention does require him to ask my father. Of course, that is not a good idea. He would not give his blessing. And when I walk down the aisle I want Richard to give me away. Algernon is not happy about that.'

'So what are you going to do?'

'We don't know yet. I have at least persuaded him that we should marry in our church. We are still arguing—no, discussing—the other parts.'

'I do think you should tell your mother and Richard what is going on. They will not be against it. In fact, they would be very happy.'

'Perhaps. But with the problems between Richard and Algernon I was hoping to keep it secret until we can come to some arrangement that will not result in a massive row.'

'Do you think you can persuade Algernon to accept Richard giving you away?'

'Eventually!'

'I promise I will not say anything. Good luck!' Victoria felt a pang of jealousy. Penelope and Algernon had each other and would manage to overcome the problems. *If only Richard were free. I am sure he would want me. I can tell by the way he looks at me. I cannot just go and throw myself at him. But I am tempted. In the field before those gypsies appeared, I was ready to give myself to him and I am sure he was ready to take me. But it didn't happen and now I do not know if it ever will.*

Chapter Fourteen

Thanks to brilliant detective work by Abigail and Bridget, Victoria knew that Lord de Mornay visited Hundred Acre Farm on a Saturday morning, if he was in the area, to collect his share of the takings and indulge in the pleasures of the house. He was in business with a widow, Mrs Ambleside, who resided there. It was a clandestine business, and though it had been raided by the police and the Revenue, nothing was ever found to prove what went on there. The business had little to do with farming, though she did hire a few men to keep the place running while the other employees worked in the farmhouse, upstairs.

Victoria had no real plan. She would sit up in Magpie Wood with a good view of the farm and see if he was there or if he arrived. If she saw him leave, she would follow him. It seemed unlikely that he would do anything to implicate himself in the crimes at Eagledown, but if she could link him somehow, then it was worth trying, even if it took days of following him. *He must eventually slip up and incriminate himself.*

True to form, de Mornay came out of the farmhouse, adjusted his jacket and trousers and climbed on a horse.

Victoria followed on her horse, keeping a discreet distance between herself and her target. *I wonder where he is going?*

He rode along a bridleway that stretched from Hundred Acre Farm all the way to Winchester. As he approached a stream and an old mill he dismounted, tied the horse to a tree and went inside.

The building was derelict. *What is he up to?* Victoria tied her horse to a branch and sneaked towards the mill. Pulling herself up to look through a broken window she saw de Mornay lifting floorboards. He put something in a leather wallet under the floor and replaced the boards. She darted around the corner when he approached the window and looked out.

Her foot caught in an old rusted bucket and made a clanging sound.

De Mornay came out and around the side of the mill. Victoria hid behind a pile of wood with her heart almost in her mouth as she heard his footsteps. It was the first place he would look. Her hand gripped the deer's-foot handle of her knife in her boot.

A feral cat shot out of the woodpile. Victoria heard de Mornay curse and through a gap saw him climb on his horse and trot away, leaving Victoria with a madly beating heart and a dilemma. *Should I follow him or should I look under the floorboards?*

It took her a little time to find the right floor boards, but with perseverance she found them and pulled them up.

She found a map of Eagledown, showing in detail where the dam was weakest. The leather wallet she saw him place there bulged. With trembling fingers, she opened it and found a thick bundle of five- and ten-pound notes. *That must be from the bordello he runs.*

If I take anything from the hole and he returns, he will know that someone has found his hiding place. If I leave it here, what are the chances of his coming back for it and moving it before I see the constable?

She decided to leave everything in place and hurried off to find Constable Hemingway.

***

She found him in his garden tending his roses. 'Constable, Constable . . .

'Whatever is the matter, Miss?'

'I have found the evidence to link Lord de Mornay with what is happening at Eagledown.'

'What have you found, Miss?'

'A plan of the dam at Eagledown.'

'Where?'

'In the old Battersby mill.'

'How do we link that to Lord de Mornay?'

'I followed him there and saw him lift the floorboards.'

'Dear God, Victoria! I mean, Miss, you shouldn't be doing anything like that. Something dreadful could have happened to you. Wait here while I get my coat and the pony and trap.'

Victoria led the way to Battersby Mill.

'I saw him through this window,' she said, showing him where her vantage point gave her a view of the inside.

Together they went into the mill. Victoria showed the constable which floorboards to lift.

He reached in and pulled out the leather wallet and map.

'You can arrest him now.'

'Wish I could, Miss. I can't. This doesn't prove anything. I'll have a word with Inspector Forbes and see if he can come up with any suggestions.'

Victoria rode back to Eagledown feeling miserable. She had thought she had come so close to saving the estate from Lord de Mornay but, on reflection, she knew the constable was right. Money and a map did not provide enough evidence that would stand up in court. *Hopefully, Inspector Forbes will think of something.*

***

Inspector Forbes sat in a white-washed interview room at Winchester police station. Opposite sat Lord de Mornay and his solicitor, Mr McKenzie, a dour Scotsman with a big grey beard. A worn wooden table stood between Forbes and the other two.

'This is an outrage,' said de Mornay.

'You have not been arrested. You are simply here to answer a few questions,' said Inspector Forbes.

'Well get on with it then, man,' said McKenzie.

Forbes lifted a brown paper bag from the floor at his side. He emptied the contents onto the table: a wad of ten- and five-pound notes, a leather wallet and a plan of a dam.

'Have you seen any of these before?' said Forbes.

'No, I've already told you that.'

'We have a witness who saw you put these in a hiding place in a disused water mill.'

'Whoever says that, he is lying. Who is it? I demand to know. I will sue him for libel. '

'There are one thousand and fifty pounds here,' said Forbes.

'So? What has that to do with me?'

'If it isn't your money, it will go into the county's coffers until the owner turns up. Now you wouldn't want to lose all that money, would you?'

'I am sure you know perfectly well that I am bankrupt, and if I did indeed have any money, it would be seized by the bailiffs.'

'All the more reason to hide it in the mill, then.'

'You have nothing, Inspector. I do not think my client needs to answer any more questions,' said McKenzie, stroking his beard.

'This is a plan of the dam at Eagledown that was blown up, killing workers at the estate,' said Forbes, holding up the plan.

McKenzie took it from him. 'It is a plan of something, somewhere, perhaps, but how do we know it is a plan of a particular dam. There is nothing on it to identify it.'

'I can assure you it is the dam at Eagledown,' said Forbes.

'Well, it would not be me you have to convince, Inspector. It would be a court,' said de Mornay. 'And there is nothing to connect it to me.'

'I have a witness,' said Forbes.

'You have a witness? You keep telling me that. One man's word against another's. Who is this man?' said de Mornay.

'If that will be all, Inspector, my client and I have other matters to attend to,' said McKenzie.

***

Humphreys showed Inspector Forbes into the drawing room where Victoria and Richard waited.

'I've done all I'm legally allowed to do and a little bit more, but I can't prove Lord de Mornay had anything to do with blowing up the dam or had anything to do with the other incidents. There is insufficient to get a conviction. I questioned him but I do not have the evidence to proceed.'

'Thank you for trying,' said Richard.

'I understand that the chief constable has told him who gave the information to the police. You must be very careful, Victoria. I really mean that. He is a very dangerous man.'

'I am going away for a few months to tour Europe with Lady Luisa and Lady Adele and Penelope. I doubt he would be following me.'

'I doubt it too, but you must keep alert,' said Inspector Forbes.

'At least we now know who is behind all this, even if we cannot prove it,' said Richard.

'Your father is probably behind all or most of what is happening here, but I am a police officer and I have to keep an open mind. As you told me before, you are not short of people who could mean you harm.'

'To be honest, Inspector, I do not think any of the others would sink to these depths,' said Richard.

'Probably not. But, as I said, I must keep an open mind.'

***

Victoria strolled along the main basement corridor looking for Jane to help her with her packing. The European trip had been arranged before she saw Lord de Mornay at the mill. Now the idea seemed even more prescient.

As she passed the gunroom, she spotted Richard cleaning a shotgun. She stepped into the large, windowless room through an open, iron-barred gate. 'Looks like a prison cell.'

'Have you experience of such places?' said Richard with a smile. Then he frowned. 'I am sorry. That was stupid of me.'

Victoria smiled through the terrible memory of being incarcerated in the orphanage. Then she looked around the room. There were several rifles and shotguns on shelves. Other shelves held photographic equipment and photographs of African wildlife. 'I would like to learn how to shoot.'

'What? People or animals?'

'Four unescorted women on our European trip may attract unwelcome attention. I would just like to make sure we cover all eventualities. And if your father comes after me I want to know that I have protection.'

'I am not sure that my mother or aunt would approve of your carrying a firearm on your holiday.'

'Then perhaps it will best if we do not tell them.'

'I don't know, Victoria; if you were to shoot someone abroad, you could find yourself in serious trouble with the law there.'

'And we could find ourselves in serious trouble if we have no defence. Please, Richard, show me how to use a gun.'

'This gun has a hefty kick on it. Do you think you could manage it?' He offered the shotgun to Victoria.

'Probably, but I was more interested in shooting one of your pistols. I do not think I could reasonably be expected to conceal that thing about my person.' They both chuckled. Victoria loved his chuckle. In fact, she had come to realise that she loved him.

Richard opened a drawer in a bulky oak chest. He lifted out a Colt Navy thirty-six black-powder revolver and passed it to Victoria. She took it from him and nearly dropped it when she felt the weight.

'This has a mighty kick on it too.'

'What about that one?' she said, looking at a peculiar revolver with the hammer to one side of the barrel.

'That is an unusual one. It is a Kerr's thirty-six. They were made in London mainly for the Confederate cavalry. It doesn't kick as much as the Colt but it does kick, I can assure you.'

'May I try it?'

Richard rummaged around in the drawer and found a box of cartridges. He dropped the cylinder of the pistol and placed five bullets into the five slots. The remainder he put in his pocket. 'Come on, then. We will give it a go outside.'

'You do not take part in the shoots. Why do you have so many guns?'

'I don't take pleasure from killing. I am interested in how mechanical things work. Some of these were given to me and some belonged to my grandfather.'

'Are you not tempted to shoot your father?'

'Certainly not. That would be murder.'

'Sometimes you have to fight for what you believe in.'

'I agree, but there are many ways of fighting that do not include shooting people.'

'You are a man of sound principles, Richard. Perhaps too much so for your own good.'

'We are what we are, Victoria.'

He led Victoria to the back of the stables where a massive pile of horse manure decayed. Richard found a broken bucket and embedded it in the manure. Then he pointed to a spot five yards from the target.

'Why here? Am I not too close?' said Victoria, holding her nose against the steaming odour from the pile.

'Pistols are not very accurate over long distances. And when you are learning, if you miss, the bullet will stay in that stinking pile rather than flying off to injure someone.'

'Oh, of course.'

Richard stood behind Victoria and put his arms around her to hold the gun in both his hands. 'Now take the weapon from me, carefully.'

She transferred it into her own hands and held it tight in a two-handed grip. Richard adjusted her hands so she held it firmly but not too tightly. She could feel his breath on her neck. A few butterflies cavorted around inside her. Since their encounter in the field was disturbed by the gypsies, they had not spent any time together, alone. He guided her hands until she was looking down the five-inch barrel. Hitting the bucket was the last thing on her mind. Being engulfed in his strong arms was all she wanted.

'Now squeeze the trigger, gently.'

She eased back the trigger until suddenly a deafening bang went off and the gun kicked upwards in her hands. The noise made her ears ring. 'Did I hit it?'

'Well, you hit the manure about three feet to the right of the bucket.'

Richard still had his arms around Victoria. He guided her hands back to the shooting position. Carefully she squeezed the trigger and then closed her eyes just before the bang.

'How was that?'

'Two feet above. You closed your eyes. Keep them open!'

Her third shot tore into the manure just below the bucket; the fourth and fifth hit the target. Richard clipped five more bullets from his pocket with one hand while keeping the other arm around Victoria. She leant back against him. She knew it was not a gun barrel she could feel pressing against her. It sent a tingle of excitement down her spine. *He wants me and I want him. To hell with convention.*

Now with two arms back around her, Richard reloaded the pistol and put it back into her hands. She lowered it to her side and turned in his arms to face him. She slipped her free arm around his waist.

'Richard, we cannot go on ignoring what we both feel.'

'I agree, absolutely. I know it is wrong for us to be together until I am no longer married. But I do not want to wait any longer. We must be very careful to protect your reputation. I confess, Victoria, I have fallen in love with you.'

'I love you too, Richard.' *Thank goodness his halo has slipped!*

He pulled her to him. Gently their lips met.

Victoria felt a wave of joy surge through her body. *At last! At last!*

The sound of horses' hooves and the metal rims of carriage wheels on the stable-yard cobblestones made them quickly separate.

'Bonnie and your mother are back.'

'Damn! Sorry!' said Richard, taking the pistol from her hand. He slipped the gun into his jacket pocket.

'We need to talk,' said Victoria.

'I know. Could you come to my room before dinner this evening? I have something crucial that I need to tell you about Peggy.'

'Yes. I wish you were coming away with us. I will miss you terribly.'

'And I you.'

And then a shot of guilt ran through her. 'But Richard, you are married. I am not sure . . . I know you are going to divorce but . . .' And then the memory of that kiss and what she felt took over. 'Yes, Richard. Yes, I will be there. Please do not be shocked. I do not want to wait for the divorce. It is so far in the future.'

'I will explain everything this evening. You will understand.'

Victoria's head was in a spin from the kiss. She hardly took in a word that Bonnie said or took notice of the results of their London shopping trip to buy clothes for the holiday, even though there was a stunning white dress for her in the bundle.

***

Victoria bathed in her three inches of water and dressed in a light-blue dress that was not quite up to the image she wanted to show that evening to Richard. Her finest clothes had been packed already by Jane.

With her ear to her bedroom door to listen if the coast was clear, Victoria had to take deep breaths to calm her excitement. All quiet. She opened her door and hurried along the corridor.

Bonnie's door opened and out she stepped. 'Ah, Victoria, I am so glad you are ready early. Come with me. Penelope cannot decide which dress to take for the opera and I thought you would have a better idea than I regarding what suits her.'

Victoria was stuck. Hiding her disappointment from Bonnie, she followed her to Penelope's room.

A beautiful canary-yellow dress lay on Penelope's bed alongside an equally elegant burgundy one. 'What do you think, Victoria? There isn't enough room to take both,' said Penelope.

'The yellow,' said Victoria, trying hard to sound interested.

'Splendid. I thought so too,' said Bonnie. 'I'll get Jane to pack it for you. Well, come along girls. Time for dinner and I do believe we should all have an early night. Tomorrow will be a long day.'

A daydream flitted around Victoria's brain. Tonight, she would lie with Richard in his bed, even it meant hell and damnation for this sin. *I must find the opportunity to tell him I will come to him later.*

The three women made their way along the corridor to the stairs. Adele joined them. Richard came out of his room as they passed and looked at Victoria. She managed to raise her eyebrows without her companions seeing.

She sipped her pre-dinner champagne in the drawing room with Richard so tantalisingly close, but it was impossible to talk privately. The thoughts of what would happen later kept creeping into her mind, making her feel warm all over. She hoped Bonnie and Lady Adele would not notice. *I wonder what he wants to tell me about Peggy? I do not care. I just want him to make love to me.*

Dinner seemed to drag on for hours. All the talk was about their adventure starting the next morning. Adele was looking forward to Vienna while Bonnie had La Scala, Milan, at the top of her list. Penelope could not hide her excitement that they would be in Venice and possibly ride in a gondola. All Victoria wanted to do was get the trip over quickly and come back to Richard. She settled for saying she would enjoy Lake Como and the mountain air. Four months they would be away. It sounded like a lifetime to Victoria.

Eventually, they finished the meal. 'Off to bed, ladies,' said Bonnie with a laugh. 'We have to be at the railway station at seven.'

As Victoria said goodnight to Richard, she whispered, 'Sorry I could not come earlier. I shall come tonight when the house goes quiet.' His smile made her heart sing.

Victoria undressed, hung up her dress and slipped on her nightgown and dressing gown. She would sit up and wait for the house to go quiet and then sneak along the corridor to Richard's room. She knew it may lead to something. She hoped it would. She had been hoping since the gun practice that afternoon. The guilt that he was married still lay deep down within her, but the stirring of love mixed with not a little lust had taken over.

The thought of his making love to Rawnie if he had the opportunity while she was away clawed at her insides. *If he makes love to me then he would not want to make love to the gypsy. Not after me. He would not do that.* She winced when she realised that jealousy had not been one of her faults, but love seemed to have brought it out.

A commotion in the corridor outside sent her running for the door. Victoria looked out into the hallway. Bonnie and Jane stood outside Bonnie's bedroom door. 'It's all right,' said Bonnie. 'Just an accident with the hot coals in the bed warmer. I am afraid my bed is ruined.'

Richard came to his door wearing a long, silk dressing gown. Victoria wondered if he were naked beneath and it sent shivers of expectancy all over her body.

'It is fine, Richard. Go back to bed.' Bonnie looked up the corridor to Victoria. 'If you do not mind, Victoria, I will share with you tonight. No point in making up a bed in one of the guestrooms at this time of night.'

Victoria shot a glance at Richard. He raised his eyebrows slightly. 'Of course, Bonnie,' said Victoria, trying hard not to reveal her deep disappointment.

The next morning she had no opportunity to speak to Richard alone before all four ladies boarded the pony and trap for the railway station.

He stood at the door of Eagledown House and waved to them as they departed.

Victoria waved back, wondering how long four months would feel until she could return and see Richard. The ominous thought of Rawnie being available and probably willing, or even predatory towards Richard, cast a shadow on her European adventure.

Chapter Fifteen

Richard rode Solomon hard through the cut fields. Four weeks had gone by since Victoria and the others departed for their European tour. He had received two letters from her but they were evidently written in the presence of Bonnie, Penelope or his mother. At least he hoped they had been written in someone else's presence as they contained nothing intimate; nothing that would suggest their love and raw passion for each other.

He pulled up at Peggy's farm, tied the horse to a post and patted Napoleon, the dog. A rap on the door brought the maid.

'It's you, Sir. Madam is expecting you.' She stood aside and took Richard's riding crop and hat as he came through the door.

Richard found Peggy and Luke in the living room playing with Alice. Luke stood, shook hands with Richard and then hoisted the little girl onto his shoulders and left the room.

'You wanted to see me?' said Richard, kissing Peggy on the cheek.

'Yes. How is it progressing ... being caught *in flagrante delicto*?'

'I will do it soon, I promise. I think we are both in a hurry to get on with our lives.'

'Aye, Richard. I'd rather get it over as quickly as possible so we can settle down to a proper family life. As it is, it will take two years from filing the papers. Do you have someone in mind for the "other woman"?'

'Yes. She has been away for a few weeks but she's back now. It is a little difficult as I wanted to explain to Victoria what was happening before she got the wrong idea. I am afraid I failed to do that before she left for Europe. But yes, I do have someone ready. I will do it tomorrow night at the Coach and Horses.'

'I wondered about you and Victoria. I'm so pleased for you, Richard. She would make an excellent wife.' Peggy kissed him on the cheek.

'Yes. I miss her. It will be another three months before she returns.'

'I'm relieved it won't be her reputation that's sullied in this scheme of ours.'

'Do not worry, Peggy. I would not cause a scandal for any society ladies. I will do it tomorrow evening at eight o'clock if my plan works out, and I believe it will. Have you a solicitor ready?'

'Aye. I'm using old Johnson.'

'Are you sure the excitement won't kill him?' They both giggled like naughty children.

'What name will you use?'

'I am known there. I will use my own. The landlord rents the rooms by the hour so he will not be a problem.' Her inquisitive smile made him laugh. 'That's what I understand. I have no personal knowledge. Honest!'

'Just joking.' She kissed him on the cheek again. 'You're sure this won't cause a problem for the woman? Are you using a . . .'

'Professional? No. I am using someone who will not worry about what people say or think and who will appreciate the money.'

'I'm intrigued that you know such a woman, Richard.'

'It is not what you are thinking, Peggy! Honest!'

'If it is or isn't what I am thinking, it is no business of mine. I'm only concerned that we don't ruin someone's reputation for our own benefit.'

The maid brought tea and biscuits. When she left, Richard said, 'There has been some suggestion that Algernon may somehow be connected with my problems. I am sure my father is at the bottom of most of it, but there may be more than one person trying to ruin me.'

Peggy touched his arm. 'Richard, he has nothing to do with what has been happening over at Eagledown. He's a good man, even if he is a little headstrong at times.'

'You are right, Peggy. It is wrong of me to think he would lower himself to that level, even though he hates me.'

'He's still in love with Penelope. How do you feel about that?'

'They have been seen talking. To have Algernon as a brother-in-law would please me immensely, but due to the circumstances I do not think that is possible at present.'

'It would be if we told him the truth.'

'I know, but he is so headstrong he would react violently and end up on the gallows. No, Peggy. We agreed.'

***

Richard galloped to the gypsy camp in Priory Wood. He could see the rising campfire smoke before he crested Clay Hill and then the camp itself as he trotted Solomon down the far side.

There were only three caravans instead of the usual four. He hoped Rawnie would be there. As he dismounted, a man with a face like the leather on Solomon's saddle looked up from a campfire where he held a skinned rabbit on a stick, roasting over the embers. He saw two other men in dirty white shirts with red neckerchiefs sitting around a second fire, drinking from tin mugs and smoking clay pipes.

'Is Rawnie here?' Richard said to Leather Face.

'Who wants her?'

'I do.'

'What for?'

'I just want to talk to her.'

'She's in there.' The man nodded towards a green caravan with roses painted on the sides. A well-polished copper milk churn stood by a set of three wooden steps that led up to the caravan's door.

Richard strode over to the caravan.

He looked around to see Leather Face standing by his fire with a wicked-looking knife in one hand and the rabbit still in the other. The two men at the second fire slowly climbed to their feet.

'I just want to talk to her.'

He could feel their eyes on his back as he climbed the steps. At the green-painted door with mullioned windows, he peered through to see Rawnie sitting in a rocking chair. He tapped gently on the glass.

She looked up. Her long, black hair hung about her bare, tanned shoulders and stood out against the clean, white blouse that just reached the top of her ample bosom. Her long, red dress was pulled up to her knees, showing off her long legs. She smiled and waved for him to come in.

The small, immaculately clean interior of the caravan contained the rocking chair, a bunk bed at the far end, a table with a crystal ball and two chairs. It smelled of lavender as he entered and closed the door behind him.

'Hello,' she said in her throaty voice. 'What can I do for you, my good looking friend? Have you come to hire me for that little escapade we talked about?' She let out a deep laugh that made Richard smile.

Richard looked out through the glass in the door to see Leather Face standing outside with the knife in his hand.

He did not look as if he would come in, though there was no doubt in Richard's mind that the man would use the knife if he thought Rawnie was in trouble.

***

Richard, bare chested but covered by a sheet up to his waist, sat up in the big, double bed that boasted a canopied top and four posts. Weighty red curtains at a sash window hung down to a red-and-black Persian carpet. An oak door with black metal fittings allowed access to this grey-stone walled room.

He checked his timepiece, lying on a mahogany bedside table that also held a candle, his wallet, a bottle of wine and two empty glasses. 'Anytime now,' he said to Rawnie, lying naked on the covers at his side.

The door burst open. Peggy strode in, followed by old Johnson who indeed looked as if the excitement may cause him to expire.

'You bounder. You cad. You miserable adulterer,' screamed Peggy.

Old Johnson cleared his throat. 'Obviously you are caught, Sir. Do not try to deny you are an adulterer!'

The landlord, a man in his forties with a big belly and port nose, dashed into the room.

'What kind of place is this, Sir, that you allow such base behaviour on your premises,' said old Johnson to the landlord.

'I thought they were man and wife,' said the landlord.

'That harlot may be somebody's wife, but she ain't his. I am,' said Peggy with all the indignation she could muster.

Rawnie just lay there and smiled. Richard gave her a dig with his foot under the sheet.

Rawnie said. ''Ere, who you calling a harlot?'

'I've seen enough. You, Mr Johnson, and you, landlord, are witnesses to my husband's infidelity. Now please let us leave this den of iniquity.'

She gently pushed old Johnson out of the door. The landlord had already gone. Peggy turned to Richard, winked, flounced out and slammed the door.

Richard looked at Rawnie as she spread herself out on her back on top of the sheet, without any sign of modesty. Her tanned, strong body, in contrast to the white sheet, and her mouth so soft and inviting made Richard long to roll over on top of her and take what clearly was on offer. He quickly looked away, picked up the wine bottle and poured out a glass of red wine that he downed in one.

He lifted his wallet from the table.

'No,' said Rawnie. She ran her tongue over her cherry-red lips.

'But the agreement was five pounds.'

Rawnie turned over on to her front and lifted herself up on her elbows. 'I'm not a whore. I know the money means nothing to men like you. You have plenty. But I'll take your money if you get out of bed now, dress and leave. If you stay, I want no payment.'

'Rawnie, I cannot get involved with you. First of all, you know I wanted this so my wife could divorce me and marry her lover and I would be free to ask a woman I love to marry me.' He took a five-pound note from his wallet. 'Please, take the money.'

'Get involved with me? Richard, the last thing I want in this world is to "get involved" with someone who'd keep me in some mansion and make me live the life your people do. My ambition is far higher than that. I'm a free woman and I bow to no man. But you do have something I want tonight and it's not money or commitment. If that shocks you, I'm not sorry. I'm going to Canada or America to the wide open spaces. I can't live in a mansion and make small talk with stupid fat ladies. So don't flatter yourself that I want to get involved with you. Take what I'm offering you with no commitment, or pay me.'

'Then please take the money. In fact, I will make it twenty pounds to help you cross the ocean as long as you stay around long enough to be named as co-respondent in the divorce case.'

'If I'm going to perjure myself in court to get you a divorce, I need a promise from you that you won't tell anyone—I mean anyone—that nothing happened. It'd get me gaol time and you know what happens to women like me.'

'Of course I won't tell anyone.'

'How can I trust you?'

'I give you my word.'

'Not good enough. Swear on your mother's life.'

'Rawnie, I am Church of England. We do not do that sort of swearing.'

'Well, if you want me to lie to the court you're going to have to.'

Richard took a deep breath. 'All right. I swear on my mother's life that I will not tell anyone that nothing happened. I promise . . . I swear that I will say we had sexual intercourse. Is that good enough?'

'Yes.'

'Good. Take the money.'

'I don't need your money. But I'll take it. Get out of bed first.' She rolled over onto her back and sat propped up against the bed head with her legs crossed. She smiled. Her lips parted to reveal perfect white teeth. She put her forefinger in her mouth and sucked.

Richard took a deep breath and lifted three more five-pound notes from his wallet. He looked at her. His mind was confused, but his body was reacting as a healthy young man would in these circumstances.

'Well?' she said. 'Are you going to fuck me or pay me?'

***

Richard looked across the highly polished desk at Peggy sitting demurely alongside old Johnson, who had a sheaf of papers in front of him.

'Are you sure you do not wish to have your own solicitor present?' said old Johnson, rubbing his arthritic hands together.

'Yes, Mr Johnson, I am sure,' said Richard.

'Then the leasehold of the farm currently owned by Eagledown shall be transferred to Lady Margaret de Mornay freehold, together with the two hundred acres south of Bevois Wood. Is that correct?'

'Yes,' said Richard.

'Are you sure that you wish to settle for this?' said Johnson.

'Aye, for sure I am,' said Peggy.

'And you realise that if you remarry, your new husband will have control of the farm?'

'Yes, I realise that. I have nothing to fear.'

'I am sure Peggy, er. . . Lady Margaret does not have anything to worry about, Mr Johnson, but I can assure you that if there were any problems, then I would see to it that she is well provided for.'

'You seem to be a very generous man, Sir Richard,' said Johnson.

'Peggy and I are fond of each other.'

'Now about the child,' said Johnson.

'Peggy will have custody and I will make whatever provisions are necessary for her.'

'We need to put this in writing,' said Johnson.

'Not necessary. I trust Richard,' said Peggy.

'It's not my place to put difficulties in your path if this is the course you desire to take. It's the strangest divorce I've handled,' said Johnson. 'The parties are usually at each other's throats.'

'How long before the divorce will be granted?' said Peggy.

'The courts don't like to be rushed. About two years is usual if there are no problems, but do not hold me to that. Now what about the other matter. Adultery is not enough for a woman to divorce a man though it is for a man to divorce a woman.'

'As we agreed,' said Richard. 'Desertion. I went off to Africa for four years, leaving her behind, and since I have returned, I have not allowed her to come to Eagledown to live. That should be sufficient, I believe.'

'I believe so too,' said Johnson. 'I must warn you that the court does not appreciate being duped into granting a divorce. This law is only a few years old. Before that, you needed an Act of Parliament to get divorced. The judges are loathe to open the floodgates and allow the easy dissolution of families. The penalties are quite strict for fraud.'

'I understand,' said Richard.

***

Richard and Peggy stepped out onto the pavement in Jewry Street near Winchester city centre.

Luke, leaning on the solicitor's wall next to its brass plaque, straightened up.

'Thank goodness that's all over,' she said.

Richard kissed Peggy on the cheek and shook Luke's hand. He watched as his soon to be ex-wife and her lover walked away towards the railway station.

He stepped out into the street towards a little coffee house, deep in thought. His reverie suddenly vanished when he heard a shout, looked up to see two shire horses about eighteen hands high, pulling a brewer's dray loaded with barrels, bearing down on him. The drayman pulled on the reins. The horses stopped. The dray's metal-rimmed wheels slid sideways on the cobbles. The barrels tumbled into the street, broke and flooded the road with sticky ale.

'Bloody lunatic!' The driver, a huge Irishman with red hair and a beard, jumped from his dray and stuck his face in Richard's.

'Sorry, will this cover it?' Richard took out his wallet. The drayman's face lit up and he stepped aside after snatching the four five-pounds notes offered.

Richard abandoned the coffee and headed for the city centre, where he found the jeweller's shop he was looking for in a little road off the High Street.

He could smell the beeswax on the heavily polished mahogany counter as he watched the bespectacled craftsman come out of a workroom into the shop. The gentle ticking of many clocks on the wall and a steady *tick tick* from a grandfather clock reminded Richard of the nights in the veldt when he would lie awake in the camp listening to the insects.

The jeweller put a small, leather-bound box on the counter and lifted the lid. Richard's face showed his delight. The raw, opaque diamond given to him by the Xhosa warrior for saving his son from lions had been transformed. It sparkled in the sunlight that came through the window, resting in a band of gold made from the nuggets given to him by the warrior.

'A pleasure to work on, Sir.'

'Thank you. You have done an excellent job.'

The jeweller stepped into the workroom and returned with a bill. Richard wrote a cheque and left with his engagement ring in the leather box, safely tucked into the bottom of his pocket.

***

Victoria felt butterflies in her tummy as she saw Eagledown in the distance through the carriage window. Would Richard be waiting?

No. But Humphreys stood by the entrance steps and helped Bonnie from the carriage, closely followed by Penelope and Victoria. Adele was the last to alight. Victoria noticed that Humphreys seemed to hold Adele's hand longer than necessary to help her down the steps. A whole series of incidents began to make more sense, particularly his brave defence of her against Lord de Mornay. But whatever may have been going on between them, it was clear from his expression that something grave had happened while they were away.

'Where's Richard?' said Victoria, her tummy sick with worry.

Humphreys took a sharp intake of breath. 'He's in Winchester, Miss.'

'What's happened?' said Bonnie with concern.

'I'm afraid it is all rather sudden, Ma'am. He had hoped that you would be home before the matter came to public notice.'

'Please, what's happened?' said Adele.

Victoria could not speak. Her hands trembled. What on earth had happened to put Humphreys into such a state?

'Sir Richard and Peggy ... er Lady Peggy ... are getting divorced.'

Victoria felt an immense relief. From thinking something horrible had happened to Richard she now realised that he would no longer be married. They could be together without any guilt. He would be free to marry her. She hoped he would marry her. Her feet almost glided up the steps to the house.

He is getting divorced. It will take two years and I understand that, but I will wait for him. Well, I will not wait two years before making love to him. I wonder what grounds were given for the divorce. Adultery? No, not Richard. No, it cannot be. With whom would he be adulterous? Me, if I got the chance! He wouldn't have gone with Rawnie. Not now he knows how I feel about him. Victoria had little knowledge of such matters, but from conversations she had picked up she believed divorce was a very long and complicated process. *Oh my goodness! Poor Richard.* She had heard rumours about Peggy and a man who lived at her farm. Nobody at Eagledown spoke about it.

So Richard is divorcing Peggy. That was what he wanted to tell me before we went abroad. Perhaps he feels guilty about damaging Peggy's reputation by accusing her. He would not do that. But he has. He has done it so he can marry me. I must go to Peggy and beg her forgiveness. She does not deserve to be shamed. But . . . Oh joy, I can have Richard.

In the drawing room, the travellers took afternoon tea served by Humphreys. When they finished, Adele and Bonnie went upstairs to supervise the unpacking. Penelope went to her room to practice her violin, leaving Victoria alone. She picked up a book from a table and thumbed through *Madame Bovary*. Were there similarities in that book to Peggy? Perhaps not. Victoria could not help feeling sorry for her. To be divorced for adultery was indeed shameful among the gossiping women in the area. *I will not gossip or cast stones. I had been prepared to commit adultery with Richard and only serendipity stopped me.*

She was still flicking through *Madame Bovary* when she heard the main door open and the sound of boots on the wooden floor. It had to be Richard. Nobody else strode with such vigour. Well, nobody else who lived at Eagledown. *I will sit quietly and await his entrance. I will pretend to know nothing of why he has been in Winchester. He will tell me in his own way and in his own time.*

Richard came through the door. She jumped out of her chair and threw her arms around him, checked that nobody was looking and followed that with a kiss. *So much for sitting quietly.*

'I have heard the news. Mr Humphreys told us. Richard, I am so happy. We can be together. I do feel so sorry for Peggy and I will go to her and offer her my sympathy. But oh, Richard, I could not hope for a better homecoming.'

Richard looked worried. 'Humphreys told you everything?'

'Yes . . . yes, Richard.'

'And you do not mind? I mean, you are not disgusted with me?'

'Richard ... my dear Richard ... I am sad that Peggy had to have her reputation sullied. I will do all that I can to ensure that the gossips are put in their place. I would rather you had waited and used some other means of obtaining a divorce instead of accusing Peggy of adultery ... But Richard, I must confess that I am overjoyed at my good fortune.'

Richard sat down, hard, on a sofa. 'Come and sit next to me, Victoria.'

Victoria sat down and linked her arm through his.

'Victoria, I did not divorce Peggy for her adultery. She is divorcing me because of mine.'

Victoria felt as if the prize bull had kicked her in the stomach. She could not speak at first but eventually managed to say, 'With whom?'

'Rawnie.'

'The gypsy?' Victoria slapped him across the face, jumped to her feet and dashed up to her bedroom, where she slammed the door shut, bolted it and threw herself on the bed to sob. They were the first sad tears to fall from her eyes since Edward drowned.

She refused to open the door for Richard, then Bonnie, then Adele and finally Penelope. She did eventually open it for Humphreys when he brought her a cup of hot milk and a biscuit.

Humphreys took hold of her hand and squeezed. 'Richard is a good man. He could not shame Peggy by divorcing her. It is customary for the man to provide the evidence for his wife to divorce him in these circumstances.'

'But why with the gypsy girl? Why not with me? Does that shock you?'

'No, Miss. Nothing shocks me. He would not have wished to tarnish your reputation either.'

'So that is what these high-born people do?'

'Miss, Richard is a wonderful man. Remember that, always.'

Chapter Sixteen

Victoria came down to breakfast, her eyes bloodshot, her face pallid and her mood black. Bonnie, Penelope and Adele were just finishing. All three looked up at her as she entered.

Bonnie said, 'Victoria . . .'

Victoria turned, dashed out through the door, along the corridor and out into the stable yard. She marched into the stables, found Phoebe, the horse she had been given by Richard to replace Tess. Quickly, she found her tack, saddled the mare and led her out into the stable yard, where she jumped on and cantered off into the countryside.

The fields were ploughed and barren. High above a red kite circled. Victoria had no thoughts for the wonders of nature. Her tears blurred her vision. She had no idea how long she had ridden but realised she must have been going around in a wide circle because she found herself just outside the nearest village to Eagledown, Martinsfield. She trotted the horse into the small community with its rickety houses around a patchy green. At the far end she saw Constable Hemingway standing by his gate in his blue police shirt without its collar, his braces hanging loosely by his plump sides.

He waved. She made her way over.

'Good day, Miss.'

The jolly policeman didn't seem at all jolly. In fact, he looked sadder than she felt.

'Is everything all right, Constable?'

'I wish it were, Miss. It's the missus. She's gone down with the fever. Scarlet fever said the doc. I don't know how I'm going to cope.'

'Is there nobody in the village who will help you?'

'No, Miss. They is all scared of catching it themselves. I don't blame them. I understand. But she's a funny one is my missus. If you'll pardon me being . . . well . . . I don't know how to say it.'

'What?' Victoria jumped down from her horse and tied the reins to a fence post.

'Well . . . you know. She has to do her . . . her . . . It's like this, Miss. She don't want me to see to her . . . Well, she's sort of embarrassed, even though we've been wed for nigh on twenty-five years.'

'I think I understand, Constable. Perhaps I can help.'

'I don't know, Miss. I'd never forgive myself if you caught it.'

'You know my history, Constable. I grew up in an orphanage where scarlet fever came too often. I have looked after the other orphans with it. I even went down with it once but I recovered. A doctor said I could not get it again.'

'Even so, Miss, the things my missus needs doing for her ain't the sort of work a lady should be doing. But I'm desperate, Miss. If you could find me someone to help, I'd be much obliged.'

'Take me to see Mrs Hemingway.'

'Are you sure, Miss?'

'Now, please!' Victoria needed to drive the bitter disappointment from her heart. Looking after a gravely ill woman would fill her troubled mind, though she would have looked after Mrs Hemingway even if she was not heartbroken.

Victoria followed the constable through his garden with its vegetables, roses and perfect borders. He pushed open the heavy wooden door that looked as if it would keep a marauding army at bay. They crossed a stone-flagged floor to an unsteady staircase. She followed him upstairs.

On the small landing were two doors. One stood slightly ajar and Mrs Hemingway lay inside on a brass bed with at least two quilts covering her. Even from that distance she could see the scarlet hue of her face.

Victoria marched through the door.

Mrs Hemingway looked up with dull eyes and tried to speak but could only manage a groan.

'I am here to see if I can help you. The first thing we need to do is get you washed and some clean bedding. Constable!'

'Yes, Miss,' said the constable, peering through the open door.

'Bring me clean sheets, please.'

The constable disappeared, happy to be following orders rather than having to decide what to do. He returned quickly with two linen sheets.

'Thank you. Now bring me a bucket of hot water and some towels.'

'I'll have to boil the water on the fire, Miss.'

'I know. Please get on with it.'

He disappeared again.

Victoria cleaned and washed Mrs Hemingway. When she had her charge comfortable, Victoria went downstairs and checked the kitchen. She found some onions, potatoes and a leek that looked as though they had just been picked from the constable's garden.

A knock on a neighbour's door elicited a cooked chicken leg. Victoria boiled up the vegetables and chicken leg into a broth. She gave a bowl to the constable, who gratefully accepted it. She fed Mrs Hemingway.

Next, Victoria sent a boy to fetch Bridget and to tell Bonnie where she was and that she would not be home for a couple of days.

Bridget arrived with a bag full of potions which she showed Victoria how to administer. Though she wanted to stay to help, Victoria sent her home to look after her own family.

After three nights of nursing, Mrs Hemingway recovered. Victoria looked at the love that passed between Mrs Hemingway and the constable as he sat on the bed holding her hand. It was a love that ran deep. It made her sad to think that she nearly had such a love, but Richard had deceived her and slept with the gypsy, Rawnie. He was not the man she thought he was and he was not worthy of her. Still, it cut deeply into her heart that she had lost him forever.

When she was about to leave the Hemingways, the constable spoke with tears of gratitude in his eyes. 'I shall never forget what you've done for us, Miss Victoria. Someday I hope to be able to repay your kindness.'

She kissed him on the cheek and made her way back to Eagledown. As the building came into sight, she found it had lost its appeal.

***

The next few weeks were difficult, with Victoria avoiding Richard or ignoring him at meal times.

As Victoria sat combing her hair before going to bed, Bonnie came into the room.

'Victoria, I have had enough of all this. You have been brought up to behave like a lady and you will do so. Sulking and bad moods are unbecoming. Pull yourself together and get on with your life. So Richard slept with the gypsy woman? That is what men do. Go and find yourself another man if you don't want him, but I will not have you behaving like this.'

Victoria broke down in tears. Bonnie hugged her.

At breakfast the following morning Victoria came into the room. Richard and Penelope were already eating.

'Good morning, Richard, Penelope. A beautiful day isn't it? I was thinking of going for a ride. Would either of you care to accompany me?'

They both looked at her in surprise and then smiled.

'Yes,' said Penelope.

'That would be excellent,' said Richard.

'I am so sorry for being a bore,' said Victoria.

Penelope got to her feet. 'I have just remembered, I cannot go. I have to practice the violin for a concert.'

Victoria appreciated the lie.

With only Richard and Victoria left in the dining room, he said, 'I am so sorry. I wanted to explain . . .'

'Richard, I am sorry too, but what we nearly had was only nearly. I am afraid I cannot think of you and I being together. The gypsy would always come into my mind. But that is no reason why we cannot be friends.'

She could not see that his heart was breaking.

***

Lord Peter sat at the head of the table in his grand dining room with its forty-candle chandelier sending light throughout the wood-panelled room. Portraits of ancestors looked down. Logs burned in the hearth of a massive stone fireplace, with carved figures of Greek goddesses on each side. On the table was a silver centrepiece of Chinese buildings and people. Three silver candelabra on the table gave off more light to illumine the well-dressed diners. At each place setting was an array of silver cutlery and finely engraved wine glasses.

Bonnie sat at the other end of the table from Lord Peter in a pale-blue evening gown with short sleeves and a low front. Her hair hung in ringlets, tied with pale-blue silk ribbons. At her neck she wore a black silk choker with a cameo holding it in place.

Between the two ends sat Richard in a black tailcoat and white tie, Penelope in a crimson evening dress with a pearl necklace, Lady Adele in a pale-green evening dress with an emerald necklace, and Victoria in an evening dress the colour of daffodils. Her hair hung in ringlets tied with yellow ribbons. At her neck she wore a gold chain with an empty gold locket in the shape of a heart.

After six courses that included soup, fish, salad, venison, cheese and a magnificent crystal-palace pudding and the best wines from the cellar, including the homegrown champagne, Lord Peter stood and clinked his glass. Everyone stopped talking and looked at him.

Victoria wondered what he was going to say. It was clearly a special occasion that had brought them together in their finery, and the meal was exceptional.

'Dear friends,' began Lord Peter, 'I am not one for long, drawn-out speeches so I shall not bother you with one this evening. It is my great honour and pleasure to announce that Luisa has gracefully accepted my offer of marriage.'

'That is wonderful,' said Adele, jumping to her feet and putting her arms around her sister.

'Indeed it is,' said Richard, standing up and raising his glass.

'I am so happy for you,' said Penelope.

'When?' said Adele.

'There is much to arrange. We have not yet set a date but we hope it will be in about six months,' said Lord Peter.

'This really is wonderful news,' said Adele.

Victoria would have to appear happy. After all, she had in the past wanted Bonnie to marry him. But now he was a suspect in the shooting of the prize bull and her horse. Not the prime suspect. She still believed Lord de Mornay to be the real culprit, but it was possible that Lord Peter was responsible for the bull and horse, if not the other incidents. She smiled at Bonnie and raised her glass.

The ladies adjourned to the drawing room, leaving the two men with their port and cigars.

'Victoria, you are welcome to come and live here with Peter and I. If you prefer to stay at Eagledown then I am sure there will be no objection from anyone,' said Bonnie.

'Of course, we would love you to stay at Eagledown,' said Penelope.

'I agree. And I know Richard would too,' said Adele.

'Thank you,' said Victoria.

The other women began to plan the forthcoming wedding. Would it be in the little Saxon church or the bigger parish church? How many guests would there be? Where would they hold the reception? They did not notice Victoria slip out of the room.

She wandered along a corridor, heading for the kitchen to talk to Cook. Lord Peter's cook was famous for her homegrown vegetables and herbs and, not having the inclination to get involved in the wedding talk, she decided this would be a suitable diversion. She tried to convince herself that it was because she suspected Lord Peter may be the shooter, not because she was jealous that Bonnie was getting married, while she had lost the man she loved because of her pride and his infidelity. Though she tried, she did not fool herself.

As she passed an open door, she saw a light on in a room and an array of guns lined up along the wall. An old man dressed in a green apron was sitting on a stool, cleaning a shotgun at a table. Though she did not know his name she knew he was the gamekeeper for Lord Peter. She walked in.

'Oh, sorry Miss,' said the man standing up. 'I'm just getting the guns ready for the shoot next week.'

'Please, carry on. I am just looking, if that is acceptable.'

'Indeed, Miss. Just ask if you need anything explaining.' He sat down again and continued cleaning the gun.

Two oil lamps in the room gave off enough light for her to read the manufacturers' names on the guns as she wandered around examining them. She found what she was looking for. A rifle with the marking 'Snider-Enfield'.

'This is an interesting rifle,' she said.

The gamekeeper put down the shotgun and came over. 'Yes, that's the Snider-Enfield. The army are using it now it's been approved by the War Office. Very accurate.'

'Are they quite common?'

'Yes, Miss. Very common.'

'Thank you.'

The gamekeeper continued his work.

A silver trophy on a shelf caught Victoria's eye. She read the inscription.

Lord Peter Abbott
Shangai: 1857

'Excuse me, what is this trophy for?'

The gamekeeper put his shotgun down and came over to Victoria. 'This one? His Lordship got it for the long-distance shooting competition. He's the best I've ever seen.'

'Thank you.'

The gamekeeper went back to his work, and Victoria left the room so deep in thought she forgot to go to the kitchen and found herself back in the drawing room. The men were there.

'Ah, here you are, Victoria. I wondered what happened to you,' said Lord Peter.

'I just went for a stroll through your lovely house.'

***

Victoria lay in bed thinking. Sleep would not come. The image of the rifle and the memory of Tess being shot from under her kept spilling around her brain.

He is probably not the one who blew the dam, and I do not think he would try to spread foot and mouth disease because it could carry over to his herd. But he could be the shooter. The bull was definitely a problem for him as it knocked him from the number one spot. He is a very good shot. It could be him. Hurting Jake and burning the barn? I do not know.

And if Bonnie does marry him, then whatever she owns will become the property of Lord Peter. Married women's property always belongs to their husbands. It is not fair, but that is the way it is. If she marries him he will have control over half of Eagledown's cattle and bulls. He could make it very difficult for Richard.

At breakfast, Victoria was the last to come down.

'Sleep well?' said Bonnie.

'Yes, thank you,' she lied.

Bonnie, Adele and Penelope finished their breakfast and left.

Now that Victoria was alone with Richard she decided to air her concerns. 'Richard, last night over at Lord Peter's I went into the gun room.'

'Whatever for?'

'I just wanted to have a look around. He has a Snider-Enfield rifle.'

'So have a lot of people.'

'He has a trophy for long-distance shooting and his gamekeeper says he is the best shot he has ever seen.'

'What are you getting at, Victoria?'

'He could be the man who shot the bull and Tess.'

'I do not think so, Victoria. Not Lord Peter. No, it just isn't possible. Why would he do that?'

'Because your bull beat his bull.'

'That is not how it works, Victoria. Lord Peter is an honourable man. Men such as he would not do that. And I know he did not do it.'

'What? Because he was born into high society? That makes him better than other people further down the social scale? Is that what you are saying, Richard? Are you suggesting that you society people are better than the rest of us?'

'Calm down. I am not suggesting that.'

'Well, that is what it sounds like. And as for your high-society morals and codes of conduct, what about your father? He is hardly a paragon of virtue. . . and your adultery.'

'I don't know what has got into you, Victoria.'

'And another thing. If Bonnie marries him, he will have control of half of Eagledown's cattle stock and whatever else she owns here. He will be able to take over. He will be able to ensure Eagledown bulls do not win in future. I am trying to warn you, Richard. Why will you not listen to me?'

'Because, Victoria, Aunt Luisa told me this morning that, on the advice of Lord Peter, she wanted to transfer the ownership of all she owns here to me before the wedding. Lord Peter does not wish to make life difficult at Eagledown. She is going to make the necessary arrangements through a solicitor in town this week. Oh, and when the bull was shot? Lord Peter was giving a lecture on the Orient at Oxford University.'

Victoria wished the floor would open up and swallow her.

***

Richard and Victoria rode through a field on the Eagledown estate.

'Touch wood, we haven't had any more attacks from the madman,' said Richard. 'I hope you agree that Lord Peter is completely above any suspicion.'

'Yes, I am sorry. I was only trying to help.'

'So we still have to find out it who is responsible.

'Your father.'

'Yes. Maybe Inspector Forbes questioning him has scared him off. I hope so.'

'Hopefully it is now at an end. It will always be hanging there, though, in the background, like the sword of Damocles.' *Just like Rawnie.*

Back at the stables they unsaddled their horses and put them in their boxes.

Victoria could sense that he wanted to say something but either could not or would not. She wondered if she had overreacted to the affair he had with Rawnie. Her pride would not let her forgive him. The reason he had done it was clear: he had to be the adulterer because it would have been ungentlemanly of him to accuse Peggy. *But why did he have to choose the beautiful Rawnie?* That was what really cut deep and made her jealous.

They parted at the back door to Eagledown. He went off to check on the cattle barn. After the fire, a new barn was under construction out of stone with as little wood as possible.

Victoria made her way to the drawing room.

Humphreys handed her an envelope on a silver platter. 'Arrived about an hour ago, Miss. I didn't see who brought it.'

'Thank you, Mr Humphreys.' She slit the envelope and took out a note as he left.

Dear Miss Sillitoe,
I am terminally ill and need to get some things off my conscience before I meet my Maker. Would you please come alone to the Bear and Ragged Staff and hear my confession? Do not tell anyone that you are coming to see me. I will expect you to swear that you haven't told a soul before I tell you what you want to know.'

Your Obedient Servant,
S. Tweedale.

Victoria screwed the note up in a ball and then unravelled it before screwing it up again.

If he thinks he can lure me by this transparent sob story, he must be stupid.

She threw the note on the fire and poked it to make sure it burnt.

But what if it is true? What if Tweedale genuinely wants to make amends? Is this an opportunity that should not be missed? Why the 'come alone' though? That is suspicious. And The Bear and Ragged Staff is three miles away from Eagledown. So many questions and not enough answers.

She thought about Jake and his terrible injuries. He was making progress, but he would never be the carefree, strong young man she remembered. The grandfather clock chimed three. *Plenty of time to go to the rendezvous and return in time for dinner. What if Tweedale can actually tell me who attacked Jake and who burnt the barn?* She resolved to find out.

On her way to the stables, she slipped the catch on the gunroom door, checked over her shoulder that nobody could see her, and stepped inside. A strong smell of gun oil and polish filled the air. She knew exactly what she wanted. The third drawer down in the oak cabinet held the .36 Kerr's revolver. It was lighter and shorter than the Navy Colt and would fit in her wrist bag without looking too obvious as it had done on her European trip. Victoria lifted the pistol and checked the five-shot cylinder; loaded, just as she had put it away. With a thumping heart, she placed it carefully in her bag. Then she touched the deer's-foot-handle knife in her boot. *If anyone tries anything, I am prepared.*

***

Victoria saddled Phoebe. Bonnie and her sister were shopping. Richard was at the barn. Penelope, she could hear playing the violin. Victoria had complied with the instruction not to tell anyone where she was going, but a niggling doubt kept creeping into her head that it could be a trap.

Phoebe did not like to hurry, however much Victoria tried to make her, so off they went at a sedate trot. The route along a sunken lane and then the bridleway through Bevois Wood took half an hour. Victoria pulled Phoebe up a hundred yards short of her destination so she could look down from the hill at the country pub nestling in a fold. Smoke rose from a chimney. Outside the door were two tables with benches, unoccupied. The pub sign swung lightly in a breeze and bore the bear and ragged staff of the establishment's name.

Victoria walked Phoebe the last hundred yards to the pub and tied her to a post outside. Through a window, she peered inside. She could not see much, though some light came in through this window and another on the far side of the public bar. It was not enough to make out who she would find inside.

With a deep breath, Victoria took hold of the metal latch on the heavy door and shoved it open. The stench of stale beer and old smoke filled her nostrils. One customer stood at the bar with a pewter mug in his hand and his back to her. The landlord, Allington, turned to look at her as she crossed the stone-flagged floor. The customer turned. She did not know him but had seen him around in the village and at the agricultural show.

She knew Allington slightly. He provided the beer tent at the agricultural show every year. He stroked his mutton-chop whiskers and pulled in his belly. 'What can I do for you, Miss?'

'I believe you have a Mr Tweedale staying here. I understand he is sick. May I see him, please?'

'He's upstairs in bed. Second door on the left,' said Allington, pointing his chin at a flight of wooden stairs.

Victoria nodded a thank you and climbed the stairs. She found the second room on the left and knocked on the door.

'Come in,' said a wheezy voice from within.

Victoria felt the pistol in her bag and opened the door. In the small room with a sloping ceiling, she saw an iron bedstead with Tweedale sitting propped up on a black-striped, dirty pillow.

'Good of you to come. Didn't think you would.'

'I am not here for small talk. You said in the note that you had information about what was happening at Eagledown. First of all, tell me why you want to give me this information.' She looked at him more carefully. He had never looked a well man, but now he looked pale, drawn and very sick.

'I'm dying. To tell you the truth I'm scared. I'm going to meet my Maker and I've done some dreadful things in my time. If I can get one person I've wronged to forgive me, I may stand a chance of staying out of Hell in the next life.'

'And now tell me why I had to come alone.'

'I'm going to make a confession to you. If I did it with anyone else present you'd have enough evidence to have me arrested and I would spend my last days in prison. Maybe I'd even live long enough to hang. This way it's your word against mine if you go to the police while I live.'

'Before we discuss what you want to tell me, I want to know what happened to my mother. According to your Bible she is recorded as dying. There is no record at the church or at the undertaker's place of business. What happened to her?'

'It was all a long time ago.'

'I still want to know.'

'What was her name?'

'Do you mean you don't remember?'

'As I said, it was all a long time ago. Sillitoe, Sillitoe. I remember you, but your mother? I'm not sure. Was it Mary Sillitoe?'

'Yes, Mary Sillitoe. What happened to her?'

'I can't remember. I think she died. No, wait a minute. No, she left. I can't remember why.'

'You have nothing to lose by telling me the truth.'

'I know that. It's just that I don't remember.'

'Why not? Were there so many girls you disposed of to Woodward that you are unable to recall all of them?'

'That's about it, I'm afraid. It's the truth. I may have sold her to Woodward. I honestly can't remember.'

'So what do you want to tell me?'

'Swear to me that you came alone and that you haven't told anyone where you were going. There's a Bible on the bedside table.'

Victoria picked up the Bible and swore.

'I blew up the dam. I didn't know people would die. Honestly, I didn't.'

'I do not believe you. You blew up the dam to kill me.'

'It's true that I would've liked to kill you. But no, you were not the target.'

'What do you mean?'

'I was paid to blow up the dam so it would cost a lot of money to repair and help to bankrupt Eagledown.'

'Why did you want to bankrupt Eagledown?'

'I didn't. The person who paid me to blow it up wanted to bankrupt the estate.'

'And who was that? As if I don't know.'

'I shall tell you shortly. Those two idiots who were caught trying to infect the cattle with foot and mouth; I hired them.'

'Why?'

'Again, I was hired to find someone who could not be traced back to—shall we call him the client? If the herd went down with foot and mouth, it would be a financial disaster for the estate.'

'So stop waffling on and tell me who hired you.'

'In a moment. I didn't shoot the bull or your horse. That was the client himself. And I did not burn the barn or club your workman. That was the client himself again.'

'So who was it?'

'Can you forgive me?'

'First tell me who the client is, and then I will consider whether I forgive you or not.'

'It was Lord ... No!' Tweedale stared in horror at something behind her.

Then all went dark for Victoria as something was thrown over her head. It was a blanket. Arms pulled her down to the floor. She was pinioned by someone strong with a knee across her chest, but she could also hear someone else in the room. Her bag was wrenched from her wrist. Still she could not see anything.

'There's a gun in here. Use this one. It'll be more evidence of what she did,' said a voice that sent a chill through her body. Only a few words, but they were enough for her to recognise the owner. Woodward. That gruff voice had haunted her nightmares and she remembered it too well from the time in the orphanage when Tweedale had tried to sell her to him.

'No, no, no,' Tweedale pleaded.

Then she heard five shots. With all her strength, she reached down to her boot. She managed to grasp the knife and stab Woodward in the leg. She was sure it was him.

She caught the word, 'Bitch,' and felt a blow to the side of her head. Her knife was wrenched from her grip. Still she could not see what was happening.

Then the hands that held her let go. She heard the door open and two sets of footsteps run down the wooden stairs. Victoria threw off the blanket and jumped to her feet. In the bed was Tweedale, with what she knew must be bullet holes in his chest, four of them. There was another bullet hole in the wall just above his head. And then she saw her knife sticking in his neck. Blood spattered the wall, pillow and blanket. She could see he was dead as mutton. The Kerr's revolver lay on the bed. She looked at her dress: blood all over it from the assailant she had stabbed.

The door burst open and in dashed Allington and the customer from downstairs.

'Jesus Christ. Freddy, go fetch the constable,' he said to the customer, who raced out of the room.

'Don't move,' said Allington to Victoria.

She could see he meant it. He looked mean and ready for trouble. It suddenly dawned on her that he thought she had murdered Tweedale.

'Did you see who those men were?' said Victoria.

'What men?'

'The ones that ran downstairs. Are they still here?'

'I don't know what you're talking about. I've not seen anyone else.'

Victoria felt her stomach sink. She inched towards the revolver, forgetting she had heard five shots and the gun only held five bullets. Allington stepped into her path. He did not touch the gun, but his presence prevented her from doing so too.

She would not be able to overcome Allington. She would wait for the police and then everything would be sorted out. Allington and the customer must have seen the murderers when they ran downstairs. They would have to tell the truth. Or were they on the side of the murderers?

Victoria and the landlord stood looking at each other for fifteen minutes. Victoria's heart pounded in her chest. *What was it that Tweedale had said? 'Lord,' that was all. He must have meant Lord de Mornay, but it was not enough. Still not enough.*

Constable Hemingway arrived out of breath with the customer, Freddy. 'What happened?'

'I do not know. I came into the room to speak to Mr Tweedale. Someone threw a blanket over me, took my gun and shot him. Then they stabbed him with my knife. I managed to stab one of them, too. That is where all this blood came from. I think I stabbed him in the leg.'

The constable looked at Allington and the customer.

'What?' said Allington.

'I'm looking to see if you have any injuries.'

'Now you just wait a minute, Constable. We were downstairs when we heard shots from up here. We ran up and found her, alone, covered in blood. Isn't that right, Freddy?'

Freddy nodded his head.

'You, Freddy, if that's your name, get to the telegraph at the railway station. Tell the station master to send a message to Inspector Forbes at Winchester police station, telling him to come here immediately. There's been a murder. Got that?'

Freddy nodded and ran down the stairs.

She saw the constable peering at her dress. 'Oh my God, you think I did it.' Her hands began to shake.

'Right, everybody downstairs. We'll wait for the inspector,' said the constable.

They left the room. Constable Hemingway closed the door behind him and followed the other two downstairs into the public bar.

'Drink, Constable?' said Allington.

'No.'

'Could I have a glass of water please,' said Victoria.

Allington stepped into a back room. She could hear him pumping water from an inside well.

'You'd better tell me what this is all about, Miss,' said the constable.

'I had a note from Tweedale asking me to come here. It turned out he wanted to make a confession and tell me who was involved in the sabotage at Eagledown.'

'Why would he want to do that?'

'He said he was dying and wanted to atone before he met his Maker.'

'Never thought of Tweedale as the religious type.'

'He was, in some strange and perverted way.'

'And did he tell you?'

'He just said "Lord" and then all hell broke loose.'

'Did you see who shot him or stabbed him?'

'No, I had a blanket over my head and I was being held down on the floor. But I know who had me pinned down. It was a man called Woodward. I recognised his voice from the orphanage.'

The constable got to his feet, waddled over to the heavy oak door and bolted it. 'Closed for business,' he said as Allington came out of the back room carrying a glass of water.

'You can't close me down.'

'Just did. Now sit down, shut up and wait.'

An hour later Inspector Forbes arrived with a doctor and two constables. He smiled at Victoria. 'I'll be with you in a moment, Victoria. What's it all about?' he asked Constable Hemingway.

Hemingway took the inspector to the far side of the room out of earshot of the others. Victoria could see that he was bringing him up to date. The two other constables stayed near the door. Victoria had the impression they were making sure she did not leave. Then

Inspector Forbes, Constable Hemingway and the doctor went upstairs.

A few minutes later the inspector came back down, took Victoria by the elbow and led her from her seat to a side room that contained three round tables with a few chairs around each of them. He sat Victoria down and took a chair opposite.

'Victoria, tell me what happened.'

She repeated what she had told Constable Hemingway. Then she told him that Tweedale had confessed to blowing up the dam and putting Edwin and Billy up to contaminating the herd. The inspector listened intently.

'Why did you bring a gun?'

'I thought it may be a trap.'

'Did you tell anyone that you were coming here?'

'No, the note said not to. I asked Tweedale why he wanted that. He said it was to protect him. If there were any witnesses to what he told me he could be arrested and maybe hanged before he died from his disease.'

'Can I see the note?'

'I burnt it.'

'Why?'

'I was not going to come and then I changed my mind.'

'But why burn it?'

'I was angry.'

'Who delivered the note?'

'I do not know. Mr Humphreys found it and brought it to me.'

'Did you show it to anyone?'

'No. Look, Inspector, you must know I would not kill anyone.'

'I'm sure you would not, Victoria, but all the evidence seems to be pointing at you. You have blood all over your dress. You say you stabbed one of your assailants and the blood on your dress is from him, but neither Allington nor Freddy have any injuries. They say nobody else came down the stairs and nobody else was in the room when they came in. Only you covered in blood. So there must have been at least a third person involved.'

'There must have been, but I did not see him. I do know who had me pinned down on the floor. It was a man called Woodward.'

'Yes, the constable told me. Do you know where this Woodward lives?'

'No. He's a sea captain.'

'You did not see him, you only recognised his voice?'

'That's right. I will never forget his voice. Tweedale tried to sell me to him.'

'I have no choice, Victoria. I must arrest you for the murder of Tweedale.'

Victoria felt sick. With all the dignity she could muster she climbed to her feet. 'I understand, Inspector.'

'PC Hemingway, please take Victoria to Winchester police station and have her booked in with the station sergeant for the murder of Tweedale.'

'What?'

'Do as I say. We have no choice.' He looked at the two other constables by the door. 'One of you go with him.'

***

Victoria stood in a daze before the station sergeant in Winchester police station.

'Name?' said the sergeant.

'Victoria Sillitoe.'

'Address?'

'Eagledown House, Hampshire.'

In a dark corridor with a stone-flagged floor, Victoria walked in front of a fat, greasy woman gaoler. The smell of cooking fat and sweat assaulted Victoria's nostrils. She stopped at an open cell door. The gaoler pushed her into the cell and slammed the door. Victoria looked around the eight-feet-by-eight-feet cell with its arched ceiling. The barred window that was too high to see out let in the evening light to illuminate the whitewashed walls. A bucket with a lid stood in the corner next to a bunk with a single grey blanket.

She sat on the bunk, staring at the white wall until the darkness crept into the cell. She lay down and covered herself with the blanket. After many hours, sleep finally came.

Chapter Seventeen

Charlie and Mary Powell arrived at Gravestoke House in a hansom cab. Charlie's sturdy frame belied the hard life and near starvation of his past life and, at the age of thirty-eight, his once-curly brown hair had turned to grey.

Mary's physical bearing also stood testament to a life of hardship, though her beauty was still apparent under the suntanned complexion. Her rough hands were a sharp contrast to her fashionable blue-and-white dress under her long black cloak. Her greying hair hung in ringlets under a black bonnet.

'Please wait for us,' said Charlie to the coachman, climbing down from the two-seater carriage and helping Mary down.

'Yes, Guv'nor,' said the driver, holding the solid, chestnut mare in the reins.

Charlie felt the pistol in the inside pocket of his expensive grey suit and Mary fingered a knife tucked into the pocket of her dress.

Charlie rapped on the door of the orphanage.

A boy answered. He surprised Charlie and Mary with his happy smile.

'We want to see the master,' said Charlie.

The boy stood aside, still smiling.

The visitors did not wait to be shown to the master's quarters. They marched along the corridor but checked their steps when three giggling children ran along the passage ahead of them playing catch.

Mr Jolyon was at his desk when his door burst open.

'We're looking for Tweedale,' said Charlie.

'He no longer works here. I'm the master of Gravestoke House. How may I help you?'

'Where is he?'

'I suspect in Hell. He was murdered a few weeks ago. Who are you?' asked Mr Jolyon.

'Charlie and Mary Powell.'

'And what business do you have with Gravestoke House, may I inquire?'

'We used to live here,' said Mary.

'Orphans?'

'Yes,' said Charlie.

'Well, I think you'll find the place has changed considerably since your time.'

'I could tell that by the face of the boy who opened the door for us. And children are playing in corridors. That would never have been allowed before,' said Mary.

'So, at the risk of repeating myself, what business do you have with Gravestoke House?'

'I want to know where my twins are,' said Mary.

'Twins?'

'Yes. I had twins. A boy and a girl. They were taken from me when I was sold to Woodward.'

'Captain Woodward?'

'Yes. That's him,' said Mary.

'Sold?'

'Yes, sold. Perhaps Tweedale has gone to Hell but what about Woodward? Does he still come here?' asked Mary.

'Most certainly he does not. Why are you interested him?'

'Because Tweedale sold us to him and then the bastard sold us into slavery. That's what it was. Slavery! Down in Australia. I'll kill the bastard when I find him, but for now I want to know what happened to my twins,' said Mary.

Mr Jolyon peered over the half-moon spectacles he'd taken to wearing lately. 'Would you mind helping me with some information?'

'What information?' said Charlie.

Mr Jolyon walked over to the shelf holding the Bible and lifted it down. Turning the pages, he came to the register of names. 'What year was it you were sold to Woodward?'

Eighteen forty-six,' said Mary.

Mr Jolyon turned the pages to that year and ran his finger down the list until he came to:

> *Edward Sillitoe: born 24.6.1846:* Alongside this entry in different ink was written *died from drowning: 16.5.1855.*

> *Victoria Sillitoe: born 24.6.1846:* Next to this entry in different ink was written *left to make her way in the world: 24.6.1862.*
> *Mary Sillitoe: died 27.8.1846 aged 16 years.*
> *Charles Powell: left to make his way in the world 27.8.1846 aged 16 years.*

'For all his faults, Tweedale was a meticulous bookkeeper. Well, as far as recording what he wanted to record,' said Mr Jolyon.

'Aye, he was that,' said Charlie. 'A lyin' no good bastard of a bookkeeper.'

'Mrs Powell, what was your maiden name?'

'Sillitoe.'

Mr Jolyon drew a sharp intake of breath. 'I have some terrible news for you.' He turned the Bible around for her to see the entries.

'Oh my God!' Mary staggered backwards, almost in a faint.

Charlie and Mr Jolyon helped her to a chair. She came around slowly as they sat her down.

'That was stupid of me,' said Mr Jolyon, fanning Mary's face with his handkerchief.

Charlie shook his head. 'It says the boy is dead but then it says Mary is too. Do you know if he really is dead?'

'I'm afraid so. Charles Powell, is that you?'

'Yes.'

'May I ask if you are you the father of the twins?'

'Yes, I am.'

Mary managed to look up. 'What happened to my daughter, Victoria? It says she left to make her way in the world. Has she been sold too?'

'No, Mrs Powell. Your daughter has grown up into a lady.'

'Thank God. Where is she? I must see her,' said Mary.

'I'm afraid I have further bad news for you. I said Tweedale was murdered. I'm afraid your daughter Victoria is facing trial for his murder.'

Mary nearly fainted again. Charlie put his arms around her.

'She murdered Tweedale? Then she had good cause if she grew up in this orphanage with him as the master,' said Charlie.

'She did not murder him though if she had, I agree with you. From what I have heard of Tweedale and his rule in this orphanage there would be a queue waiting to kill him,' said Mr Jolyon.

'You said . . .' began Mary.

'Victoria did not kill Tweedale, but she has been accused of it and I suspect she will be convicted. The cards are stacked against her.'

'If she didn't kill Tweedale, then who did?' said Charlie.

'Either Lord de Mornay or Captain Woodward.'

'Then I will see both of them and make them tell the truth,' said Mary.

'I think that may be difficult. I suggest you go to Eagledown House and see Sir Richard de Mornay. He is trying to gather evidence to prove Victoria's innocence.'

'What is he to this Lord de Mornay?' said Charlie.

'His son.'

'And he's trying to prove his father is a murderer?' said Mary.

'Yes.'

'There's obviously a long story in all this. I take it that this Richard de Mornay will enlighten us?' said Charlie.

'I'm sure he will.'

'Where is she now?' said Mary.

'In Winchester prison.'

'We must go to the prison and see her, Charlie.'

'Yes, we must. But first we must see this Richard de Mornay to find out what's going on.'

'Thank you, Sir, for your help and kindness. I can see that this orphanage is now somewhere where children may grow up safely,' said Mary.

'You can thank your daughter for that. She's the one that has ensured it's a safe place. She's a lady now, but I fear she is doomed. There are plenty of people who want to help her. Sir Richard is coordinating plans.'

***

Charlie and Mary stood inside the hall of Eagledown House.

'Strange to think that our daughter lived here,' said Mary.

'Lives here,' said Charlie.

'Yes, Charlie, lives here. We won't give up hope and we won't give in. We got through those years in Australia without giving in and I'm damned if I'll give in now.'

'That's right.'

Humphreys appeared. 'Please follow me. Sir Richard is at home,' said Humphreys.

Humphreys showed Charlie and Mary into the drawing room. 'Mr and Mrs Charles Powell, Sir.' Humphreys turned and left.

Richard stood, bowed to Mary and offered his hand to Charlie. 'Humphreys tells me, Mr Powell, that you have come on business regarding Victoria.'

'I have,' said Charlie. 'I am her father and this is her mother.'

Richard blinked. 'I don't understand. I thought she was an orphan.' He ushered them both to a sofa and sat them down.

'Mr de Mornay, sorry, Sir Richard, less than two months after Victoria and her twin brother were born we were sold by Tweedale to a Captain Woodward and taken to Australia where we were sold on as indentured labourers. In fact, we were virtually slaves. We have returned to take our revenge, only to find that Tweedale is dead and our daughter accused of his murder.'

Mary's hands still shook. 'That's right. Mr Jolyon at the orphanage said you were trying to help her.'

'I believe that she did not kill Tweedale, but I would not blame her if she had,' said Richard.

'I understand you're coordinating attempts to clear her name,' said Mary, at last managing to contain her shakes.

'Yes, I am.'

'How can we help?'

'I have made inquiries and Woodward is due in Liverpool Docks from Spain in one week's time. If Victoria is convicted— and I fear she will be—it would help if you found Woodward and brought him back to Winchester. There is an inspector there, Forbes, who is also doing all he can to clear her name. He is a policeman so I doubt he will have the freedom to persuade Woodward to tell the truth . . . On the other hand, you . . .'

'Understood. We'll do it. When is the trial?' said Mary.

'Tomorrow,' said Richard.

'Is there anything else we can do?' asked Charlie.

'I don't think so at present. Please, stay here at Eagledown while we work something out.'

'Sir, I have to ask you what the relationship is between my daughter and you. If you get my meaning, Sir,' said Charlie.

'Charlie!' said Mary.

Richard looked at Charlie for a moment. 'Er ... oh! No, Sir. Your daughter was taken in by my aunt and brought up here while I was in Africa. Please, Sir, I can assure you that there is nothing but the utmost propriety involved with your daughter's residence in this house.'

'That's good enough for me, Sir. We'd like to take your offer of accommodation here if we may.'

'I wish to go to Winchester Prison to see Victoria if that's possible,' said Mary.

'I will get someone to take you.' Richard pulled the cord by the fireplace. Humphreys appeared at the drawing-room door soon afterwards.

'Humphreys, Mr and Mrs Powell will be staying here at Eagledown. Please tell Jane to make up one of the guest rooms. And please arrange for Jake to take Mr and Mrs Powell to Winchester Prison to see their daughter, Victoria.'

Humphreys hesitated for a moment.

'That's right, Humphreys. Victoria is their daughter.'

'If I am speaking out of turn, Sir, Ma'am, please forgive me, but I must say that your daughter is an exceptional young woman of whom you should be immensely proud. She fills any room she is in with sunshine. All the people here on the estate and those who know her in the towns and villages will do everything in their power to save her. And so will I.'

'Thank you,' said Mary. 'It means so much to us that she's managed to grow up and become a lady, in spite of her humble beginning.'

Charlie put his arm around his wife. 'It sounds as if she's just like you.'

Mary kissed him on the cheek.

'We have a hansom cab outside,' said Charlie.

'Humphreys, please pay the driver and send him away. You are my guests. Jake will take you to Winchester.'

***

Charlie and Mary waited outside the front door of Eagledown.

Around the corner clopped a pony and trap driven by Jake. He climbed down slowly from the driver's seat and with his speech slightly slurred said, 'Sir, Ma'am, please climb aboard and I'll take you to the prison. It should take about an hour and a half. Your daughter is well loved by everyone. She saved my life and she taught me and others on the estate how to read and write. We'll not let anything happen to her, you have my word.'

'Thank you,' said Charlie, smiling.

As the pony and trap trotted along the drive to the main gates, Arthur the shepherd and his wife Bridget were coming through. Bridget carried a basket of herbs while Arthur's sheepdog was at his heels.

Jake pulled on the reins. The horse came to a stop.

Arthur touched his forelock and Bridget bobbed a curtsey to the two passengers in the trap.

'Excuse me, Ma'am, Sir, but I'd like you to meet two of our people who know your daughter very well and are going to help. This is Arthur and his wife, Bridget.'

'G'day,' said Charlie.

Bridget looked on nonplussed.

'They are Miss Victoria's parents,' said Jake.

'I thought she was an . . .' said Bridget.

'Orphan? Yes, she very nearly was thanks to that evil man in the orphanage,' said Mary.

'Pleased to meet you, Sir, Ma'am. Don't mind Arthur 'ere. He don't speak,' said Bridget. 'We is so grateful to Miss Victoria. We was down on our luck and out of work. She took us on without knowing us and gave us somewhere to live and work. Miss Victoria is an angel and no mistake.'

'Thank you,' said Mary, smiling at them.

Jake drove the pony and trap on.

As they came around a bend not far from Eagledown, they came across Constable Hemingway puffing his way along the lane.

Jake brought the trap to a halt. 'Constable, these are Miss Victoria's parents. I'm taking them to visit her in the prison.'

'I thought she were a . . .'

'Orphan?' said Mary. 'Nearly.'

'She's a grand lass is your daughter, Ma'am. She'd do anything for anybody. Saved my wife's life when she was taken with the scarlet fever she did. And she's done so much to help others. It's damned . . . Er, sorry. It's criminal what they is doing to the poor lass.'

'Thank you, Constable,' said Charlie.

'I don't know what we is going to do about the trial. Sir Richard is trying hard to come up with something but I fear the evidence is rigged against the poor girl. We'll all do whatever it takes to make sure she is all right, though.'

Jake drove the pony and trap on. They came past the gates of Squire Galbraith's estate. 'The gentleman who lives there,' said Jake, pointing at an Elizabethan mansion on the other side of the gates. 'He is very important in the area. He has contacts in London and elsewhere. If the trial goes against Miss Victoria, he will make representations on her behalf.'

'I'm amazed at the good my daughter has done for the people living here. What did she do for the squire?' said Mary.

'Nothing, other than always having a smile and words of encouragement for him. He's a cantankerous old gentleman but he always stands up for the underdog.'

Jake drove the pony and trap on to Winchester where he pulled into the livery stables of Mr Belchamber.

Jamie Hardcastle took the horse by the halter while Jake climbed down.

'Jamie, these are Miss Victoria's parents and I'm taking them up to the prison to visit her. Will you look after the horse and trap for me, please?'

'Of course, Jake. Anything for Miss Victoria but I thought she was . . .'

'An orphan?' said Charlie climbing down, and then helping Mary.

'Yes, Sir.'

'Well it's a long story, young man, but she's not an orphan and we're going to see her for the first time since she was a tiny baby,' said Mary.

'It's a real cruel thing they're doing to her, Ma'am. Miss Victoria wouldn't hurt a fly. I know she wouldn't. She helps everyone and anyone who needs it. She got me this job when I was out of work and starving. There'll be a riot if they try to do anything to Miss Victoria. So there will. And I'll be in it.'

Jake led Charlie and Mary up West Hill towards the red-brick and dismal prison.

***

A hatch opened in the massive doors of Winchester prison in response to Jake's banging.

'What do you want?' said a face at the opening.

'Visitors for Miss Victoria Sillitoe,' said Jake.

'Ain't visiting time,' said the face.

Jake pushed a leather pouch through the open hatch. 'Sir Richard de Mornay's compliments, and it is visiting time.'

The face moved away as the sound of jangling coins came through the door. 'All right,' said the face.

A small door in the massive doors opened. Jake, Charlie and Mary stepped through.

The face belonged to a heavy-set man in a navy-blue serge jacket and trousers. Mutton-chop whiskers bordered his ruddy complexion. 'Follow me.'

Jake, Charlie and Mary followed the guard across a cobbled courtyard to a flight of iron steps that led up to a door in the red-brick façade of the main building. Rows of barred windows on three levels spread along the side wall.

The guard used a key to unlock the door at the top of the stairs. He ushered the visitors inside and along a white-painted corridor to a green door. 'In there,' he said.

The visitors went in. The guard locked the door from the outside. They waited.

***

Victoria, in a grey shift and looking pale and tired, was led by a female warder with big hips and a weasel face into a small room with a pine table, with two chairs on one side and a single chair on the other.

The warder closed the door and stood against the wall, leaving her charge standing in the middle of the room.

'Jake, good to see you,' said Victoria, looking from him to the other two visitors. The woman looked familiar but she could not remember ever seeing her before. It was something in the way she looked and stood.

'Please, sit down. We have something to tell you,' said the woman.

Victoria shot a glance at Jake. He nodded.

She sat on the single chair while the man and woman sat on the others. Jake stood quietly in a corner.

'This is going to come as a shock to you, Victoria,' said the woman.

Victoria wondered what it could be. Whatever it was, it was important to bring them here outside visiting hours.

'I am Mary Powell and this is my husband, Charlie. We are your parents.'

At first, the words were beyond her comprehension. She simply sat looking at the woman who claimed to be her mother. Then, as the enormity of what she had heard sank in, she blinked and sucked in a deep breath. 'Mr Jolyon was right. You didn't die.'

'No, I didn't die. We, your father and me, were sold by Tweedale to Captain Woodward and taken to Australia.'

'He was going to do that to me but I escaped,' said Victoria, still staring from one parent to the other.

'We had a hard time in Australia. We were prisoners. But when our time was up we vowed we would come back for you and your brother,' said Charlie.

'Edward is . . .' said Victoria.

'Yes, I know. Mr Jolyon told us,' said Mary.

Charlie said, 'But we couldn't get back because we had no money. So we went to work in the coalfields near Newcastle in New South Wales, but all we could earn was enough to keep a roof over our heads and barely enough for food in our bellies, so we left and went gold mining.'

'It took years of hard labour,' said Mary, 'but eventually, we struck gold. It meant more years of hard work, but we managed to build up our fortune and then we returned to deal with Tweedale and find our children, only to discover Edward had drowned, Tweedale was dead and you were charged with his murder.'

'I did not do it,' said Victoria.

'I wouldn't blame you if you had,' said Charlie. 'I would have killed him had I found him alive.'

Mary's hand went slowly across the table. Victoria's hand moved towards it.

'No touching,' bellowed the warder.

They pulled back their hands.

'My trial is tomorrow.'

'We know. We'll be there. We've met many people who you've helped. You are a truly kind and loved person. They're all supporting you. Don't despair, Victoria,' said Charlie.

'I am trying not to but it is hard. This place is not as bad as the orphanage but it is difficult. There are so many sad people in here and I am sure many of them are victims rather than offenders. If I ever get out of this, I shall do something to help them.'

'For now, we just have to think about you, Victoria,' said Charlie.

'Whatever happens to me, I am so glad I got to meet you both. I always wondered what you were like and now I know,' said Victoria.

'I hope we're not a disappointment to you,' said Mary.

'Certainly you are not. If I have any strength at all, I know I have it from you. I can only begin to imagine what you must have been through in Australia. And you have survived. I thank God that I have lived long enough to meet you.'

'Time up,' said the warder.

Victoria stood up. So did Mary. The two women looked at each other for a moment, and then they flung their arms around each other and hugged as tightly as they could.

'Let go,' screamed the warder, stepping forward with a wooden truncheon in her hand.

Jake shuffled forward. Though slow he still looked big and strong. 'I wouldn't do that if I were you,' he said.

The warder backed off.

Victoria and her mother held on to each other for several minutes. Then the warder led Victoria away.

Chapter Eighteen

Victoria stepped from the cart that had brought her down West Hill from Winchester Prison to the Great Hall of the Hampshire Assizes. She looked at the ancient stone building. A warm dress and shawl that Bonnie had brought to the prison kept out the icy wind but not the cold finger of fear. Her education at Eagledown had taught her about the Bloody Assizes of Winchester and Dorchester, where the followers of Monmouth were hanged, drawn and quartered nearly two hundred years before. She knew her fate if convicted would be hanging, as drawing and quartering were no longer practised. It was no less a horrible end to her young life.

Two prison matrons helped her into the Great Hall where she had to shuffle along under the restraint of manacles and shackles. They removed her chains when she reached the dock. As she sat down, she looked out across the stone-walled court. On the far wall hung a massive, round tabletop that legend said had been King Arthur's.

There was no mistaking her mother in the public gallery, mopping a tear. Though the woman's hard life was engrained into her features, she kept traces of the beauty that she had passed on to her daughter. Victoria smiled at her and the man next to her, her father. *How cruel for this to happen when at last I have met my parents. Shall I die before I may really get to know them?*

Richard, Bonnie and Lady Adele were also in the public gallery. Her QC, Roger Hepple, looked up and smiled at her from his position in front of the raised judge's bench, with the Royal Coat of Arms on the wall behind. He had a quiet manner. Victoria thought he was not yet thirty. Next to Mr Hepple was a tall man with a stoop, wearing the same QC uniform of a black gown and wig. This she knew would be Sir George Pitter, the famous prosecutor with many convictions and executions to his 'credit'. Victoria thought he must be at least sixty.

She looked across at two rows of six men. Would they, the jury, believe her? She did not recognise any of them. Mr Hepple had told her they were brought up from Southampton, as too many people in Winchester and the surrounding area knew her and could not be relied on to be impartial, according to the prosecution.

A voice called out, 'All rise.'

Victoria climbed to her feet along with everyone else in the courtroom.

Judge Herbert Phillips squeezed his fat belly between the wall and the three chairs for the bench. He took his place at the centre in a chair with a high and ornate leather back. He adjusted his long wig and sat down. Two men, wigless and in black frock coats, sat on the two chairs each side of him.

Victoria listened, still standing, as the charge was read out to her by yet another bewigged gentleman from a table in front of the bench, facing towards the defence and prosecuting counsel. 'Victoria Sillitoe, you are charged that on the seventh of August this year you did feloniously, wilfully, and with malice aforethought kill and murder Samuel Tweedale. Do you plead guilty or not guilty?'

'Not guilty, Sir,' said Victoria as loudly and firmly as she could muster.

A matron tugged her arm for her to sit. She sat quietly and listened to the evidence from the doctor who had arrived at the Bear and Ragged Staff with Inspector Forbes. Then she heard the pathologist give his testimony that Tweedale had been shot four times and stabbed in the neck. The probable cause of death was a bullet in the heart, but the other bullets and the knife wound would on their own likely have resulted in death, he said.

Doctor O'Reilly took the witness stand. Victoria wondered why he had been called.

'Doctor, are you acquainted with Eagledown House?' asked Pitter.

'I am, Sir.'

'Are you a regular visitor, socially?'

'I am, Sir. And I am also the physician for the family there.'

'Have you ever heard anyone at that house threaten the life of Mr Tweedale?'

Victoria saw the panic on the doctor's face.

'Please answer the question,' said Pitter.

'I don't know what you mean.'

'It is a very simple question, Doctor. Have you ever heard anyone at Eagledown threaten Mr Tweedale's life?'

The doctor did not reply.

'Let me help you, Doctor. Were you in discussion with Squire Galbraith in the Martinsfield coffee house shortly after an incident in which the barn at Eagledown was burnt and a person killed?'

'Er . . .'

'Answer the question,' said the judge.

Hepple stood up. 'That is hearsay evidence, M'lud, and not admissible.'

'Don't tell me what is admissible. Sit down,' said the judge.

'Did you discuss with Squire Galbraith your concerns that Victoria Sillitoe had threatened Mr Tweedale's life?'

'Er . . .'

'I shall hold you in contempt if you do not answer,' said the judge.

'Yes I did, but it was just a conversation and I do not . . .'

'What exactly did Miss Sillitoe say?'

'I do not recall.'

'Doctor, I'm warning you,' said the judge.

'It was just an idle threat about shooting Tweedale. She didn't mean it.'

'How do you know?' said Pitter.

'Because she wouldn't kill anyone.'

'That will be all,' said Pitter.

Hepple stood up. 'Doctor, have you told anyone other than Squire Galbraith about this alleged statement by Miss Sillitoe?'

'Of course not. And I doubt that Squire Galbraith would have done so either. Someone must have overheard the private conversation.'

'Thank you,' said Hepple.

Squire Galbraith took the witness stand.

Pitter stood up. 'Squire Galbraith, do you recall a conversation with Doctor O'Reilly in a coffee house in Martinsfield when he told you he had heard Victoria Sillitoe threaten the life of Mr Tweedale.'

'What are you getting at?'

Hepple stood up. 'That is definitely hearsay evidence, M'lud, and I must vigorously protest.'

'Shut up and sit down,' said the judge.

'Answer the question,' said Pitter.

'No.'

'Is that "no" you didn't have such a conversation?' said Pitter.

'It is "no" I will not answer questions about private conversations,' said the squire.

'I shall hold you in contempt,' said the judge.

'I could not give a fig, you jumped-up, poor excuse for a judge. I know Lord de Mornay has something on you to blackmail you into this miscarriage of justice and I will not be a party to it. Do you hear me? I will not be a party to it! And no! A private conversation is a private conversation!' said the squire, huffing and puffing.

The judge banged his gavel on the desk, went red in the face and shouted, 'Take that man down for contempt.'

A young constable at the back of the court stepped forward, shaking slightly.

'All right, I'll go quietly,' said the squire, walking beside the constable to the door. When he reached it, he turned and said, 'You are making a big mistake if you think you can push this case against Miss Sillitoe through without conducting the trial in accordance with the law. I shall see to it that you are disbarred, you damned fool. And the local population will not countenance it. That I can say with confidence.'

The judge's temple looked fit to burst and his face turned from red to almost purple. 'Take him down, now!'

'God bless you, Squire,' said a woman's voice from the gallery. All eyes turned to the origin, Bonnie.

'Thank you,' said another woman, and eyes turned to Victoria's mother.

A rumble of stamping feet began in the public gallery.

'Quiet or I shall clear the court,' bellowed the judge.

The noise subsided.

A captain from the Royal Ordnance Depot at Woolwich gave evidence that the bullets found in Tweedale matched the type that the Kerr's revolver used.

Allington gave evidence.

Pitter said, 'Mr Allington, please tell us what happened at your public house on the seventh of August this year.'

'I was in the public bar with Freddy Mills when Miss Sillitoe came in looking for Tweedale. I told her he was upstairs in bed, sick. She went upstairs. A few minutes later I heard several shots. I don't know how many. More than three. We dashed upstairs and found Miss Sillitoe standing in the bedroom. She were covered in blood. I saw a revolver on the bed. In the bed, I saw Mr Tweedale with what looked like bullet holes in him and a knife stuck in his neck.'

'Was anyone else in the room other than you, Mr Mills and Miss Sillitoe?'

'Yes, Sir.'

'And who was that?'

A surge of optimism streaked through Victoria. He was going to tell the truth!

'Mr Tweedale, but he were dead.'

The optimism vanished like a stone thrown into a pond.

'I meant any other living person?'

'No, Sir.'

'Between hearing the shots and dashing up the stairs, did you see or hear anyone coming down the stairs?'

'No, Sir.'

'Is there any other way out of the bedroom to the outside other than down the stairs?'

'No, Sir. I have the windows nailed shut to stop the thieving gyp . . . to stop thieves getting in.'

Pitter sat down. 'Your witness.'

Hepple stood up. 'Mr Allington, I put it to you that you are mistaken.'

'What about?'

'Not hearing anyone come down the stairs.'

'No, I'm not mistaken. Only Miss Sillitoe went up them stairs and nobody came down them.'

'Did the deceased give you a note for Miss Sillitoe?'

'No.'

'Are you aware of the deceased giving anyone a note for Miss Sillitoe?'

'No.'

'Then pray tell me why Miss Sillitoe should come to the inn if she had not been sent for.'

'Objection, M'lud,' said Pitter, rising to his feet and holding his lapels. 'The witness is not clairvoyant.'

'Indeed, he is not,' said the judge.

'Mr Allington, are you acquainted with Lord de Mornay and Captain Woodward?' said Hepple.

'No.'

'You have never met Lord de Mornay or Captain Woodward?'

'Not that I know of. I keep an inn. Lots of people come in but I don't know all their names.'

'No further questions, M'Lud.'

Allington stepped down from the witness box.

Victoria saw him cast a glance around the room as if looking for someone.

'Call Constable Hemingway,' said the court clerk.

The constable wobbled in and climbed the steps to the witness box. 'I swear by Almighty God that the evidence I shall give shall be the truth, the whole truth and nothing but the truth,' he said in his deep, loud voice, with his right hand on the New Testament.

Pitter rose to his feet. 'Constable, please tell the court what you saw when you arrived at The Bear and Ragged Staff on the seventh of August this year.'

'I entered the public house to find nobody in the public area. I made my way upstairs to a bedroom. There I found the body of the deceased, Mr Tweedale, lying in bed. It appeared that he had been shot four times in the body and stabbed in the neck.'

'Were you accompanied by anyone?'

'Yes, Sir, Freddy Mills. He had come to my police house to fetch me.'

'When you entered the bedroom did you find anyone else in the room?'

'Yes, Sir, I saw the landlord Allington and Miss Sillitoe.'

'Was there anything unusual in Miss Sillitoe's appearance?'

Hemingway hesitated.

'Constable Hemingway, please answer my question. Was there anything unusual in Miss Sillitoe's appearance?'

'She had blood on her dress.'

'I'm sorry, I'm not sure that the jury could hear that reply. Would you repeat what you just said, please?'

'I said that she had blood on her dress.'

'Did Mr Allington have any sign of blood on his clothing or any sign of any injury?'

'No, Sir.'

'Pardon?'

'I said, no, Sir.'

'Did Mr Mills have any sign of blood on his clothing or any sign of any injury?'

'No, Sir.'

'And what did you do next?'

'I took Allington and Miss Sillitoe down to the public bar and sent Freddy Mills to the railway station to summon Inspector Forbes by telegraph.'

'Thank you, Constable. Please remain there while my learned friend cross examines you.' Pitter sat down.

'Constable,' Hepple began, 'what was the demeanour of the defendant when you entered the room where the deceased lay?'

'How do you mean, Sir?'

'What was her mood? How did she appear? Angry? Afraid?'

'She looked scared. Miss Victoria would never harm a fly.'

'Constable, restrict your answers to the questions asked,' said the judge.

'Did she have the demeanour of someone who had just murdered someone?' asked Hepple.

'No, Sir.'

'Objection, M'Lud. Unless the constable has medical or psychiatric training, this is unfounded opinion.'

'I agree,' said the judge. 'The jury will disregard that comment and I warn you, Constable, to keep your evidence to fact, not opinion.

'Well, to blazes with it. Miss Victoria is innocent!'

'Constable! One more remark like that and I shall hold you in contempt.'

'You can't lock everyone up who opposes this travesty of justice,' shouted Mary from the public gallery.

'Constable, remove that woman,' bellowed the judge.

A constable in the public gallery stepped towards Mary Powell. Charlie stood up between Mary and the policeman.

'No, it's all right, Charlie. No trouble today. We'll save it for later.' Mary walked out of the public gallery.

'No more questions, M'Lud,' said Hepple.

Hemingway left the witness box and managed to smile at Victoria.

Inspector Forbes marched into the courtroom and stood in the witness box. He took the oath.

'Inspector Forbes, did you attend a public house called The Bear and Ragged Staff on the seventh of August this year?'

'Yes, Sir.'

'Did you examine a crime scene there?'

'Yes, Sir.'

'And what did you find?'

'In a bedroom, I found the body of Mr Tweedale. He had been shot four times and stabbed in the neck. A fifth bullet was embedded in the wall above his head.'

'Did you find any weapons in the bedroom?'

'Yes, Sir.'

'What were they?'

'A Kerr's thirty-six revolver.'

'Is this the revolver?' Pitter handed a pistol to Forbes.

'I believe so.'

'Was there any other weapon?'

'A knife.'

'This knife?' Pitter passed Victoria's knife with the deer's-foot handle to him.

'I believe so, Sir.'

'And where did you find it?'

'In Mr Tweedale's neck.'

'And did you subsequently arrest Miss Sillitoe for the murder of Mr Tweedale?'

'Yes, Sir.'

'Why?'

'What do you mean, Sir?'

'Why did you arrest her?'

'She had blood on her dress.'

'Is that all?'

'No, Sir, I made inquiries first.'

'And what did your investigations reveal, Inspector?'

'Miss Sillitoe had brought the Kerr's revolver with her to the public-house and the knife belonged to her.'

'Did you subsequently find a Mr Woodward?'

'Yes, Sir.'

'Why did you go in search of Mr Woodward?'

'Miss Sillitoe recognised the voice of the man who pinned her down in the bedroom while Tweedale was murdered. She said it was Woodward.'

'Indeed, Inspector? And you say you did find the said Mr Woodward?'

'Yes, Sir.'

'Then please tell the court why Mr Woodward does not appear before it, charged with complicity in the murder.'

'He had an alibi, Sir.'

'He had an alibi? Did you check that alibi out, Inspector?'

'Of course.'

'And what was his alibi?'

'He was in Portugal, Sir.'

'He was in Portugal? Is that something he claims or did you verify it?'

'I questioned six men who claim to have been there with him. They say he was.'

'Are you sure the Woodward you found was the same Woodward that Miss Sillitoe alleges held her down while Mr Tweedale was murdered?'

Forbes did not answer.

'Answer the question,' said the judge.

'Yes, Sir.'

'So Mr Woodward could not possibly have been at the Bear and Ragged Staff if he was in Portugal, could he, Inspector?'

'I believe he was lying and his alibis were lying.'

'Really, Inspector? And on what evidence do you base that statement?'

'I know Miss Sillitoe. I know she would not kill anyone. And I know that she does not lie. If she says she heard Woodward's voice, then she heard Woodward's voice.'

'Inspector, restrict your evidence to the facts, not opinion,' said the judge.

'I do believe there is more to your relationship with Miss Sillitoe than is . . . shall we say, appropriate? Has she offered you favours for making such an unfounded statement?' asked Pitter.

'Do not be disgusting. How dare . . .'

The judge intervened. 'Inspector, control yourself. Mr Pitter is merely offering a plausible reason why you should be so adamant about Miss Sillitoe's innocence in spite of all the evidence to the contrary.'

Hepple jumped to his feet. 'I object to your statement, M'lud. It is a clear assumption of her guilt before the trial has taken its course.'

'Shut up and sit down. Do not dare criticise me.'

Hepple sat down, red in the face with his temple throbbing.

'Thank you, Inspector. Please remain there while my learned friend cross-examines you.'

Hepple took up the questioning. 'We can clear up one thing, Inspector. Please tell the court why you are supportive of Miss Sillitoe.'

'She saved my life.'

'In what circumstances?'

'She risked her life to stop a train I was travelling on from being blown up by anarchists attempting to kill a very important person.'

'And who was that very important person?'

'I'm afraid that is something I am not at liberty to divulge.'

'You will disclose the name to this court, Inspector, or I shall hold you in contempt,' said the judge.

'I shall write down the name for you, M'Lud, but it must not be divulged to the court or there will be grave consequences for you, I can assure you of that.'

'Do not dare threaten me.'

Forbes wrote down 'Queen Victoria', folded the piece of paper and handed it to the judge. Judge Phillips swallowed hard when he read it and slipped it into his pocket. 'We shall adjourn for lunch.'

***

Hepple sat in a cell with Victoria. 'Allington is obviously lying if you are telling the truth, but there's no point in antagonising the judge or the jury by accusing Allington at this stage.'

'How many murder trials have you defended in?' said Victoria.

'Two.'

'And how many did you win?'

'None.'

Victoria took a deep breath. 'I appreciate that you are doing your best but I don't understand why all the other more experienced barristers contacted by Richard and Lady Luisa refused to defend me.'

'I'm afraid you are stuck with me, Victoria. All the others have been persuaded that it would not be good for their careers if they defended you.'

'Can they do that? I mean, how can they do that?'

'In this case, they did. I think, as the squire implied, de Mornay has something to blackmail the judge into pushing this trial through so that the outcome is guilty.'

'Can we find out what that is?'

'I don't think so.'

'Well, there must be grounds to appeal if this goes through,' said Victoria with more hope than belief.

'No. The judge will make sure the records are as he wants them and any appeal will have to follow what is recorded. And the evidence against you is very strong.'

'I did not do it.'

'I know that.'

'So tell me, Mr Hepple, why are you risking your career defending me?'

'Because I believe in justice. It is as simple as that.'

***

Back in the court after lunch, it was Victoria's turn to give evidence. She climbed into the witness box with a matron standing close by. Looking up at the public gallery she saw that her mother had regained her seat. It gave her strength to see her parents there.

'Please give the court your account of the incident at The Bear and Ragged Staff public house on seventh of August this year,' said Hepple.

'I received a note from Tweedale asking me to visit that place. When I arrived, I found him in bed upstairs. He asked me to forgive him for the harm that he had done to me in the past and what he had done to the Eagledown estate.'

'Please tell us what harm he had done to you.'

'He was the master at the orphanage where I lived until I was sixteen. He tried to sell me to a man called Woodward who was going to sell me into . . . into prostitution. I escaped. When I was a child at the orphanage, he beat me with a cane on my back and I still have the scars.'

A gasp came from some of the jury members.

'And the harm he did to Eagledown?'

'He blew up the dam killing seven people to bankrupt the estate. He paid two men to contaminate the herd with foot and mouth. He told me he was working with someone who killed a prize bull and my horse. The man burnt down the barn and seriously injured one of the farmworkers. He killed the gamekeeper. Tweedale was going to tell me who the man was when I was attacked from behind and covered with a blanket. But he did manage to say the man's name was "Lord" before he was silenced. And he meant Lord de Mornay.'

'Objection, M'Lud. He could have meant Lord anybody,' said Pitter.

'Agreed,' said the judge. 'Keep your answers to the facts.'

'Then what happened?' said Hepple.

Someone took my gun from my bag and shot Tweedale. They took my knife from me and stabbed him in the neck. Then they let me go. I heard them run downstairs.'

'How many were there?'

'At least two.'

'Did you recognise any of them?'

'I couldn't see because I had a blanket thrown over me and I was pinned to the floor. I know it was Woodward who pinned me down. I recognised his voice.'

'How did you get blood on your dress?'

'I stabbed Woodward. I think it was in his leg.'

'Did you kill Mr Tweedale?'

'No.'

'Please remain there while my learned friend cross examines you.'

Pitter stood up. 'Let me see if I have this correct. Did you go to the Bear and Ragged Staff to see Mr Tweedale?'

'Yes.'

'Why?'

'I have already said. He sent me a note telling me he wanted to give me some information about who was causing the problems at Eagledown and that he wanted my forgiveness.'

'And where is the note?'

'I burnt it.'

'Why?'

'I thought it was a trap.'

'But you went anyway?'

'I changed my mind and decided to go.'

'Did you tell anyone where you were going?'

'No.'

'Why?'

'The note told me not to tell anyone.'

'What note?'

'The one I burnt.'

'Ah yes. The note that told you that Mr Tweedale wanted to make some sort of confession and give you the name of someone causing harm to Eagledown. A note that you conveniently burnt.'

Victoria looked at Pitter. This was not a question so she waited.

'Did you take a gun to the Bear and Ragged Staff?' asked Pitter.

'Yes.'

'Where did you get the gun from?'

'The gunroom at Eagledown.'

'Did you tell anyone that you were taking the gun?'

'No.'
'Why?'
'Because the note told me not to tell anyone where I was going.'
'What note?'
'Please, I've told you twice already. The note that I burnt.'
'Oh yes. The note that you burnt.'
Again she waited for a proper question.
'And you had a knife?'
'Yes.'
'Where did you keep that knife?'
'In my boot.'
'Why?'
'For protection.'
'From whom?'
'From whoever was trying to ruin Eagledown.'
'And you believed that was Mr Tweedale?'
'I know it was. He told me it was.'
'So you take a gun and a knife to see someone whom you believe is trying to ruin the estate where you live and whom you believe has killed several people?'

Victoria stared at Pitter.

Judge Phillips said, 'Please answer the question, Miss Sillitoe.'

'Er . . . yes . . . Sir.'

'And in anger, you shot Mr Tweedale and then stabbed him?'

'No, Sir.'

'I'm sorry. Perhaps I have it wrong. You stabbed him and then you shot him?'

'No . . . no . . . no. I did not kill Tweedale.'

'M'lud, I have no more questions for this witness.'

The clerk said, 'Call Mr Humphreys.'

Humphreys marched into the courtroom with all the bearing that years in the military had taught him. He took his position in the witness box and gave the oath.

'Mr Humphreys,' said Hepple. 'Please tell the court where you were on the seventh of August this year.'

'At Eagledown House, Sir.'

'What is your role there?'

'I'm the butler, Sir.'

'Was Miss Sillitoe at home?'

'Yes, Sir.'

'Did a note arrive addressed to her?'

'Yes, Sir.'

'And how was that note delivered to the house?'

'I don't know, Sir. I found it on the floor of the hallway as I was walking through.'

'How did it get there?'

'I do not know, Sir. It's possible that it was shoved through between the door and the architrave. There's a gap there that needs to be filled due to the warping of the wood.'

'Please describe this note.'

'It was an envelope with a paper inside but sealed so I can't say what was in the note.'

'To whom was it addressed?'

'Miss Sillitoe.'

'And you gave it to her?'

'Yes, Sir. She was in the drawing room.'

'So, Mr Humphreys. You are confirming that there was a note addressed to Miss Sillitoe on the seventh of August?'

'Yes, Sir.'

'No further questions, M'Lud.'

'You say you did not see the contents of the note, Mr Humphreys,' said Pitter.

'That's correct, Sir. The envelope was sealed.'

'So that note could have contained anything.'

'It contained what Miss Sillitoe says it contained. She does not lie.'

'What happened to the note after you gave it to Miss Sillitoe?'

'I don't know.'

'Did you see it again?'

'No, Sir.'

'And what did Miss Sillitoe do after you gave her the note?'

'I don't know. I left her alone.'

'And did the defendant leave the house shortly afterwards?'

'Yes.'

'Did she say where she was going?'

'No.'

'Thank you. No further questions, M'Lud.'

The judge looked at a large clock on the wall above the jury. 'It's four o'clock. The prosecution will close its case followed by the defence. And keep it short.'

Pitter launched into his speech but Victoria sat in a daze and heard none of it, or that of Hepple's.

The judge said, 'The jury will retire and reach its verdict, if possible, this evening.'

***

Victoria sat in a cell below the court with Hepple. 'What are my chances?'

'It's hard to say. The evidence against you is very strong.'

A matron rattled a bunch of keys at the door. 'Jury's ready.'

She escorted Victoria to the dock.

'All rise,' said the clerk as the judge came into the court.

He took his seat and signalled everyone to be seated.

'Gentlemen of the jury, have you reached a unanimous verdict in the case of Regina versus Sillitoe?' asked the clerk.

A bespectacled man in a dark-grey suit and matching tie stood up. 'Yes, we have.'

The judge peered down. 'And what is your verdict?'

'Guilty,' said the man. 'But we urge clemency, M'Lud, given the poor character of the deceased and the good character of the young defendant.'

Victoria saw the judge glance across at Lord de Mornay, who seemed to be staring back with a threatening expression. 'The jury's role is to find the prisoner guilty or not guilty. The sentence is my role.'

'The prisoner will stand,' said the clerk.

Victoria stood up.

The judge donned a black cap. 'Victoria Sillitoe, you have been found guilty of the murder of Samuel Tweedale. You will be taken from here to a place where you will await execution. Then you will be hanged by the neck until you are dead. May God have mercy on your soul.'

Victoria gripped the side of the dock.

'No, no, no,' screamed Mary from the public gallery.

Then more cries of 'No, no' from the other spectators echoed around the room.

'Silence or I'll have you all arrested,' shouted the judge over the din, but it did not stop. He got up quickly and went to the judges' chambers, slamming the door and locking it.

Another matron joined her colleague in the dock and together they dragged Victoria down the steps to the cells.

Charlie Powell reached into his jacket and curled his fingers around the handle of his gun.

'No, Charlie, not here. They'll take you too,' said Mary. 'We won't let this happen. We need to get Woodward. You can't help me if you're in gaol.'

Chapter Nineteen

Inspector Forbes twiddled with his watch chain as he waited in a corridor outside the drawing-room door in Osborne House on the Isle of Wight. Two footmen stood guard. For the seventh time in as many minutes, he flipped open the silver cover of his timepiece. *Five past eight. Her Majesty will be going in for dinner.*

'I must see Her Majesty soon or I shall miss the last ferry back to Portsmouth.'

The footmen looked straight ahead, inscrutable. Not even a flicker of recognition that they heard his plea.

Another minute passed like an hour. The door opened. Out stepped a man in a major's scarlet dress uniform. 'Inspector Forbes? I'm Major Fortescue-d'Angelo. An audience at this hour is most unusual. Her Majesty seems to hold you in some esteem so she will see you now, but I must insist that you are brief. She is to dine with the prime minister and home secretary.'

The policeman marched in and bowed to Queen Victoria, sitting by a window, looking out on the last of the setting sun.

'I'm very pleased to see you again, Inspector. Now, what may I do for you that is so urgent?'

'Ma'am, you will remember an incident several years ago when a young orphan saved all our lives by flagging down the train before it was blown up.'

'Yes, indeed. I have my own sources of information and from those I understand that the girl in question is now facing execution for murder.'

'Yes, Ma'am. She's innocent. Of that I have no doubt.'

'I had my people make inquiries. I'm afraid the evidence is far too strong for me to intervene. For me to interfere in the justice system would create considerable problems. I am so sorry it has come to this. I owe the girl my life, but I owe a greater duty to the country.'

'I am not asking for a pardon, Ma'am. I understand that you cannot grant one in these circumstances. I am asking for your Royal

Prerogative of Mercy. I will prove her innocence eventually but first I have to stop the execution.'

'I believe the execution is scheduled for the day after tomorrow. Is that correct?'

'Yes, Ma'am.'

The Queen turned to the major. 'Please ask the prime minister and home secretary to join us.'

Forbes recognised both men immediately in their white ties and tails. The Earl of Derby came in first, closely followed by the Home Secretary Gathorne Hardy.

'Gentlemen,' said the Queen, 'you will recall I have already discussed with you the case of Victoria Sillitoe.'

Both men nodded.

'Inspector Forbes believes she is innocent.'

'Do you have any evidence of this?' said the Earl of Derby to Inspector Forbes.

'She is known to me. I have no doubt that she is innocent of the crime.'

Hardy intervened. 'Are you suggesting irregularities in the trial?'

'I'm suggesting, Sir, that there has been a miscarriage of justice. I'm sure prosecution witnesses lied.'

'Have you any evidence to uphold that claim,' said Hardy.

'Not yet, Sir, but I'm confident I shall find such evidence.'

'Ma'am,' said Hardy, 'as we discussed earlier, if the condemned has been through a lawful trial and convicted then unless there is evidence to refute that conviction it must stand and with it the judge's decision on the death penalty. We must not undermine the independent judiciary.'

'I know that, Mr Hardy. I am not considering a pardon. I am considering exercising my Royal Prerogative of Mercy.'

'My advice, Ma'am, in the light of the current political climate, with several Fenians awaiting execution, would be to let the law take its course. I am sorry, Ma'am, but sparing one convicted murderer and allowing others to die would not be tolerated by the public,' said Hardy.

'I concur, Ma'am,' said the Earl of Derby.

'I can assure you that the public in Hampshire are completely behind Miss Sillitoe. They would be very pleased if she were given mercy,' said Forbes.

'Indeed that may be so, Inspector. I understand she is a very popular young woman because of the good work she has done for so many people. But the people in London, in Yorkshire and in Dublin do not know her. They would not take kindly to someone in her elevated position being spared while others from more lowly positions were hanged,' said Hardy.

'Thank you, gentlemen. I need to think this over. The execution is in two days' time. Inspector, I will give you my decision in the morning.'

Major Fortescue-d'Angelo escorted Forbes from the room.

***

Victoria woke from her fitful sleep at seven. From her window in the small cell, she looked out across Winchester in contemplation of her death in twenty-four hours. How cruel to die for a crime she had not committed, but self-pity was not in her repertoire. In her mind, she resolved to go to her death with dignity.

The cell door opened. A cadaverous-looking man slithered in. 'I'm Perkins, the hangman, my dear.'

'Well, I cannot say I am pleased to meet you.'

'Now it's like this, my dear. For a little monetary consideration, I can use the long rope. Otherwise, it will be the short rope.'

'I have not the faintest idea what you are talking about. Go away and leave me alone. You shall have my complete attention tomorrow but in the meantime, please leave me alone.'

'My dear, if I use the long rope, when you fall through the trap you will fall ten feet. Your weight will snap your neck and you will die immediately.'

'I said go away.' She turned her back but her heart beat like an African drum and a sick feeling spread through her stomach.

Perkins continued with his pitch. 'But if I use the short rope, when the trap door opens you will fall only inches. Then you will strangle to death slowly. Your eyes will pop, your tongue will swell and you will gasp and gasp for breath, but none will come. It usually takes about three to four minutes to die this way. It's very painful, I can assure you.'

Victoria turned to face him. 'Mr Perkins, whether my death is to be quick or slow I have no intention of paying you anything. I have been taught to be polite and ladylike but I feel at this moment I must revert to my early years and say, fuck off.'

Her look convinced Perkins it would be wise to leave. As he went out, he said, 'It's the short rope for you, you murdering bitch.'

The door clanged shut. Victoria sat on her bunk and put her face in her hands. No tears came.

**

From a silver tray, Humphreys lifted bacon and eggs onto Richard's plate as he sat in the dining room wondering if his rescue plan stood any chance of success. He had to try. But was it fair to risk everyone else?

The Powells were going to kidnap Woodward and make him tell the truth. If he did not, and it was unlikely that he would, then the plan to spring Victoria at the scaffold was in place. It would involve a lot of people who loved Victoria creating a diversion while Constable Hemingway pulled her away and hid her in a cattle truck adapted by Mr Belchamber. Jake would be in charge of the cattle truck. She would be taken to the docks with Richard and put aboard a ship with the Powells to start a new life in Australia. That was the plan. Richard hoped it would work.

Humphreys answered Richard's silent thoughts. 'Sir Richard, all of us will do our part willingly. Do not worry about us. We know what we are doing and we will face the consequences.'

'I do not know how to thank you, Humphreys.'

'Save Miss Victoria and live a long and happy life in Australia. That's all the thanks I want or need, Sir. All any of us want.'

To Richard's surprise, Humphreys stepped forward and put his hand on his shoulder and squeezed. 'I have watched you grow up, Richard. You are a good man. Someday, you will return to Eagledown and take your rightful place with Victoria by your side. Until then, your mother, aunt and I will keep it running smoothly. Do not worry.'

'Well, she won't have any choice but to come with me. When we get there, I am not sure she will want to stay with me.'

'I think she will, Richard.'

Richard wondered why Humphreys, the butler, had called him 'Richard' rather than 'Sir'. He took no offence because the man was risking his liberty to help him, but it seemed strange. He had always felt an affinity with Humphreys, particularly in his younger years, but he had never before called him Richard. He decided it must be the pressure and strain of the impending escape attempt that for a moment had broken the barriers between master and servant.

***

Charlie and Mary Powell waited outside the chandler's store in Liverpool docks. Woodward sauntered out with a brass telescope under his arm.

'Ah, Captain Woodward, long time no see,' said Charlie.

'I'm sorry. Do I know you?'

'As I said, it's been a long time.'

'More than twenty years,' said Mary.

'What do you want? Who are you?'

'You sold us into slavery,' said Charlie.

'I've never sold anyone into slavery. Get out of my way.' Woodward tried to push past Charlie but stopped in his tracks when he felt the barrel of a pistol in his ribs.

'You sold us as indentured labourers in Australia. That's what you did, Captain Woodward. But now we're back,' said Mary.

'It's not my fault. If you're from the orphanage, it's not my fault. Blame Tweedale.'

'What do you mean, if we're from the orphanage? How many other places were you kidnapping children from?' said Charlie.

'Honest, I had nothing to do with it. Go see Tweedale.'

'He's dead,' said Mary.

'Oh.'

'You should know. You witnessed his murder,' said Charlie.

'No I didn't. I was in Portugal. I have witnesses. Clear off and leave me alone before I call the police.'

'I would like you to tell us what actually happened when Tweedale was killed,' said Mary.

'I told you, I was in Portugal.'

'You're beginning to try my patience,' said Mary, pulling her knife.

Woodward swallowed hard and stepped backwards but he was against a wall. 'What are you going to do?'

Mary waved the knife in his face.

'I've not yet decided. I may stab you and throw you in the dock. Maybe my husband will shoot you. On the other hand, we may take you to the police and tell them about you selling children down in Australia.'

'If you shoot me there are witnesses who will hear it and you'll hang. If you tell the police, they won't believe you. You have no evidence.'

'He's got a point,' said Charlie.

'You're right,' said Mary. 'It'll have to be the knife.'

'You're crazy. You wouldn't dare,' said Woodward through trembling lips.

'So I'll just castrate him then,' said Charlie, handing the revolver to Mary and taking her knife.

'Good idea,' said Mary. 'Over there, Woodward.' Mary pointed to an alley.

'I won't go with you.' Woodward's hands shook and his face broke out in a cold sweat.

Charlie stuck the knife point in Woodward's backside. He moved towards the alley.

In the dark alley Charlie said, 'Now, about Tweedale. What happened?'

'That girl, Victoria Sillitoe, shot him.'

'All right, I've had enough. Castrate him,' said Mary, grabbing hold of his pants and yanking them down. She saw a wound in his thigh. It had partly healed but her knowledge of such injuries told her it was about six weeks since it was inflicted. 'And there's evidence that she stabbed you, as she claimed.'

'Wait, wait. All right. All right. Lord de Mornay shot Tweedale.' Woodward pulled up his pants.

'And you saw that?' said Charlie.

'Yes.'

'You're coming with us to Winchester to tell the judge and the police. We don't have much time. We have to get there before tomorrow morning,' said Charlie.

'Can we get back in time?' asked Mary.

'Yes, I've checked the train times. But we must leave now.'

'And don't think of changing your mind, Woodward. We have other people involved and if you don't tell the truth when we get there and try to get us arrested you'll meet a painful death from our friends. Is that understood?' said Mary.

***

Tucker, Mills, Jonesy and Tommy sat on a wall outside the prison, careful not to get their white militia breeches dirty.

They stood to attention when Captain Harry Ratcliffe in his smart officer's uniform strode across the road towards the prison with Lord de Mornay and Judge Phillips.

Ratcliffe returned the militiamen's salute, sticking out his puny chest in pride at his elevated status.

'So what's up?' said Tommy as the delegation went through the prison gates.

'Dunno any more than you. Captain Ratcliffe said for us to meet him here at ten for a job. Expect it's to escort someone,' said Mills.

'Who's doin' the escort tomorrow for Miss Victoria? Hope I'm not called in. Poor lass,' said Jonesy.

'Aye you're right there,' said Tucker.

'Damned shame if you ask me,' said Tommy. 'She helped my missus by paying for the medicine for our little Alice when she were took ill and then showed her how to look after the child, at risk of catching something herself.'

'Well, let's hope none of us are on that escort. I couldn't see the lass hang. I would have to do something,' said Tucker. 'She got me leave to go up country to see my dad when he were dying. Made such a fuss with the adjutant he had to let me go.'

'Aye, the lass is an angel and no mistake,' said Mills.

'No point in talkin' about it. We can't do nuthin', said Jonesy. 'But I'm damned if I'll see her hang without trying something, even it gets me flogged.'

Constable Hemingway dashed out of the prison and ran down the hill to the laughter of the militiamen as they watched his ample form disappear.

The prison clocked chimed eleven. Still the militiamen waited. Constable Hemingway made his way back up the hill, slowly and puffing.

'What's going on, Constable?' said Tommy as the overweight policeman came past on his way back into the prison.

'They're going to hang Miss Victoria today.'

The militiamen looked at each other in shock.

'There'll be a crowd and trouble at the scaffold. It's market day and the town is full of people,' said Jonesy. 'I'm not sure I'm willing to intervene if the mob tries to free her.'

'No, they're taking her to Gallows Hill and using that one. There won't be any crowd there. They're going to take her out quietly,' said the constable.

'That's why we're here then?' said Tucker.

'That's right,' said the constable and headed for the prison gates.

***

Richard trotted Solomon along the Winchester road deep in thought. He would tell Victoria about the rescue to give her hope and strength to face the coming ordeal tomorrow. He wondered about the ring he still kept in his pocket: the one made from gold and a diamond given to him by the Xhosa warrior. *Should I give it to her? Will she accept it?*

Thundering towards him on a horse he saw young Jamie Hardcastle. He was about to fly past Richard when he suddenly pulled up his horse.

'Sir Richard! Sir Richard! Constable Hemingway sent me to tell you. They've brought the hanging forward. It's going to be at Gallows Hill and they'll be on their way now.'

The shock went through Richard fast as a lightning strike. 'Ride to Eagledown, find Humphreys and tell him what you have told me.' The plan was in tatters. Even if Humphreys could gather the team together, by the time they reached Gallows Hill it would be too late. But he must give them a chance just in case, by some miracle, they made it.

Richard looked out across the Downs. He could see Gallows Hill in the distance. It would take him half an hour to get there at full gallop. With a kick in the side, Solomon took off. They jumped ditches and fences, and raced across open ground with Richard holding on tight.

***

With one militiaman in each corner on top, a carriage pulled by four horses rumbled along a country lane towards Gallows Hill. Inside, Victoria sat calmly with Reverend Beckett. Her hands pinioned behind her back made it difficult to keep her balance with every jolt and bump. Captain Ratcliffe followed on his horse. Behind him, another carriage carried Judge Phillips, Lord de Mornay, two magistrates and the prison governor. Perkins sat on top next to the driver.

Victoria looked out of the window. She could see Gallows Hill coming closer. They would be there within ten minutes.

Her heart beat fast and her hands felt clammy, but she would not let anyone see her fear. *This is my final journey and I shall go to the scaffold with my head held high, not bowed or subdued.* She prayed silently for the strength to carry her through her coming ordeal.

As her life was about to end, Victoria thought of what might have been. *I was too proud and judgemental about Richard. Now I realise he did what he did with Rawnie to free Peggy so she could marry and so he could marry me. I was too selfish and stupid to realise that and let jealousy rule me. It is too late now for me to tell him that I love him. I have nothing to forgive. He did what he did with Rawnie and I have no right to judge him. How could I have been so shallow and selfish?*

***

Inspector Forbes paced up and down the corridor outside the drawing room of Osborne House. Another look at his timepiece told him it was ten o'clock. The door opened and out stepped Major Fortescue-d'Angelo.

'Inspector, Her Majesty will see you now.'

Forbes stepped into the drawing room and bowed to the Queen.

She sat looking out on the fine, cold morning. 'Inspector, I have given your request a considerable amount of thought. The home secretary advises me that I should not grant the Royal Prerogative of Mercy in this case. The victim, in his sick bed, was shot four times and stabbed. There can be no suggestion that it was anything other than cold-blooded murder. She admits she had the murder weapon in her handbag and it was her knife.'

Inspector Forbes' heart sank. The Queen was his only hope to give him time to prove Victoria's innocence.

'Why are you so convinced of her innocence?' said Her Majesty.

'I know Victoria Sillitoe, Ma'am. I believe she is incapable of murder.'

'You are asking me to risk serious repercussions by granting the stay of execution just because you do not think she is guilty, in spite of all the evidence to the contrary?'

'Yes, Ma'am.'

'Inspector, do you not think you ask too much of me?'

'Ma'am, she saved your life and mine.'

'Indeed she did, Inspector. But I may not grant mercy because of that. It would be misinterpreted by my opponents and they are not a few in number.'

'Ma'am . . .'

'Enough, Inspector. I have made my decision.' She rang a small bell on her desk. The major stepped back into the room. 'Summon my secretary.'

The detective felt sick in his stomach. He had failed to convince Her Majesty. Victoria Sillitoe would hang for a crime he knew she had not committed. Now the Queen was moving on to other business without even dismissing him from her presence. He bowed and turned to leave.

'Where are you going?'

'Ma'am, I'm sorry. I thought my audience had come to an end.'

A wiry little fellow in round spectacles and a frock coat entered the room from a side door.

'Mr Cattermole, please make out a warrant for a Royal Prerogative of Mercy for one Miss Victoria Sillitoe. Substitute "life imprisonment" for the death penalty. Inspector, this may cause some problems. I am relying on you to prove the girl's innocence.'

Inspector Forbes felt like kissing the Queen but decided that would be most unwise. She definitely would not be amused.

I can get to the prison by this afternoon and have the execution for tomorrow cancelled

***

Charlie looked at his fob watch while Mary prodded Woodward along on the way to the railway station.

'We will be back this evening. The execution will be cancelled when Woodward tells his story,' said Charlie.

***

The coach with its cargo of sorrow arrived at Gallows Hill. A north-westerly cut across the hills, swaying the tall grass and bending the few trees on that exposed hill. Saturday's condemned man still hung in a metal cage from the gibbet. The crows had taken his eyes.

Harry Ratcliffe ordered his men to take down the body and put it back up there alongside the body of Victoria after the execution.

The Reverend Beckett mumbled away.

It seemed like a dream but Victoria knew it was for real. A shudder went through her whole body when she looked at the half-eaten face of the hanged man. *Will I soon look like that too?* Constable Hemingway stood by her side.

'Constable, I have a favour to ask,' she said.

'I will do anything I can for you, Miss.'

'Please go to Richard and tell him that I love him. I understand now that he did what he did for the sake of others, not for himself. Tell him I am sorry for being such a foolish, jealous woman.'

'I know that Sir Richard loves you too. He loves you very much. Since the verdict and sentence he's been struggling to find a way to save you. We were all in on a plan to rescue you, but they've thwarted it by bringing the execution forward and changing the location. I hope this is of some comfort now for you to know that so many people wanted to help. You are loved by many people, Victoria, so many.'

'Thank you.'

Perkins checked the gallows. A smile crossed his unpleasant face as he found the equipment in good working order. He made a point of selecting the shortest rope from his collection on the roof of the coach.

Judge Phillips climbed out of his coach. He avoided eye contact with her as he stood looking out across the view.

Lord de Mornay did not avoid eye contact with her. He was gloating.

The prison governor tried to make small talk with the two magistrates. He, too, was avoiding eye contact with her.

'Ready,' Perkins shouted from the scaffold.

Ratcliffe stepped forward and took Victoria by the elbow. Her hands were still manacled behind her.

The constable dithered. He was outnumbered. He took the other elbow and, with Ratcliffe, escorted Victoria to the scaffold.

The Reverend intoned his prayers.

Perkins approached with a hood to put over Victoria's head.

She shook it away. 'I'll die looking at the sky.'

Perkins slipped the noose over Victoria's head and settled it around her delicate neck. 'Short rope,' he hissed in her ear.

Victoria took a deep breath, wondering if that would be her last. So far she had managed to keep her dignity and stay resolute, but the tension had begun to erode her resolve. The fear spread up from her stomach to her chest. Her legs felt wobbly. She hoped and prayed that she could stand up until the trapdoor opened and she fell to her death. Victoria lifted up her eyes to the sky for one last look.

Constable Hemingway kept hold of her arm.

Lord de Mornay climbed up onto the scaffold, his face contorted in what passed for a smile of triumph. 'It only came to me the other day. I knew I had seen you somewhere before when I returned from Africa and saw you at Eagledown. It took me a long time to realise that you are the guttersnipe who stabbed me in the leg in Southampton. Well, I have to say that today is going to be very pleasurable. I shall see you die slowly, and Richard will come and see you hanging there with your eyes eaten by the crows. I always win in the end.'

Victoria looked away. She had no fight left in her. All she wanted now was for it to be over as quickly as possible.

Judge Phillips said, 'Proceed.'

Perkins took hold of the lever that dropped the trapdoor to send Victoria to the afterlife. 'You had your chance. It could have been the long rope. Goodbye!'

Constable Hemingway said a silent prayer while keeping hold of her arm.

'Tell the constable to let her go,' said Perkins. 'I don't want him interfering.'

'Let go of her,' ordered the judge.

Hemingway stroked Victoria's arm and then let go. 'I'm so sorry, Victoria.'

'You will tell Richard that I love him, please.'

'I promise.'

Perkins pulled the lever. The trapdoor fell open. Victoria dropped only three inches. The noose tightened around her neck. She gasped for breath, but none would come. Her feet kicked the air but found no support.

***

In desperation, the constable grabbed the hanging body of Victoria and held her up, taking the weight off the rope. He had no idea what to do next. 'I don't care if they shoot me, I'll not stand by while they murder you.'

'What the hell?' Ratcliffe strode forward and then checked his step at the sight of the large constable.

He shouted down to his four men to take the constable prisoner.

In the distance, a rider on a black horse galloped towards the gallows. 'Oh shit,' said Ratcliffe.

'Do something, you blithering idiot,' said Lord de Mornay to the terrified militia officer.

'Shoot the rider,' said Ratcliffe.

All four militiamen kneeled and pointed their rifles at the oncoming rider.

Lord de Mornay made an attempt to pull Victoria from the grasp of the constable but got a kick in his bad leg from the sweating policeman.

Bang. Bang. Bang. Bang.

The first bullet scared a crow fifty feet above Richard's head. The other three missed by even more.

Ratcliffe jumped off the scaffold and grabbed a rifle from the nearest man. He pointed it at the oncoming horse. Jonesy barged into his back, causing him to lose his aim. He recovered, with Richard now only about twenty yards away. For all his faults and cowardice, Ratcliffe was still an excellent shot and could not miss at that range. And he would not have. But the hammer of the weapon came down on the spent cartridge from the previous shot. 'Shit.'

The judge and magistrates backed away.

Perkins hid under the scaffold.

Lord de Mornay grabbed Ratcliffe's sword from where he had discarded it in favour of the rifle. He ran it into the constable's chest. A bayonet stabbed de Mornay in the leg. He went down screaming in pain.

Constable Hemingway's strength oozed from his body with his blood. He could not hold Victoria up much longer. He summoned up his last ounce of strength to keep her from choking. He could not release the noose as he needed two hands to hold her up.

Richard jumped from his horse.

Ratcliffe backed away.

The militiamens' smiles told Richard he need not fear them. He climbed the scaffold.

'Thank God,' said Hemingway, now staggering under the weight and loss of blood.

Richard pulled the rope from Victoria's neck.

Constable Hemingway collapsed. She bent down to help him though she was still coughing and gasping for breath. Richard stood over them.

Jonesy stepped up to the scaffold, put his hands up to show he meant no harm and bent down next to the injured policeman. The other three militiamen formed a guard on the scaffold.

Jonesy said, 'Get her out of here, Guv'nor. We'll take care of the copper.'

Victoria kissed the constable on the forehead. 'Thank you,' she said.

'Get away, Miss. Get away,' said Constable Hemingway. 'But before you go, Sir Richard, I gave Victoria a promise that I would tell you that she loves you. I have kept my promise.' The constable's eyes closed and his breathing became shallow. Victoria stroked his cheek.

'Please, Miss. Get the hell out of here before it's too late. We'll care for the constable,' said Jonesy.

'Thank you. Thank you all,' said Victoria.

Ratcliffe had managed to put a good fifty yards between himself and the scaffold. 'You'll all pay for this,' he shouted.

***

Richard carried Victoria to Solomon, lifted her onto the horse's back, climbed up behind her and, with a wave of thanks to the militia, cantered away.

Richard's plan had gone disastrously wrong. He could not go to Eagledown as that would be the first place searched. The rendezvous point would not be ready to conceal them in the waggon. They would have to travel on Solomon. A hue and cry would be raised. They had no chance of getting through to the ship before the alert was given.

Then Richard remembered his childhood hiding place in Midge Dell. Not even Penelope or Peggy knew of it. Only he and Algernon had ever been there and they kept it secret from the girls because . . . Well, they did not know why. They just wanted a secret hideout to annoy the girls.

There would be no need to travel on any roads or public paths. He could get from Gallows Hill to the hideaway by crossing Starling Wood and on past Blackstone Lake.

It took half an hour of careful riding to negotiate the route. Richard felt his heart beat so loudly he was sure Victoria could hear it. He found the cave in Midge Dell with difficulty. Years had passed since last he had been there and nature had contrived to keep its secret by growing all over the entrance.

He helped Victoria from the horse, slipped off his riding jacket and put it around her bare shoulders. 'We'll be safe here until I work out what to do,' said Richard. He tethered Solomon to a fallen oak branch.

'Richard, you have thrown everything you have away for me. You are a fugitive now like me. If we are caught, they may hang you too.'

'Then we had best not get caught. I had a plan, but it all went wrong when they brought the execution forward. Do not worry. We have many friends.'

Richard pulled branches and twigs from the cave entrance and led Victoria inside. He helped her keep her balance over rocks as her hands were still manacled behind her. The cave seemed smaller to him than he remembered. It went back into the hillside for about twenty feet but was only five feet high, so even Victoria had to duck.

In the light that filtered in from the entrance, Richard could see signs of the cave's previous occupation by him and Algernon when they were small boys. A wooden sword stood on one side and a hearth of stones still held burnt wood. A hammer and chisel lay, rusted, next to a boulder carved with the initials 'RDM' and 'AC', together with the year '1852'.

'You must have been ten,' said Victoria looking at the year. 'AC?'

'Algernon Crabtree.'

He sat her on a boulder so she could lean against the cave wall while he examined the hammer and chisel. Though rusty on the outside, he smiled when he found they were still serviceable.

'Can you slip your hands around to the front?'

'I do not know.' She struggled and managed to get her manacled hands over her feet. 'You will cut my hands off.'

She was staring at the hammer and chisel.

'Do not worry. I won't hurt you. Put your hands each side of this rock.'

Victoria took a deep breath and did as requested. It took Richard six blows to separate a chain link and free her hands, though he could not take the bracelets off for fear of injuring her.

For a long time, they just sat in the cave looking out, not saying anything, lost in their own thoughts. Eventually, Richard said, 'We are going to have to stay here for a few days until I work out a plan.'

'I am so sorry I have ruined your life by getting you involved in my troubles,' said Victoria.

'I would not have it any other way. And it is you who has been caught up in my troubles.'

'I have not treated you well. I am sorry for that. We all have our weaknesses and I have more than most. The way you treated Peggy, leaving her and your child to go off to Africa, and then taking up with that woman at the inn . . . You must have had your reasons. It is not right that I judged you. I have no right to judge you. I was jealous. I am sorry.'

'Victoria . . .'

She put her finger to his lips. 'You have saved my life and as a result ruined your own. You have nothing to explain. And I want to say—and this is not because you have saved my life—I want to say that I love you, Richard. If this is too forward, I do not care. Our chances of coming through this alive are poor. I know that. I have loved you since I first saw you. I do not want to die without your knowing.'

Love and tears welled up within him at the same time. He took her hand in his and kissed her lips.

They stayed locked in an embrace for a long time before they, by some strange communion, separated and looked into each other's eyes.

'We will make it through. I promise,' said Richard. He believed it, but he had no idea how he would achieve it.

***

Inspector Forbes arrived at the prison late that afternoon, armed with the Prerogative of Mercy from Queen Victoria. He checked his fob watch. Ten past four. He had made good time.

A flap in the heavy door slid open. 'Yes?' said the door warden, looking the policeman up and down.

'I have an important document for the prison governor. It's a stay of execution signed by Her Majesty for Victoria Sillitoe.'

'Too late.'

Forbes' heart sank. 'What do you mean, too late? The execution is not until tomorrow.'

'They brought it forward to this morning. Took her to Gallows Hill to avoid trouble. You're too late.' He slid the flap shut, leaving the inspector standing in front of the door, feeling dizzy and sick.

He watched, in a daze, as a coach came along the Romsey road towards the prison. It pulled into the courtyard and stopped by the gates. The inspector watched the prison governor and Lord de Mornay climb out. De Mornay leant heavily on a stick with a bandage around his lower leg where the breeches had been cut away.

With leaden feet, he walked over to the coach. 'Governor, I've come from Her Majesty. I have a Prerogative of Mercy signed by her for Victoria Sillitoe. I've just been informed that I'm too late. I demand that I receive her body for burial. She is not to be left on the gibbet. Have you left her there?'

De Mornay scowled at the inspector and limped over to sit on a small wall.

The prison governor looked at the policeman and shook his head. 'That will not be possible. You cannot have the body.'

'It damned well will be possible. I will ask you only once again before I make such a fuss with Her Majesty that you will end up a warder on some God-forsaken fever island. Where is her body?'

The governor sighed. 'She escaped.'

Forbes could not stop his grin spreading from ear to ear. He strode off to Winchester police station to make his inquiries.

There he found the superintendent in a state of frenzy, organising search parties of soldiers, militia and police. The senior officer informed Inspector Forbes that he had no intention of calling off the search. The condemned may have had her sentence commuted, but she was still a murderer and to be held for life imprisonment with hard labour.

In the cells, Forbes found the four militiamen, unrepentant even though they faced a flogging at best and gaol at worst. They gave him an honest account of the events and told him Constable Hemingway was in the hospital with a life-threatening wound after his courageous stand.

The inspector strode over to the hospital and found Hemingway unattended and unconscious in a general ward. He called Matron out of her quarters and demanded that Hemingway receive the very best treatment and a private room. By the time he left, Matron's moustache was twitching alarmingly, but she made sure she followed the inspector's instructions. He was clearly on a mission and looked as though he would brook no argument from anybody, not even someone as fierce as Matron.

Then he went back to the police station to see how he was going to either prove Victoria's innocence or help her stay free.

He was studying statements by oil lamp when Charlie and Mary arrived at eight o'clock that evening with Woodward.

Forbes briefed the two on the events of that morning, while the station sergeant locked Woodward up in a cell next to the four militiamen.

Charlie and Mary set off in the dark for Eagledown.

Forbes dragged Woodward out of his cell and into an interview room.

'I've been kidnapped. I'm not saying anything. I want a lawyer,' said Woodward.

'I know you lied about Miss Sillitoe shooting Tweedale and I can prove it. And you admitted your guilt to the people who brought you here.'

'They threatened to kill me. I only said that to save my life. I had nothing to do with Tweedale's death. I was in Portugal.'

Forbes hoped his bluffing was not too obvious. 'You will hang for his murder if you do not tell the truth. Now stop lying and do something to save yourself.'

'How do I know that you'll keep your word and not get me hanged anyway?'

'You'll hang for sure if you don't turn Queen's evidence. Now come on.'

'I'm saying nothing, so bugger off.'

Forbes steepled his hands and looked at Woodward. If he could not make Woodward talk, he would never prove Victoria's innocence. Something inside him snapped. He grabbed Woodward and propelled him against the white, stone wall so hard it knocked the breath from the prisoner.

He raised his fist with such anger in his soul that Woodward nearly wet himself.

'All right. All right. Queen's evidence you said. I'll tell you.'

The red mist settled in Forbes' eyes and he calmed down. He dropped Woodward back into his chair.

'It was as she said at the trial. But I didn't kill Tweedale. It was de Mornay. I didn't know he was going to kill him. I swear it. We knew Tweedale was going to rat on de Mornay, but I thought the plan was to scare him and the woman. Only scare them so he didn't rat.'

'So the landlord, Allington, was lying. He did see you come down the stairs.'

'Yeah.'

'And the six men who gave you an alibi were lying?'

'Yeah.'

'How did you know that Miss Sillitoe was going to be at the Bear and Ragged Staff?'

'Tweedale gave a boy a letter to deliver to her. De Mornay got hold of it and read it. He decided to get rid of Tweedale before he could implicate him in the murders and at the same time get his revenge on his son by having Miss Victoria hanged for the murder. He knew his son was in love with her.

Forbes wrote a statement and Woodward signed it. With Woodward back in his cell after the confession, Forbes had the militia released.

He climbed into a pony and trap and set off for the Bear and Ragged Staff. Allington jumped in fright when the heavy oak door burst open and in stormed Inspector Forbes. The customers parted as if they were the Red Sea and Forbes was Moses. He took hold of Allington by the throat and dragged him to the pony and trap. A fist in Allington's stomach persuaded him to get aboard. Soon Forbes had Allington back at the police station.

It took less than three minutes to get the confession from the landlord.

By the time the inspector had finished with the paperwork, it was past midnight. The superintendent called off the search for the fugitives for the night and cancelled it when Forbes gave him the result of his inquiries.

***

Outside the cave, the sounds of the night disturbed the silence. An owl hooted. Somewhere a vixen called like a woman in distress. Far away a hound howled at the full moon.

Richard reached into his pocket and pulled out the leather box he had kept since collecting it from the jeweller's shop in Winchester.

'It may be too late but I had this made from a diamond and gold given to me by a Xhosa warrior. You know what it means. Whether we survive or not, I would very much like to know your answer.'

'The answer is yes, Richard. It is something I have dreamed of for so long.'

He slipped the ring on her finger.

Victoria snuggled up close to Richard's warm body. His arms engulfed her. She took his hand and held it to her breast. Their lips touched and then a long gentle kiss followed. She leant back to look at his face in the faint light. 'This is not how I imagined it would be for us the first time. Not here in a cave, fugitives. But I do not want to die before sharing our love.'

He unbuttoned her dress.

***

The next morning a mist lay across the fields as Inspector Forbes cantered his rented horse towards Eagledown House in the distance. There was a smile on his face. Throwing Lord de Mornay into a cell earlier had made his day. He arrived with mud spatters on his thick, leather coat and boots, tied his horse up to a rail outside the stables and marched to the servants' entrance. The door swung open before he got there.

'Thank God she's safe,' said Humphreys, standing in the doorway with Charlie and Mary behind him.

'She's in the clear. I have all the evidence needed for her release. Now we just have to find them. Have you any idea where they may be?'

They all shook their heads.

Bonnie strode out of the stables. 'Inspector, thank you for all you have done.'

'Have you any idea where they may be or who may know?' said Forbes.

'No. Wait . . . Algernon. He and Richard were great friends when they were young. He may know a hiding place. If they do not know they are no longer wanted by the police, then they may be hiding, waiting to get in touch so they can escape to Australia as planned.'

'That would be Algernon Crabtree?' said Forbes.

'Yes. I will come with you,' said Bonnie.

'Me too,' said Humphreys.

'And us,' said Mary.

Penelope dashed out of the house. 'Don't leave me behind.'

Lady Adele rushed out to join the posse.

They piled into a carriage and took off towards Peggy's farm. There they found Peggy and Luke.

'I heard. Fantastic news,' said Peggy.

'Is Algernon around?' said Bonnie.

'He's in the stables,' said Luke, just as Algernon stepped out of the stables carrying a saddle and pulling his horse behind him.

'Algernon, we need to find Richard and Victoria. They may be hiding somewhere. Do you have any idea where he would go to lie low for a few days?' asked Bonnie.

'I'm very happy that they're not going to hang Victoria. I like her. But why should I do anything to help Richard after what he did to Peggy?'

'Please, Algernon. Do it for me,' said Penelope, stepping forward.

'Inspector, can you guarantee that Lord de Mornay will not be released?' said Peggy.

'He's going to hang. There's more than enough evidence. He will not be getting out even with his connections. They wouldn't dare with Her Majesty involved in making sure justice is done.'

'Then, Algernon, I'll tell you why you should help Richard.' Peggy took Algernon by the hand and led him to the stable.

A few moments later Algernon dashed out of the stables, threw his saddle on his horse and shouted, 'Follow me. I have an idea. Penelope, you come with me.'

Penelope hitched up her skirts and climbed upon Algernon's horse to sit astride. He jumped up behind and put his arms around her as she leant back into him.

Lady Adele smiled.

The search party careered along a path through the woods and past the gypsy encampment. Rawnie stood by a campfire and called out, 'What's happening?'

The inspector called back. 'We're off to find Victoria and Richard. She's been cleared and is free.'

Rawnie leapt on the back of her horse, bareback, and joined the charge through the woods.

Off they went at a gallop, Algernon and Penelope out in front on his horse, the inspector galloping close behind, then the carriage careering along, followed by Rawnie, getting the best out of her nag until they all arrived at a hill that the carriage could not climb. Algernon jumped from his horse, handed the reins to Penelope and rushed up the hill. The others struggled up after him.

***

Inside the cave, Richard and Victoria lay on his shirt and breeches with her dress and his coat over the top of them. Richard heard the voices first. He looked around the cave for a weapon, but only the wooden sword and the rusty chisel could be used for defence.

'I am so sorry,' said Richard.

'If I am to die then at least I die having known you, Richard. Last night was the most beautiful night in my whole life.'

They hurriedly dressed.

'Richard, Richard, come out.'

Richard recognised the voice. His old friend had betrayed him. There could be no escape. He took Victoria by the hand, kissed her and they walked to the cave entrance to meet their fate.

Early morning sunshine for a moment blinded him. He looked out and could see several figures, but not who they were.

As his eyes grew accustomed to the light, he saw Algernon and Inspector Forbes. He could hear others struggling up the hill.

Algernon stepped forward and stuck out his hand. Richard looked in bewilderment.

'Peggy told me what happened. You married her to save her reputation when your father drugged her and . . . and . . . made her pregnant. And you did it because you knew I would have killed him and hanged for it had I known what he did.'

The two men threw their arms around each other.

'And Victoria is in the clear. Your father is locked up for murder and I have all the evidence needed to hang him,' said the inspector.

At that moment, Lady Adele and Humphreys reached the cave.

'Actually, Richard, Lord de Mornay is not your father,' said Adele. She linked Humphreys' arm. 'He is. And when Lord de Mornay has hanged we will marry. We should have done so many years ago, but circumstances prevailed against us.'

Richard's jaw dropped. Victoria stood behind and smiled, until Rawnie pushed through.

'Shut your ears, copper. I don't want to be done for perjury. Miss ... Victoria, is it not? I just thought I had to come along to warn you about Richard. He's a grade one pain in the arse. Useless. He hires me to go to bed with him so his missus can divorce him. There am I, all ready, willing and waiting and what does the clown do? Nothing. He gets out of bed and leaves me there. Anyhow he paid me, so I lied to the court after making him swear that he wouldn't tell anyone I lied. So if you're looking for some action between the sheets don't bother with him.'

Richard and Rawnie's eyes met. Rawnie turned and climbed back down the hill with a grin on her face, and her ticket to America in her pocket.

Victoria called out after her. 'Thank you, Rawnie. Good luck!'

The End

If you enjoyed Honourable Lies you may like Fran Connor's novel, 'Someone to Watch Over Me'. Please see the first chapter below. It is available from Amazon.

Chapter One

Madrid June 1936

Damn this rain; it's going down my neck. It's the last thing I need tonight. If I had a car, I wouldn't be arriving like a drowned rat. If this useless government knew how to govern, we wouldn't have a taxi strike. If… if… if… Stop bloody moaning; be grateful even if you are sopping wet.

I wish I were back in Andalusia; it hardly ever rains there. It hardly ever rains here in the summer either. Just my bloody luck.

Can I do it? Dare I do it?

Through the puddles I slosh.

It's been a long, dry summer so far. Though I could do without the rain tonight, it is at least laying the dust. I can smell the freshness in the air. I don't know if it's the thunder and lightning or my anticipation, but I feel an electric charge in the atmosphere. I'm so excited, and I'm no schoolgirl.

Will Pablo be there or is he going to chicken out?

The delicious smell of meat roasting over charcoal wafts out of Felipe's Restaurant. That's what I love here. There's so much to enjoy just walking through the streets and picking up the scents and the buzz of the city. Well, when it isn't raining so damned hard. Inside the restaurant, I see diners at candlelit tables lingering over their dinner and each other. I don't think I could eat tonight; I'm too excited.

This is it. A black door heavily studded with square iron pegs around a metal grille. It could have guarded El Cid's castle; instead it stands as the gateway to what I hope will be a triumph and not a nightmare.

Bang, bang, bang. Don't exaggerate. It's more of a slight thud, thud, thud as my soft kid-glove demands entry.

A metal flap scrapes open behind the grille and a pair of dark eyes, stark against their whites, peer out. "Yes?"

"Alicia Carter for the Lindy Hop."

A jangle of keys, the clank of a massive lock turning and the ancient door creaks open. A blast of warm air escapes into the sodden and deserted street.

The owner of the eyes is Sebastian. Well, that's what it says on his name badge stuck to the lapel of his white tuxedo. The big African looks the perfect person to keep out unwanted visitors with his arms as thick as my bronzed thighs. My bronzed thighs! Soon everyone will see them. It gives me a funny feeling inside.

He smiles with a grin that lights up the dingy entrance hall and points to a well- worn flight of stone steps leading down to a corridor vaulted in red brick. It all looks so wicked and degenerate. I hear the rhythm of a drumbeat, a trumpet, a sax and, in the background, a piano. My heart quickens and my steps too, leaving a trail of water on the bare stone floor.

At the end of the corridor I find the ladies' cloakroom and push open the peeling painted door. A heavy smell hangs in the air, a mixture of the entire range of cheap perfume available in the city, the less pleasant odour of sweat and a rank toilet. A row of dressing tables with light bulbs around the mirrors stands against the far wall; several bulbs have blown, making the arches they form resemble mouths in need of dental attention. I hate dentists. There are no windows. A half-opened door reveals a cracked toilet bowl, the source of one of the smells. Even though it is disgusting the excitement means I'll have to use it. A row of coat hangers holds various outdoor clothes with boots, galoshes and wellingtons lined up below. Beside the coat hangers, against an algae infested yellow wall, lies a bank of once well-varnished lockers, some closed without protruding keys and some open with the keys still in the locks.

I'm alone in here. Quickly I throw off the mac, galoshes and sou'wester. Mama insisted I took the sou'wester with me to Madrid for the rain. She even embroidered my name on it so it wouldn't get lost. I slip off my calf-length, pale-blue dress that's more suitable for afternoon tea at the Ritz in London than this place. I know that. I spent a weekend at the Ritz, but not with a lover; with my Mama and Papa. It would be heaven to go back there with a lover. I will someday.

I catch a reflection of myself in the mirror. Am I vain to think how good I look in my white silk underwear that contrasts so with my tanned body? I may be half English, but I don't want to be a pale English rose. I want to be Carmen! Sure as hell I don't want to end up like her though; murdered by a man she spurned. It would have made a better story had she killed him. Why is the woman always the victim? I'll never be one. At least, I'll do everything I can to make sure that fate does not befall me.

There's something erotic about my black stockings. How many men have seen me in this state of undress? Not many. The two I dined with at Felipe's and, to be honest, just two more. I will have more men. I'm not ready to settle down and be the little woman at home waiting for my man. But I shall choose when and with whom I go to bed. I'm a modern woman. Why shouldn't I be the one to choose?

I pull the stockings carefully off each shaved leg and replace them with white ankle socks. I may not wish to be an English rose, but I certainly don't want to be hairy like some of the girls at the university. Then I wriggle into the pleated short, white skirt and pull on the white blouse. A quick brush of the hair and: ready!

I hang the dress neatly. I slide my shoulder bag into one of the lockers. My .32 Smith and Wesson revolver lies snug in its pocket inside the bag alongside a torch. A strange present from Papa, a gun; he worries about me being in Madrid. He knows I would use it only in self-defence.

I look around for where to put the locker key and decide to hide it inside my galoshes.

It's time. I step out of the ladies' changing room into the corridor and follow it for about ten yards where it opens out into a vast cavern of a cellar. It's the size of a crypt in a cathedral. This is about as wicked and degenerate as it gets in Madrid outside of the bordellos.

A different fug, tobacco and something sweet, fills the air here; it's packed tight with bodies of every shape, colour and sex although the gender of some is not immediately evident.

On the far side I see the raised stage and a band of tuxedo-clad black men, with a white man sitting at a piano. A foot-stomping tune vibrates around the walls. There isn't enough room to Lindy Hop, but that doesn't stop the dancers from trying.

Where's Pablo? I can't see him.

I find a chair by an alcove in the red brick wall and step up to see across the dance floor. There he is!

I step down.

"Hey, be careful," says a woman's voice.

Damn! I've stepped on a woman's foot protruding from the alcove. Oh no! I see a man on top of her pumping away with his bare backside on public view without concern for anyone who may be watching.

Well really! "Sorry!"

Someone takes hold of my arm, just above the right elbow. I turn quickly, ready to slap if needed. No need. It's Jose. He smiles, showing his crooked front teeth in a pinched face with a thin moustache under a hooked nose. His white suit is in need of cleaning and pressing. I don't dislike him though he doesn't attract me either. He is one who will never share my bed. Poor Jose, he's so short for a man. I don't like being taller than my escort.

"Dance?" he says.

"Thank you no, Jose, I'm busy."

"Maybe later?"

"Maybe." Not likely.

At least he's not as unpleasant as his father, the police chief back in our hometown of Jerez de la Frontera. Colonel Lopez has a grudge against Papa. Papa thinks it's because he's English and maybe because he could afford to send me to an expensive school in England. He also sent me to finishing school in Switzerland and now Madrid University, all paid for honestly through his sherry business. Colonel Lopez makes his money from bribes and extortion to pay for Jose's education and his own peccadillos.

I gently take my arm from Jose and zigzag through the dance crowd to where I saw Pablo. He leans on the red brick wall, a languorous stance that belies his high-octane dance prowess. And there's his lover Gregor, a huge Russian with a beard Rasputin would have coveted, standing by his side smoking a cheroot.

"Pablo, are you ready?" I shout, just as the thunderous tune belting out stops and the band, except for the piano player, traipse off.

Pablo looks at his white pants and sleeveless shirt, backhands his curly black hair, slicked with Brylcreem, and says, "You don't think I usually dress like this, darling!"

Gregor lets out a guffaw that makes a woman in front of him jump in fright.

"Darling, you look divine," says Pablo.

"When are we on?"

"They said they'd start at about ten o'clock, so we have ten minutes. Let's get a drink."

"Da," says Gregor.

"We'd best go light on the booze with the dance coming up," I say.

Pablo shrugs.

We skirt the stage to the bar on the far right and leave it to Gregor to force his way to the front and come back with three large vodkas.

Three other couples prepare nearby, dressed like Pablo and me. The competition looks fierce as I try to check them out without being obvious.

My gaze turns to the piano player: a slim man, probably in his early thirties in a white tuxedo and black dress trousers with a silk stripe down the sides. His hair is neat, well cut, black with a slight greying at the temples and natural, not slicked with pomade. I like the look of him. What's that tune he's playing? I don't know it. It's soft and gentle. The crowd dance to the music while locked in their lovers' arms.

I look at the vast array of love on display. It's my final year at university; in fact it's my last night. With all the work I had to do I've been celibate for the last year, but I have my degree. I shall use it to build irrigation systems in Andalusia. There are plenty of men I can have now. Doing the Lindy Hop was my release from the study and Pablo doesn't complicate things.

Pablo sees me looking at the pianist. "He's called Alphonse, darling. More your type than mine."

A strikingly good-looking black woman sashays onto the stage to the rapturous applause of the audience. I've heard about this singer from America; she now lives in France and she's taken the European jazz scene by storm. She's in a long, silver evening dress; her hair, tied up in a bun like a flamenco dancer, has a gardenia tucked in just above her left ear. She's gorgeous. I hate her! Not really.

The piano player begins a tune I've heard before, but never like this, never with so much feeling. Perhaps it's the expectant atmosphere in the cellar that one could cut with a knife. Or is it the way the pianist plays and the singer sways? Or is it just the pianist?

There's a somebody I'm longin' to see
I hope that he, turns out to be
Someone who'll watch over me

I'm a little lamb who's lost in the wood
I know I could, always be good
To one who'll watch over me

Still she sways at the microphone. A lull falls into the cellar as she stops singing. The pianist plays a verse, and she accompanies with a gentle humming; then she comes back in with:

Although he may not be the man some
Girls think of as handsome
To my heart he carries the key
Won't you tell him please to put on some speed?
Follow my lead, oh, how I need
Someone to watch over me
Someone to watch over me

The crowd erupts in applause and cheers. She takes an elegant bow.

I think about the words. No, I don't want someone to watch over me. I want to be free. Having someone to watch over you; it sounds as if one would have a jailer. No, I'm going to make my own way in life, do what I want to do, go where I want to go and sleep with whom I want to sleep.

The band comes back. The singer gives a fantastic rendition of a scat song to the stomping sound from the band.

My eyes meet the pianist's for an instant, perhaps less than a second but long enough for me to know that there is a mutual attraction. Oh my goodness, I've butterflies in my tummy.

The song and the deafening din of the crowd's appreciation over, the singer takes the microphone from its stand and sidles over to the pianist. "A big hand please for Alphonse here who stepped in at such short notice when my guy fell ill this morning. I'm sure you'll agree; he knows his jazz!" She strokes his neck.

Why the hell am I jealous?

He smiles up at her. "And now the Lindy Hop competition you've been waiting for," she says, making way at the microphone for the trumpet player.

The trumpeter smiles and looks around the room. His eyes fall on Pablo and me. "There's two of them. Yes and the rest are there too. Make way, please."

The crowd pull back from the stage to leave the area in front clear for about ten feet.

"C'mon folks," says the trumpeter. "We gotta get back further than that."

Another ten feet is won, stretching from one side of the stage to the other.

It'll be tight with four couples dancing this frenetic dance in that space, but we've practised.

"One two three four." The trumpeter brings in the band while the singer takes a seat at the side of the stage to watch.

All the competitors burst into the available space and begin. Pablo and I start with some Charleston steps and our penguinesque moves bring applause and laughter from the crowd. Then we go into a throw. I sail over Pablo's head feet first to land behind him while still in step with the beat. I come back through his legs to face him. Wow! We're doing it. Some shimmying, twirls and a lot of footsteps force us to concentrate on each other. There's no time to worry about what the other entrants are doing; though I can't help stealing an occasional glance at them and the men in the audience.

I twist and turn and somersault. I hope my white pants against tanned thighs exude the eroticism of this crazy dance. I know some of the men out there will want to have me, and it feels great. On a turn, I catch sight of Jose in his crinkled, white suit jacket. He's just given me a creepy look. I don't want to raise his hopes.

The music stops.

The first elimination takes out a pair I saw in practice. I thought they were the primary challengers. The woman rubs her elbow. If her eyes could kill, her partner would be dead. I didn't see what happened; they must have had a fall.

"One two three four," says the trumpeter and off we go again at the frenetic pace.

I manage three somersaults in this section and some serious hip swinging before the music stops.

I hold my breath and Pablo's hand, waiting with my heart still pumping from the exertion and with hope that we're still in the competition. The trumpeter casts his judge's eyes over the remaining competitors.

We survive this cut, and now we're down to two couples. I see the pianist looking at me from the stage. He smiles. I smile back. Don't get distracted, you stupid girl. And then the music starts.

With only two couples left on the floor, we throw everything into the final routine we've rehearsed for the last three months. I sail through the air over his head and land perfectly on my feet. I manage a spin that would delight a prima donna. I throw Pablo over my head, catching his hands and glide him between my legs. The crowd goes wild.

The music stops.

Panting, I look up to the stage but not at the trumpeter, though he holds the decision. I glance—no, it's a stare—at the piano player and feel warm and gooey inside when he looks back at me and smiles.

Everything else seems distant, so it's a surprise when Pablo pokes me in the back and gently pushes me up the steps to the stage to receive the first prize. I take the trophy: two gold-coloured dancers on a plinth that bears the inscription:

Fernando's Lindy Hop Competition 1936; First Prize.

The trophy comes with a wad of pesetas that I hand to Pablo. I have no need of more money with my generous allowance from Papa, and we agreed I should keep the trophy if we won.

"Can we have that dance now?"

I look up from admiring the trophy to see Jose staring at me. "I'm sorry, Jose; I'm off home now. I've a few things to sort out before I leave tomorrow." I feel guilty about the lie, but I couldn't bring myself to let him touch me. I've danced with him before and didn't like the feel of his clammy hands or the way he pressed his lower body hard against me. I feel sorry for him; it doesn't extend to getting too close.

I make my way back to the ladies' changing room, slip on my coat over the dancing clothes and put my dress inside the shoulder bag. I'll change when I get home. I'd like to stay and meet the piano player, but I know I have no chance of doing that; he'll be off to a party somewhere with that stunning singer.

I hope the rain has stopped. Walking home is bad enough but this is not a nice area and could be dangerous at night. That's why I carry a revolver.

Sebastian opens the outer door; I leave after thanking him. Damn! The rain is even heavier, and the clap of thunder with flashes of lightning makes the prospect of a taxi ride the best option. Oh shit! I remember. The taxis are on strike.

I pull up my coat and with my sou'wester pulled down I set off under the umbrella with the trophy under my arm.

Hello, who's that following me? A new black Ford stops by me. With one hand on the umbrella and the other holding the trophy, I can't easily reach my gun.

"Can I give you a lift?"

Oh, it's all right. It's Jose. "I didn't know you had a car, Jose. How long have you had this?"

"Not long. Jump in."

He's harmless, and it's raining hard. He's just creepy but I can handle him. "Thanks." I open the passenger door and climb in out of the rain. The leather seats smell new. I put my shoulder bag on the floor in front of me and place the trophy next to it. I chuck the sou'wester onto the back seat with my furled umbrella.

"I'm just off the Grand Via," I say.

"Yes, I know."

How does he know? That's creepy. He won't try anything though. He isn't the type. But I pull my bag with my gun up against my seat.

"Congratulations on winning the first prize."

"Thanks."

The windscreen wiper isn't having much impact on the downpour. I hope Jose has a better view of the road ahead because I can see bugger all.

"When are you going back to Jerez?" he asks.

"In the morning. What about you?"

"I've finished my course. Not sure if I want to go back to Jerez. I want to do something. Jerez is nothing but sherry. I'm now a qualified civil engineer so I may go abroad and build bridges or dams."

"That sounds interesting. Where abroad? Africa? South America?"

"Don't know yet. We could work together on something."

"Maybe." No chance.

Jose brings the car to a halt. Good, we must be at my place. It's dark; he's turned off the lights. Where are the street lights?

"Are we here already? Thanks, Jose. It's much appreciated."

I pull the handle on the door and push it open. With one foot on the running board I hesitate; a flash of lightning lights up the surroundings; we're in a derelict square with ruined houses. I don't like this.

"Jose…"

A hand on the collar of my coat drags me back. Suddenly, in another lightning flash, I see the contorted face of Jose in front of me and… Oh God no! A knife.

"Jose…"

"You always were a bitch to me. Now I'm going to have you and if you struggle I'll cut your throat."

He's on top of me now. His free hand roams my body. I smell stale tobacco and booze on his breath. On a one to one I could knock him down but he has a knife and he looks crazy enough to use it. Jesus! I'm going to end up like Carmen.

"Jose…"

"Shut up and get your panties off."

"Jose, don't! You don't want to do this. I've never done anything bad to you."

"Shut up and get ready. I'm going to have you. If you make it good, I may let you live."

"All right, all right, Jose. Be careful with the knife, Jose. I'm doing it."

I reach down towards my panties. It's difficult to breath with him on top of me. My hand slides into the bag and grips the handle of my revolver. Slowly I pull it out and bend my finger around the trigger.

If I threaten to shoot him he could stick the knife in my throat before I fire. If I shoot him in the leg, he may still be able to hurt me. I have to shoot to kill. It's my only chance.

"Jose, please, I beg you. Don't do it. You'll regret it. Please, Jose, no."

"It's your last chance. Get your panties off." His free hand goes down to his belt while his other holds the knife against my throat.

I raise the pistol. He can't see it. I don't want to do this, but I have no choice. Why me? Should I let him do it? I don't want to let him do it, and he may kill me afterwards to stop me talking. Why should I give in? Fuck it, I won't be a victim.

The sound rings in my ears.

His whole body lurches back towards the windscreen. I open my eyes and, with the pistol still in my right hand, knock the knife from his right hand with my left.

A flash of lightning is enough for me to see the shocked expression on his face. He slumps forward on me. In a fearful panic I wriggle out from underneath and jump from the car.

The rain soon soaks my hair and runs down my neck. My right hand feels sticky. In the darkness I can just make out Jose lying face down against the front passenger seat. I suck in a deep breath and reach under his legs for my bag, drag it from the car and lift out my torch.

My heart's beating as if it's going to explode.

I shine the torch on Jose. Blood covers the seat, and I can see the entry wound in his chest. My knowledge of physiology is scant but the hole, I know, is near his heart. That's exactly where I intended to shoot him.

I can hear him gurgling as the blood pours from his wound. How can I stop it? I grab my bag and find a silk paisley scarf that Mama gave to me. Gingerly I lift Jose back from the seat and ram the scarf into the wound. It's stemmed the bleeding; at least, it's stopped the flow, but I know he may still be bleeding internally. He's not conscious. That's a blessing for him and me.

I step back from the car. On my hand I can see what the sticky feeling was: blood. Dear God, it's his blood. Though the rain pours, it won't wash the blood away. I look down at my coat; it's bloody, and so are my clothes underneath. Where the hell am I?

I must call an ambulance and the police. I don't know where I am. Shall I leave him here in the car while I go to find help? Wait. If I call the police, will they accuse me of shooting him? I did shoot him, but it was self-defence. His father will make trouble. A rapist or attempted rapist; no, he'll never allow that. What the hell am I going to do? Is he going to die?

The lyrics of the song 'Someone To Watch Over Me'
by George and Ira Gershwin are copyright.

They are reproduced in this novel under license issued by:

Troy Schreck: (USA and the rest of the world except Europe)
Contract and Licensing Administrator
Alfred Music
P.O. Box 10003 • Van Nuys, CA 91410-0003
(818) 891-5999 x183 | (818) 895-4875 fax

Christine Cullen: (Europe)
Warner / Chappell Music Ltd
Electric Lighting Station
46 Kensington Court
London
W8 5DA

Printed in Great Britain
by Amazon